THE
SEVEN HUSBANDS
OF
EVELYN HUGO

ALSO BY TAYLOR JENKINS REID

Forever, Interrupted
After I Do
Maybe in Another Life
One True Loves

THE SEVEN HUSBANDS OF EVELYN HUGO

a novel

TAYLOR JENKINS REID

ATRIA PAPERBACK

NEW YORK   LONDON   TORONTO   SYDNEY   NEW DELHI

ATRIA

Atria
An Imprint of Simon & Schuster, Inc.
1230 Avenue of the Americas
New York, NY 10020

ATRIA and colophon are trademarks of Simon & Schuster, Inc.

Interior design by Carly Loman

Manufactured in the United States of America

ISBN 978-1501139239

For Lilah
Smash the patriarchy, sweetheart

THE
SEVEN HUSBANDS
OF
EVELYN HUGO

Evelyn Hugo to Auction Off Gowns

BY PRIYA AMRIT   MARCH 2, 2017

Film legend and '60s It Girl Evelyn Hugo has just announced that she will auction off 12 of her most memorable gowns through Christie's to raise money for breast
cancer research.

At the age of 79, Hugo has long been an icon of glamour and elegance. She is known for a personal style both
sensual and restrained, and many of Hugo's most famous
looks are considered touchstones of the fashion and Hollywood archives.

Those looking to own a piece of Hugo history will be
intrigued not only by the gowns themselves but also by
the context in which they were worn. Included in the sale
will be the emerald-green Miranda La Conda that Hugo
wore to the 1959 Academy Awards, the violet soufflé and
organdy scoop-neck she donned at the premiere of *Anna
Karenina* in 1962, and the navy-blue silk Michael Maddax
that she was wearing in 1982 when she won her Oscar for
All for Us.

Hugo has weathered her share of Hollywood scandals,
not the least of which being her seven marriages, including
her decades-long relationship with film producer Harry
Cameron. The two Hollywood insiders shared a daughter,
Connor Cameron, who is no doubt the influence for the
auction. Ms. Cameron passed away last year from breast
cancer soon after turning 41.

Born Evelyn Elena Herrera in 1938, the daughter of

Cuban immigrants, Hugo grew up in the Hell's Kitchen neighborhood of New York City. By 1955, she had made her way to Hollywood, gone blond, and been rechristened Evelyn Hugo. Almost overnight, Hugo became a member of the Hollywood elite. She remained in the spotlight for more than three decades before retiring in the late '80s and marrying financier Robert Jamison, older brother of three-time Oscar-winning actress Celia St. James. Now widowed from her seventh husband, Hugo resides in Manhattan.

Preternaturally beautiful and a paragon of glamour and daring sexuality, Hugo has long been a source of fascination for moviegoers the world over. This auction is expected to raise upward of $2 million.

C AN YOU COME INTO MY office?"
      I look around at the desks beside me and then back at Frankie, trying to confirm to whom, exactly, she's talking. I point to myself. "Do you mean me?"

Frankie has very little patience. "Yes, Monique, you. That's why I said, 'Monique, can you come into my office?'"

"Sorry, I just heard the last part."

Frankie turns. I grab my notepad and follow her.

There is something very striking about Frankie. I'm not sure that you'd say she was conventionally attractive—her features are severe, her eyes very wide apart—but she is nevertheless someone you can't help but look at and admire. With her thin, six-foot-tall frame, her short-cropped Afro, and her affinity for bright colors and big jewelry, when Frankie walks into a room, everyone takes notice.

She was part of the reason I took this job. I have looked up to her since I was in journalism school, reading her pieces in the very pages of the magazine she now runs and I now work for. And if I'm being honest, there is something very inspiring about having a black woman running things. As a biracial woman myself—light brown skin and dark brown eyes courtesy of my black father, an abundance of face freckles courtesy of my white mother—Frankie makes me feel more sure that I can one day run things, too.

"Take a seat," Frankie says as she sits down and gestures toward an orange chair on the opposite side of her Lucite desk.

I calmly sit and cross my legs. I let Frankie talk first.

"So, puzzling turn of events," she says, looking at her computer. "Evelyn Hugo's people are inquiring about a feature. An exclusive interview."

My gut instinct is to say *Holy shit* but also *Why are you telling me this?* "About what in particular?" I ask.

"My guess is it's related to the gown auction she's doing," Frankie says. "My understanding is that it's very important to her to raise as much money for the American Breast Cancer Foundation as possible."

"But they won't confirm that?"

Frankie shakes her head. "All they will confirm is that Evelyn has something to say."

Evelyn Hugo is one of the biggest movie stars of all time. She doesn't even have to *have* something to say for people to listen.

"This could be a big cover for us, right? I mean, she's a living legend. Wasn't she married eight times or something?"

"Seven," Frankie says. "And yes. This has huge potential. Which is why I hope you'll bear with me through the next part of this."

"What do you mean?"

Frankie takes a big breath and gets a look on her face that makes me think I'm about to get fired. But then she says, "Evelyn specifically requested you."

"Me?" This is the second time in the span of five minutes that I have been shocked that someone was interested in speaking with me. I need to work on my confidence. Suffice it to say, it's taken a beating recently. Although why pretend it was ever really soaring?

"To be honest, that was my reaction, too," Frankie says.

Now *I'll* be honest, I'm a little offended. Although, obviously, I can see where she's coming from. I've been at *Vivant* for less than a year, mostly doing puff pieces. Before that, I was blogging for the *Discourse*, a current events and culture site that calls itself a newsmagazine but is, effectively, a blog with punchy headlines. I wrote mainly for the Modern Life section, covering trending topics and opinion pieces.

After years of freelancing, the *Discourse* gig was a lifesaver. But when

Vivant offered me a job, I couldn't help myself. I jumped at the chance to join an institution, to work among legends.

On my first day of work, I walked past walls decorated with iconic, culture-shifting covers—the one of women's activist Debbie Palmer, naked and carefully posed, standing on top of a skyscraper overlooking Manhattan in 1984; the one of artist Robert Turner in the act of painting a canvas while the text declared that he had AIDS, back in 1991. It felt surreal to be a part of the *Vivant* world. I have always wanted to see my name on its glossy pages.

But unfortunately, for the past twelve issues, I've done nothing but ask old-guard questions of people with old money, while my colleagues back at the *Discourse* are attempting to change the world while going viral. So, simply put, I'm not exactly impressed with myself.

"Look, it's not that we don't love you, we do," Frankie says. "We think you're destined for big things at *Vivant*, but I was hoping to put one of our more experienced, top hitters on this. And so I want to be up front with you when I say that we did not submit you as an idea to Evelyn's team. We sent five big names, and they came back with this."

Frankie turns her computer screen toward me and shows me an e-mail from someone named Thomas Welch, who I can only assume is Evelyn Hugo's publicist.

From: Thomas Welch
To: Troupe, Frankie
Cc: Stamey, Jason; Powers, Ryan

It's Monique Grant or Evelyn's out.

I look back up at Frankie, stunned. And to be honest, a little bit star-struck that Evelyn Hugo wants anything to do with me.

"Do you *know* Evelyn Hugo? Is that what's going on here?" Frankie asks me as she turns the computer back toward her side of the desk.

"No," I say, surprised even to be asked the question. "I've seen a few of her movies, but she's a little before my time."

"You have no personal connection to her?"

I shake my head. "Definitely not."

"Aren't you from Los Angeles?"

"Yeah, but the only way I'd have any connection to Evelyn Hugo, I suppose, is if my dad worked on one of her films back in the day. He was a still photographer for movie sets. I can ask my mom."

"Great. Thank you." Frankie looks at me expectantly.

"Did you want me to ask now?"

"Could you?"

I pull my phone out of my pocket and text my mother: *Did Dad ever work on any Evelyn Hugo movies?*

I see three dots start to appear, and I look up, only to find that Frankie is trying to get a glimpse of my phone. She seems to recognize the invasion and leans back.

My phone dings.

My mother texts: *Maybe? There were so many it's hard to keep track. Why?*

Long story, I reply, *but I'm trying to figure out if I have any connection to Evelyn Hugo. Think Dad would have known her?*

Mom answers: *Ha! No. Your father never hung out with anybody famous on set. No matter how hard I tried to get him to make us some celebrity friends.*

I laugh. "It looks like no. No connection to Evelyn Hugo."

Frankie nods. "OK, well, then, the other theory is that her people chose someone with less clout so that they could try to control you and, thus, the narrative."

I feel my phone vibrate again. *That reminds me that I wanted to send you a box of your dad's old work. Some gorgeous stuff. I love having it here, but I think you'd love it more. I'll send it this week.*

"You think they're preying on the weak," I say to Frankie.

Frankie smiles softly. "Sort of."

"So Evelyn's people look up the masthead, find my name as a lower-level writer, and think they can bully me around. That's the idea?"

"That's what I fear."

"And you're telling me this because . . ."

Frankie considers her words. "Because I don't think you can be bullied around. I think they are underestimating you. And I want this cover. I want it to make headlines."

"What are you saying?" I ask, shifting slightly in my chair.

Frankie claps her hands in front of her and rests them on the desk, leaning toward me. "I'm asking you if you have the guts to go toe-to-toe with Evelyn Hugo."

Of all the things I thought someone was going to ask me today, this would probably be somewhere around number nine million. Do I have the guts to go toe-to-toe with Evelyn Hugo? I have no idea.

"Yes," I say finally.

"That's all? Just yes?"

I want this opportunity. I want to write this story. I'm sick of being the lowest one on the totem pole. And I need a win, goddammit. "Fuck yes?"

Frankie nods, considering. "Better, but I'm still not convinced."

I'm thirty-five years old. I've been a writer for more than a decade. I want a book deal one day. I want to pick my stories. I want to eventually be the name people scramble to get when someone like Evelyn Hugo calls. And I'm being underused here at *Vivant*. If I'm going to get where I want to go, something has to let up. Someone has to get out of my way. And it needs to happen quickly, because this goddamn career is all I have anymore. If I want things to change, I have to change how I do things. And probably drastically.

"Evelyn wants me," I say. "You want Evelyn. It doesn't sound like I need to convince you, Frankie. It sounds like you need to convince *me*."

Frankie is dead quiet, staring right at me over her steepled fingers. I was aiming for formidable. I might have overshot.

I feel the same way I did when I tried weight training and started with the forty-pound weights. Too much too soon makes it obvious you don't know what you're doing.

It takes everything I have not to take it back, not to apologize profusely. My mother raised me to be polite, to be demure. I have long operated under the idea that civility is subservience. But it hasn't gotten me very far, that type of kindness. The world respects people who think they should be running it. I've never understood that, but I'm done fighting it. I'm here to be Frankie one day, maybe bigger than Frankie. To do big, important work that I am proud of. To leave a mark. And I'm nowhere near doing that yet.

The silence is so long that I think I might crack, the tension building with every second that goes by. But Frankie cracks first.

"OK," she says, and puts out her hand as she stands up.

Shock and searing pride run through me as I extend my own. I make sure my handshake is strong; Frankie's is a vise.

"Ace this, Monique. For us and for yourself, please."

"I will."

We break away from each other as I walk toward her door. "She might have read your physician-assisted suicide piece for the *Discourse*," Frankie says just before I leave the room.

"What?"

"It was stunning. Maybe that's why she wants you. It's how we found you. It's a great story. Not just because of the hits it got but because of you, because it's beautiful work."

It was one of the first truly meaningful stories I wrote of my own volition. I pitched it after I was assigned a piece on the rise in popularity of microgreens, especially on the Brooklyn restaurant scene. I had gone to the Park Slope market to interview a local farmer, but when I confessed that I didn't get the appeal of mustard greens, he told me that I sounded like his sister. She had been highly carnivorous until the past year, when she switched to a vegan, all-organic diet as she battled brain cancer.

As we spoke more, he told me about a physician-assisted suicide support group he and his sister had joined, for those at the end of their lives and their loved ones. So many in the group were fighting for the right to die with dignity. Healthy eating wasn't going to save his sister's life, and neither of them wanted her to suffer any longer than she had to.

I knew then that I wanted, very deeply, to give a voice to the people of that support group.

I went back to the *Discourse* office and pitched the story. I thought I'd be turned down, given my recent slate of articles about hipster trends and celebrity think pieces. But to my surprise, I was greeted with a green light.

I worked tirelessly on it, attending meetings in church basements, interviewing the members, writing and rewriting, until I felt confident that the piece represented the full complexity—both the mercy and the moral code—of helping to end the lives of suffering people.

It is the story I am proudest of. I have, more than once, gone home from a day's work here and read that piece again, reminding myself of what I'm capable of, reminding myself of the satisfaction I take in sharing the truth, no matter how difficult it may be to swallow.

"Thank you," I tell Frankie now.

"I'm just saying that you're talented. It might be that."

"It's probably not, though."

"No," she says. "It's probably not. But write this story well, whatever it is, and then next time it will be."

Evelyn Hugo's Coming Clean

BY JULIA SANTOS   MARCH 4, 2017

Word on the street is siren/LIVING LEGEND/world's most beautiful blonde Evelyn Hugo is auctioning off gowns *and* agreeing to an interview, which she has not done in multiple decades.

PLEASE tell me she is finally ready to talk about all those damn husbands. (I can understand four, maybe even five, six if you are really pushing it, but seven? Seven husbands? Not to mention the fact that we all know she was having an affair with Congressman Jack Easton in the early '80s. Girl. Got. A. Round.)

If she won't come clean about the husbands, let's pray she at least goes on the record about how she got those eyebrows. I mean, SHARE THE WEALTH, EVELYN.

When you see pictures of E back in the day with her brassy blond hair, those dark, straight-as-an-arrow eyebrows, that deep-tanned skin, and those golden-brown eyes, you have no choice but to stop what you are doing and stare right at her.

And don't even get me started on that body.

No ass, no hips—just huge boobs on a slim frame.

I have basically been working my entire adult life for a body like that. (Note: Am very far away. Might be the spaghetti bucatini I've been eating for lunch every day this week.)

Here is the only part that has me heated: Evelyn could have chosen anyone for this. (Ahem, me?) But instead she chose some newbie at *Vivant*? She could have had any-one. (Ahem, me?) Why this Monique Grant chick (and not me)?

Ugh, fine. I'm just bitter it's not me.

I should really get a job at *Vivant*. They get all the good stuff.

COMMENTS:

Hihello565 says: Even people at *Vivant* don't want to work at *Vivant* anymore. Corporate overlords producing censored advertiser courting bullshit.

Pppppppppps reply to Hihello565: Yeah, OK. Something tells me if the most well-respected, sophisticated magazine in the country offered you a job, you'd take it.

EChristine999 says: Didn't Evelyn's daughter die of cancer recently? I feel like I read something recently about that. So heartbreaking. BTW, that picture of Evelyn at Harry Cameron's grave? Basically ruined me for months. Beautiful family. So sad that she lost them.

MrsJeanineGrambs says: I do not care about Evelyn Hugo AT ALL. STOP WRITING ABOUT THESE PEOPLE. Her marriages, affairs, and most of her movies just go to prove one thing: Slut. *Three A.M.* was a disgrace to women. Focus your attention on people that deserve it.

SexyLexi89 says: Evelyn Hugo is maybe the most beautiful woman of all time. That shot in *Boute-en-Train* where she's coming out of the water naked and the camera cuts to black right before you see her nipples? So good.

PennyDriverKLM says: All hail Evelyn Hugo for making blond hair and dark eyebrows THE LOOK. Evelyn, I salute you.

YuppiePigs3 says: Too skinny! Not for me.

EvelynHugoIsASaint says: This is a woman who has donated MILLIONS OF DOLLARS to charities for battered women's organizations and LGBTQ+ interests, and now she's auctioning off gowns for cancer research and all you can talk about is her eyebrow game? Seriously?

JuliaSantos@TheSpill reply to EvelynHugoIsASaint: This is a fair point, I guess. SORRY. In my defense, she started making millions by being a badass business bitch back in the '60s. And she would never have had the clout to do that without her talent and beauty, and she never would have been as beautiful without DEM BROWS. But OK, fair point.

EvelynHugoIsASaint reply to JuliaSantos@TheSpill: Ugh. Sorry for being so bitchy. I skipped lunch. Mea culpa. For what it's worth, *Vivant* won't do half as well with this story as you would have. Evelyn should have chosen you.

JuliaSantos@TheSpill reply to EvelynHugoIsASaint: Right????? Who is Monique Grant anyway? BORING. I'm coming for her . . .

I'VE SPENT THE PAST FEW days researching everything I can about Evelyn Hugo. I was never a big film buff, let alone interested in any old Hollywood stars. But Evelyn's life—at least the version on record as of now—is enough for ten soap operas.

There's the early marriage that ended in divorce when she was eighteen. Then the studio-setup courtship and tumultuous marriage to Hollywood royalty Don Adler. The rumors that she left him because he beat her. Her comeback in a French New Wave film. The quickie Vegas elopement with singer Mick Riva. Her glamorous marriage to the dapper Rex North, which ended in both of them having affairs. The beautiful love story of her life with Harry Cameron and the birth of their daughter, Connor. Their heartbreaking divorce and her very quick marriage to her old director Max Girard. Her supposed affair with the much younger Congressman Jack Easton, which ended her relationship with Girard. And finally, her marriage to financier Robert Jamison, rumored to have at least been inspired by Evelyn's desire to spite former costar—and Robert's sister—Celia St. James. All of her husbands have passed away, leaving Evelyn as the only one with insight into those relationships.

Suffice it to say, I have my work cut out for me if I want to get her to talk about any of it.

After staying late at the office this evening, I finally make my way home a little before nine. My apartment is small. I believe the most appropriate term is *teeny-tiny sardine box*. But it's amazing how vast a small place can feel when half of your things are gone.

David moved out five weeks ago, and I still haven't managed to re-place the dishes he took with him or the coffee table his mother gave us last year as a wedding present. Jesus. We didn't even make it to our first anniversary.

As I walk in my front door and put my bag on the sofa, it strikes me again just how needlessly petty it was of him to take the coffee table. His new San Francisco studio came fully furnished courtesy of the generous relocation package offered with his promotion. I suspect he put the table in storage, along with the one nightstand he insisted was rightfully his and all of our cookbooks. I don't miss the cookbooks. I don't cook. But when things are inscribed to "Monique and David, for all your many years of happiness," you think of them as half yours.

I hang up my coat and wonder, not for the first time, which question gets closer to the truth: Did David take the new job and move to San Francisco *without me*? Or did I refuse to leave New York *for him*? As I take off my shoes, I resolve once again that the answer is somewhere in the middle. But then I come back to the same thought that always stings afresh: *He actually left.*

I order myself pad thai and then get in the shower. I turn the water to nearly scalding hot. I love water so hot it almost burns. I love the smell of shampoo. My happiest place might just be under a showerhead. It is here in the steam, covered in suds, that I do not feel like Monique Grant, woman left behind. Or even Monique Grant, stalled writer. I am just Monique Grant, owner of luxury bath products.

Well after I've pruned, I dry myself off, put on my sweatpants, and pull my hair away from my face, just in time for the deliveryman to make his way to my door.

I sit with the plastic container, trying to watch TV. I attempt to zone out. I want to make my brain do something, anything, other than think about work or David. But once my food is gone, I realize it's futile. I might as well work.

This is all very intimidating—the idea of interviewing Evelyn Hugo, the task of controlling her narrative, of trying to make sure she doesn't control mine. I'm often inclined to overprepare. But more to the point,

I've always been a bit like an ostrich, willing to bury my head in the sand to avoid what I don't want to face.

So, for the next three days, I do nothing but research Evelyn Hugo. I spend my days pulling up old articles about her marriages and her scandals. I spend my evenings watching her old movies.

I watch clips of her in *Carolina Sunset*, *Anna Karenina*, *Jade Diamond*, and *All for Us*. I watch the GIF of her coming out of the water in *Boute-en-Train* so many times that when I fall asleep, it plays over and over in my dreams.

And I start to fall in love with her, just the littlest bit, as I watch her films. Between the hours of eleven P.M. and two A.M., while the rest of the world is sleeping, my laptop flickers with the sight of her, and the sound of her voice fills my living room.

There is no denying that she is a stunningly beautiful woman. People often talk about her straight, thick eyebrows and her blond hair, but I can't take my eyes off her bone structure. Her jawline is strong, her cheekbones are high, and all of it comes to a point at her ever-so-swollen lips. Her eyes are huge but not so much round as an oversized almond shape. Her tanned skin next to her light hair looks beachy but also elegant. I know it's not natural—hair that blond with skin that bronze—and yet I can't shake the feeling that it *should* be, that humans should be born looking like this.

I have no doubt that's part of the reason film historian Charles Redding once said that Evelyn's face felt "inevitable. So exquisite, so nearly perfect, that when looking at her, you get the sense that her features, in that combination, in that ratio, were bound to happen sooner or later."

I pin images of Evelyn in the '50s wearing tight sweaters and bullet bras, press photos of her and Don Adler on the Sunset Studios lot shortly after they were married, shots of her from the early '60s with long, straight hair and soft, thick bangs and wearing short-shorts.

There is a photo of her in a white one-piece, sitting on the shoreline of a pristine beach, with a large, floppy black hat covering most of her face, her white-blond hair and the right side of her face illuminated by the sun.

One of my personal favorites is a black-and-white shot from the Golden Globes in 1967. She is seated on the aisle, her hair pulled into a loose updo. She is wearing a light-colored lace gown with a deep scoop neckline, her cleavage controlled but on full display and her right leg escaping through the high slit of the skirt.

There are two men seated next to her, names lost to history, who are staring at her as she looks ahead at the stage. The man next to her is staring at her chest. The one next to him is staring at her thigh. Both of them seem enraptured and hoping to see the tiniest bit farther.

Maybe I'm overthinking that photo, but I'm starting to notice a pattern: Evelyn always leaves you hoping you'll get just a little bit more. And she always denies you.

Even in her much-talked-about sex scene in *Three A.M.* from 1977, in which she writhes, reverse-cowboy style, on top of Don Adler, you see her full breasts for less than three seconds. It was rumored for years that the incredible box-office numbers for the film were because couples were going to see it multiple times.

How does she know just how much to give and just how much of herself to withhold?

And does that all change now that she's got something to say? Or is she going to play me the same way she played audiences for years?

Is Evelyn Hugo going to tell me just enough to keep me on the edge of my seat but never enough to truly reveal anything?

I WAKE UP A HALF hour before my alarm. I check my e-mails, including one from Frankie with the subject line "KEEP ME UPDATED,"
yelling at me in all caps. I make myself a small breakfast.

I put on black slacks and a white T-shirt with my favorite herringbone
blazer. I gather my long, tight curls into a bun at the top of my head. I
forgo my contacts and choose my thickest black-framed glasses.

As I look in the mirror, I notice that I have lost weight in my face
since David left. While I have always had a slim frame, my butt and
face seem to be the first to pick up any extra weight. And being with
David—during the two years we dated and the eleven months since we
married—meant I put on a few. David likes to eat. And while he would
get up in the early mornings to run it off, I slept in.

Looking at myself now, pulled together and slimmer, I feel a rush of
confidence. I look good. I feel good.

Before I make my way out the door, I grab the camel cashmere scarf
that my mother gave me for Christmas this past year. And then I put
one foot in front of the other, down to the subway, into Manhattan, and
uptown.

Evelyn's place is just off Fifth Avenue overlooking Central Park. I've
done enough Internet stalking to know she's got this place and a beach-
front villa just outside of Málaga, Spain. She's had this apartment since the
late '60s, when she bought it with Harry Cameron. She inherited the villa
when Robert Jamison died almost five years ago. In my next life, please
remind me to come back as a movie star with points on the back end.

Evelyn's building, at least from the outside—limestone, prewar, beaux arts style—is extraordinary. I am greeted, before even walking in, by an older, handsome doorman with soft eyes and a kind smile.

"How may I help you?" he says.

I find myself embarrassed even to say it. "I'm here to see Evelyn Hugo. My name's Monique Grant."

He smiles and opens the door for me. It's clear he was expecting me. He walks me to the elevator and presses the button for the top floor.

"Have a nice day, Ms. Grant," he says, and then disappears as the elevators close.

I ring the doorbell of Evelyn's apartment at eleven A.M. on the dot. A woman in jeans and a navy blouse answers. She looks to be about fifty, maybe a few years older. She is Asian-American, with straight jet-black hair pulled into a ponytail. She's holding a stack of half-opened mail.

She smiles and extends her hand. "You must be Monique," she says as I hold out my own. She seems like the sort of person who genuinely delights in meeting other people, and I already like her, despite my strict promise to myself to remain neutral to everything I encounter today.

"I'm Grace."

"Hi, Grace," I say. "Nice to meet you."

"Likewise. Come on in."

Grace steps out of the way and beckons to invite me in. I put my bag on the ground and take off my coat.

"You can put it right in here," she says, opening a closet just inside the foyer and handing me a wooden hanger.

This coat closet is the size of the one bathroom in my apartment. It's no secret that Evelyn has more money than God. But I need to work at not letting that intimidate me. She's beautiful, and she's rich, and she's powerful and sexual and charming. And I'm a normal human being. Somehow I have to convince myself that she and I are on equal footing, or this is never going to work.

"Great," I say, smiling. "Thank you." I put my coat on the hanger, slip it over the rod, and let Grace shut the closet door.

"Evelyn is upstairs getting ready. Can I get you anything? Water, coffee, tea?"

"Coffee would be great," I say.

Grace brings me into a sitting room. It is bright and airy, with floor-to-ceiling white bookcases and two overstuffed cream-colored chairs.

"Have a seat," she says. "How do you like it?"

"My coffee?" I ask, unsure of myself. "With cream? I mean, milk is fine, too. But cream is great. Or whatever you have." I get hold of myself. "What I'm trying to say is that I'd like a splash of cream if you have it. Can you tell I'm nervous?"

Grace smiles. "A little. But you don't have anything to worry about. Evelyn's a very kind person. She's particular and private, which can take some getting used to. But I've worked for a lot of people, and you can trust me when I say Evelyn's better than the rest."

"Did she pay you to say that?" I ask. I am trying to make a joke, but it sounds more pointed and accusatory than I intended.

Luckily, Grace laughs. "She did send my husband and me to London and Paris last year as my Christmas bonus. So in an indirect way, yeah, I suppose she did."

Jesus. "Well, that settles it. When you quit, I want your job."

Grace laughs. "It's a deal. And you've got coffee with a splash of cream coming right up."

I sit down and check my cell phone. I have a text from my mom wishing me luck. I tap to respond, and I am lost in my attempts to properly type the word *early* without auto-correct changing it to *earthquake* when I hear footsteps on the stairs. I turn around to see the seventy-nine-year-old Evelyn Hugo walking toward me.

She is as breathtaking as any of her pictures.

She has the posture of a ballerina. She's wearing slim black stretch pants and a long gray-and-navy striped sweater. She's just as thin as she ever was, and the only way I know she's had work done on her face is because no one her age can look like that without a doctor.

Her skin is glowing and just the littlest bit red, as if it's been rubbed clean. She's wearing false eyelashes, or perhaps she gets eyelash extensions. Where her cheeks were once angular, they are now a bit sunken. But they have just a tint of soft rosiness to them, and her lips are a dark nude.

Her hair is past her shoulders—a beautiful array of white, gray, and blond—with the lightest colors framing her face. I'm sure her hair is triple-processed, but the effect is that of a gracefully aging woman who sat out in the sun.

Her eyebrows, however—those dark, thick, straight lines that were her signature—have thinned over the years. And they are now the same color as her hair.

By the time she reaches me, I notice that she is not wearing any shoes but, instead, big, chunky knit socks.

"Monique, hello," Evelyn says.

I am momentarily surprised at the casualness and confidence with which she says my name, as if she has known me for years. "Hello," I say.

"I'm Evelyn." She reaches out and takes my hand, shaking it. It strikes me as a unique form of power to say your own name when you know that everyone in the room, everyone in the world, already knows it.

Grace comes in with a white mug of coffee on a white saucer. "There you go. With just a bit of cream."

"Thank you so much," I say, taking it from her.

"That's just the way I like it as well," Evelyn says, and I'm embarrassed to admit it thrills me. I feel as if I've pleased her.

"Can I get either of you anything else?" Grace asks.

I shake my head, and Evelyn doesn't answer. Grace leaves.

"Come," Evelyn says. "Let's go to the living room and get comfortable."

As I grab my bag, Evelyn takes the coffee out of my hand, carrying it for me. I once read that charisma is "charm that inspires devotion." And I can't help but think of that now, when she's holding my coffee for me. The combination of such a powerful woman and such a small and humble gesture is enchanting, to be sure.

We step into a large, bright room with floor-to-ceiling windows. There are oyster-gray chairs opposite a soft slate-blue sofa. The carpet under our feet is thick, bright ivory, and as my eyes follow its path, I am struck by the black grand piano, open under the light of the windows. On the walls are two blown-up black-and-white images.

The one above the sofa is of Harry Cameron on the set of a movie.

The one above the fireplace is the poster for Evelyn's 1959 version of *Little Women*. Evelyn, Celia St. James, and two other actresses' faces make up the image. All four of these women may have been household names back in the '50s, but it is Evelyn and Celia who stood the test of time. Looking at it now, Evelyn and Celia seem to shine brighter than the others. But I'm pretty sure that's simply hindsight bias. I'm seeing what I want to see, based on how I know it all turns out.

Evelyn puts my cup and saucer down on the black-lacquer coffee table. "Sit," she says as she takes a seat herself in one of the plush chairs. She pulls her feet up underneath her. "Anywhere you want."

I nod and put my bag down. As I sit on the couch, I grab my notepad.

"So you're putting your gowns up for auction," I say as I settle myself. I click my pen, ready to listen.

Which is when Evelyn says, "Actually, I've called you here under false pretenses."

I look directly at her, sure I've misheard. "Excuse me?"

Evelyn rearranges herself in the chair and looks at me. "There's not much to tell about me handing a bunch of dresses over to Christie's."

"Well, then—"

"I called you here to discuss something else."

"What is that?"

"My life story."

"Your life story?" I say, stunned and trying hard to catch up to her.

"A tell-all."

An Evelyn Hugo tell-all would be . . . I don't know. Something close to the story of the year. "You want to do a tell-all with *Vivant*?"

"No," she says.

"You don't want to do a tell-all?"

"I don't want to do one with *Vivant*."

"Then why am I here?" I'm even more lost than I was just a moment ago.

"You're the one I'm giving the story to."

I look at her, trying to decipher what exactly she's saying.

"You're going to go on record about your life, and you're going to do it with me but not with *Vivant*?"

Evelyn nods. "Now you're getting it."

"What exactly are you proposing?" There is no way that I have just walked into a situation in which one of the most intriguing people alive is offering me the story of her life for *no reason*. I must be missing something.

"I will tell you my life story in a way that will be beneficial to both of us. Although, to be honest, mainly you."

"Just how in-depth are we talking about here?" Maybe she wants some airy retrospective? Some lightweight story published somewhere of her choosing?

"The whole nine yards. The good, the bad, and the ugly. Whatever cliché you want to use that means 'I'll tell you the truth about absolutely everything I've ever done.'"

Whoa.

I feel so silly for coming in here expecting her to answer questions about dresses. I put the notebook on the table in front of me and gently put the pen down on top of it. I want to handle this perfectly. It's as if a gorgeous, delicate bird has just flown to me and sat directly on my shoulder, and if I don't make the exact right move, it might fly away.

"OK, if I understand you correctly, what you're saying is that you'd like to confess your various sins—"

Evelyn's posture, which until this point has shown her to be very relaxed and fairly detached, changes. She is now leaning toward me. "I never said anything about confessing sins. I said nothing about sins at all."

I back away slightly. I've ruined it. "I apologize," I say. "That was a poor choice of words."

Evelyn doesn't say anything.

"I'm sorry, Ms. Hugo. This is all a bit surreal for me."

"You can call me Evelyn," she says.

"OK, Evelyn, what's the next step here? What, precisely, are we going to do together?" I take the coffee cup and put it up to my lips, sipping just the littlest bit.

"We're not doing a *Vivant* cover story," she says.

"OK, that much I got," I say, putting the cup down.

"We're writing a book."

"We are?"

Evelyn nods. "You and I," she says. "I've read your work. I like the way you communicate clearly and succinctly. Your writing has a no-nonsense quality to it that I admire and that I think my book could use."

"You're asking me to ghostwrite your autobiography?" This is fantastic. This is absolutely, positively fantastic. *This* is a good reason to stay in New York. A great reason. Things like this don't happen in San Francisco.

Evelyn shakes her head again. "I'm giving you my life story, Monique. I'm going to tell you the whole truth. And you are going to write a book about it."

"And we'll package it with your name on it and tell everyone you wrote it. That's ghostwriting." I pick up my cup again.

"My name won't be on it. I'll be dead."

I choke on my coffee and in doing so stain the white carpet with flecks of umber.

"Oh, my God," I say, perhaps a bit too loudly, as I put down the cup. "I spilled coffee on your carpet."

Evelyn waves this off, but Grace knocks on the door and opens it just a crack, poking her head in.

"Everything OK?"

"I spilled, I'm afraid," I say.

Grace opens the door fully and comes in, taking a look.

"I'm really sorry. I just got a bit shocked is all."

I catch Evelyn's eye, and I don't know her very well, but what I do know is that she's telling me to be quiet.

"It's not a problem," Grace says. "I'll take care of it."

"Are you hungry, Monique?" Evelyn says, standing up.

"I'm sorry?"

"I know a place just down the street that makes really great salads. My treat."

It's barely noon, and when I'm anxious, the first thing to go is my appetite, but I say yes anyway, because I get the distinct impression that it's not really a question.

"Great," Evelyn says. "Grace, will you call ahead to Trambino's?"

Evelyn takes me by the shoulder, and less than ten minutes later, we're walking down the manicured sidewalks of the Upper East Side.

The sharp chill in the air surprises me, and I notice Evelyn grab her coat tightly around her tiny waist.

In the sunlight, it's easier to see the signs of aging. The whites of her eyes are cloudy, and the complexion of her hands is in the process of becoming translucent. The clear blue tint to her veins reminds me of my grandmother. I used to love the soft, papery tenderness of her skin, the way it didn't bounce back but stayed in place.

"Evelyn, what do you mean you'll be dead?"

Evelyn laughs. "I mean that I want you to publish the book as an authorized biography, with your name on it, when I'm dead."

"OK," I say, as if this is a perfectly normal thing to have someone say to you. And then I realize, no, that's crazy. "Not to be indelicate, but are you telling me you're dying?"

"Everyone's dying, sweetheart. You're dying, I'm dying, that guy is dying."

She points to a middle-aged man walking a fluffy black dog. He hears her, sees her finger aimed at him, and realizes who it is that's speaking. The effect on his face is something like a triple take.

We turn toward the restaurant, walking the two steps down to the door. Evelyn sits at a table in the back. No host guided her here. She just knows where to go and assumes everyone else will catch up. A server in black pants, a white shirt, and a black tie comes to our table and puts down two glasses of water. Evelyn's has no ice.

"Thank you, Troy," Evelyn says.

"Chopped salad?" he asks.

"Well, for me, of course, but I'm not sure about my friend," Evelyn says.

I take the napkin off the table and put it in my lap. "A chopped salad sounds great, thank you."

Troy smiles and leaves.

"You'll like the chopped salad," Evelyn says, as if we are friends having a normal conversation.

"OK," I say, trying to redirect. "Tell me more about this book we're writing."

"I've told you all you need to know."

"You've told me that I'm writing it and you're dying."

"You need to pay better attention to word choice."

I may feel a little out of my league here—and I may not be exactly where I want to be in life right now—but I know a thing or two about word choice.

"I must have misunderstood you. I promise I'm very thoughtful with my words."

Evelyn shrugs. This conversation is very low-stakes for her. "You're young, and your entire generation is casual with words that bear great meaning."

"I see."

"And I didn't say I was confessing any *sins*. To say that what I have to tell is a sin is misleading and hurtful. I don't feel regret for the things I've done—at least, not the things you might expect—despite how hard they may have been or how repugnant they may seem in the cold light of day."

"*Je ne regrette rien*," I say, lifting my glass of water and sipping it.

"That's the spirit," Evelyn says. "Although that song is more about not regretting because you don't live in the past. What I mean is that I'd still make a lot of the same decisions today. To be clear, there *are* things I regret. It's just . . . it's not really the sordid things. I don't regret many of the lies I told or the people I hurt. I'm OK with the fact that sometimes doing the right thing gets ugly. And also, I have compassion for myself. I trust myself. Take, for instance, when I snapped at you earlier, back at the apartment, when you said what you did about my confessing sins. It wasn't a nice thing to do, and I'm not sure you deserved it. But I don't regret it. Because I know I had my reasons, and I did the best I could with every thought and feeling that led up to it."

"You take umbrage with the word *sin* because it implies that you feel sorry."

Our salads appear, and Troy wordlessly grates pepper onto Evelyn's until she puts her hand up and smiles. I decline.

"You can be sorry about something and not regret it," Evelyn says.

"Absolutely," I say. "I see that. I hope that you can give me the benefit of the doubt, going forward, that we're on the same page. Even if there are multiple ways to interpret exactly what we're talking about."

Evelyn picks up her fork but doesn't do anything with it. "I find it very important, with a journalist who will hold my legacy in her hands, to say exactly what I mean and to mean what I say," Evelyn says. "If I'm going to tell you about my life, if I'm going to tell you what really happened, the truth behind all of my marriages, the movies I shot, the people I loved, who I slept with, who I hurt, how I compromised myself, and where it all landed me, then I need to know that you *understand* me. I need to know that you will listen to *exactly* what I'm trying to tell you and not place your own assumptions into my story."

I was wrong. This is not low-stakes for Evelyn. Evelyn can speak casually about things of great importance. But right now, in this moment, when she is taking so much time to make such specific points, I'm realizing this is *real*. This is happening. She really intends to tell me her life story—a story that no doubt includes the gritty truths behind her career and her marriages and her image. That's an incredibly vulnerable position she's putting herself in. It's a lot of power she's giving me. I don't know *why* she's giving it to me. But that doesn't negate the fact that she *is* giving it to me. And it's my job, right now, to show her that I am worthy of it and that I will treat it as sacred.

I put my fork down. "That makes perfect sense, and I'm sorry if I was being glib."

Evelyn waves this off. "The whole culture is glib now. That's the new thing."

"Do you mind if I ask a few more questions? Once I have the lay of the land, I promise to focus solely on what you're saying and what you mean, so that you feel understood at such a level that you can think of no one better suited to the task of gatekeeping your secrets than me."

My sincerity disarms her ever so briefly. "You may begin," she says as she takes a bite of her salad.

"If I'm to publish this book after you have passed, what sort of financial gain do you envision?"

"For me or for you?"

"Let's start with you."

"None for me. Remember, I'll be dead."

"You've mentioned that."

"Next question."

I lean in conspiratorially. "I hate to pose something so vulgar, but what kind of timeline do you intend? Am I to hold on to this book for years until you . . ."

"Die?"

"Well . . . yes," I say.

"Next question."

"What?"

"Next question, please."

"You didn't answer that one."

Evelyn is silent.

"All right, then, what kind of financial gain is there for me?"

"A much more interesting question, and I have been wondering why it took you so long to ask."

"Well, I've asked it."

"You and I will meet over the next however many days it takes, and I will tell you absolutely everything. And then our relationship will be over, and you will be free—or perhaps I should say bound—to write it into a book and sell it to the highest bidder. And I do mean highest. I insist that you be ruthless in your negotiating, Monique. Make them pay you what they would pay a white man. And then, once you've done that, every penny from it will be yours."

"Mine?" I say, stunned.

"You should drink some water. You look ready to faint."

"Evelyn, an authorized biography about your life, in which you talk about all seven of your marriages . . ."

"Yes?"

"A book like that stands to make millions of dollars, even if I didn't negotiate."

"But you will," Evelyn says, taking a sip of her water and looking pleased.

The question has to be asked. We've been dancing around it for far too long. "Why on earth would you do that for me?"

Evelyn nods. She has been expecting this question. "For now, think of it as a gift."

"But why?"

"Next question."

"Seriously."

"Seriously, Monique, next question."

I accidentally drop my fork onto the ivory tablecloth. The oil from the dressing bleeds into the fabric, turning it darker and more translucent. The chopped salad is delicious but heavy on the onions, and I can feel the heat of my breath permeating the space around me. What the hell is going on?

"I'm not trying to be ungrateful, but I think I deserve to know why one of the most famous actresses of all time would pluck me out of obscurity to be her biographer and hand me the opportunity to make millions of dollars off her story."

"The *Huffington Post* is reporting that I could sell my autobiography for as much as twelve million dollars."

"Jesus Christ."

"Inquiring minds want to know, I guess."

The way Evelyn is having so much fun with this, the way she seems to delight in shocking me, lets me know that this is, at least a little bit, a power play. She likes to be cavalier about things that would change other people's lives. Isn't that the very definition of power? Watching people kill themselves over something that means nothing to you?

"Twelve million is a lot, don't get me wrong . . ." she says, and she doesn't need to finish the sentence in order for it to be completed in my head. *But it's not very much to me.*

"But still, Evelyn, why? Why me?"

Evelyn looks up at me, her face stoic. "Next question."

"With all due respect, you're not being particularly fair."

"I'm offering you the chance to make a fortune and skyrocket to the top of your field. I don't have to be fair. Certainly not if that's how you're going to define it, anyway."

On the one hand, this feels like a no-brainer. But at the same time, Evelyn has given me absolutely nothing concrete. And I could lose my job by stealing a story like this for myself. That job is all I have right now. "Can I have some time to think about this?"

"Think about what?"

"About all of this."

Evelyn's eyes narrow ever so slightly. "What on earth is there to think about?"

"I'm sorry if it offends you," I say.

Evelyn cuts me off. "You haven't *offended* me." Just the very implication that I could get under her skin gets under her skin.

"There's a lot to consider," I say. I could get fired. She could back out. I could fail spectacularly at writing this book.

Evelyn leans forward, trying to hear me out. "For instance?"

"For instance, how am I supposed to handle this with *Vivant*? They think they have an exclusive with you. They're making calls to photographers this very moment."

"I told Thomas Welch not to promise a single thing. If they have gone out and made wild assumptions about some cover, that's on them."

"But it's on me, too. Because now I know you have no intention of moving forward with them."

"So?"

"So what do I do? Go back to my office and tell my boss that you're not talking to *Vivant*, that instead you and I are selling a book? It's going to look like I went behind their backs, on company time, mind you, and stole their story for myself."

"That's not really my problem," Evelyn says.

"But that's why I have to think about it. Because it's *my* problem."

Evelyn hears me. I can tell she's taking me seriously from the way she puts her water glass down and looks directly at me, leaning with her forearms on the table. "You have a once-in-a-lifetime opportunity here, Monique. You can see that, right?"

"Of course."

"So do yourself a favor and learn how to grab life by the balls, dear. Don't be so tied up trying to do the right thing when the smart thing is so painfully clear."

"You don't think that I should be forthright with my employers about this? They'll think I conspired to screw them over."

Evelyn shakes her head. "When my team specifically requested you, your company shot back with someone at a higher level. They only agreed to send you out once I made it clear that it was you or it was no one. Do you know why they did that?"

"Because they don't think I—"

"Because they run a business. And so do you. And right now, your business stands to go through the roof. You have a choice to make. Are we writing a book together or not? You should know, if you won't write it, I'm not going to give it to anyone else. It will die with me in that case."

"Why would you tell only *me* your life story? You don't even know me. That doesn't make sense."

"I'm under absolutely no obligation to make sense to you."

"What are you after, Evelyn?"

"You ask too many questions."

"I'm here to interview you."

"Still." She takes a sip of water, swallows, and then looks me right in the eye. "By the time we are through, you won't have any questions," she says. "All of these things you're so desperate to know, I promise I'll answer them before we're done. But I'm not going to answer them one minute before I want to. I call the shots. That's how this is going to go."

I listen to her and think about it, and I realize I would be an absolute moron to walk away from this, no matter what her terms are. I didn't stay in New York and let David go to San Francisco because I like the Statue of Liberty. I did it because I want to climb the ladder as high as I possibly can. I did it because I want my name, the name my father gave me, in big, bold letters one day. This is my chance.

"OK," I say.

"OK, then. Glad to hear it." Evelyn's shoulders relax, she picks up her water again, and she smiles. "Monique, I think I like you," she says.

I breathe deeply, only now realizing how shallow my breathing has been. "Thank you, Evelyn. That means a lot."

E VELYN AND I ARE BACK in her foyer. "I'll meet you in my office in a half hour."

"OK," I say as Evelyn heads down the corridor and out of sight. I take off my coat and put it in the closet.

I should use this time to check in with Frankie. If I don't reach out to update her soon, she'll track me down.

I just have to decide how I'm going to handle it. How do I make sure she doesn't try to wrestle this away from me?

I think my only option is to pretend everything is going according to plan. My only plan is to lie.

I breathe.

One of my earliest memories from when I was a child was of my parents bringing me to Zuma Beach in Malibu. It was still springtime, I think. The water hadn't yet warmed enough for comfort.

My mom stayed on the sand, setting down our blanket and umbrella, while my dad scooped me up and ran with me down to the shoreline. I remember feeling weightless in his arms. And then he put my feet in the water, and I cried, telling him it was too cold.

He agreed with me. It *was* cold. But then he said, "Just breathe in and out five times. And when you're done, I bet it won't feel so cold."

I watched as he put his feet in. I watched him breathe. And then I put my feet back in and breathed with him. He was right, of course. It wasn't so cold.

After that, my dad would breathe with me anytime I was on the verge of tears. When I skinned my elbow, when my cousin called me an Oreo, when my mom said we couldn't get a puppy, my father would sit and breathe with me. It still hurts, all these years later, to think about those moments.

But for now, I keep breathing, right there in Evelyn's foyer, centering myself as he taught me.

And then, when I feel calm, I pick up my phone and dial Frankie.

"Monique." She answers on the second ring. "Tell me. How's it going?"

"It's going well," I say. I'm surprised at how even and flat my voice is. "Evelyn is pretty much everything you'd expect from an icon. Still gorgeous. Charismatic as ever."

"And?"

"And . . . things are progressing."

"Is she committing to talk about any other topics than the gowns?"

What can I say now to start covering my own ass? "You know, she's pretty reticent about anything other than getting some press for the auction. I'm trying to play nice at the moment, get her to trust me a bit more before I start pushing."

"Will she sit for a cover?"

"It's too early to tell. Trust me, Frankie," I say, and I hate how sincere it sounds coming out of my mouth, "I know how important this is. But right now, the best thing for me to do is make sure Evelyn likes me so that I can try to garner some influence and advocate for what we want."

"OK," Frankie says. "Obviously, I want more than a few sound bites about dresses, but that's still more than any other magazine has gotten from her in decades, so . . ." Frankie keeps talking, but I've stopped listening. I'm far too focused on the fact that Frankie's not even going to get sound bites.

And I'm going to get far, far more.

"I should go," I say, excusing myself. "She and I are talking again in a few minutes."

I hang up the phone and breathe out. *I've got this shit.*

As I make my way through the apartment, I can hear Grace in the kitchen. I open the swinging door and spot her cutting flower stems.

"Sorry to bother you. Evelyn said to meet her in her office, but I'm not sure where that is."

"Oh," Grace says, putting down the scissors and wiping her hands on a towel. "I'll show you."

I follow her up a set of stairs and into Evelyn's study area. The walls are a striking flat charcoal gray, the area rug a golden beige. The large windows are flanked by dark blue curtains, and on the opposite side of the room are built-in bookcases. A gray-blue couch sits facing an over-sized glass desk.

Grace smiles and leaves me to wait for Evelyn. I drop my bag on the sofa and check my phone.

"You take the desk," Evelyn says as she comes in. She hands me a glass of water. "I can only assume the way this works is that I talk and you write."

"I suppose," I say, sitting in the desk chair. "I've never attempted to write a biography before. After all, I'm not a biographer."

Evelyn looks at me pointedly. She sits opposite me, on the sofa. "Let me explain something to you. When I was fourteen years old, my mother had already died, and I was living with my father. The older I got, the more I realized that it was only a matter of time until my father tried to marry me off to a friend of his or his boss, someone who could help his situation. And if I'm being honest, the more I developed, the less secure I was in the idea that my father might not try to take something of me for himself.

"We were so broke that we were stealing the electricity from the apartment above us. There was one outlet in our place that was on their circuit, so we plugged anything we needed to use into that one socket. If I needed to do homework after dark, I plugged in a lamp in that outlet and sat underneath it with my book.

"My mother was a saint. I really mean it. Stunningly beautiful, an incredible singer, with a heart of gold. For years before she died, she would always tell me that we were gonna get out of Hell's Kitchen and go straight to Hollywood. She said she was going to be the most famous woman in the world and get us a mansion on the beach. I had this fantasy of the two of us together in a house, throwing parties, drinking champagne. And then she died, and it was like waking up from a dream. Suddenly, I was in a world where none of that was ever going to happen. And I was going to be stuck in Hell's Kitchen forever.

"I was gorgeous, even at fourteen. Oh, I know the whole world prefers a woman who doesn't know her power, but I'm sick of all that. I turned heads. Now, I take no pride in this. I didn't make my own face. I didn't give myself this body. But I'm also not going to sit here and say, 'Aw, shucks. People really thought I was pretty?' like some kind of prig.

"My friend Beverly knew a guy in her building named Ernie Diaz who was an electrician. And Ernie knew a guy over at MGM. At least, that was the rumor going around. And one day, Beverly told me she heard that Ernie was up for some job rigging lights in Hollywood. So that weekend, I made up a reason to go over to Beverly's, and I 'accidentally' knocked on Ernie's door. I knew exactly where Beverly was. But I knocked on Ernie's door and said, 'Have you seen Beverly Gustafson?'

"Ernie was twenty-two. He wasn't handsome by any means, but he was fine to look at. He said he hadn't seen her, but I watched as he continued to stare at me. I watched as his eyes started at mine and grazed their way down, scanning every inch of me in my favorite green dress.

"And then Ernie said, 'Sweetheart, are you sixteen?' I was fourteen, remember. But do you know what I did? I said, 'Why, I just turned.'"

Evelyn looks at me with purpose. "Do you understand what I'm telling you? When you're given an opportunity to change your life, be ready to do whatever it takes to make it happen. The world doesn't *give* things, you *take* things. If you learn one thing from me, it should probably be that."

Wow. "OK," I say.

"You've never been a biographer before, but you are one starting now."

I nod my head. "I got it."

"Good," Evelyn says, relaxing into the sofa. "So where do you want to begin?"

I grab my notebook and look at the scribbled words I've covered the last few pages with. There are dates and film titles, references to classic images of her, rumors with question marks after them. And then, in big letters that I went over and over with my pen, darkening each letter until I changed the texture of the page, I've written, "Who was the love of Evelyn's life???"

That's the big question. That's the hook of this book.

Seven husbands.

Which one did she love the best? Which one was the *real* one?

As both a journalist and a consumer, that's what I want to know. It won't be where the book begins, but maybe that is where she and I should begin. I want to know, going into these marriages, which is the one that matters the most.

I look up at Evelyn to see her sitting up, ready for me.

"Who was the love of your life? Was it Harry Cameron?"

Evelyn thinks and then answers slowly. "Not in the way you mean, no."

"In what way, then?"

"Harry was my greatest friend. He invented me. He was the person who loved me the most unconditionally. The person I loved the most purely, I think. Other than my daughter. But no, he was not the love of my life."

"Why not?"

"Because that was someone else."

"OK, who *was* the love of your life, then?"

Evelyn nods, as if this is the question she has been expecting, as if the situation is unfolding exactly as she knew it would. But then she shakes her head again. "You know what?" she says, standing up. "It's getting late, isn't it?"

I look at my watch. It's midafternoon. "Is it?"

"I think it is," she says, and she walks toward me, toward the door.

"All right," I say, standing up to meet her.

Evelyn puts her arm around me and leads me out into the hallway. "Let's pick up again on Monday. Would that be OK?"

"Uh . . . sure. Evelyn, did I say something to offend you?"

Evelyn leads me down the stairs. "Not at all," she says, waving my fears aside. "Not at all."

There is a tension that I can't quite put my finger on. Evelyn walks with me until we hit the foyer. She opens the closet. I reach in and grab my coat.

"Back here?" Evelyn says. "Monday morning? What do you say we start around ten?"

"OK," I say, putting my thick coat around my shoulders. "If that's what you'd like."

Evelyn nods. She looks past me for a moment, over my shoulder, but appearing not to actually be looking at anything in particular. Then she opens her mouth. "I've spent a very long time learning how to . . . spin the truth," she says. "It's hard to undo that wiring. I've gotten too good at it, I think. Just now, I wasn't exactly sure *how* to tell the truth. I don't have very much practice in it. It feels antithetical to my very survival. But I'll get there."

I nod, unsure how to respond. "So . . . Monday?"

"Monday," Evelyn says with a long blink and a nod. "I'll be ready then."

I walk back to the subway in the chilly air. I cram myself into a car packed with people, holding on to the handrail above my head. I walk to my apartment and open my front door.

I sit on my couch, open my laptop, and answer some e-mails. I start to order something for dinner. And it is only when I go to put my feet up that I remember there is no coffee table. For the first time since he left, I have not come into this apartment immediately thinking of David.

Instead, what plays in the back of my mind all weekend—from my Friday night in to my Saturday night out and my Sunday morning at the park—isn't *How did my marriage fail?* but rather *Who the hell was Evelyn Hugo in love with?*

I AM ONCE AGAIN IN Evelyn's study. The sun is shining directly into the windows, lighting Evelyn's face with so much warmth that it obscures her right side from view.

We're really doing this. Evelyn and me. Subject and biographer. It begins now.

She is wearing black leggings and a man's navy-blue button-down shirt with a belt. I'm wearing my usual jeans, T-shirt, and blazer. I dressed with the intention of staying here all day and all night, if need be. If she keeps talking, I will be here, listening.

"So," I say.

"So," Evelyn says, her voice daring me to go for it.

Sitting at her desk while she is on the couch feels adversarial somehow. I want her to feel as if we are on the same team. Because we are, aren't we? Although I get the impression you never know with Evelyn.

Can she really tell the truth? Is she capable of it?

I take a seat in the chair next to the sofa. I lean forward, with my notepad in my lap and a pen in my hand. I take out my phone, open the voice memo app, and hit record.

"You sure you're ready?" I ask her.

Evelyn nods. "Everyone I loved is dead now. There's no one left to protect. No one left to lie for but me. People have so closely followed the most intricate details of the fake story of my life. But it's not . . . I don't . . . I want them to know the real story. The real me."

"All right," I say. "Show me the real you, then. And I'll make sure the world understands."

Evelyn looks at me and briefly smiles. I can tell I have said what she wants to hear. Fortunately, I mean it.

"Let's go chronologically," I say. "Tell me more about Ernie Diaz, your first husband, the one who got you out of Hell's Kitchen."

"OK," Evelyn says, nodding. "It's as good a place to start as any."

Poor Ernie Diaz

♦

M Y MOTHER HAD BEEN A chorus girl off Broadway. She'd emi-grated from Cuba with my father when she was seventeen. When I got older, I found out that *chorus girl* was also a euphemism for a prostitute. I don't know if she was or not. I'd like to think she wasn't—not because there's any shame in it but because I know a little bit about what it is to give your body to someone when you don't want to, and I hope she didn't have to do that.

I was eleven when she died of pneumonia. Obviously, I don't have a lot of memories of her, but I do remember that she smelled like cheap vanilla, and she made the most amazing *caldo gallego*. She never called me Evelyn, only *mija*, which made me feel really special, like I was hers and she was mine. Above all else, my mother wanted to be a movie star. She really thought she could get us out of there and away from my father by getting into the movies.

I wanted to be just like her.

I've often wished that on her deathbed she'd said something moving, something I could take with me always. But we didn't know how sick she was until it was over. The last thing she said to me was *Dile a tu padre que estaré en la cama.* "Tell your father I'll be in bed."

After she died, I would cry only in the shower, where no one could see me or hear me, where I couldn't tell what were my tears and what was the water. I don't know why I did that. I just know that after a few months, I was able to take a shower without crying.

And then, the summer after she died, I began to develop.

My chest started growing, and it wouldn't stop. I had to rifle through my mom's old things when I was twelve years old, looking to see if there was a bra that would fit. The only one I found was too small, but I put it on anyway.

By the time I was thirteen, I was five foot eight, with dark, shiny brown hair, long legs, light bronze skin, and a chest that pulled at the buttons of my dresses. Grown men were watching me walk down the street, and some of the girls in my building didn't want to hang out with me anymore. It was a lonely business. Motherless, with an abusive father, no friends, and a sexuality in my body that my mind wasn't ready for.

The cashier at the five-and-dime on the corner was this boy named Billy. He was the sixteen-year-old brother of the girl who sat next to me in school. One October day, I went down to the five-and-dime to buy a piece of candy, and he kissed me.

I didn't want him to kiss me. I pushed him away. But he held on to my arm.

"Oh, come on," he said.

The store was empty. His arms were strong. He grasped me tighter. And in that moment, I knew he was going to get what he wanted from me whether I let him or not.

So I had two choices. I could do it for free. Or I could do it for free candy.

For the next three months, I took anything I wanted from that five-and-dime. And in exchange, I saw him every Saturday night and let him take my shirt off. I never felt I had much choice in the matter. Being wanted meant having to satisfy. At least, that was my view of it back then.

I remember him saying, in the dark, cramped stockroom with my back against a wooden crate, "You have this power over me."

He'd convinced himself that his wanting me was my fault.

And I believed him.

Look what I do to these poor boys, I thought. And yet also, *Here is my value, my power.*

So when he dumped me—because he was bored with me, because

he'd found someone else more exciting—I felt both a deep relief and a very real sense of failure.

There was one other boy like that, whom I took my shirt off for because I thought I had to, before I started realizing that *I* could be the one doing the choosing.

I didn't want anyone; that was the problem. To be perfectly blunt, I'd started to figure my body out quickly. I didn't need boys in order to feel good. And that realization gave me great power. So I wasn't interested in anyone sexually. But I did want *something*.

I wanted to get far away from Hell's Kitchen.

I wanted out of my apartment, away from my father's stale tequila breath and heavy hand. I wanted someone to take care of me. I wanted a nice house and money. I wanted to run, far away from my life. I wanted to go where my mom had promised me we'd end up someday.

Here's the thing about Hollywood. It's both a place and a feeling. If you run there, you can run toward Southern California, where the sun always shines and the grimy buildings and dirty sidewalks are replaced by palm trees and orange groves. But you also run toward the way life is portrayed in the movies.

You run toward a world that is moral and just, where the good guys win and the bad guys lose, where the pain you face is only in an effort to make you stronger, so that you can win that much bigger in the end.

It would take me years to figure out that life doesn't get easier simply because it gets more glamorous. But you couldn't have told me that when I was fourteen.

So I put on my favorite green dress, the one I had just about grown out of. And I knocked on the door of the guy I heard was headed to Hollywood.

I could tell just by the look on his face that Ernie Diaz was glad to see me.

And that's what I traded my virginity for. A ride to Hollywood.

Ernie and I got married on February 14, 1953. I became Evelyn Diaz. I was just fifteen by that point, but my father signed the papers. I have to think Ernie suspected I wasn't of age. But I lied right to his face about it, and that seemed good enough for him. He wasn't a bad-looking guy, but he also wasn't particularly book-smart or charming. He wasn't going to get many chances to marry a beautiful girl. I think he knew that. I think he knew enough to grab the chance when it swung his way.

A few months later, Ernie and I got into his '49 Plymouth and drove west. We stayed with some friends of his as he started his job as a grip. Pretty soon we had saved enough to get our own apartment. We were on Detroit Street and De Longpre. I had some new clothes and enough money to make us a roast on the weekends.

I was supposed to be finishing high school. But Ernie certainly wasn't going to be checking my report cards, and I knew school was a waste of time. I had come to Hollywood to do one thing, and I was going to do it.

Instead of going to class, I would walk down to the Formosa Cafe for lunch every day and stayed through happy hour. I had recognized the place from the gossip rags. I knew famous people hung out there. It was right next to a movie studio.

The red building with cursive writing and a black awning became my daily spot. I knew it was a lame move, but it was the only one I had. If I wanted to be an actress, I would have to be discovered. And I wasn't sure how you went about that, except by hanging around the spots where movie people might be.

So I went there every day and nursed a glass of Coke.

I did it so often and for so long that eventually the bartender got sick of pretending he didn't know what gamble I was running.

"Look," he said to me about three weeks in, "if you want to sit around here hoping Humphrey Bogart shows up, that's fine. But you need to make yourself useful. I'm not giving up a paying seat for you to sip a soda."

He was older, maybe fifty, but his hair was thick and dark. The lines on his forehead reminded me of my father's.

"What do you want me to do?" I asked him.

I was slightly worried that he'd want something from me that I had already given to Ernie, but he threw a waiter's pad at me and told me to try my hand at taking orders.

I had no clue how to be a waitress, but I certainly wasn't going to tell him that. "All right," I said. "Where should I start?"

He pointed at the tables in the place, the booths in a tight row. "That's table one. You can figure out the rest of the numbers by counting."

"OK," I said. "I got it."

I stood up off the bar stool and started walking over to table two, where three men in suits were seated, talking, their menus closed.

"Hey, kid?" the bartender said.

"Yes?"

"You're a knockout. Five bucks says it happens for you."

I took ten orders, mixed up three people's sandwiches, and made four dollars.

Four months later, Harry Cameron, then a young producer at Sunset Studios, came in to meet with an exec from the lot next door. They each ordered a steak. When I brought the check, Harry looked up at me and said, "Jesus."

Two weeks later, I had a deal at Sunset Studios.

I WENT HOME and told Ernie that I was shocked that anyone at Sunset Studios would be interested in little old me. I said that being an actress would just be a fun lark, a thing to do to pass the time until my real job of being a mother began. Grade-A bullshit.

I was almost seventeen by that point, although Ernie still thought I was older. It was late 1954. And I would get up every morning and head to Sunset Studios.

I didn't know how to act my way out of a paper bag, but I was learning. I was an extra in a couple of romantic comedies. I had one line in a war picture.

"And why shouldn't he?" That was the line.

I played a nurse taking care of a wounded soldier. The doctor in the scene playfully accused the soldier of flirting with me, and I said, "And why shouldn't he?" I said it like a child in a fifth-grade play, with a slight New York accent. Back then, so many of my words were accented. English spoken like a New Yorker. Spanish spoken like an American.

When the movie came out, Ernie and I went to see it. Ernie thought it was funny, his little wife with a little line in a movie.

I had never made much money before, and now I was making as much as Ernie after he was promoted to key grip. So I asked him if I could pay for acting classes. I'd made him arroz con pollo that night, and I specifically didn't take my apron off when I brought it up. I wanted him to see me as harmless and domestic. I thought I'd get further if I didn't threaten him. It grated on my nerves to have to ask him how I could spend my own money. But I didn't see another choice.

"Sure," he said. "I think it's a smart thing to do. You'll get better, and who knows, you might even star in a picture one day."

I *would* star.

I wanted to punch his lights out.

But I've since come to understand that it wasn't Ernie's fault. None of it was Ernie's fault. I'd told him I was someone else. And then I started getting angry that he couldn't see who I really was.

Six months later, I could deliver a line with sincerity. I wasn't great by any means, but I was good enough.

I'd been in three more movies, all day-player roles. I'd heard there was a part open to play Stu Cooper's teenage daughter in a romantic comedy. And I decided I wanted it.

So I did something that not many other actresses at my level would have had the guts to do. I knocked on Harry Cameron's door.

"Evelyn," he said, surprised to see me. "To what do I owe the pleasure?"

"I want the Caroline part," I said. "In *Love Isn't All.*"

Harry motioned for me to sit down. He was handsome, for an executive. Most producers around the lot were rotund, a lot of them losing their hair. But Harry was tall and slim. He was young. I suspected he didn't even have a decade on me. He wore suits that fit him nicely and always complemented his ice-blue eyes. There was something vaguely midwestern about him, not so much in how he looked but in the way he approached people, with kindness first, then strength.

Harry was one of the only men on the lot who didn't stare directly at my chest. It actually bothered me, as if I'd been doing something wrong to not get his attention. It just goes to show that if you tell a woman her only skill is to be desirable, she will believe you. I was believing it before I was even eighteen.

"I'm not going to bullshit you, Evelyn. Ari Sullivan is never going to approve you for that part."

"Why not?"

"You're not the right type."

"What's that supposed to mean?"

"No one would believe you were Stu Cooper's daughter."

"I certainly could be."

"You could not."

"Why?"

"*Why?*"

"Yes, I want to know why."

"Your name is Evelyn Diaz."

"So?"

"I can't put you in a movie and try to pretend you're not Mexican."

"I'm Cuban."

"For our purposes, same difference."

It was not the same difference, but I saw absolutely no merit in trying to explain that to him. "OK," I said. "Then how about the movie with Gary DuPont?"

"You can't play a romantic lead with Gary Dupont."

"Why not?"

Harry looked at me as if to ask if I was really going to make him say it.

"Because I'm *Mexican*?" I asked.

"Because the movie with Gary DuPont needs a nice blond girl."

"I could be a nice blond girl."

Harry looked at me.

I tried harder. "I want it, Harry. And you know I can do it. I'm one of the most interesting girls you guys have right now."

Harry laughed. "You're bold. I'll give you that."

Harry's secretary knocked on the door. "I'm sorry to interrupt, but Mr. Cameron, you need to be in Burbank at one."

Harry looked at his watch.

I made one last play. "Think about it, Harry. I'm good, and I can be even better. But you're wasting me in these small roles."

"We know what we're doing," he said, standing up.

I stood up with him. "Where do you see my career a year from now, Harry? Playing a teacher with three lines?"

Harry walked past me and opened his door, ushering me out. "We'll see," he said.

Having lost the battle, I resolved to win the war. So the next time I saw Ari Sullivan at the studio dining hall, I dropped my purse in front of him and "accidentally" gave him an eyeful as I bent down to pick it up. He made eye contact with me, and then I walked away, as if I wanted nothing from him, as if I had no idea who he was.

A week later, I pretended I was lost in the executive offices, and I ran into him in the hallway. He was a portly guy, but it was a weight that suited him. He had eyes that were so dark brown it was hard to make out the irises and the kind of five o'clock shadow that was permanent. But he had a pretty smile. And that was what I focused on.

"Mrs. Diaz," he said. I was both surprised and not surprised to find that he had learned my name.

"Mr. Sullivan," I said.

"Please, call me Ari."

"Well, hello, Ari," I said, grazing my hand on his arm.

I was seventeen. He was forty-eight.

That night, after his secretary left for the day, I was laid across his desk, with my skirt around my hips and Ari's face between my legs. It turned out Ari had a fetish for orally pleasing underage girls. After about seven minutes of it, I pretended to erupt in reckless pleasure. I couldn't tell you whether it was any good. But I was happy to be there, because I knew it was going to get me what I wanted.

If the definition of enjoying sex means that it is pleasurable, then I've had a lot of sex that I didn't enjoy. But if we're defining it as being happy to have made the trade, then, well, I haven't had much I hated.

When I left, I saw the row of Oscars that Ari had sitting in his office. I told myself that one day I'd get one, too.

Love Isn't All and the Gary DuPont movie I'd wanted came out within a week of each other. *Love Isn't All* tanked. And Penelope Quills, the woman who'd gotten the part I'd wanted opposite Gary, got terrible reviews.

I cut out a review of Penelope and sent it by interoffice mail to Harry and Ari, with a note that said, "I would have knocked it out of the park."

The next morning, I had a note from Harry in my trailer: "OK, you win."

Harry called me into his office and told me that he had discussed it with Ari, and they had two potential roles for me.

I could play an Italian heiress as the fourth lead in a war romance. Or I could play Jo in *Little Women*.

I knew what it would mean, playing Jo. I knew Jo was a white woman. And still, I wanted it. I hadn't gotten on my back just to take a baby step.

"Jo," I said. "Give me Jo."

And in so doing, I set the star machine in motion.

Harry introduced me to studio stylist Gwendolyn Peters. Gwen bleached my hair and cut it into a shoulder-length bob. She shaped my eyebrows. She plucked my widow's peak. I met with a nutritionist, who made me lose six pounds exactly, mostly by taking up smoking and replacing some meals with cabbage soup. I met with an elocutionist, who got rid of the New York in my English, who banished Spanish entirely.

And then, of course, there was the three-page questionnaire I had to fill out about my life until then. What did my father do for a living? What did I like to do in my spare time? Did I have any pets?

When I turned in my honest answers, the researcher read it in one sitting and said, "Oh, no, no, no. This won't do at all. From now on, your mother died in an accident, leaving your father to raise you. He worked as a builder in Manhattan, and on weekends during the summer, he'd take you to Coney Island. If anyone asks, you love tennis and swimming, and you have a Saint Bernard named Roger."

I sat for at least a hundred publicity photos. Me with my new blond hair, my trimmer figure, my whiter teeth. You wouldn't believe the things they made me model. Smiling at the beach, playing golf, running down the street being tugged by a Saint Bernard that someone borrowed from a set decorator. There were photos of me salting a grapefruit, shooting a bow and arrow, getting on a fake airplane. Don't even get me started on the holiday photos. It would be a sweltering-hot September day, and I'd be sitting there in a red velvet dress, next to a fully lit Christmas tree, pretending to open a box that contained a brand-new baby kitten.

The wardrobe people were consistent and militant about how I was dressed, per Harry Cameron's orders, and that look always included a tight sweater, buttoned up just right.

I wasn't blessed with an hourglass figure. My ass might as well have been a flat wall. You could hang a picture on it. It was my chest that kept men's interest. And women admired my face.

To be honest, I'm not sure when I figured out the exact angle we were all going for. But it was sometime during those weeks of photo shoots that it hit me.

I was being designed to be two opposing things, a complicated image that was hard to dissect but easy to grab on to. I was supposed to be both naive *and* erotic. It was as if I was too wholesome to understand the un-wholesome thoughts you were having about me.

It was bullshit, of course. But it was an easy act to put on. Sometimes I think the difference between an actress and a star is that the star feels comfortable being the very thing the world wants her to be. And I felt comfortable appearing both innocent and suggestive.

When the pictures got developed, Harry Cameron pulled me into his office. I knew what he wanted to talk about. I knew there was one remaining piece that needed to be put into place.

"What about Amelia Dawn? That has a nice ring to it, doesn't it?" he said. The two of us were sitting in his office, him at his desk, me in the chair.

I thought about it. "How about something with the initials EH?" I asked. I wanted to get something as close to the name my mother gave me, Evelyn Herrera, as I could.

"Ellen Hennessey?" He shook his head. "No, too stuffy."

I looked at him and sold him the line I'd come up with the night before, as if I'd just thought of it. "What about Evelyn Hugo?"

Harry smiled. "Sounds French," he said. "I like it."

I stood up and shook his hand, my blond hair, which I was still getting used to, framing my sight.

I turned the knob to his door, but Harry stopped me.

"There's one more thing," he said.

"OK."

"I read your answers to the interview questions." He looked at me directly. "Ari is very happy with the changes you've made. He thinks you have a lot of potential. The studio thinks it would be a good idea if you went on a few dates, if you were seen around town with some guys like Pete Greer and Brick Thomas. Maybe even Don Adler."

Don Adler was the hottest actor at Sunset. His parents, Mary and Roger Adler, were two of the biggest stars of the 1930s. He was Hollywood royalty.

"Is that going to be a problem?" Harry asked.

He wasn't going to mention Ernie directly, because he knew he didn't have to.

"Not a problem," I said. "Not at all."

Harry nodded. He handed me a business card.

"Call Benny Morris. He's a lawyer over in the bungalows. Handled Ruby Reilly's annulment from Mac Riggs. He'll help you straighten it out."

I went home and told Ernie I was leaving him.

He cried for six hours straight, and then, in the wee hours of the night, as I lay beside him in our bed, he said, "*Bien*. If that's what you want."

The studio gave him a payout, and I left him a heartfelt letter telling him how much it hurt me to leave him. It wasn't true, but I felt I owed it to him to finish out the marriage as I'd started it, pretending to love him.

I'm not proud of what I did to him; it didn't feel casual to me, the way I hurt him. It didn't then, and it doesn't now.

But I also know how badly I'd needed to leave Hell's Kitchen. I know what it feels like to not want your father to look at you too closely, lest he decides he hates you and hits you or decides he loves you a little too much. And I know what it feels like to see your future ahead of you—the husband who's really just a new version of your father, surrendering to him in bed when it's the last thing you want to do, making only biscuits and canned corn for dinner because you don't have money for meat.

So how can I condemn the fourteen-year-old girl who did whatever she could to get herself out of town? And how can I judge the eighteen-year-old who got herself out of that marriage once it was safe to do so?

Ernie ended up remarried to a woman named Betty who gave him eight children. I believe he died in the early '90s, a grandfather many times over. He used the payout from the studio to put a down payment on a house in Mar Vista, not far from the Fox lot. I never heard from him again.

So if we are going by the metric that all's well that ends well, then I guess it's safe to say that I'm not sorry.

E VELYN," GRACE SAYS AS SHE comes into the room. "You have a
dinner with Ronnie Beelman in an hour. I just wanted to remind
you."

"Oh, right," Evelyn says. "Thank you." She turns to me once Grace has
left. "How about we pick this up tomorrow? Same time?"

"Yeah, that's fine," I say, starting to gather my things. My left leg has
fallen asleep, and I tap it against the hardwood to try to wake it up.

"How do you think it's going so far?" Evelyn asks as she gets up and
walks me out. "You can make a story out of it?"

"I can do anything," I say.

Evelyn laughs and says, "Good girl."

"HOW ARE THINGS?" my mom asks the moment I pick up the phone.
She says "things," but I know she means *How is your life without
David?*

"Fine," I say as I set my bag on the couch and walk toward the refrigerator. My mother cautioned me early on that David might not be
the best man for me. He and I had been dating a few months when I
brought him home to Encino for Thanksgiving.

She liked how polite he was, how he offered to set and clear the table.
But in the morning before he woke up on our last day in town, my mom
told me she questioned whether David and I had a meaningful connection. She said she didn't "see it."

I told her she didn't need to see it. That I *felt* it.

But her question stuck in my head. Sometimes it was a whisper; other times it echoed loudly.

When I called to tell her we'd gotten engaged a little more than a year later, I was hoping my mother could see how kind he was, how seamlessly he fit into my life. He made things feel effortless, and in those days, that seemed so valuable, so rare. Still, I worried she would air her concerns again, that she would say I was making a mistake.

She didn't. In fact, she was nothing but supportive.

Now I'm wondering if that was more out of respect than approval.

"I've been thinking . . ." my mom says as I open the refrigerator door. "Or I should say I've hatched a plan."

I grab a bottle of Pellegrino, the plastic basket of cherry tomatoes, and the watery tub of burrata cheese. "Oh, no," I say. "What have you done?"

My mom laughs. She's always had such a great laugh. It's very carefree, very young. Mine is inconsistent. Sometimes it's loud; sometimes it's wheezy. Other times I sound like an old man. David used to say he thought my old-man laugh was the most genuine, because no one in their right mind would *want* to sound like that. Now I'm trying to remember the last time it happened.

"I haven't done anything yet," my mom says. "It's still in the idea phase. But I'm thinking I want to come visit."

I don't say anything for a moment, weighing the pros and cons, as I chew the massive chunk of cheese I just put in my mouth. Con: she will critique every single outfit I wear in her presence. Pro: she will make macaroni and cheese and coconut cake. Con: she will ask me if I'm OK every three seconds. Pro: for at least a few days, when I come home, this apartment will not be empty.

I swallow. "OK," I say finally. "Great idea. I can take you to a show, maybe."

"Oh, thank goodness," she says. "I already booked the ticket."

"Mom," I say, groaning.

"What? I could have canceled it if you'd said no. But you didn't. So great. I'll be there in about two weeks. That works, right?"

I knew this was going to happen as soon as my mom partially retired from teaching last year. She spent decades as the head of the science department at a private high school, and the moment she told me she was stepping down and only teaching two classes, I knew that extra time and attention would have to go somewhere.

"Yeah, that works," I say as I cut up the tomatoes and pour olive oil on them.

"I just want to make sure you're OK," my mom says. "I want to be there. You shouldn't—"

"I know, Mom," I say, cutting her off. "I know. I get it. Thank you. For coming. It will be fun."

It won't be *fun*, necessarily. But it will be good. It's like going to a party when you've had a bad day. You don't want to go, but you know you should. You know that even if you don't enjoy it, it will do you good to get out of the house.

"Did you get the package I sent?" she says.

"The package?"

"With your dad's photos?"

"Oh, no," I say. "I didn't."

We are quiet for a moment, and then my mom gets exasperated by my silence. "For heaven's sake, I've been waiting for you to bring it up, but I can't wait any longer. How's it going with Evelyn Hugo?" she says. "I'm dying to know, and you're not offering anything!"

I pour my Pellegrino and tell her that Evelyn is somehow both forthright and hard to read. And then I tell her that she isn't giving me the story for *Vivant*. That she wants me to write a book.

"I'm confused," my mom says. "She wants you to write her biography?"

"Yeah," I say. "And as exciting as it is, there's something weird about it. I mean, I don't think she ever considered doing a piece with *Vivant* at all. I think she was . . ." I trail off, because I haven't figured out exactly what it is I'm trying to say.

"What?"

I think about it more. "Using *Vivant* to get to me. I don't quite know. But Evelyn is very calculating. She's up to something."

"Well, I'm not surprised she wants you. You're talented. You're bright . . ."

I find myself rolling my eyes at my mother's predictability, but I do still appreciate it. "No, I know, Mom. But there's another layer here. I'm convinced of it."

"That sounds ominous."

"I guess so."

"Should I be worried?" my mom asks. "I mean, are *you* worried?"

I hadn't thought about it in such direct terms, but I suppose my answer is no. "I think I'm too intrigued to be worried," I say.

"Well, then, just make sure you share the real juicy stuff with your mother. I did suffer through a twenty-two-hour labor for you. I deserve this."

I laugh, and it comes out, just a little bit, like an old man. "All right," I say. "I promise."

"OK," EVELYN SAYS. "Are we ready?"

She is back in her seat. I am in my spot at the desk. Grace has brought us a tray with blueberry muffins, two white mugs, a carafe of coffee, and a stainless-steel creamer. I stand up, pour my coffee, add my cream, walk back to the desk, press record, and then say, "Yes, ready. Go for it. What happened next?"

Goddamn Don Adler

◆

*L*ITTLE *W*OMEN TURNED OUT TO be a carrot dangled in front of me. Because as soon as I became "Evelyn Hugo, Young Blonde," Sunset had all sorts of movies they wanted me to do. Dumb sentimental comedy stuff.

I was OK with it for two reasons. One, I had no choice but to be all right with it because I didn't hold the cards. And two, my star was rising. Fast.

The first movie they gave me to star in was *Father and Daughter*. We shot it in 1956. Ed Baker played my widowed father, and the two of us were falling in love with people at the same time. Him with his secretary, me with his apprentice.

During that time, Harry was really pushing for me to go out on a few dates with Brick Thomas.

Brick was a former child star and a matinee idol who honest-to-God thought he might be the messiah. Just standing next to him, I thought I might drown in the self-adoration cascading off him.

One Friday night, Brick and I met, with Harry and Gwendolyn Peters, a few blocks from Chasen's. Gwen put me in a dress, hose, and heels. She put my hair in an updo. Brick showed up in dungarees and a T-shirt, and Gwen put him in a nice suit. We drove Harry's brand-new crimson Cadillac Biarritz the half mile to the front door.

People were taking pictures of Brick and me before we even got out of the car. We were escorted to a circular booth, where the two of us packed ourselves in tight together. I ordered a Shirley Temple.

"How old are you, sweetheart?" Brick asked me.

"Eighteen," I said.

"So I bet you had my picture up on your wall, huh?"

It took everything I had not to grab my drink and throw it right in his face. Instead, I smiled as politely as possible and said, "How'd you know?"

Photographers snapped shots as we sat together. We pretended not to see them, making it look as if we were laughing together, arm in arm.

An hour later, we were back with Harry and Gwendolyn, changing into our normal clothes.

Just before Brick and I said good-bye, he turned to me and smiled. "Gonna be a lot of rumors about you and me tomorrow," he said.

"Sure are."

"Let me know if you want to make 'em true."

I should have kept quiet. I should have just smiled nicely. But instead, I said, "Don't hold your breath."

Brick looked at me and laughed and then waved good-bye, as if I hadn't just insulted him.

"Can you believe that guy?" I said. Harry had already opened my door and was waiting for me to get into the car.

"*That guy* makes us a lot of money," he said as I sat down.

Harry got in on the other side and turned the key in the ignition but didn't start driving. Instead, he looked at me. "I'm not saying you should be dallying around too much with these actors you don't like," he said. "But it would do you some good, if you liked one, if things progressed past a photo op or two. The studio would like it. The fans would like it."

Naively, I had thought I was done pretending to like the attention of every man I came across. "OK," I said, rather petulantly. "I'll try."

And while I knew it was the best thing to do for my career, I grinned through my teeth on dates with Pete Greer and Bobby Donovan.

But then Harry set me up on a date with Don Adler, and I forgot why I would ever have resented the idea in the first place.

Don Adler invited me out to Mocambo, without a doubt the hottest club in town, and he picked me up at my apartment.

I opened the door to see him in a nice suit, with a bouquet of lilies.

He was just a few inches taller than me in my heels. Light brown hair, hazel eyes, square jaw, the kind of smile that, the moment you saw it, made you smile. It was the smile his mother had been famous for, now on a handsomer face.

"For you," he said, just a bit shyly.

"Wow," I said, taking them from him. "They're gorgeous. Come in. Come in. I'll put them in some water."

I was wearing a boatneck sapphire-blue cocktail dress, my hair up in a chignon. I grabbed a vase from underneath the sink and turned the water on.

"You didn't have to do all this," I said as Don stood in my kitchen, waiting for me.

"Well," he said, "I wanted to. I've been hounding Harry to meet you for a while. So it was the least I could do to make you feel special."

I put the flowers on the counter. "Shall we?"

Don nodded and took my hand.

"I saw *Father and Daughter*," he said when we were in his convertible and headed over to the Sunset Strip.

"Oh yeah?"

"Yeah, Ari showed me an early cut. He says he thinks it's going to be a big hit. Says he thinks *you're* going to be a big hit."

"And what did *you* think?"

We were stopped at a red light on Highland. Don looked at me. "I think you're the most gorgeous woman I've ever seen in my life."

"Oh, stop," I said. I found myself laughing, blushing even.

"Truly. And a real talent, too. When the movie ended, I looked right at Ari and said, 'That's the girl for me.'"

"You did not," I said.

Don put up his hand. "Scout's honor."

There's absolutely no reason a man like Don Adler should have a different effect on me from the rest of the men in the world. He was no more handsome than Brick Thomas, no more earnest than Ernie Diaz, and he could offer me stardom whether I loved him or not. But these things defy reason. I blame pheromones, ultimately.

That and the fact that, at least at first, Don Adler treated me like a person. There are people who see a beautiful flower and rush over to pick it. They want to hold it in their hands, they want to own it. They want the flower's beauty to be theirs, to be within their possession, their control. Don wasn't like that. At least, not at first. Don was happy to be near the flower, to look at the flower, to appreciate the flower simply *being*.

Here's the thing about marrying a guy like that—a guy like Don Adler, back then. You're saying to him, "This beautiful thing you've been happy to simply appreciate, well, now it's yours to own."

Don and I partied the night away at the Mocambo. It was a real scene. Crowds outside, packed tight as sardines trying to get in. Inside, a celebrity playground. Tables upon tables filled with famous people, high ceilings, incredible stage acts, and birds everywhere. Actual live birds in glass aviaries.

Don introduced me to a few actors from MGM and Warner Brothers. I met Bonnie Lakeland, who had just gone freelance and made it big with *Money, Honey*. I heard, more than once, someone refer to Don as the prince of Hollywood, and I found it charming when he turned to me after the third time someone said it and whispered, "They are underestimating me. I'll be king one of these days."

Don and I stayed at Mocambo well past midnight, dancing together until our feet hurt. Every time a song ended, we said we were going to sit down, but once a new one started, we refused to leave the floor.

He drove me home, the streets quiet at the late hour, the lights dim all over town. When we got to my apartment, he walked me to my door. He didn't ask to come in. He just said, "When can I see you again?"

"Call Harry and make a date," I said.

Don put his hand on the door. "No," he said. "Really. Me and you."

"And the cameras?" I said.

"If you want them there, fine," he said. "If you don't, neither do I." He smiled, a sweet, teasing smile.

I laughed. "OK," I said. "How about next Friday?"

Don thought about it a second. "Can I tell you the truth about something?"

"If you must."

"I'm scheduled to go to the Trocadero with Natalie Ember next Friday night."

"Oh."

"It's the name. The Adler name. Sunset's trying to squeeze all the fame out of me that they can."

I shook my head. "I don't think it's just the name," I told him. "I've seen *Brothers in Arms*. You're great. The whole audience loved you."

Don looked at me shyly and smiled. "You really think so?"

I laughed. He knew it was true; he just liked hearing it come out of my mouth.

"I won't give you the satisfaction," I said.

"I wish you would."

"Enough of that," I told him. "I've told you when I'm free. You do with it what you will."

He stood tall, listening to what I'd said as if I'd given him orders. "OK, I'll cancel Natalie, then. I'll pick you up here on Friday at seven."

I smiled and nodded. "Good night, Don," I said.

"Good night, Evelyn," he said.

I started to shut the door, and he put his hand up, stopping me.

"Did you have a good time tonight?" he asked me.

I thought about what to say, how to say it. And then I lost control of myself, giddy to feel excited by someone for the first time. "One of the better nights of my life," I said.

Don smiled. "Me too."

The next day, our picture appeared in *Sub Rosa* magazine with the caption "Don Adler and Evelyn Hugo make quite the pair."

*F*ATHER AND *D*AUGHTER WAS A huge hit. And as a show of just how excited Sunset was about my new persona, they credited me in the beginning of the movie as "Introducing Evelyn Hugo." It was the first, and only, time my name was under the marquee.

On opening night, I thought of my mother. I knew that if she could have been there with me, she would have been beaming. *I did it*, I wanted to tell her. *We're both out of there.*

When the movie did well, I thought Sunset would certainly green-light *Little Women*. But Ari wanted Ed Baker and me in another movie as fast as possible. We didn't do sequels back then. Instead, we would essentially just make the same movie again with a different name and a slightly different conceit.

So we commenced shooting on *Next Door*. Ed played my uncle, who had taken me in after my parents died. The two of us quickly fell into respective romantic entanglements with the widowed mother and son who lived next to us.

Don was shooting a thriller on the lot at the time, and he used to come visit me every day when his set broke for lunch.

I was absolutely smitten, in love and lust for the very first time.

I found myself brightening up the moment I set eyes on him, always finding reasons to touch him, reasons to bring him up in conversation when he wasn't around.

Harry was sick of hearing about him.

"Ev, honey, I'm serious," Harry said one afternoon in his office when the two of us were sharing a drink. "I've had it up to my eyeballs with this Don Adler talk." I visited Harry about once a day back then, just to check in, see how he was doing. I always made it seem like business, but even then I knew he was the closest thing I had to a friend.

Sure, I'd become friendly with a lot of the other actresses at Sunset. Ruby Reilly, in particular, was a favorite of mine. She was tall and lean, with a dynamite laugh and an air of detachment to her. She never minced words but she could charm the pants off almost anybody.

Sometimes Ruby and I, and some of the other girls on the lot, would grab lunch and gossip about various goings-on, but, to be honest, I would have thrown every single one of them in front of a moving train to get a part. And I think they would have done the same to me.

Intimacy is impossible without trust. And we would have been idiots to trust one another.

But Harry was different.

Harry and I both wanted the same thing. We wanted Evelyn Hugo to be a household name. Also, we just liked each other.

"We can talk about Don, or we can talk about when you're green-lighting *Little Women*," I said teasingly.

Harry laughed. "It's not up to me. You know that."

"Well, why is Ari dragging his feet?"

"You don't want to do *Little Women* right now," Harry says. "It's better if you give it a few months."

"I most certainly *do* want to do it right now."

Harry shook his head and stood up, pouring himself another glass of scotch. He didn't offer me a second martini, and I knew it was because he knew I shouldn't have had the first one to begin with.

"You could really be big," Harry said. "Everybody's saying so. If *Next Door* does as well as *Father and Daughter* and you and Don keep going on the way you have been, you could be a big deal."

"I know," I said. "That's what I'm banking on."

"You want *Little Women* to come out just when people are thinking you only know how to do one thing."

"What do you mean?"

"You had a huge hit with *Father and Daughter*. People know you can be funny. They know you're adorable. They know they liked you in that picture."

"Sure."

"Now you're gonna do it again. You're going to show them that you can re-create the magic. You're not just a one-trick pony."

"All right . . ."

"Maybe you do a picture with Don. After all, they can't print pictures of the two of you dancing at Ciro's or the Trocadero fast enough."

"But—"

"Hear me out. You and Don do a picture. A matinee romance, maybe. Something where all the girls want to be you, and all the boys want to be *with* you."

"Fine."

"And just when everyone is thinking they know you, that they 'get' Evelyn Hugo, you play Jo. You knock everybody's socks off. Now the audience is going to think to themselves, 'I knew she was something special.'"

"But why can't I just do *Little Women* now? And they'll think that *now*?"

Harry shook his head. "Because you have to give them time to invest in you. You have to give them time to get to know you."

"You're saying I should be predictable."

"I'm saying you should be predictable and then do something unpredictable, and they'll love you forever."

I listened to him, thought about it. "You're just feeding me a line," I said.

Harry laughed. "Look, this is Ari's plan. Like it or not. He wants you in a few more pictures before he's gonna give you *Little Women*. But he is gonna give you *Little Women*."

"All right," I said. What choice did I have, really? My contract with Sunset was for another three years. If I caused too much trouble, they had an option to drop me at any time. They could loan me out, force me to take projects, put me on leave without pay, you name it. They could do anything they wanted. Sunset owned me.

"Your job now," Harry said, "is to see if you can make a real go of it with Don. It's in both of your best interests."

I laughed. "Oh, *now* you want to talk about Don."

Harry smiled. "I don't want to sit here and listen to you talk about how dreamy he is. That's boring. I want to know if the two of you might be ready to make it official."

Don and I had been seen around town, our photos taken at every hot spot in Hollywood. Dinner at Dan Tana's, lunch at the Vine Street Derby, tennis at the Beverly Hills Tennis Club. And we knew what we were doing, parading around in public.

I needed Don's name mentioned in the same sentences as mine, and Don needed to look like he was a part of the New Hollywood. Photos of the two of us double-dating with other stars went a long way toward solidifying his image as a man-about-town.

But he and I never talked about any of that. Because we were genuinely happy to be around each other. The fact that it was helping our careers felt like a bonus.

The night of the premiere of his movie *Big Trouble*, Don picked me up wearing a slick dark suit and holding a Tiffany box.

"What's this?" I asked him. I was wearing a black-and-purple floral Christian Dior.

"Open it," Don said, smiling.

Inside was a giant platinum and diamond ring. It was braided on the sides with a square-cut jewel in the middle.

I gasped. "Are you . . ."

I knew it had been coming, if only because I knew Don wanted to sleep with me so bad it was nearly killing him. I'd been resisting him despite his very overt advances. But it was getting harder to do. The more we kissed in dark places, the more we found ourselves alone in the backs of limousines, the harder it was for me to push him away.

I'd never had that feeling before, physical yearning. I'd never felt what it is to ache to be touched—until Don. I would find myself next to him, desperate to feel his hands on my bare skin.

And I loved the idea of making love to someone. I'd had sex before, but it had never meant anything to me. I wanted to *make love* to Don. I *loved* him. And I wanted us to do it right.

And here it was. A marriage proposal.

I put my hand out to touch the ring, to make sure it was all real. Don shut the box before I could. "I'm not asking you to marry me," he said.

"What?" I felt foolish. I'd allowed myself to dream too big. Here I was, Evelyn Herrera, parading around as if my name was Evelyn Hugo and I could marry a movie star.

"At least, not yet."

I tried to hide my disappointment. "Have it your way, then," I said, turning away from him to grab my clutch.

"Don't be sour," Don said.

"Who's sour?" I said. We walked out of my apartment, and I shut the door behind me.

"I'm going to ask you tonight." His voice was pleading, nearly apologetic. "At the premiere. In front of everyone."

I softened.

"I just wanted to make sure . . . I wanted to know . . ." Don grabbed my hand and got down on one knee. He didn't open the ring box again. He just looked at me sincerely. "Will you say yes?"

"We should go," I said. "You can't be late to your own movie."

"Will you say yes? That's all I need to know."

I looked right at him and said, "Yes, you dumb fool. I'm mad for you."

He grabbed me and kissed me. It hurt a little. His teeth hit my lower lip.

I was going to get married. To someone I loved this time. To someone who made me feel the way I was pretending to feel in the movies.

What could be any further from that tiny sad apartment in Hell's Kitchen than this?

An hour later, on the red carpet, in a sea of photographers and publicists, Don Adler got down on one knee. "Evelyn Hugo, will you marry me?"

I cried and nodded. He stood up and put the ring on my finger. And then he picked me up and spun me in the air.

As Don put me back down, I saw Harry Cameron by the theater door, clapping for us. He gave me a wink.

DON AND EV, FOREV!

You heard it here first, folks: Hollywood's newest It Couple, Don Adler and Evelyn Hugo, are tying the knot!

The Most Eligible of Eligible Bachelors has chosen none other than the sparkling blond starlet to be his bride. The two have been seen canoodling and cavorting all over, and now they've decided to make it official.

Rumor has it that Mary and Roger Adler, Don's oh-so-proud parents, couldn't be happier to have Evelyn joining the family.

You can bet your bottom dollar that the nuptials will be the event of the season. With a Hollywood family this glamorous and a bride this beautiful, the whole town will be talking.

We had a beautiful wedding. Three hundred guests, hosted by Mary and Roger Adler. Ruby was my maid of honor. I wore a jewel-necked taffeta gown, covered with rose-point lace, with sleeves down to my wrists and a full lace skirt. It was designed by Vivian Worley, the head costumer for Sunset. Gwendolyn did my hair, pulled back into a simple but flawless bun, to which my tulle veil was attached. There wasn't much of the wedding that was planned by us; it was controlled almost entirely by Mary and Roger and the rest by Sunset.

Don was expected to play the game exactly the way his parents wanted it played. Even then I could tell he was eager to get out of their shadow, to eclipse their stardom with his own. Don had been raised to believe that fame was the only power worth pursuing, and what I loved about him was that he was ready to become the most powerful person in any room by becoming the most adored.

And while our wedding might have been at the whim of others, our love and our commitment to each other felt sacred. When Don and I looked into each other's eyes and held hands as we said "I do" at the Beverly Hills Hotel, it felt like it was just the two of us up there, despite being surrounded by half of Hollywood.

Toward the end of the night, after the wedding bells and our announcement as a married couple, Harry pulled me aside. He asked me how I was doing.

"I'm the most famous bride in the world right now," I said. "I'm great."

Harry laughed. "You'll be happy?" he asked. "With Don? He's going to take good care of you?"

"I have no doubt about it."

I believed in my heart that I'd found someone who understood me, or at least understood the me I was trying to be. At the age of nineteen, I thought Don was my happy ending.

Harry put his arm around me and said, "I'm happy for you, kid."

I grabbed his hand before he could pull it away. I'd had two glasses of champagne, and I was feeling fresh. "How come you never tried anything?" I asked him. "We've known each other a few years now. Not even a kiss on the cheek."

"I'll kiss you on the cheek if you want," Harry said, smiling.

"Not what I mean, and you know it."

"Did you want something to happen?" he asked me.

I wasn't attracted to Harry Cameron. Despite the fact that he was a categorically attractive man. "No," I said. "I don't think I did."

"But you wanted me to want something to happen?"

I smiled. "And what if I did? Is that so wrong? I'm an actress, Harry. Don't you forget that."

Harry laughed. "You have 'actress' written all over your face. I remember it every single day."

"Then why, Harry? What's the truth?"

Harry took a sip of his scotch and took his arm off me. "It's hard to explain."

"Try."

"You're young."

I waved him off. "Most men don't seem to have any problem with a little thing like that. My own husband is seven years older than me."

I looked over to see Don swaying with his mother on the dance floor. Mary was still gorgeous in her fifties. She'd come to fame during the silent-film era and did a few talkies before retiring. She was tall and intimidating, with a face that was striking more than anything.

Harry took another swig of his scotch and put the glass down. He looked thoughtful. "It's a long and complicated story. But suffice it to say, you've just never been my type."

The way he said it, I knew he was trying to tell me something. Harry wasn't interested in girls like me. Harry wasn't interested in girls at all.

"You're my best friend in the world, Harry," I said. "Do you know that?"

He smiled. I got the impression he did so because he was charmed and because he was relieved. He'd revealed himself, however vaguely. And I was meeting him with acceptance, however indirectly.

"Am I really?" he asked.

I nodded.

"Well, then, you'll be mine."

I raised my glass to him. "Best friends tell each other everything," I said.

He smiled, raising his own glass. "I don't buy that," he teased. "Not for one minute."

Don came over and interrupted us. "Would you mind terribly, Cameron, if I danced with my bride?"

Harry put his hands up, as if in surrender. "She's all yours."

"That she is."

I took Don's hand, and he twirled me around the dance floor. He looked right into my eyes. He really looked at me, really saw me.

"Do you love me, Evelyn Hugo?" he asked.

"More than anything in the world. Do you love me, Don Adler?"

"I love your eyes, and your tits, and your talent. I love the fact that you've got absolutely no ass on you. I love everything about you. So to say yes would be an understatement."

I laughed and kissed him. We were surrounded by people, packed onto the dance floor. His father, Roger, was smoking a cigar with Ari Sullivan in the corner. I felt a million miles away from my old life, the old me, that girl who needed Ernie Diaz for anything at all.

Don pulled me close and put his mouth to my ear, whispering, "Me and you. We will rule this town."

We were married for two months before he started hitting me.

S IX WEEKS INTO OUR MARRIAGE, Don and I shot a weepie on location in Puerto Vallarta. Called *One More Day*, it was about a rich
girl, Diane, who spends the summer with her parents at their second
home, and the local boy, Frank, who falls in love with her. Naturally, they
can't be together, because her parents don't approve.

The first weeks of my marriage to Don had been nearly blissful. We
bought a house in Beverly Hills and had it decorated in marble and
linen. We had pool parties nearly every weekend, drinking champagne
and cocktails all afternoon and into the night.

Don made love like a king, truly. With the confidence and power of
someone in charge of a fleet of men. I melted underneath him. In the
right moment, for him, I'd have done anything he wanted.

He had flipped a switch in me. A switch that changed me from a
woman who saw making love as a tool into a woman who knew that
making love was a need. I needed him. I needed to be seen. I came alive
under his gaze. Being married to Don had shown me another side of
myself, a side I was just getting to know. A side I liked.

When we got to Puerto Vallarta, we spent a few days in town before
shooting. We took our rented boat out into the water. We dived into the
ocean. We made love in the sand.

But as we started shooting and the daily stresses of Hollywood started
fracturing our newlywed cocoon, I could tell the tide was turning.

Don's last movie, *The Gun at Point Dume*, wasn't doing well at the
box office. It was his first time in a Western, his first crack at playing

an action hero. *PhotoMoment* had just published a review saying, "Don Adler is no John Wayne." *Hollywood Digest* wrote, "Adler looks like a fool holding a gun." I could tell it was bothering him, making him doubt himself. Establishing himself as a masculine action hero was a vital part of his plan. His father had mostly played the straight man in madcap comedies, a clown. Don was out to prove he was a cowboy.

It did not help that I had just won an Audience Appreciation Award for Best Rising Star.

On the day we shot the final good-bye, where Diane and Frank kiss one last time on the beach, Don and I woke up in our rented bungalow, and he told me to make him breakfast. Mind you, he did not *ask* me to make him breakfast. He barked the order. Regardless, I ignored his tone and called down to the maid.

She was a Mexican woman named Maria. When we had first arrived, I was unsure if I should speak Spanish to the local people. And then, without ever making a formal decision about it, I found myself speaking slow, overenunciated English to everyone.

"Maria, will you please make Mr. Adler some breakfast?" I said into the phone, and then I turned to Don and said, "What would you like? Some coffee and eggs?"

Our maid back in Los Angeles, Paula, made his breakfast every morning. She knew just how he liked it. I realized in that moment that I'd never paid attention.

Frustrated, Don grabbed the pillow from under his head and smashed it over his face, screaming into it.

"What has gotten into you?" I said.

"If you're not going to be the kind of wife who is going to make me breakfast, you can at least know how I like it." He escaped to the bathroom.

I was bothered but not entirely surprised. I had quickly learned that Don was only kind when he was happy, and he was only happy when he was winning. I had met him on a winning streak, married him as he was ascending. I was quickly learning that sweet Don was not the only Don.

Later, in our rented Corvette, Don backed out of the driveway and started heading the ten blocks toward set.

"Are you ready for today?" I asked him. I was trying to be uplifting.

Don stopped in the middle of the road. He turned to me. "I've been a professional actor for longer than you've been alive." This was true, albeit on a technicality. He was in one of Mary's silent movies as a baby. He didn't act in a movie again until he was twenty-one.

There were a few cars behind us now. We were holding up traffic. "Don . . ." I said, trying to encourage him to move forward. He wasn't listening. The white truck behind us started pulling around, trying to get past us.

"Do you know what Alan Thomas said to me yesterday?" Don said.

Alan Thomas was his new agent. Alan had been encouraging Don to leave Sunset Studios, to go freelance. A lot of actors were navigating their careers on their own. It was leading to big paychecks for big stars. And Don was getting antsy. He kept talking about making more for one picture than his parents had made their whole careers.

Be wary of men with something to prove.

"People around town are asking why you're still going by Evelyn Hugo."

"I changed my name legally. What do you mean?"

"On the marquee. It should say 'Don and Evelyn Adler.' That's what people are saying."

"Who is saying that?"

"People."

"What people?"

"They think you wear the pants."

My head fell into my hands. "Don, you're being silly."

Another car came up around us, and I watched as they recognized Don and me. We were seconds away from a full page in *Sub Rosa* magazine about how Hollywood's favorite couple were at each other's throat. They'd probably say something like "The Adlers Gone Madlers?"

I suspected Don saw the headlines writing themselves at the same time I did, because he started the car and drove us to set. When we pulled onto the lot, I said, "I can't believe we're almost forty-five minutes late."

And Don said, "Yeah, well, we're Adlers. We can be."

I found it absolutely repugnant. I waited until the two of us were in his trailer, and I said, "When you talk like that, you sound like a horse's ass. You shouldn't say things like that where people can hear you."

He was taking off his jacket. Wardrobe was due in any moment. I should have just left and gone to my own trailer. I should have let him be.

"I think you have gotten the wrong impression here, Evelyn," Don said.

"And how is that?"

He came right up into my face. "We are not equals, love. And I'm sorry if I've been so kind that you've forgotten that."

I was speechless.

"I think this should be the last movie you do," he said. "I think it's time for us to have children."

His career wasn't turning out the way he wanted. And if he wasn't going to be the most famous person in his family, he surely wasn't going to allow that person to be me.

I looked right at him and said, "Absolutely. Positively. Not."

And he smacked me across the face. Sharp, fast, strong.

It was over before I even knew what happened, the skin on my face stinging from the blow I could barely believe had come my way.

If you've never been smacked across the face, let me tell you something, it is humiliating. Mostly because your eyes start to tear up, whether you mean to be crying or not. The shock of it and the sheer force of it stimulate your tear ducts.

There is no way to take a smack across the face and look stoic. All you can do is remain still and stare straight ahead, allowing your face to turn red and your eyes to bloom.

So that's what I did.

The way I'd done it when my father hit me.

I put my hand to my jaw, and I could feel the skin heating up under my hand.

The assistant director knocked on the door. "Mr. Adler, is Miss Hugo with you?"

Don was unable to speak.

"One minute, Bobby," I said. I was impressed by how unstrained my voice was, how confident it seemed. It sounded like the voice of a woman who had never been hit a day in her life.

There were no mirrors I could get to easily. Don had his back to them, blocking them. I pushed my jaw forward.

"Is it red?" I said.

Don could barely look at me. But he glanced and then nodded his head. He was boyish and ashamed, as if I were asking him if he'd been the one to break the neighbor's window.

"Go out there and tell Bobby I'm having lady troubles. He'll be too embarrassed to ask anything else. Then tell your wardrobe person to meet you in my dressing room. Have Bobby tell mine to meet me in here in a half hour."

"OK," he said, and then grabbed his jacket and slipped out.

The minute he was out the door, I locked myself inside and slumped down against the wall, the tears coming fast the moment no one could see them.

I had made my way three thousand miles from where I was born. I had found a way to be in the right place at the right time. I'd changed my name. Changed my hair. Changed my teeth and my body. I'd learned how to act. I'd made the right friends. I'd married into a famous family. Most of America knew my name.

And yet . . .

And yet.

I got up off the floor and wiped my eyes. I gathered myself.

I sat down at the vanity, three mirrors in front of me lined with lightbulbs. How silly is it that I thought that if I ever found myself in a movie star's dressing room, that meant I'd have no troubles?

A few moments later, Gwendolyn knocked on the door to do my hair.

"One second!" I yelled out.

"Evelyn, we have to move quickly. You guys are already behind schedule."

"Just one second!"

I looked at myself in the mirror and realized I couldn't force the redness to go away. The question was whether I trusted Gwen. And I decided I did, I had to. I stood up and opened the door.

"Oh, sweetheart," she said. "You look a fright."

"I know."

She looked more closely at me and realized what she was seeing. "Did you fall?"

"Yes," I said. "I did. I fell right over. Onto the counter. Jaw caught the worst of it."

We both knew I was lying.

And to this day, I'm not sure whether Gwen asked me if I fell in order to spare me the need to lie or to encourage me to keep quiet.

I wasn't the only woman being hit back then. A lot of women were negotiating the very same things I was at that moment. There was a social code for these things. The first rule being to shut up about it.

An hour later, I was being escorted to set. We were to film a scene just outside a mansion on the beach. Don was sitting in his chair, the four wooden legs digging into the sand, behind the director. He ran up to me.

"How are you feeling, sweetheart?" His voice was so chipper, so consoling, that for a moment I thought he had forgotten what happened.

"I'm fine. Let's get on with it."

We took our places. The sound guy mic'ed us. The grips made sure we were lit properly. I put everything out of my head.

"Hold on, hold on!" the director yelled. "Ronny, what's going on with the boom . . ." Distracted by a conversation, he walked away from the camera.

Don covered his mic and then put his hand on my chest and covered mine.

"Evelyn, I'm so sorry," he whispered into my ear.

I pulled back and looked at him, stunned. No one had ever apologized for hitting me before.

"I never should have laid a hand on you," he said. His eyes were filling with tears. "I'm ashamed of myself. For doing anything at all to hurt you." He looked so pained. "I will do anything for your forgiveness."

Maybe the life I thought I had wasn't so far away after all.

"Can you forgive me?" he asked.

Maybe this was all a mistake. Maybe it didn't mean anything had to change.

"Of course I can," I said.

The director ran back to the camera, and Don leaned back, taking his hands off our mics.

"And . . . action!"

Don and I were both nominated for Academy Awards for *One More Day*. And I think the general consensus was that it didn't matter how talented we were. People just loved seeing us together.

To this day, I have no idea if either of us is actually any good in it. It is the only movie I've ever shot that I cannot bring myself to watch.

A MAN HITS YOU ONCE and apologizes, and you think it will never happen again.

But then you tell him you're not sure you ever want a family, and he hits you once more. You tell yourself it's understandable, what he did. You were sort of rude, the way you said it. You do want a family someday. You truly do. You're just not sure how you're going to manage it with your movies. But you should have been more clear.

The next morning, he apologizes and brings you flowers. He gets down on his knees.

The third time, it's a disagreement about whether to go out to Romanoff's or stay in. Which, you realize when he pushes you into the wall behind you, is actually about the *image* of your marriage to the public.

The fourth time, it's after you both lose at the Oscars. You are in a silk, emerald-green, one-shoulder dress. He's in a tux with tails. He has too much to drink at the after-parties, trying to nurse his wounds. You're in the front seat of the car in your driveway, about to go inside. He's upset that he lost.

You tell him it's OK.

He tells you that you don't understand.

You remind him that you lost, too.

He says, "Yeah, but your parents are trash from Long Island. No one expects anything from you."

You know you shouldn't, but you say, "I'm from Hell's Kitchen, you asshole."

He opens the parked car's door and pushes you out.

When he comes crawling to you in tears the next morning, you don't actually believe him anymore. But now this is just *what you do.*

The same way you fix the hole in your dress with a safety pin or tape up the crack in a window.

That's the part I was stuck in, the part where you accept the apology because it's easier than addressing the root of the problem, when Harry Cameron came to my dressing room and told me the good news. *Little Women* was getting the green light.

"It's you as Jo, Ruby Reilly as Meg, Joy Nathan as Amy, and Celia St. James is playing Beth."

"Celia St. James? From Olympian Studios?"

Harry nodded. "What's with the frown? I thought you'd be thrilled."

"Oh," I said, turning further toward him. "I am. I absolutely am."

"You don't like Celia St. James?"

I smiled at him. "That teenage bitch is gonna act me under the table."

Harry threw his head back and laughed.

Celia St. James had made headlines earlier in the year. At the age of nineteen, she played a young widowed mother in a war-period piece. Everyone said she was sure to be nominated next year. Exactly the sort of person the studio would want playing Beth.

And exactly the sort of person Ruby and I would hate.

"You're twenty-one years old, you're married to the biggest movie star there is right now, and you were just nominated for an Academy Award, Evelyn."

Harry had a point, but so did I. Celia was going to be a problem.

"It's OK. I'm ready. I'm gonna give the best goddamn performance of my life, and when people watch the movie, they are going to say, 'Beth who? Oh, the middle sister who dies? What about her?'"

"I have absolutely no doubt," Harry said, putting his arm around me. "You're fabulous, Evelyn. The whole world knows it."

I smiled. "You really think so?"

This is something that everyone should know about stars. We like to be told we are adored, and we want you to repeat yourself. Later in my life, people would always come up to me and say, "I'm sure you don't want to hear me blabbering on about how great you are," and I always say, as if I'm joking, "Oh, one more time won't hurt." But the truth is, praise is just like an addiction. The more you get it, the more of it you need just to stay even.

"Yes," he said. "I really think so."

I stood up from my chair to give Harry a hug, but as I did, the lighting highlighted my upper cheekbone, the rounded spot just below my eye.

I watched as Harry's gaze ran across my face.

He could see the light bruise I was hiding, could see the purple and blue under the surface of my skin, bleeding through the pancake makeup.

"Evelyn . . ." he said. He put his thumb up to my face, as if he needed to feel it to know it was real.

"Harry, don't."

"I'll kill him."

"No, you won't."

"We're best friends, Evelyn. Me and you."

"I know," I said. "I know that."

"You said best friends tell each other everything."

"And you knew it was bullshit when I said it."

I stared at him as he stared at me.

"Let me help," he said. "What can I do?"

"You can make sure I look better than Celia, better than all of 'em, in the dailies."

"That's not what I mean."

"But it's all you can do."

"Evelyn . . ."

I kept my upper lip stiff. "There's no move here, Harry."

He understood what I meant. I couldn't leave Don Adler.

"I could talk to Ari."

"I love him," I said, turning away and clipping my earrings on.

It was the truth. Don and I had problems, but so did a lot of people.

And he was the only man who had ever ignited something in me. Sometimes I hated myself for wanting him, for finding myself brightening up when his attention was on me, for still needing his approval. But I did. I loved him, and I wanted him in my bed. And I wanted to stay in the spotlight.

"End of discussion."

A moment later, there was another knock on my door. It was Ruby Reilly. She was shooting a drama where she played a young nun. She was standing in front of the two of us in a black tunic and a white cowl. Her hood was in her hand.

"Did you hear?" Ruby said to me. "Well, of course you heard. Harry's here."

Harry laughed. "You both start rehearsals in three weeks."

Ruby hit Harry on the arm playfully. "No, not that part! Did you hear Celia St. James is playing Beth? That tart's gonna show us all up."

"See, Harry?" I said. "Celia St. James is going to ruin everything."

THE MORNING WE STARTED REHEARSALS for *Little Women*, Don woke me up with breakfast in bed. Half a grapefruit and a lit cigarette. I found this highly romantic, because it was exactly what I wanted.

"Good luck today, sweetheart," he said as he got dressed and headed out the door. "I know you'll show Celia St. James what it really means to be an actress."

I smiled and wished him a good day. I ate the grapefruit and left the tray in bed as I got into the shower.

When I got out, our maid, Paula, was in the bedroom cleaning up after me. She was picking the butt of my cigarette off the duvet. I'd left it on the tray, but it must have fallen.

I didn't keep a neat house.

My clothes from last night were on the floor. My slippers were on top of the dresser. My towel was in the sink.

Paula had her work cut out for her, and she didn't find me particularly charming. That much was clear.

"Can you do that later?" I said to her. "I'm terribly sorry, but I'm in a rush to get to set."

She smiled politely and left.

I wasn't in a rush, really. I just wanted to get dressed, and I wasn't going to do that in front of Paula. I didn't want her to see that there was a bruise, dark purple and yellowing, on my ribs.

Don had pushed me down the stairs nine days before. Even as I say it all these years later, I feel the need to defend him. To say that it wasn't as bad as it sounds. That we were toward the bottom of the stairs, and he gave me a shove that bumped me down about four steps and onto the floor.

Unfortunately, the table by the door, where we kept the keys and the mail, is what caught my fall. I landed on it on my left side, the handle on the top drawer getting me right in the rib cage.

When I said that I thought I might have broken a rib, Don said, "Oh, no, honey. Are you all right?" as if he wasn't the one who pushed me.

Like an idiot, I said, "I think I'm fine."

The bruise wasn't going away quickly.

Paula burst back in through the door a moment later.

"Sorry, Mrs. Adler, I forgot the—"

I panicked. "For heaven's sake, Paula! I asked you to leave!"

She turned around and walked out. And what pissed me off more than anything was that if she was going to sell a story, why wasn't it that one? Why didn't she tell the world that Don Adler was beating his wife? Why, instead, did she come after *me*?

TWO HOURS LATER, I was on the set of *Little Women*. The soundstage had been turned into a New England cabin, complete with snow on the windows.

Ruby and I were united in our fight against Celia St. James stealing the movie from us, despite the fact that anyone who plays Beth leaves the audience reaching for the hankies.

You can't tell an actress that a rising tide lifts all boats. It doesn't work that way for us.

But on the first day of rehearsals, as Ruby and I hung out by craft services and drank coffee, it became clear that Celia St. James had absolutely no idea how much we all hated her.

"Oh, God," she said, coming up to Ruby and me. "I'm so scared."

She was wearing gray trousers and a pale pink short-sleeved sweater. She had a childlike, girl-next-door kind of face. Big, round, pale blue eyes, long lashes, Cupid's bow lips, long strawberry-red hair. She was simplicity perfected.

I was the sort of beautiful that women knew they could never truly emulate. Men knew they would never even get close to a woman like me.

Ruby was the elegant, aloof sort of beauty. Ruby was cool. Ruby was chic.

But Celia was the sort of beautiful that felt as if you could hold it in your hands, like if you played your cards right, you might just get to marry a girl like Celia St. James.

Ruby and I both were aware of what kind of power that is, accessibility.

Celia toasted a piece of bread at the craft services table and slathered it with peanut butter and then bit into it.

"What on earth are you scared of?" Ruby said.

"I have no idea what I'm doing!" Celia said.

"Celia, you can't really expect us to fall for this 'aw shucks' routine," I said.

She looked at me. And the way she did it made me feel as if no one had ever really looked at me before. Not even Don. "That hurts my feelings," she said.

I felt a little bit bad. But I certainly wasn't going to let on. "I didn't mean anything by it," I said.

"Yes, you absolutely did," Celia said. "I think you're a bit of a cynic."

Ruby, that fair-weather friend, pretended to hear the AD calling for her and took off.

"I just have a hard time believing a woman the entire town is saying will be nominated next year is doubting her ability to play Beth March. It's the chewiest, most likable role in the whole thing."

"If it's such a sure thing, then why didn't *you* take it?" she asked me.

"I'm too old, Celia. But thank you for that."

Celia smiled, and I realized I'd played right into her hands.

That's when I started to take a liking to Celia St. James.

LET'S PICK UP HERE TOMORROW," Evelyn says. The sun set long ago. As I look around, I notice the remains of breakfast, lunch, and dinner scattered across the room.

"OK," I say.

"By the way," she adds as I start to pack up. "My publicist got an e-mail today from your editor. Inquiring about a photo shoot for the June cover."

"Oh," I say. Frankie has checked in on me a few times now. I know I need to call her back, update her on this situation. I'm just . . . not sure of my next move.

"I take it you haven't told them the plan," Evelyn says.

I place my computer in my bag. "Not yet." I hate the slight tint of sheepishness that comes out when I say it.

"That's fine," Evelyn says. "I'm not judging you, if that's what you're worried about. God knows I'm no defender of the truth."

I laugh.

"You'll do what you need to do," she says.

"I will," I say.

I just don't know what, exactly, that is yet.

WHEN I GET home, the package from my mother is sitting just inside my building's door. I pick it up, only to realize that it's incredibly heavy. I end up pushing it across the tile floor with my foot. I pull it, one step at a time, up the stairs. And then I drag it into my apartment.

When I open the box, it's filled with some of my father's photo albums.

The front of each is embossed with "James Grant" in the bottom right-hand corner.

Nothing can stop me from sitting down, right on the floor where I am, and looking through the photos one by one.

On-set still photos of directors, famous actors, bored extras, ADs—you name it, they are all in here. My dad loved his job. He loved taking pictures of people who weren't paying attention to him.

I remember once, about a year before he died, he took a two-month job in Vancouver. My mom and I went to visit him twice while he was up there, but it was so much colder than L.A., and he was gone for what felt like so long. I asked him why. Why couldn't he just work at home? Why did he have to take this job?

He told me he wanted to do work that invigorated him. He said, "You have to do that, too, Monique. When you're older. You have to find a job that makes your heart feel big instead of one that makes it feel small. OK? You promise me that?" He put out his hand, and I shook it, like we were making a business deal. I was six. By the time I was eight, we'd lost him.

I always kept what he said in my heart. I spent my teenage years with a burning pressure to find a passion, one that would expand my soul in some way. It was no small task. In high school, long after we had said good-bye to my father, I tried theater and orchestra. I tried joining the chorus. I tried soccer and debate. In a moment of what felt like an epiphany, I tried photography, hoping that the thing that expanded my father's heart might expand my own.

But it wasn't until I was assigned to write a profile piece on one of my classmates in my composition class freshman year at USC that I felt anything close to a swelling in my chest. I liked writing about real people. I liked finding evocative ways of interpreting the real world. I liked the idea of connecting people by sharing their stories.

Following that part of my heart led me to J school at NYU. Which led to my internship at WNYC. I followed that passion to a life of freelancing for embarrassing blogs, living check to check and hand to mouth, and then, eventually, to the *Discourse*, where I met David when he was working on the site's redesign, and then to *Vivant* and now to Evelyn.

One small thing my dad said to me on a cold day in Vancouver has essentially been the basis of my entire life's trajectory.

For a brief moment, I wonder if I would have listened to him if he hadn't died. Would I have clung to his every word so tightly if his advice had felt unlimited?

At the end of the last photo album, I come across candids that don't appear to be from a movie set. They were taken at a barbecue. I recognize my mom in the background of some of them. And then, at the very end, is one of me with my parents.

I can't be more than four years old. I am eating a piece of cake with my hand, looking directly into the camera, as my mother holds me and my father has his arm around us. Most people still called me by my first name, Elizabeth, back then. Elizabeth Monique Grant.

My mom assumed I'd grow up to be a Liz or a Lizzy. But my father had always loved the name Monique and couldn't help but call me by it. I would often remind him that my name was Elizabeth and he would tell me that my name was whatever I wanted it to be. When he passed away, it became clear to both my mother and me that I should be Monique. It eased our pain ever so slightly to honor every last thing about him. So my pet name became my real name. And my mother often reminds me that my name was a gift from my father.

Looking at this picture, I am struck by how beautiful my parents were together. James and Angela. I know what it cost them to build a life, to have me. A white woman and a black man in the early '80s, neither of their families being particularly thrilled with the arrangement. We moved around a lot before my father died, trying to find a neighborhood where my parents felt at ease, at home. My mother didn't feel welcome in Baldwin Hills. My father didn't feel comfortable in Brentwood.

I was in school before I met another person who looked like me. Her name was Yael. Her father was Dominican, and her mother was from

Israel. She liked to play soccer. I liked to play dress-up. We could rarely agree on anything. But I liked that when someone asked her if she was Jewish, she said, "I'm half Jewish." No one else I knew was *half* something.

For so long, I felt like two halves.

And then my father died, and I felt like I was one-half my mother and one-half lost. A half that I feel so torn from, so incomplete without.

But looking at this picture now, the three of us together in 1986, me in overalls, my father in a polo, my mother in a denim jacket, we look like we *belong* together. I don't look like I am half of one thing and half of another but rather one whole thing, theirs. Loved.

I miss my dad. I miss him all the time. But it's moments like this, when I'm on the precipice of finally doing work that might just expand my heart, that I wish I could at least send him a letter, telling him what I'm doing. And I wish that he could send me one back.

I already know what he would write. Something like "I'm proud of you. I love you." But still, I'd like to get one anyway.

"ALL RIGHT," I say. My spot at Evelyn's desk has become my second home. I've come to rely on Grace's morning coffee. It has replaced my usual Starbucks habit. "Let's pick up where we left off yesterday. You're about to start *Little Women*. Go."

Evelyn laughs. "You've become an old hand at this," she says.

"I learn quickly."

A WEEK INTO REHEARSALS, DON and I were lying in bed. He was asking how it was going, and I admitted that Celia was just as good as I'd thought she'd be.

"Well, *The People of Montgomery County* is going to be number one again this week. I'm at the top of my game again. And my contract is up at the end of this year. Ari Sullivan is willing to do whatever I want to make me happy. So just say the word, baby, and *poof*, she's out of there."

"No," I said to him, putting my hand on his chest and my head on his shoulder. "It's OK. I'm the lead. She's supporting. I'm not going to worry too much. And anyway, there's something I like about her."

"There's something I like about you," he said, pulling me on top of him. And for a moment, all my worries completely disappeared.

The next day, when we broke for lunch, Joy and Ruby went off to get turkey salads. Celia caught my eye. "There's no chance you'd want to cut out and grab a milk shake, is there?" she asked.

The nutritionist at Sunset would not have liked me getting a milk shake. But what he didn't know wouldn't kill him.

Ten minutes later, we were in Celia's baby-pink 1956 Chevy, making our way to Hollywood Boulevard. Celia was a terrible driver. I gripped the door handle as if it was capable of saving my life.

Celia stopped at the light at Sunset Boulevard and Cahuenga. "I'm thinking Schwab's," she said with a grin.

Schwab's was the place everybody hung around during the day back then. And everybody knew that Sidney Skolsky, from *Photoplay*, worked out of Schwab's almost every day.

Celia wanted to be seen there. She wanted to be seen there with me.

"What kind of game are you playing?" I asked.

"I'm not playing any game," she said, falsely insulted that I'd suggest such a thing.

"Oh, Celia," I said, dismissing her with a wave of my hand. "I've been at this a few more years than you. You're the one who just fell off the turnip truck. Don't confuse us."

The light turned green, and Celia gunned it.

"I'm from Georgia," she said. "Just outside of Savannah."

"So?"

"I'm just saying, I didn't fall off a turnip truck. I was scouted by a guy from Paramount back home."

I found it somewhat intimidating—maybe even threatening—that someone had flown out to woo her. I had made my way to town through my own blood, sweat, and tears, and Celia had Hollywood running *to* her before she was even somebody.

"That may be so," I said. "But I still know what game you're running, honey. Nobody goes to Schwab's for the milk shakes."

"Listen," she said, the tone of her voice changing slightly, becoming more sincere. "I could use a story or two. If I'm going to star in my own movie soon, I need some name recognition."

"And this milk shake business is all just a ruse to be seen with me?" I found it insulting. Both being used and being underestimated.

Celia shook her head. "No, not at all. I wanted to go get a milk shake with you. And then, when we pulled out of the lot, I thought, *We should go to Schwab's.*"

Celia stopped abruptly at the light at Sunset and Highland. I realized at that point that was just how she drove. A lead foot on both the gas and the brake.

"Take a right," I said.

"What?"

"Take a right."

"Why?"

"Celia, take the goddamn right before I open this car door and throw myself out of it."

She looked at me like I was nuts, which was fair. I had just threatened to kill myself if she didn't put on her blinker.

She turned right on Highland.

"Take a left at the light," I said.

She didn't ask questions. She just put on her blinker. And then she spun onto Hollywood Boulevard. I instructed her to park the car on a side road. We walked to CC Brown's.

"They have better ice cream," I said as we walked in.

I was putting her in her place. I wasn't going to be photographed with her unless I wanted to be, unless it was my idea. I certainly wasn't going to be pushed around by somebody less famous than I was.

Celia nodded, feeling the sting.

The two of us sat down, and the guy behind the counter came up to us, momentarily speechless.

"Uh . . ." he said. "Do you want menus?"

I shook my head. "I know what I want. Celia?"

She looked at him. "Chocolate malt, please."

I watched the way his eyes fixed on her, the way she bent forward slightly with her arms together, emphasizing her chest. She seemed unaware of what she was doing, and that mesmerized him even more.

"And I'll have a strawberry milk shake," I said.

When he looked at me, I saw his eyes open wider, as if he wanted to see as much of me as he could at one time.

"Are you . . . Evelyn Hugo?"

"No," I said, and then I smiled and looked him right in the eye. It was ironic and teasing, with the same tone and inflection I'd used countless times when I was recognized around town.

He scattered away.

"Cheer up, buttercup," I said as I looked at Celia. She was staring down at the glossy counter. "You're getting a better milk shake out of the deal."

"I upset you," she said. "With the Schwab's thing. I'm sorry."

"Celia, if you're going to be as big as you clearly want to be, you need to learn two things."

"And what are they?"

"First, you have to push people's boundaries and not feel bad about it. No one is going to give you anything if you don't ask for it. You tried. You were told no. Get over it."

"And the second thing?"

"When you use people, be good at it."

"I wasn't trying to use you—"

"Yes, Celia, you were. And I'm fine with that. I wouldn't have a moment's hesitation in using you. And I wouldn't expect you to have a second thought about using me. Do you know the difference between the two of us?"

"There are a lot of differences between the two of us."

"Do you know the one in particular I'm talking about?" I said.

"What is it?"

"That I know I use people. I'm fine with the idea of using people. And all of that energy that you spend trying to convince yourself that you're *not* using people I spend getting better at it."

"And you're proud of that?"

"I'm proud of where it's gotten me."

"Are you using me? Now?"

"If I was, you'd never know."

"That's why I'm asking."

The guy behind the counter came back with our milk shakes. He appeared to have to give himself a pep talk just to give them to us.

"No," I said to Celia, once he was gone.

"No what?"

"No, I'm not using you."

"Well, that's a relief," Celia said. It struck me as painfully naive, the way she so easily, so readily believed me. I was telling the truth, but still.

"Do you know *why* I'm not using you?" I said.

"This should be good," Celia said as she took a sip of her shake. I laughed, surprised by both the world-weariness in her voice and the speed with which she spoke.

Celia would go on to win more Oscars than anybody else in our circle back then. And it was always for intense, dramatic roles. But I always thought she'd be dynamite in a comedy. She was so quick.

"The reason I'm not using you is that you have nothing to offer me. Not yet, at least."

Celia took a sip of her shake again, stung. And then I leaned forward and took a sip of mine.

"I don't think that's true," Celia said. "I'll give you that you're more famous than me. Being married to Captain Hollywood can have that effect on a person. But other than that, we're at the same place, Evelyn. You've turned in a couple of good performances. So have I. And now we're in a movie together, which both of us took on because we want an Academy Award. And let's be honest, I have a leg up on you in that regard."

"And why is that?"

"Because I'm a better actress."

I stopped sipping the thick shake through the straw and turned myself toward her.

"How do you figure that?"

Celia shrugged. "It's not something we can measure, I suppose. But it's true. I've seen *One More Day*. You're really good. But I'm better. And you know I'm better. That's why you and Don almost had me kicked off the project."

"No, we didn't."

"Yes, you did. Ruby told me."

I wasn't mad at Ruby for telling Celia what I'd told her, the same way you're not mad at a dog for barking at a mailman. That's just what they do.

"Oh, fine. So you're a better actress than me. And sure, maybe Don and I discussed getting you fired. So what? Big deal."

"Well, that's just my point exactly. I'm more talented than you, and you're more powerful than me."

"So?"

"So you're right, I'm not very good at using people. So I'm trying this a different way. Let's help each other out."

I sipped my milk shake again, mildly intrigued. "How so?" I said.

"After hours, I'll help you with your scenes. I'll teach you what I know."

"And I go with you to Schwab's?"

"You help me do what you've done. Become a star."

"But then what?" I said. "We both end up famous and talented? Competing for every job in town?"

"I suppose that is one option."

"And the other?"

"I really like you, Evelyn."

I looked at her sideways.

She laughed at me. "I know that's probably not something most actresses mean in this town, but I don't want to be like most actresses. I really like you. I like watching you on-screen. I like how the moment you show up in a scene, I can't look at anything else. I like the way your skin is too dark for your blond hair, the way the two shouldn't go together and yet seem so natural on you. And to be honest, I like how calculating and awful you kind of are."

"I am not awful!"

Celia laughed. "Oh, you definitely are. Getting me fired because you think I'll show you up? Awful. That's just awful, Evelyn. And walking around bragging about how you use people? Just terrible. But I really like it when you talk about it. I like how honest you are, how unashamed. So many women around here are full of crap with everything they say and do. I like that you're full of crap only when it gets you something."

"This laundry list of compliments seems to have a lot of insults in it," I said.

Celia nodded, hearing me. "You know what you want, and you go after it. I don't think there is anyone in this town doubting that Evelyn Hugo is going to be the biggest star in Hollywood one of these days. And that's not just because you're something to look at. It's because you decided you wanted to be huge, and now you're going to be. I want to be friends with a woman like that. That's what I'm saying. Real friends. None of this Ruby Reilly, backstabbing, talking-about-each-other-behind-our-backs crap. Friendship. Where each of us gets better, lives better, because we know the other."

I considered her. "Do we have to do each other's hair and stuff like that?"

"Sunset pays people to do that. So no."

"Do I have to listen to your man troubles?"

"Certainly not."

"So what, then? We choose to spend time together and try to be there for each other?"

"Evelyn, have you never had a friend before?"

"Of course I've had friends before."

"A real one, a close friend? A true friend?"

"I have a true friend, thank you very much."

"Who is it?"

"Harry Cameron."

"Harry Cameron is your friend?"

"He's my best friend."

"Well, fine," Celia said, putting out her hand for me to shake. "I will be your second-best friend, next to Harry Cameron."

I took her hand and shook it firmly. "Fine. Tomorrow I'll take you to Schwab's. And afterward, we can rehearse together."

"Thank you," she said, and she smiled brightly, as if she'd gotten everything she'd ever wanted in the world. She hugged me, and when we broke away, the man behind the counter was staring at us.

I asked for the check.

"It's on the house," he said, which I thought was the dumbest thing, because if there is anyone that should be getting free food, it isn't rich people.

"Will you tell your husband I loved *The Gun at Point Dume*?" the man said as Celia and I got up to leave.

"What husband?" I said as coyly as possible.

Celia laughed, and I flashed her a grin.

But what I was really thinking was, *I can't tell him that. He'll think I'm making fun of him, and he'll smack me.*

COLD, COLD EVELYN

Why would a beautiful couple with a gorgeous five-bedroom home not be interested in filling it up with a brood of children? You'd have to ask Don Adler and Evelyn Hugo that question.

Or maybe you'd just have to ask Evelyn.

Don wants a baby, and certainly we've all been waiting with bated breath to find out when the progeny of those two beautiful creatures will make his or her way into the world. We know any child they have would be sure to send us into fits of swooning.

But Evelyn's saying no.

Instead, all Evelyn talks about is her career, including her new movie, *Little Women*.

More than that, Evelyn doesn't even attempt to keep a clean house or mind her husband's simple requests, and she can't be bothered to be kind to the help.

Instead, she's out at Schwab's with single girls like Celia St. James!

Poor Don's at home, yearning for a child, while Evelyn's out having the time of her life.

It's all *Evelyn, Evelyn, Evelyn* in that house.

And she's left a *very* unsatisfied husband.

I S THIS REALLY HAPPENING?" I said as I threw the magazine onto Harry's desk. But of course, he'd already seen it.

"It's not that bad."

"It's not good."

"No, it's not."

"Why didn't anyone take care of this?" I asked.

"Because *Sub Rosa* isn't listening to us anymore."

"What do you mean?"

"They don't care about the truth or access to stars. They are just printing whatever they want."

"They care about money, don't they?"

"Yes, but they will make way more by pontificating about the ins and outs of your marriage than we can afford to pay them."

"You are Sunset Studios."

"And if you haven't noticed, we aren't making nearly as much money as we used to."

My shoulders slumped. I sat in one of the chairs facing Harry's desk. There was a knock.

"It's Celia," she said through the door.

I walked over and opened it for her.

"I take it you've seen the piece," I said.

Celia looked at me. "It's not that bad."

"It's not good," I said.

"No, it's not."

"Thank you. You both are a pair of aces."

Celia and I had finished shooting *Little Women* the week before. The two of us, along with Harry and Gwendolyn, had gone out for celebratory steaks and cocktails at Musso & Frank the day after we finished.

Harry had given Celia and me the good news that Ari thought we were both shoo-ins for nominations.

Every night after shooting, Celia and I would stay late in my trailer and rehearse our scenes. Celia was Method. She tried to "become" her character. That wasn't really my speed. But she did teach me how to find moments of emotional truth in false circumstances.

It was a strange time in Hollywood. There seemed to be two tracks running parallel to each other at the same time back then.

There was the studio game, with studio actors and studio dynasties. And then there was the New Hollywood making its way into the hearts of audiences, Method actors in gritty movies with antiheroes and untidy endings.

It wasn't until those evenings with Celia, the two of us sharing a pack of cigarettes and a bottle of wine for dinner, that I even started paying attention to the new stuff.

But whatever influence she had on me was a good one, because Ari Sullivan thought I could win an Oscar. And that made me like Celia all the more.

Our weekly outings to hot spots like Rodeo Drive weren't even feeling like a favor anymore. I did it happily, attracting attention for her simply because I enjoyed her company.

So as I sat there in Harry's office, pretending to be pissed at both of them for not being very helpful, I knew I was with my two favorite people.

"What does Don say about it?" Celia asked.

"I'm sure he's going all around the lot trying to find me."

Harry looked at me pointedly. He knew what might happen if Don read it in a bad mood. "Celia, are you shooting today?" he asked.

She shook her head. "*The Pride of Belgium* doesn't start until next week. I just have some wardrobe fittings later, after lunch."

"I'll move your wardrobe fittings. Why don't you and Evelyn go out shopping? We can call over to *Photoplay*, let them know you'll be on Robertson."

"And be seen out around town with single gal Celia St. James?" I said. "That sounds like the perfect example of what I shouldn't do."

My mind kept racing through the contents of that stupid article. *She can't be bothered to be kind to the help.*

"That little rat," I said when I figured it out. I hit my fist on the arm of the chair.

"What are you talking about?" Harry said.

"My damn maid."

"You think your maid talked to *Sub Rosa*?"

"I'm positive my maid talked to *Sub Rosa.*"

"All right, well, she's fired," Harry says. "I can have Betsy go over there today and let her go. She'll be gone by the time you get home."

I thought about my options.

The last thing I needed was America not wanting to see my movies because I wouldn't give Don a baby. I knew, of course, that most moviegoers would never say as much. They might not even realize they *thought* as much. But they would read something like this, and the next time one of my pictures came out, they'd think to themselves that there was something about me they never liked, they just couldn't put their finger on it.

People don't find it very sympathetic or endearing, a woman who puts herself first. Nor do people respect a man who can't keep his wife in line. So it didn't look good for Don, either.

"I need to talk to Don," I said, standing up. "Harry, can you have Dr. Lopani ring my house this evening? Sometime around six?"

"Why?"

"I need him to call me, and when Paula answers, he needs to sound serious, like he has very important news to tell me. He has to sound concerned enough for her to be intrigued."

"OK . . ."

"Evelyn, what are you up to?" Celia said, looking up at me.

"When I get on the phone, he has to say exactly this," I said, and I took a piece of paper and started scribbling.

Harry read it and then handed the paper to Celia. She looked at me.

There was a knock on the door, and without even being welcomed, Don came in.

"I've been looking all over for you," he said. His voice showed neither anger nor affection. But I knew Don, and I knew that with him, there was no lukewarm. The absence of warmth was a chill. "I assume you've read this bullshit?" He had the magazine in his hand.

"I have a plan," I said.

"You're goddamn right you have a plan. Somebody better have a plan. I'm not walking around this town looking like a henpecked ass-hole. Cameron, what happened here?"

"I'm dealing with it, Don."

"Good."

"But in the meantime, I think you should hear Evelyn's plan. I think it's important you're on board before she moves forward."

Don took a seat in the chair opposite Celia. He nodded at her. "Celia."

"Don."

"With all due respect, I feel like this is a matter for the three of us to discuss?" he said.

"Of course," Celia said, stepping up from the chair.

"No," I said, putting my hand out to stop her. "Stay."

Don looked at me.

"She's my friend."

Don rolled his eyes and shrugged. "So what's the plan, Evelyn?"

"I'm going to fake a miscarriage."

"What on earth for?"

"They'll hate me and probably lose respect for you if they think I won't give you a baby," I said, despite the fact that it was exactly what was going on between us. That was the elephant in the room, of course. This was all sort of true.

"But they'll pity you both if they think she can't," Celia said.

"Pity? What are you talking about, pity? I don't want to be pitied. There's no power in pity. You can't sell movies with pity."

And then Harry spoke up and said, "Like hell you can't."

WHEN THE PHONE rang at ten after six, Paula answered and then rushed into the bedroom to tell me the doctor was calling.

I picked up the line with Don beside me.

Dr. Lopani read the script written for him.

I started crying, as loudly as I could on the off chance that Paula had decided to mind her own business for once.

A half hour later, Don went downstairs and told Paula we had to let her go. He wasn't nice about it; in fact, he was just mean enough to piss her off.

Because you *might* run to the tabloids to tell them about the miscarriage of your employers. But you'll *definitely* run to the tabloids and tell them about the miscarriage of the people who just fired you.

BLESS DON AND EVELYN! THEY NEED IT!

The couple who has everything but can't have what they truly want . . .

In the home of Don Adler and Evelyn Hugo, things are not what they seem. It may appear that Evelyn is putting off Don's advances when it comes to baby making, but the truth turns out to be quite a different tale.

Because all this time we thought Evelyn was pushing Don away, it turns out she was working overtime. Evelyn and Don desperately want a little Don and Evelyn running around the house, but nature has not been kind.

It seems every time they find themselves "in the family way," things take a sad turn—a tragedy that has befallen them this month for the third time.

Let's send Don and Evelyn our best wishes.

It just goes to show that money can't buy happiness, folks.

THE NIGHT AFTER THE NEW article came out, Don was not convinced that it had been the right move, and Harry was busy but wouldn't say with what, which I knew meant he was seeing someone.

And I wanted to celebrate.

So Celia came over to the house, and we split a bottle of wine.

"You've got no maid," Celia said as she was searching around the kitchen for a corkscrew.

"No," I said, sighing. "Not until the studio is done vetting all the applicants."

Celia found the corkscrew, and I handed her a bottle of cabernet.

I never spent much time in the kitchen, and it was sort of surreal to be there without someone looking over my shoulder, offering to make me a sandwich or find whatever I was looking for. When you are rich, parts of your house don't really feel like they are yours. The kitchen was one of them for me.

I looked through my own cabinets, trying to remember where the wineglasses were. "Ah," I said when I found them. "Here."

Celia looked at what I was handing her. "Those are champagne flutes."

"Oh, right," I said, putting them back where I'd found them. We had two other sizes. I showed one of each to Celia. "Which?"

"The rounder. Do you not know glassware?"

"Glassware, serving ware, I don't know any of it. Remember, honey, I'm new money."

Celia laughed as she poured our drinks.

"I've either not been able to afford it or have been so rich someone would do it for me. Never anywhere in between."

"I love that about you," Celia said as she took a full glass and handed it to me. She took the other for herself. "I've had money my whole life. My parents act as if there is a recognized nobility in Georgia. And all of my brothers and sisters, with the exception of my older brother, Robert, are just like my parents. My sister Rebecca thinks my being in movies is an embarrassment to the family. Not so much because of the Hollywood aspect but because I'm 'working.' She says it's undignified. I love them, and I hate them. But that's family, I guess."

"I don't know," I said. "I . . . don't have much family. Any, really." My father and the rest of the relatives I had back in Hell's Kitchen had not succeeded in contacting me, if they had even tried at all. And I hadn't lost one night of sleep thinking about them.

Celia looked at me. She appeared to neither pity me nor feel uncomfortable for all that she'd had growing up that I didn't have. "All the more reason for me to admire you the way I do," she said. "Everything you have you went out and got for yourself." Celia leaned her glass into mine and clinked. "To you," she said. "For being absolutely unstoppable."

I laughed and then drank with her. "Come," I said, leading her out of the kitchen and into the living room. I put my drink down on the hairpin-leg coffee table and walked over to the record player. I pulled out Billie Holiday's *Lady in Satin* from the bottom of the stack. Don hated Billie Holiday. But Don wasn't there.

"Do you know her real name is Eleanora Fagan?" I said to Celia. "Billie Holiday is just so much prettier."

I sat down on one of our blue tufted sofas. Celia sat on the one opposite me. She folded her legs underneath her, her spare hand on her feet.

"What's yours?" she asked. "Is it really Evelyn Hugo?"

I grabbed my wineglass and confessed the truth. "Herrera. Evelyn Herrera."

Celia didn't react really. She didn't say, "So you *are* Latin." Or "I knew you were faking it," as I feared she might be thinking. She didn't say that it explained why my skin was darker than hers or Don's. In fact, she said nothing at all until she said, "That's beautiful."

"And yours?" I asked. I stood up and moved over to the couch where she was sitting, to close the gap between us. "Celia St. James . . ."

"Jamison."

"What?"

"Cecelia Jamison. That's my real name."

"That's a great name. Why did they change it?"

"I changed it."

"Why?"

"Because it sounds like a girl who might live next door to you. And I've always wanted to be the kind of girl you feel lucky just to lay your eyes on." She tilted her head back and finished her wine. "Like you."

"Oh, stop."

"You stop. You know damn well what you are. How you affect the people around you. I'd kill for a chest like that and full lips like yours. You make people think of undressing you just by showing up in a room fully clothed."

I felt flushed hearing her talk about me like that. Having her talk about the way men saw me. I'd never heard a woman talk about me that way before.

Celia took my glass out of my hand. She threw the wine back into her own throat. "We need more," she said, waving the glass in the air.

I smiled and took both glasses into the kitchen. Celia followed me. She leaned against my Formica counter as I poured.

"The first time I saw *Father and Daughter*, do you know what I thought?" she said. Billie Holiday was now faintly playing in the background.

"What?" I said, handing her her glass. She took it and put it down for a moment, then hopped up onto the counter and picked it up. She was wearing dark blue capri pants and a white sleeveless turtleneck.

"I thought you were the most gorgeous woman who had ever been created and we should all stop trying." She inhaled half the contents of her glass.

"No, you did not," I said.

"Yes, I did."

I took a sip of my wine. "It makes no sense," I told her. "You admiring me like you're any different. You're a knockout, plain and simple. With your big blue eyes and your hourglass figure . . . I think together we really give the guys a wild sight."

Celia smiled. "Thank you."

I finished my glass and put it down on the counter. Celia took it as a challenge to do the same with hers. She wiped her mouth with her fingertips when she was done. I poured us more.

"How did you learn all the underhanded, sneaky stuff you know?" Celia asked.

"I have absolutely no idea what you're talking about," I said coyly.

"You're smarter than you let on to just about anybody."

"Me?" I said.

Celia was starting to get goose bumps, so I suggested we go back into the living room, where it was warmer. The desert winds had swooped in and turned this June night into a chilly one. When I started to get cold, too, I asked her if she knew how to make a fire.

"I've seen people do it," she said, shrugging.

"Me too. I've seen Don do it. But I've never done it."

"We can do it," she said. "We can do anything."

"All right!" I said. "You go open another bottle of wine, and I'll start trying to guess how to get it started."

"Great idea!" Celia flung the blanket off her shoulders and ran into the kitchen.

I knelt down in front of the fireplace and started poking the ashes. And then I took two logs and laid them perpendicular to each other.

"We need newspaper," she said when she came back. "And I've decided there's no point in glasses anymore."

I looked up to see her swigging the wine out of the bottle.

I laughed, grabbed the newspaper off the table, and threw it in. "Even better!" I said, and I ran upstairs and grabbed the copy of *Sub Rosa* that had called me a cold bitch. I raced back down to show her. "We'll burn this!"

I threw the magazine into the fireplace and lit a match.

"Do it!" she said. "Burn those jerks."

The flame curled the pages, held steady for a moment, and then sputtered out. I lit another match and threw it in.

I somehow managed a few embers and then a very small flame as some of the newspaper caught.

"All right," I said. "I feel confident that this is slowly coming along."

Celia came over and handed me the bottle of wine. I took it and sipped from it. "You have a little catching up to do," she said as I tried to give it back to her.

I laughed and put the bottle back up to my lips.

It was expensive wine. I liked drinking it as if it was water, as if it meant nothing to me. *Poor girls from Hell's Kitchen can't drink this kind of wine and treat it like it's nothing.*

"All right, all right, give it back," Celia said.

I teasingly held on to it, not letting it out of my grasp.

Her hand was on mine. She pulled with the same force I did. And then I said, "OK, it's all yours." But I said it too late, and I let go too soon.

Wine went all over her white shirt.

"Oh, God," I said. "I'm sorry."

I took the bottle, put it down on the table, took her hand, and pulled her up the stairs. "You can borrow a shirt. I have just the perfect one for you."

I led her into my bedroom and straight into my closet. I watched as Celia looked around, taking in the surroundings of the bedroom I shared with Don.

"Can I ask you something?" she said. Her voice had an airiness to it, a wistfulness. I thought she might ask me if I believed in ghosts or love at first sight.

"Sure," I said.

"And you'll promise to tell the truth?" she asked as she took a seat on the corner of the bed.

"Not particularly," I said.

Celia laughed.

"But go ahead and ask the question," I said. "And we'll see."

"Do you love him?" she asked.

"Don?"

"Who else?"

I thought about it. I had loved him once. I'd loved him very much. But did I love him anymore? "I don't know," I said.

"Is it all for publicity? Are you just in it to be an Adler?"

"No," I said. "I don't think so."

"What, then?"

I walked over and sat down on the bed. "It's hard to say I do or don't love him or to say that I'm with him for one reason over another. I love him, and a lot of the time I hate him. And I'm with him because of his name but also because we have fun. We used to have fun a lot, and now we still do sometimes. It's hard to explain."

"Does he do it for you?" she said.

"Yes, very much. Sometimes I find myself aching to be with him so much it embarrasses me. I don't know if a woman is supposed to want a man as much as I find myself wanting Don."

Don may have taught me that I was capable of loving someone and desiring him. But he also taught me that you could desire someone even when you don't like him, that you can desire someone *especially* when you don't like him. I believe today they call it hate-fucking. But it's a crude name for something that is a very human, sensual experience.

"Forget I asked," Celia said, standing up from the bed. I could tell she was bothered.

"Let me get the shirt," I said, walking toward the dresser.

It was one of my favorite shirts, a lilac button-down blouse with a silvery sheen to it. But it didn't fit me well. I could barely fasten it around my chest.

Celia was smaller than me, more delicate.

"Here," I said, handing it to her.

She took it from me and looked at it. "The color is gorgeous."

"I know," I said. "I stole it from the set of *Father and Daughter*. But don't tell anyone."

"I hope you know by now that all of your secrets are safe with me," Celia said as she started unbuttoning it to put it on.

I think for her it was a throwaway line. But it meant a lot to me. Not because she said it, I suppose. But because *when* she said it, I realized I believed her.

"I do," I said. "I do know that."

People think that intimacy is about sex.

But intimacy is about truth.

When you realize you can tell someone your truth, when you can show yourself to them, when you stand in front of them bare and their response is "You're safe with me"—that's intimacy.

And by those standards, that moment with Celia was the most intimate one I'd ever had with anyone.

It made me so appreciative, so grateful, that I wanted to wrap my arms around her and never let go.

"I'm not sure it will fit me," Celia said.

"Try it on. I bet it will, and if it does, it's yours."

I wanted to give her a lot of things. I wanted what I had to be hers. I wondered if this was what it felt like to love someone. I already knew what it meant to be *in love* with someone. I'd felt it, and I'd acted it. But to *love* someone. To care for them. To throw your lot in with theirs and think, *Whatever happens, it's you and me.*

"All right," Celia said. She threw the shirt on the bed. As she pulled off her own shirt, I found myself looking at the paleness of the skin stretched across her ribs. I gazed at the bright whiteness of her bra. I noticed the way her breasts, instead of being lifted by the bra like mine, appeared as if the bra were there merely for decoration.

I followed the tiny trail of dark brown freckles that ran along the side of her right hip.

"Well, hello," Don said.

I jumped. Celia gasped and scrambled to put her shirt back on.

Don started laughing. "What on earth is going on in here?" he teased.

I walked over to him and said, "Absolutely nothing."

LIFE OF THE PARTY GIRL

Celia St. James is really making a name for herself around town! And it's not just because she's proving to be a swell actress. The Georgia Peach knows how to make all the right friends.

The most high-profile of which is everyone's favorite starlet Evelyn Hugo. Celia and Evelyn have been seen all over town, shopping, chatting, and even finding time for a round or two of ladies' golf at the Beverly Hills Golf Club.

And to make matters even more perfect, it seems the best friends will be going on plenty of double dates in the near future. Celia has been spotted at the Trocadero with none other than Robert Logan, close friend of Evelyn's hubby, Don Adler.

A handsome date, glamorous friends, and talk of a statuette in her future—it's a good time to be Celia St. James!

I DON'T WANT TO DO this," Celia said.

    She was wearing a tailored black dress with a deep-V neckline. It was the kind of dress I could never wear out of the house or I'd be picked up on a prostitution charge. She had on a diamond necklace that Don had persuaded Sunset to loan to her.

Sunset wasn't in the business of helping freelance actresses, but Celia wanted the diamonds, and I wanted Celia to have anything she wanted. And Don wanted me to have anything I wanted, at least most of the time.

Don had just starred in his second Western, *The Righteous*, after he had lobbied Ari Sullivan hard for one more crack at bat. This time, however, the reviews were telling a different story. Don had "manned up." He was convincing everyone, on his sophomore try, that he was a formidable action star.

Which translated into Don having the number one movie in the country and Ari Sullivan giving Don anything he asked for.

That's how those diamonds made their way onto Celia's neck, the large center ruby resting at the top of her breasts.

I was in emerald green again. It was a look that was starting to become my signature. This time, it was off the shoulder and made of peau de soie, with a cinched waist, full skirt, and beading on the neckline. My hair was down in a brushed-under bob.

I looked over at Celia, who was looking in the mirror at my vanity, fiddling with her bouffant.

"You have to do this," I said.

"I don't want to. Doesn't that count for anything?"

I picked up my clutch, made to match my dress. "Not really," I said.

"You're not the boss of me, you know," she said.

"Why are we friends?" I asked her.

"Honestly? I don't even remember," she said.

"Because our whole is greater than the sum of our parts."

"And so what?"

"And so when it comes to what acting roles to take and how to play them, who's in charge?"

"I am."

"And now, when it's the opening of our movie? Who's in charge then?"

"I suppose you are."

"You suppose right."

"I really hate him, Evelyn," Celia said. She was messing with her makeup.

"Put the rouge down," I said. "Gwen made you look gorgeous. Don't mess with perfect."

"Did you listen to me? I said I hate him."

"Of course you hate him. He's a weasel."

"There's no one else?"

"Not at this hour."

"And I can't go alone?"

"To your own premiere?"

"Why can't you and I just go together?"

"I'm going with Don. You're going with Robert."

Celia frowned and turned back to the mirror. I saw her eyes narrow and her lips purse, as if she was thinking of how mad she was.

I grabbed her bag and handed it to her. It was time to go.

"Celia, would you cut it out? If you're not willing to do what it takes to get your name in the paper, then why the hell are you here?"

She stood up, ripped the bag out my hand, and walked out the door. I watched her go down my stairs, into my living room with a grand smile, and then run into Robert's arms as if she thought he was the savior of all mankind.

I walked up to Don. He always cleaned up nicely in his tux. There was no denying that he was going to be the most handsome man there. But I was tiring of him. What's that saying? Behind every gorgeous woman, there's a man sick of screwing her? Well, it works both ways. No one mentions that part.

"Shall we go?" Celia said, as if she couldn't possibly wait to show up to the movie on Robert's arm. She was a great actress. No one has ever denied that.

"I don't want to waste a minute more," I said, looping my arm into Don's and holding on for dear life. He looked down at my arm and then at me, as if pleasantly surprised by my warmth.

"Let's see our little women in *Little Women*, shall we?" Don said. I nearly smacked him across the face. He was owed a smack or two. Or fifteen.

Our cars picked us up and drove us to Grauman's Chinese Theatre.

Parts of Hollywood Boulevard had been blocked off for our arrival. The driver pulled up just behind Celia and Robert outside the theater. We were the last in a line of four cars.

When you are one of an ensemble of female stars in a movie and the studio wants to make a big show, they make sure you all show up at the same time, in four separate cars, with four eligible bachelors for dates—except, in my case, the eligible bachelor was my husband.

Our dates stepped out first, each standing by and offering a hand. I waited as I watched Ruby step out, then Joy, then Celia. I waited just a beat longer than the rest of them. And then I stepped out, leg first, onto the red carpet.

"You're the most beautiful woman here," Don said into my ear as I stood next to him. But I already knew he thought I was the most gorgeous woman there. I knew, very acutely, that if he did not believe that, he would not have been with me.

Men were almost never with me for my personality.

I'm not suggesting that charming girls should take pity on the pretty ones. I'm just saying it's not so great being loved for something you didn't do.

The photographers started calling our names as we all walked in. My head was a jumble of words being thrown in my direction. "Ruby! Joy! Celia! Evelyn!" "Mr. and Mrs. Adler! Over here!"

I could barely hear myself think over the din of cameras snapping and the crowd buzzing. But, as I had long ago trained myself to do, I pretended as if I felt perfectly calm inside, as if being treated like a tiger at the zoo was my most comfortable situation.

Don and I held hands and smiled for every flashing bulb. At the end of the red carpet stood a few men with microphones. Ruby was speaking to one. Joy and Celia were speaking to another. The third put his mic in my face.

He was a short guy with small eyes and a bulbous, gin-blossomed nose. A face made for radio, as they say.

"Miss Hugo, are you excited for this picture to come out?"

I laughed as kindly as I could to disguise what a stupid question he was asking. "I've waited my whole life to play Jo March. I'm incredibly excited for tonight."

"And you seem to have made a good friend during filming," he said.

"What's that?"

"You and Celia St. James. You seem like you're great friends."

"She's wonderful. And wonderful in the film. Absolutely."

"She and Robert Logan seem to be getting hot and heavy."

"Oh, you'd have to ask them about that. I don't know."

"But didn't you set them up?"

Don stepped in. "I think that's all for questions," he said.

"Don, when are you and the Mrs. going to start a family?"

"I said it was enough, friend. And it's enough. Thank you."

Don pushed me forward.

We got to the doors, and I watched as Ruby and her date, followed by Joy and hers, walked through.

Don opened the door in front of us, waiting for me. Robert held the one on the other side for Celia.

And I got an idea.

I took Celia's hand and turned us around.

"Wave to the crowd," I said, smiling. "Like we're the goddamn queens of England."

Celia smiled brightly and did exactly as I did. We stood there, in black and green, redhead and blonde, one of us all ass and the other all tits, waving to the crowd as if we ruled them.

Ruby and Joy were nowhere to be seen. And the crowd roared for *us*.

We turned around and headed into the theater. We made our way to our seats.

"Big moment," Don said.

"I know."

"In just a few months, you'll win for this, and I'll win for *The Righteous*. And then the sky's the limit."

"Celia is going to be nominated, too," I whispered into his ear.

"People are going to leave this movie talking about you," he said. "I have no doubt."

I looked over to see Robert whispering into Celia's ear. She was laughing as if he actually had anything funny to say. But it was me who got her those diamonds, me who got her that gorgeous picture of the two of us that would make headlines the next day. Meanwhile, she was acting as if he was about to charm her dress off. All I could think was that he didn't know about that line of freckles on her hip. I knew about them, and he didn't.

"She's really talented, Don."

"Oh, get over her," Don said. "I'm sick of hearing her name all the damn time. They shouldn't be asking you about her. They should be asking you about *us*."

"Don, I—"

He waved me off, determining, before I'd even said anything, that whatever I had to say was useless to him.

The lights dimmed. The crowd quieted. The credits started to roll. And my face appeared on the screen.

The entire audience stared at me on-screen as I said, "Christmas won't be Christmas without any presents!"

But by the time Celia said, "We've got Father and Mother, and each other," I knew it was all over for me.

Everyone was going to walk out of this theater talking about Celia St. James.

It should have made me afraid or jealous or insecure. I should have been plotting to one-up her in some way by planting a story that she was a prude or sleeping around. That is the fastest way to ruin a woman's reputation, after all—to imply that she has not adequately threaded the needle that is *being sexually satisfying* without ever appearing to *desire sexual satisfaction.*

But instead of spending the next hour and forty-five minutes nursing my wounds, I spent the time holding back a smile.

Celia was going to win an Oscar. It was as plain as the nose on her face. And it didn't make me jealous. It made me happy.

When Beth died, I cried. And then I reached over Robert's and Don's laps and squeezed her hand.

Don rolled his eyes at me.

And I thought, *He's going to find an excuse to hit me later. But it will be for this.*

I WAS STANDING in the middle of Ari Sullivan's mansion at the top of Benedict Canyon. Don and I had made it up the winding streets without saying much of anything to each other.

I suspected he knew the same thing I did once he saw Celia in that movie. That no one cared about anything else.

After our driver dropped us off and we made our way inside, Don said, "I need to find the john," and disappeared.

I looked for Celia but couldn't find her.

Instead, I was surrounded by brown-nosing losers, hoping to rub elbows with me while they drank their sugary cocktails and talked about Eisenhower.

"Would you excuse me?" I said to a woman in a hideous bubble cut. She was waxing on about the Hope Diamond.

Women who collected rare jewels seemed exactly the same as men who were desperate to have just one night with me. The world was about objects to them; all they wanted to do was possess.

"Oh, there you are, Ev," Ruby said when she found me in the hallway.

She had two green cocktails in her hand. Her voice was lukewarm, a bit hard to read.

"Having a good night?" I asked.

She looked over her shoulder, put the stems of both glasses in one hand, and then pulled me by the elbow, spilling as she did.

"Ow, Ruby," I said, noticeably perturbed.

She nodded covertly to the laundry room to the right of us.

"What on earth . . ." I said.

"Would you just open the goddamn door, Evelyn?"

I turned the handle, and Ruby stepped in and dragged me with her. She shut the door behind us.

"Here," she said, handing me one of the cocktails in the dark. "I was getting it for Joy, but you have it. It matches your dress, anyway."

As my eyes adjusted, I took the drink from her. "You're *lucky* it matches my dress. You nearly poured half the drink on it."

With one of her hands now free, Ruby tugged on the pull chain of the light above us. The tiny room lit up and stung my eyes.

"You have absolutely no decorum tonight, Ruby."

"You think I'm worried about what you think of me, Evelyn Hugo? Now, listen, what're we going to do?"

"What are we going to do about what?"

"About what? About Celia St. James, that's what."

"What about her?"

Ruby hung her head in frustration. "Evelyn, I swear."

"She gave a great performance. What can we do?" I said.

"This is exactly what I told Harry would happen. And he said it wouldn't."

"Well, what do you want me to do about it?"

"You're losing out, too. Or do you not see that?"

"Of course I see it!" I cared, obviously. But I also knew I could still win Best Actress. Celia and Ruby would be competing for Best Supporting. "I don't know what to tell you, Ruby. We were all right about Celia. She's talented and gorgeous and charming, and when you've been bested, sometimes it's good to recognize it and move on."

Ruby looked at me as if I had slapped her.

I had nothing else to say, and she was blocking my way out of the room. So I put the drink to my mouth and downed it in two gulps.

"This is not the Evelyn I know and respect," Ruby said.

"Oh, Ruby, put a lid on it."

She finished her drink. "People have been saying all sorts of things about the two of you, and I didn't believe it. But now . . . I don't know."

"People have been saying all sorts of things like what?"

"You know."

"I assure you, I haven't the faintest."

"Why do you make things so difficult?"

"Ruby, you've pulled me into a laundry room against my will, and you're barking at me about things I can't control. I'm not the difficult one."

"She's a *lesbian*, Evelyn."

Until that point, the sounds of the party going on around us had been muted but still distinct. But the minute Ruby said what she said, the minute I heard the word *lesbian*, my blood started beating so fast that my pulse was all I could hear. I was not paying attention to what was flying out of Ruby's mouth. I could only catch certain words, like *girl* and *dyke* and *twisted*.

The skin on my chest felt hot. My ears burned.

I did my best to calm myself. And when I did, when I focused on Ruby's words, I finally heard the other piece of what she was trying to tell me.

"You should probably get a better handle on your husband, by the way. He's in Ari's bedroom getting a blow job from some harpy from MGM."

When she said it, I did not think, *Oh, my God. My husband is cheating on me.* I thought, *I have to find Celia.*

E VELYN GETS UP OFF THE sofa and picks up the phone, asking Grace to order us dinner from the Mediterranean place on the corner.

"Monique? What would you like? Beef or chicken?"

"Chicken, I guess." I watch her, waiting for her to sit back down and resume her story. But when she does sit, she merely looks at me. She neither acknowledges what she has just told me nor admits what I've been suspecting for some time now. I have no choice but to be direct. "Did you know?"

"Did I know what?"

"That Celia St. James was gay?"

"I'm telling you the story as it unfolded."

"Well, yes," I say. "But . . ."

"But what?" Evelyn is calm, perfectly composed. And I can't tell if it's because she knows what I suspect and she's finally ready to tell the truth or because I'm dead wrong and so she has no idea what I'm thinking.

I'm not sure I want to ask the question before I know the answer.

Evelyn's lips are together in a straight line. Her eyes are focused directly on me. But I notice, as she's waiting for me to speak, that her chest is rising and falling at a rapid pace. She's nervous. She's not as confident as she's letting on. She's an actress, after all. I should know well enough by now that what you see isn't always what you get with Evelyn.

So I ask her the question in a way that lets her tell me as much, or as little, as she's ready to say. "Who was the love of your life?"

Evelyn looks me in the eye, and I know she needs one more tiny push. "It's OK, Evelyn. Really."

It's a big deal. But it is OK. Things are different now from how they were then. Although still not entirely safe, either, I have to admit.

But still.

She can say it.

She can say it to me.

She can admit it, freely. Now. Here.

"Evelyn, who was your great love? You can tell me."

Evelyn looks out the window, breathes in deeply, and then says, "Celia St. James."

The room is quiet as Evelyn lets herself hear her own words. And then she smiles, a bright, wide, deeply sincere smile. She starts laughing to herself and then refocuses on me. "I feel like I spent my entire life loving her."

"So this book, your biography . . . you're ready to come out as a gay woman?"

Evelyn closes her eyes for a moment, and at first I think she is processing the weight of what I've said, but once she opens her eyes again, I realize she is trying to process my stupidity.

"Haven't you been listening to a single thing I've told you? I loved Celia, but I also, before her, loved Don. In fact, I'm positive that if Don hadn't turned out to be a spectacular asshole, I probably never would have been capable of falling in love with someone else at all. I'm bisexual. Don't ignore half of me so you can fit me into a box, Monique. Don't do that."

This stings. Hard. I know how it feels for people to assume things about you, to prescribe a label for you based on how you appear to them. I have spent my life trying to explain to people that while I look black, I am biracial. I have spent my life knowing the importance of allowing people to tell you who they are instead of reducing them to labels.

And here I've gone and done to Evelyn what so many people have done to me.

Her love affair with a woman signaled to me that she was gay, and I did not wait for her to tell me she was bisexual.

This is her whole point, isn't it? This is why she wants to be so acutely understood, with such perfect word choices. Because she wants to be seen exactly as she truly is, with all the nuance and shades of gray. The same way I have wanted to be seen.

So this is my fuckup. I just fucked up. And despite my desire to blow past it or to reduce it to nothing, I know the stronger move here is to apologize.

"I'm sorry," I say. "You're absolutely right. I should have asked you how you identify instead of assuming I knew. So let me try again. Are you prepared to come out, in the pages of this book, as a bisexual woman?"

"Yes," she says, nodding. "Yes, I am." Evelyn seems pleased with my apology, if not still slightly indignant. But we are back in business.

"And how exactly did you figure it out?" I ask. "That you loved her? After all, you could have found out she was interested in women and just as easily not realized you were interested in her."

"Well, it helped that my husband was upstairs cheating on me. Because I was sickeningly jealous on both accounts. I was jealous when I found out Celia was gay, because it meant that she was with other women, or had been with other women, that her life wasn't just *me*. And I was jealous that my husband was with a woman upstairs at the very party I was at, because it was embarrassing and threatened my way of life. I had been living in this world where I thought I could have this closeness with Celia and this distance with Don and neither of them would need anything else from anyone else. It was this odd bubble that just up and burst."

"I would imagine, back then, it wasn't a conclusion you'd come to easily—being in love with someone of the same sex."

"Of course not! Maybe if I'd spent my whole life fighting off feelings for women, then I might have had a template for it. But I didn't. I was taught to like men, and I had found—albeit temporarily—love and lust with a man. The fact that I wanted to be around Celia all the time, the fact that I cared about her enough that I valued her happiness over my own, the fact that I liked to think about that moment when she stood in front of me without her shirt on—now, you put those pieces together, and you say, one plus one equals I'm in love with a woman. But back then, at least for me, I didn't have that equation. And if you don't even realize that there's a formula to be working with, how the hell are you supposed to find the answer?"

She goes on. "I thought I finally had a friendship with a woman. And I thought my marriage was down the tubes because my husband was an asshole. And by the way, both those things were true. They just weren't the whole truth."

"So what did you do?"

"At the party?"

"Yeah, who did you go to first?"

"Well," Evelyn says, "one of them came to me."

R UBY LEFT ME THERE, NEXT to the dryer, with an empty cocktail glass in my hand.

I needed to go back to the party. But I stood there, frozen, thinking, *Get out of here.* I just couldn't turn the doorknob. And then the door opened on its own. Celia. The raucous, bright-lit party behind her.

"Evelyn, what are you doing?"

"How did you find me?"

"I ran into Ruby, and she said I could find you drinking in the laundry room. I thought it was a euphemism."

"It wasn't."

"I can see that."

"Do you sleep with women?" I asked.

Celia, shocked, shut the door behind her. "What are you talking about?"

"Ruby says you're a lesbian."

Celia looked over my shoulder. "Who cares what Ruby says?"

"Are you?"

"Are you going to stop being friends with me now? Is that what this is about?"

"No," I said, shaking my head. "Of course not. I would . . . never do that. I would never."

"What, then?"

"I just want to know is all."

"Why?"

"Don't you think I have the right to know?"

"Depends."

"So you are?" I asked.

Celia put her hand on the doorknob and prepared to leave. Instinctively, I leaned forward and grabbed her wrist.

"What are you doing?" she said.

I liked the feel of her wrist in my hand. I liked the way her perfume permeated the whole tiny room. I leaned forward and kissed her.

I did not know what I was doing. And by that I mean that I was not fully in control of my movement and that I was physically *unaware* of how to kiss her. Should it be the way I kissed men, or should it be different somehow? I also did not understand the emotional scope of my actions. I did not truly understand their significance or risk.

I was a famous woman kissing a famous woman in the house of the biggest studio head in Hollywood, surrounded by producers and stars and probably a good dozen people who ratted to *Sub Rosa* magazine.

But all I cared about in that moment was that her lips were soft. Her skin was without any roughness whatsoever. All I cared about was that she kissed me back, that she took her hand off the doorknob and, instead, put it on my waist.

She smelled floral, like lilac powder, and her lips felt humid. Her breath was sweet, spiked with the taste of cigarettes and crème de menthe.

When she pushed herself against me, when our chests touched and her pelvis grazed mine, all I could think was that it wasn't so different and yet it was different entirely. She swelled in all the places Don went flat. She was flat in the places Don swelled.

And yet that sense that you can feel your heart in your chest, that your body tells you it wants more, that you lose yourself in the scent, taste, and feel of another person—it was all the same.

Celia broke away first. "We can't stay in here," she said. She wiped her lips on the back of her hand. She took her thumb and rubbed it against the bottom of mine.

"Wait, Celia," I said, trying to stop her.

But she left the room, shutting the door behind her.

I closed my eyes, unsure how to get a handle on myself, how to quiet my brain.

I breathed in. I opened the door and walked right up the steps, taking them two at a time.

I opened every single door on the second floor until I found who I was looking for.

Don was getting dressed, shoving the tail of his shirt into his suit pants, as a woman in a beaded gold dress put her shoes on.

I ran out. And Don followed me.

"Let's talk about this at home," he said, grabbing my elbow.

I yanked it away, searching for Celia. There was no sign of her.

Harry came in through the front door, fresh-faced and looking sober. I ran up to him, leaving Don on the staircase, cornered by a tipsy producer wanting to talk to him about a melodrama.

"Where have you been all night?" I asked Harry.

He smiled. "I'm going to keep that to myself."

"Can you take me home?"

Harry looked at me and then at Don still on the stairs. "You're not going home with your husband?"

I shook my head.

"Does he know that?"

"If he doesn't, he's a moron."

"OK," Harry said, nodding with confidence and submission. Whatever I wanted was what he would do.

I got into the front seat of Harry's Chevy, and he started backing out just as Don came out of the house. He ran to my side of the car. I did not roll down the window.

"Evelyn!" he yelled.

I liked how the glass between us took the edge off his voice, how it muffled it enough to make him sound far away. I liked the control of being able to decide whether I listened to him at full volume.

"I'm sorry," he said. "It isn't what you think."

I stared straight ahead. "Let's go."

I was putting Harry in a tough spot, making him take sides. But to Harry's credit, he didn't bat an eyelash.

"Cameron, don't you dare take my wife away from me!"

"Don, let's discuss it in the morning," Harry called through the window, and then he plowed out, into the roads of the canyon.

When we got to Sunset Boulevard and my pulse had slowed, I turned to Harry and started talking. When I told him that Don had been upstairs with a woman, he nodded as if he'd expected no less.

"Why don't you seem surprised?" I asked as we sped through the intersection of Doheny and Sunset, the very spot where the beauty of Beverly Hills started to show. The streets widened and became lined with trees, and the lawns were immaculately manicured, the sidewalks clean.

"Don has always had a penchant for women he's just met," Harry says. "I wasn't sure if you knew. Or if you cared."

"I didn't know. And I do care."

"Well, then, I'm sorry," he said, looking at me briefly before putting his eyes back on the road. "In that case, I should have told you."

"I suppose there are lots of things we don't tell each other," I said, looking out the window. There was a man walking his dog down the street.

I needed someone.

Right then, I needed a friend. Someone to tell my truths to, someone to accept me, someone to say that I was going to be OK.

"What if we really did it?" I said.

"Told each other the truth?"

"Told each other everything."

Harry looked at me. "I'd say that's a burden I don't want to put on you."

"It might be a burden for you, too," I said. "I have skeletons."

"You're Cuban, and you're a power-hungry, calculating bitch," Harry said, smiling at me. "Those secrets aren't so bad."

I threw my head back and laughed.

"And you know what I am," he said.

"I do."

"But right now, you have plausible deniability. You don't have to hear about it or see it."

Harry turned left, into the flats instead of the hills. He was taking me to his house instead of my own. He was scared of what Don would do to me. I sort of was, too.

"Maybe I'm ready for that. To be a real friend. True blue," I said.

"I'm not sure that's a secret I want you to have to keep, love. It's a sticky one."

"I think that secret's much more common than either of us is pretending," I said. "I think maybe all of us have at least a little bit of that secret within us. I think I just might have that secret in me, too."

Harry took a right and pulled into his driveway. He put the car in park and turned to me. "You're not like me, Evelyn."

"I might be a little," I said. "I might be, and Celia might be, too."

Harry turned back to the wheel, thinking. "Yes," he said finally. "Celia might be, too."

"You knew?"

"I suspected," he said. "And I suspected she might have . . . feelings for you."

I felt like I was the last person on earth to know what was right in front of me.

"I'm leaving Don," I said.

Harry nodded, unsurprised. "I'm happy to hear it," he said. "But I hope you know the full extent of what it means."

"I know what I'm doing, Harry." I was wrong. I didn't know what I was doing.

"Don's not going to take it sitting down," Harry said. "That's all I mean."

"So I should continue this charade? Allow him to sleep around and hit me when he feels like it?"

"Absolutely not. You know I would never say that."

"Then what?"

"I want you to be prepared for what you're going to do."

"I don't want to talk about this anymore," I said.

"That's fine," Harry said. He opened his car door and got out. He came around to my side and opened my door.

"Come, Ev," he said kindly. He put his hand out. "It's been a long night. You need some rest."

I suddenly felt very tired, as if once he pointed it out, I realized it had been there all along. I followed Harry to his front door.

His living room was sparse but handsome, furnished with wood and leather. The alcoves and doorways were all arched, the walls stark white. Only a single piece of art hung on the wall, a red and blue Rothko above the sofa. It occurred to me then that Harry wasn't a Hollywood producer for the paycheck. Sure, his house was nice. But there wasn't anything ostentatious about it, nothing performative. It was merely a place to sleep for him.

Harry was like me. Harry was in it for the glory. He was in it because it kept him busy, kept him important, kept him sharp.

Harry, like me, had gotten into it for the ego.

And we were both fortunate that we'd found our humanity in it, even though it appeared to be somewhat by accident.

The two of us walked up the curved stairs, and Harry set me up in his guest room. The bed had a thin mattress with a heavy wool blanket. I used a bar of soap to wash my makeup off, and Harry gently unzipped the back of my dress for me and gave me a pair of his pajamas to wear.

"I'll be just next door if you need anything," he said.

"Thank you. For everything."

Harry nodded. He turned away and then turned back to me as I was folding down the blanket. "Our interests aren't aligned, Evelyn," he said. "Yours and mine. You see that, right?"

I looked at him, trying to determine if I *did* see it.

"My job is to make the studio money. And if you are doing what the studio wants, then my job is to make you happy. But more than anything, Ari wants to—"

"Make Don happy."

Harry looked me in the eye. I got the point.

"OK," I said. "I see it."

Harry smiled shyly and closed the door behind him.

You'd think I'd have tossed and turned all night, worried about the future, worried about what it meant that I had kissed a woman, worried about whether I should really leave Don.

But that's what denial is for.

The next morning, Harry drove me back to my house. I was bracing myself for a fight. But when I got there, Don was nowhere to be seen.

I knew that very moment that our marriage was over and that the decision—the one I thought was mine to make—had been made for me.

Don hadn't been waiting for me, hadn't been planning to fight for me. Don was off somewhere else, leaving me before I could leave him.

Instead, right on my doorstep, was Celia St. James.

Harry waited in the driveway until I made my way up to her. I turned and waved for him to go.

When he was gone, and my beautiful treelined street was as quiet as you'd expect in Beverly Hills at just past seven in the morning, I took Celia's hand and led her inside.

"I'm not a . . ." Celia said when I shut the door behind us. "I just . . . there was a girl in high school, my best friend. And she and I—"

"I don't want to hear about it," I said.

"OK," she said. "I'm just . . . I'm not . . . there's nothing wrong with me."

"I know there's nothing wrong with you."

She looked at me, looking to understand exactly what I wanted from her, exactly what she should confess.

"Here is what I know," I said. "I know that I used to love Don."

"I know that!" she said defensively. "I know you love Don. I've always known that."

"I said I *used* to love Don. But I don't think I've loved him for some time now."

"OK."

"Now the only person I think about is you."

And with that, I went upstairs and packed my bags.

I HID OUT IN CELIA'S apartment for a week and a half, in purgatory. Celia and I slept, chastely, side by side in her bed every night.

During the day, I stayed in her apartment and read books while she went to work on her new movie for Warner Brothers.

We did not kiss. We occasionally lingered a little too long when our arms brushed, when our hands touched, never locking eyes. But in the middle of the night, after we both had appeared to fall asleep, I would feel her body against my back and I would push myself into her, feeling the warmth of her stomach against me, her chin in the crook of my neck.

Some mornings I would wake up in a pile of her hair and inhale deeply, trying to breathe in as much of her as I could.

I knew that I wanted to kiss her again. I knew that I wanted to touch her. But I didn't know exactly what I was supposed to do or how it was supposed to work. It was easy to think of that one kiss in a dark laundry room as a fluke. It wasn't even that hard to tell myself that the feelings I had for her were simply platonic.

As long as I only indulged my thoughts about Celia *sometimes*, then I could tell myself it wasn't real. Homosexuals were misfits. And while I didn't think that made them bad people—after all, I loved Harry like a brother—I wasn't ready to be one of them.

So I told myself that the spark between Celia and me was just a quirk we had. Which was convincing as long as it remained quirky.

Sometimes reality comes crashing down on you. Other times reality simply waits, patiently, for you to run out of the energy it takes to deny it.

And that is what happened to me one Saturday morning when Celia was in the shower and I was making eggs.

There was a knock at the door, and when I opened it, I saw the only face I was happy to see on that side of the threshold.

"Hi, Harry," I said, leaning in to hug him. I was careful not to get my runny spatula on his nice oxford shirt.

"Look at you," he said. "Cooking!"

"I know," I said as I moved out of the way and invited him in. "Hell has frozen over, I guess. Would you like some eggs?"

I led him toward the kitchen. He peeked into the pan. "How well have you mastered breakfast?" he asked.

"If you're asking if your eggs will be burned, the answer is probably."

Harry smiled and put a large, heavy envelope on the dining room table. The *thwap* it made as it hit the wood was all the clue I needed to what it contained.

"Let me guess," I said. "I'm getting a divorce."

"It would appear you are."

"On what grounds? I assume his lawyers didn't check the boxes for adultery or cruelty."

"Abandonment."

I raised my eyebrows. "Clever."

"The grounds don't matter. You know that."

"I know."

"You should read through it, have a lawyer read through it. But there's essentially one big highlight."

"Tell me."

"You get the house and your money and half of his."

I looked at Harry as if he was trying to sell me the Brooklyn Bridge. "Why would he do that?"

"Because you are forbidden to talk to anyone at any time about anything that happened during your marriage."

"Is he also forbidden?"

Harry shook his head. "Not in writing, no."

"So I can't talk, and he can blab all over town? What makes him think I'll go for that?"

Harry looked down at the table for a moment and then back up at me, sheepish.

"Sunset's dropping me, aren't they?"

"Don wants you out of the studio. Ari's planning to loan you out to MGM and Columbia."

"And then what?"

"And then you're on your own."

"Well, that's fine. I can do that. Celia's freelance. I'll get an agent, like her."

"You can," Harry said. "And I think you should try, but . . ."

"But what?"

"Don wants Ari to blackball you from getting an Oscar nod, and Ari's agreeing to it. I think he's gonna loan you out and purposefully put you in flops."

"He can't do that."

"He can. And he will, because Don's the goose that laid the golden egg. The studios are all hurting. People aren't going to the movies as much; they are waiting for the next episode of *Gunsmoke*. Sunset's been in decline from the minute we were forced to sell off our theaters. We're staying afloat because of stars like Don."

"And stars like me."

Harry nodded. "But—and I'm sorry to say it, but I think it's important that you see the big picture—Don's worth a lot more asses in the seats than you are."

I felt about two inches tall. "That hurts."

"I know," Harry said. "And I'm sorry."

The water in the bathroom turned off, and I heard Celia step out of the shower. There was a breeze coming in from the window. I wanted to shut it, but I didn't move. "So that's it. If Don doesn't want me, no one does."

"If Don doesn't want you, he doesn't want anyone else to have you. I realize it's a subtle difference, but . . ."

"But it is vaguely reassuring."

"Good."

"So that's his play? Don ruins my life and buys my silence with a house and less than a million dollars?"

"That's a lot of money," Harry said, as if it mattered, as if it helped.

"You know I don't care about money," I said. "At least, not primarily."

"I know."

Celia came out of the bathroom in a robe, her hair wet and straight. "Oh, hi, Harry," she said. "I'll just be a minute."

"No need to hurry on my account," he said. "I was just leaving."

Celia smiled and walked into the bedroom.

"Thank you for bringing it," I said.

Harry nodded.

"I did it once, I can do it again," I said to him as we walked to the door. "I can build the whole thing back up from scratch."

"I have never doubted that you could do a single thing you put your mind to." Harry put his hand on the doorknob, ready to go. "I'd like it if . . . I hope that we can still be friends, Evelyn. That we can still—"

"Oh, shut up," I said. "We're best friends. Who may or may not tell each other everything. That doesn't change. You still love me, right? Even though I'm about to be on the outs?"

"I do."

"And I still love you. So that's the end of it."

Harry smiled, relieved. "OK," he said. "It's me and you."

"Me and you, true blue."

Harry walked out of the apartment, and I watched him go down the street and get into his car. Then I turned around and rested my back against the door.

I was going to lose everything I had built my life on.

Everything except the money.

I still had the money.

And that was something.

And then I realized there was something else waiting for me, something I wanted that I was free to have.

It was there, with my back against the door of her apartment, on the brink of my divorce from the most popular man in Hollywood, that I realized that lying to myself about what I wanted took far more energy than I had.

So instead of wondering what it meant and what it made me, I stood up and walked into Celia's room.

She was in her robe still, drying her hair in front of her vanity.

I walked up to her and looked into her gorgeous blue eyes, and I said, "I think that I love you."

And then I took the tie of her robe and pulled it open.

I did it slowly. I did it so slowly that she could have stopped me a million times before it broke free. But she didn't.

Instead, she sat up straighter, looked at me more boldly, and put her hand on my waist as I did it.

The sides of the robe broke free of each other the moment the tension slacked, and then there she was, naked and sitting in front of me.

Her skin was creamy and pale. Her breasts were fuller than I'd anticipated, her nipples pink. Her flat stomach rounded just the littlest bit underneath her belly button.

And when my eyes moved down to her legs, she parted them just the littlest bit.

Instinctively, I kissed her. I put my hands on her breasts, touching them the way I wanted to and then the way I liked my own to be touched.

When she moaned, I throbbed.

She kissed my neck and the top of my chest.

She pulled my shirt off over the top of my head.

She looked at me, my breasts exposed.

"You're gorgeous," she said. "Even more gorgeous than I imagined."

I blushed and put my head in my hands, embarrassed by how out of control I felt, how out of my league it all was.

She took my hands off my face and looked at me.

"I don't know what I'm doing," I said.

"It's OK," she said. "I do."

That night, Celia and I slept nude, holding each other. We no longer pretended to touch by accident. And when I woke up in the morning with her hair in my face, I inhaled, loudly and proudly.

Within those four walls, we were unashamed.

ADLER AND HUGO KAPUT!

Don Adler, Hollywood's Most Eligible Bachelor?

Don and Evelyn are calling it quits! After two years of marriage, Don has filed for divorce from Evelyn Hugo.

We are sad to see the lovebirds part ways, but we'd be lying if we said we were surprised. We've heard rumblings that Don's star is set to rise even higher, and Evelyn was getting jealous and catty.

Luckily for Don, he's renewed his contract with Sunset Studios—which must have head honcho Ari Sullivan smiling wide—and has three films slated for release this year. That Don never misses a beat!

Meanwhile, while Evelyn's newest movie, *Little Women*, showed boffo B.O. numbers and great critical reception, Sunset has pulled her out of the upcoming *Jokers Wild* and replaced her with Ruby Reilly.

Has the sun set on Evelyn's time with Sunset?

HOW DID YOU REMAIN SO confident? So steadfast in your resolve?" I ask Evelyn.

"When Don left me? Or when my career went down the tubes?"

"Both, I guess," I say. "I mean, you had Celia, so it's a little different,
but still."

Evelyn cocks her head slightly. "Different from what?"

"Hm?" I say, lost in my own thoughts.

"You said I had Celia, so it was a little different," Evelyn clarifies. "Different from what?"

"Sorry," I say. "I was . . . in my own head." I have momentarily let my own
relationship problems seep into what should be a one-way conversation.

Evelyn shakes her head. "No need to be sorry. Just tell me different
from what."

I look at her and realize that I've opened a door that can't really be
shut. "From my own impending divorce."

Evelyn smiles, almost like the Cheshire Cat. "Now things are getting
interesting," she says.

It bothers me, her cavalier attitude toward my own vulnerability. It's
my fault for bringing it up. I know that. But she could treat it with more
kindness. I've exposed myself. I've exposed a wound.

"Have you signed the papers?" Evelyn asks. "Perhaps with a tiny
heart above the *i* in Monique? That's what I would do."

"I guess I don't take divorce as lightly as you," I say. It comes out
flatly. I consider softening, but . . . I don't.

"No, of course not," Evelyn says kindly. "If you did, at your age, you'd be a cynic."

"But at your age?" I ask.

"With my experience? A realist."

"That, in and of itself, is awfully cynical, don't you think? Divorce is loss."

Evelyn shakes her head. "Heartbreak is loss. Divorce is a piece of paper."

I look down to see that I have been doodling a cube over and over with my blue pen. It is starting to tear through the page. I neither pick up my pen nor push harder. I merely keep running the ink over the lines of the cube.

"If you are heartbroken right now, then I feel for you deeply," Evelyn says. "That I have the utmost respect for. That's the sort of thing that can split a person in two. But I wasn't heartbroken when Don left me. I simply felt like my marriage had failed. And those are very different things."

When Evelyn says this, I stop my pen in place. I look up at her. And I wonder why I needed Evelyn to tell me that.

I wonder why that sort of distinction has never crossed my mind before.

On my walk to the subway this evening, I see that Frankie has called me for the second time today.

I wait until I've ridden all the way to Brooklyn and I'm heading down the street toward my apartment to respond. It's almost nine o'clock, so I decide to text her: *Just getting out of Evelyn's now. Sorry it's so late. Want to talk tomorrow?*

I have my key in my front door when I get Frankie's response: *Tonight is fine. Call as soon as you can.*

I roll my eyes. I should never bluff Frankie.

I put my bag down. I pace around the apartment. What am I going to tell her? The way I see it, I have two choices.

I can lie and tell her everything's going fine, that we're on track for the June issue and that I'm getting Evelyn to talk about more concrete things.

Or I can tell the truth and potentially get fired.

At this point, I'm starting to see that getting fired might not be so bad. I'll have a book to publish in the future, one for which I'd most likely make millions of dollars. That could, in turn, get me other celebrity biography opportunities. And then, eventually, I could start finding my own topics, writing about anything I want with the confidence that any publisher would buy it.

But I don't know when this book will be sold. And if my real goal is to set myself up to be able to grab whatever story I want, then credibility matters. Getting fired from *Vivant* because I stole their major headline would not bode well for my reputation.

Before I can decide what, exactly, my plan is, my phone is ringing in my hand.

Frankie Troupe.

"Hello?"

"Monique," Frankie says, her voice somehow both solicitous and irritated. "What's going on with Evelyn? Tell me everything."

I keep searching for ways in which Frankie, Evelyn, and I all leave this situation getting what we want. But I realize suddenly that the only thing I can control is that *I* get what *I* want.

And why shouldn't I?

Really.

Why *shouldn't* it be me who comes out on top?

"Frankie, hi, I'm sorry I haven't been more available."

"That's fine, that's fine," Frankie says. "As long as you're getting good material."

"I am, but unfortunately, Evelyn is no longer interested in sharing the piece with *Vivant*."

The silence on Frankie's end of the phone is deafening. And then it is punctuated with a flat, dead "What?"

"I've been trying to convince her for days. That's why I've been unable to get back to you. I've been explaining to her that she has to do this piece for *Vivant*."

"If she wasn't interested, why did she call us?"

"She wanted me," I say. I do not follow this up with any sort of qualification. I do not say *She wanted me and here is why* or *She wanted me and I'm so sorry about all this.*

"She used us to get to you?" Frankie says, as if it's the most insulting thing she can think of. But the thing is, Frankie used me to get to Evelyn, so . . .

"Yes," I say. "I think she did. She's interested in a full biography. Written by me. I've gone along with it in the hopes of changing her mind."

"A *biography*? You're taking our story and turning it into a book instead?"

"It's what Evelyn wants. I've been trying to convince her otherwise."

"And have you?" Frankie asks. "Convinced her?"

"No," I say. "Not yet. But I think I might be able to."

"OK," Frankie says. "Then do that."

This is my moment.

"I think I can deliver you a massive, headline-making Evelyn Hugo story," I say. "But if I do, I want to be promoted."

I can hear skepticism enter Frankie's voice. "What kind of promotion?"

"Editor at large. I come and go as I please. I choose the stories I want to tell."

"No."

"Then I have no incentive to get Evelyn to allow the piece to be in *Vivant*."

I can practically hear Frankie weighing her options. She is quiet, but there is no tension. It is as if she does not expect me to speak until she has decided what she will say. "If you get us a cover story," she says finally, "*and* she agrees to sit for a photo shoot, I'll make you a writer at large."

I consider the offer, and Frankie jumps in as I'm thinking. "We only have one editor at large. Bumping Gayle out of the spot she has earned doesn't feel right to me. I'd think you could understand that. Writer at large is what I have to give. I won't exert too much control over what you can write about. And if you prove yourself quickly there, you'll move up as everyone else does. It's fair, Monique."

I think about it for a moment further. Writer at large seems reasonable. Writer at large sounds great. "OK," I say. And then I push just a little bit further. Because Evelyn said, at the very beginning of all this, that I have to insist on being paid top dollar. And she's right. "And I want a raise commensurate with the title."

I cringe as I hear myself asking for money so directly. But I relax my shoulders the moment I hear Frankie say, "Yes, sure, fine." I breathe out. "But I want confirmation from you tomorrow," she continues. "And I want the photo shoot booked by next week."

"OK," I say. "You've got it."

Before Frankie gets off the phone, she says, "I'm impressed, but I'm also pissed off. Please make this so good that I have to forgive you."

"Don't worry," I say. "I will."

W HEN I WALK INTO EVELYN'S office the next morning, I'm so
nervous that my back is sweating and a shallow pool is forming
along my spine.

Grace puts down a charcuterie platter, and I can't stop staring at the
cornichons as Evelyn and Grace are talking about Lisbon in the summer.

The moment Grace is gone, I turn to Evelyn.

"We need to talk," I say.

She laughs. "Honestly, I feel like that's all we do."

"About *Vivant*, I mean."

"OK," she says. "Talk."

"I need to know some sort of timeline for when this book might be
released." I wait for Evelyn to respond. I wait for her to give me something, *anything*, resembling an answer.

"I'm listening," she says.

"If you don't tell me when this book could realistically be sold, then
I'm running the risk of losing my job for something that might be years
away. Decades, even."

"You certainly have high hopes for my life span."

"Evelyn," I say, somewhat discouraged that she still isn't taking this
seriously. "I either need to know when this is coming out or I need to
promise *Vivant* an excerpt of it for the June issue."

Evelyn thinks. She is sitting cross-legged on the sofa opposite me, in
slim black jersey pants, a gray shell tank, and an oversized white cardigan. "OK," she says, nodding. "You can give them a piece of it—whatever

piece you like—for the June issue. If, and only if, you shut up about this timeline business."

I don't let my joy show on my face. I'm halfway there. I can't rest until I'm done. I have to push her. I have to ask and be willing to be told no. I have to know my worth.

After all, Evelyn wants something from me. She needs me. I don't know why or what for, but I know I wouldn't be sitting here if that weren't the case. I have value to her. I know that. And now I have to use it. Just as she would if she were me.

So here we go.

"You need to sit for a photo shoot. For the cover."

"No."

"It's nonnegotiable."

"Everything is negotiable. Haven't you gotten enough? I've agreed to the excerpt."

"You and I both know how valuable new images of you would be."

"I said no."

OK. Here we go. I can do this. I just have to do what Evelyn would do. I have to "Evelyn Hugo" Evelyn Hugo. "You agree to the cover photo, or I'm out."

Evelyn sits forward in her chair. "Excuse me?"

"You want me to write your life story. I want to write your life story. But these are my terms. I'm not going to lose my job for you. And the way I keep my job is I deliver an Evelyn Hugo feature with a cover. So you either persuade me to lose my job over this—which is only possible if you tell me *when* this book is being sold—or you do this. Those are your options."

Evelyn looks at me, and I get the impression that I am more than she bargained for. And I feel good about that. There's a smile forming that is hard to keep in.

"You're having fun with this, aren't you?" she says.

"I'm trying to protect my interests."

"Yes, but you're also good at it, and I think you're delighting in it a bit."

I finally let the smile out. "I'm learning from the best."

"Yes, you are," Evelyn says. She scrunches her nose. "A cover?"

"A cover."

"Fine. A cover. And in exchange, starting Monday, I want you here every waking moment. I want to tell you all I have to say as soon as possible. And from now on, when I don't answer a question the first time, you don't ask it again. Do we have a deal?"

I get up from behind the desk, walk over to Evelyn, and put out my hand. "Deal."

Evelyn laughs. "Look at you," she says. "You keep this up, you might just rule your own part of the world one day."

"Why, thank you," I say.

"Yeah, yeah, yeah," she says, not unkindly. "Sit down at the desk. Start recording. I don't have all day."

I do as I'm told, and then I look at her. "All right," I say. "So you're in love with Celia, you've divorced Don, it looks like your career is down the tubes. What's next?"

Evelyn takes a second to answer, and in that moment I realize that she has just agreed to the very thing she swore she would never do—a *Vivant* cover—just so I won't walk.

Evelyn wants me for something. And she wants it bad.

And now I'm finally starting to suspect that I should be scared.

Gullible Mick Riva

◆

EVELYN, GREEN'S NOT YOUR COLOR

Evelyn Hugo showed up to the 1960 Audience Appreciation Awards on the arm of producer Harry Cameron last Thursday. In an emerald-green silk cocktail number, she failed to wow like she has in the past. Evelyn's signature color is starting to seem like a signature bore.

Meanwhile, Celia St. James dazzled in a stunning pale blue beaded taffeta shirtdress, updating the typical daytime look with a glamorous, fresh twist.

But the icy Evelyn didn't say a single word to her old best friend. She avoided Celia all night.

Is it because Evelyn can't handle the fact that Celia received the Most Promising Female Personality Award that night? Or is it that Celia's been nominated for an Oscar for Best Supporting Actress for their movie *Little Women*, and Evelyn didn't get a mention?

Looks like Evelyn Hugo's green with envy.

ARI DROPPED ME FROM ANY productions within Sunset and started offering to loan me out to Columbia. After being forced to do two forgettable romantic comedies—both of them so bad that it was a foregone conclusion they would fail spectacularly—the other studios didn't want much of me, either.

Don was on the cover of *Life*, gracefully coming out of the ocean onto the shore, smiling as if it was the best day of his life.

When the 1960 Academy Awards came around, I was officially persona non grata.

"You know that I would take you," Harry said when he called that afternoon to check in on me. "You just say the word, and I'll come pick you up. I'm sure you have a stunning dress you can slip on, and I'll be the envy of everybody with you on my arm."

I was at Celia's apartment, getting ready to leave before her hair and makeup people came over. She was in the kitchen, drinking lemon water, avoiding eating anything so she could fit into her dress.

"I know you would," I said into the phone. "But you and I both know it would only hurt your reputation to be aligned with me right now."

"I do mean it, though," Harry said.

"I know you do," I said. "But you also know I'm too smart to take you up on it."

Harry laughed.

"Do my eyes look puffy?" Celia asked when I got off the phone with Harry. She opened them bigger and stared at me, as if this would help me answer the question.

I saw barely anything out of the ordinary. "They look gorgeous. And anyway, you know Gwen will make you look fabulous. What are you worried about?"

"Oh, for heaven's sake, Evelyn," Celia said, teasing me. "I think we all know what I'm worried about."

I took her by the waist. She was wearing a thin satin slip, edged in lace. I was wearing a short-sleeved sweater and shorts. Her hair was wet. When Celia's hair was wet, she didn't smell like shampoo. She smelled like clay.

"You're going to win," I said, pulling her toward me. "It isn't even a contest."

"I might not. They might give it to Joy or to Ellen Mattson."

"They would no sooner give it to Ellen Mattson than throw it in the L.A. River. And Joy, bless her heart, is no you."

Celia blushed, put her head in her hands briefly, and then looked back at me. "Am I intolerable?" she said. "Obsessing over this? Making you talk to me about it? When you're . . ."

"On the skids?"

"I was going to say blackballed."

"If you are intolerable, let me be the one to tolerate you," I said, and then I kissed her and tasted the lemon juice on her lips.

I checked my watch, knowing that hair and makeup would be there any moment, and grabbed my keys.

She and I had been taking great pains not to be seen together. It was one thing when we really were just friends, but now that we had something to hide, we had to start hiding it.

"I love you," I said. "I believe in you. Break a leg."

When my hand turned the doorknob, she called to me. "If I don't win," she said, her wet hair dripping onto the spaghetti straps of her slip, "will you still love me?"

I thought she was joking until I looked directly into her eyes.

"You could be a nobody living in a cardboard box, and I'd still love you," I said. I'd never said that before. I'd never meant it before.

Celia smiled wide. "Me too. The cardboard box and all of it."

*   *   *

HOURS LATER, BACK at the home I used to share with Don but now could say was entirely my own, I made myself a Cape Codder, sat on the couch, and tuned the TV to NBC, watching all my friends and the woman I loved walk the red carpet at the Pantages Theatre.

It all seems much more glamorous on-screen. I hate to break it to you, but in person, the theater is smaller, the people are paler, and the stage is less imposing.

It's all curated to make the audience at home feel like outsiders, to make you feel like a fly on the wall of a club you aren't good enough to get into. And I was surprised by how effective it was on me, how easy it was to fall for, even for a person who had just recently been at the very center of it.

I was two cocktails in and drowning in self-pity by the time they announced Best Supporting Actress. But the minute the camera panned to Celia, I swear I sobered up and clasped my hands together as tightly as possible for her, as if the harder I pressed them together, the higher her chances of winning.

"And the award goes to . . . Celia St. James for *Little Women*."

I jumped up out of my seat and shouted for her. And then my eyes got teary as she walked up to the stage.

As she stood there, behind the microphone, holding the statuette, I was mesmerized by her. By her fabulous boatneck dress, her sparkling diamond and sapphire earrings, and that absolutely flawless face of hers.

"Thank you to Ari Sullivan and Harry Cameron. Thank you to my agent, Roger Colton. To my family. And to the amazing cast of women that I felt so lucky to be a part of, to Joy and Ruby. And to Evelyn Hugo. Thank you."

When she said my name, I swelled with pride and joy and love. I was so goddamn happy for her. And then I did something mortifyingly inane. I kissed the television set.

I kissed her right on her grayscale face.

The *clink* I heard registered before the pain. And as Celia waved to the crowd and then stepped away from the podium, I realized I'd chipped my tooth.

But I didn't care. I was too happy. Too excited to congratulate her and tell her how proud I was.

I made another cocktail and forced myself to watch the rest of the spectacle. They announced Best Picture, and as the credits rolled, I turned off the TV.

I knew that Harry and Celia would be out all night. So I shut off the lights and went upstairs to bed. I took off my makeup. I put on cold cream. I turned down the covers. I was lonely, living all alone.

Celia and I had discussed it and come to the conclusion that we could not move in together. She was less convinced of this than I was, but I was steadfast in my resolve. Even though my career was in the gutter, hers was thriving. I couldn't let her risk it. Not for me.

My head was on the pillow, but my eyes were wide open when I heard someone pull into the driveway. I looked out the window to see Celia slipping out of a car and waving good night to her driver. She had an Oscar in her hand.

"You look comfortable," Celia said, once she'd made her way to me in the bedroom.

"Come here," I said to her.

She'd had a glass or three. I loved her drunk. She was herself but happier, so bubbly I sometimes worried she'd float away.

She took a running start and hopped into the bed. I kissed her.

"I'm so proud of you, darling."

"I missed you all night," she said. The Oscar was still in her hand, and I could tell it was heavy; she kept allowing it to tip over onto the mattress. The space for her name was blank.

"I don't know if I was supposed to take this one," she said, smiling. "But I didn't want to give it back."

"Why aren't you out celebrating? You should be at the Sunset party."

"I only wanted to celebrate with you."

I pulled her closer to me. She kicked off her shoes.

"Nothing means anything without you," she said. "Everything that isn't you is a pile of dog shit."

I tossed my head back and laughed.

"What happened to your tooth?" Celia asked.

"Is it that noticeable?"

Celia shrugged. "I suppose not. I think it's just that I've memorized every inch of you."

Just a few weeks ago, I had lain naked beside Celia and let her look at me, look at every part of my body. She had told me she wanted to remember every detail. She said it was like studying a Picasso.

"It's embarrassing," I told her now.

Celia sat up, intrigued.

"I kissed the television screen," I said. "When you won. I kissed you on the TV, and I chipped my tooth."

Celia laughed so hard she cackled. The statuette fell back to the mattress with a thump. And then she rolled over on top of me and put her arms around my neck. "That's the most lovable thing anyone has ever done since the dawn of man."

"I suppose I'll make a dentist appointment first thing tomorrow."

"I suppose you will."

I picked up her Oscar. I stared at it. I wanted one myself. And if I had stuck it out with Don a little longer, I could have had one tonight.

She was still in her dress, her heels long gone. Her hair was falling out of the pins. Her lipstick was faded. Her earrings still glistened.

"Have you ever made love to an Oscar winner?" she said.

I'd done something very close with Ari Sullivan, but I didn't think that was the time to tell her. And anyway, the spirit of the question was if I'd ever experienced a moment like that one. And I absolutely had not.

I kissed her and felt her hands on my face, and then I watched as she stepped out of her dress and into my bed.

BOTH OF MY movies flopped. A romance Celia did sold out theaters. Don starred in a hit thriller movie. Ruby Reilly's reviews for *Jokers Wild* called her "stunningly perfect" and "positively incomparable."

I taught myself how to make meat loaf and iron my own slacks.

And then I saw *Breathless*. I left the theater, went straight home, called Harry Cameron, and said, "I have an idea. I'm going to Paris."

CELIA WAS SHOOTING A MOVIE on location in Big Bear for three weeks. I knew that going with her wasn't an option, nor was visiting her on the set. She insisted she would come home every weekend, but it felt too risky.

She was a single girl, after all. I was afraid the prevailing wisdom erred too close to the question *What do single girls have to go home to?*

So I decided it was the right time to go to France.

Harry had some connections to filmmakers in Paris. He made a few calls on the sly for me.

Some of the producers and directors I met with knew who I was. Some of them were clearly seeing me just as a favor to Harry. And then there was Max Girard, an up-and-coming New Wave director, who had never heard of me before.

"You are *une bombe*," he said.

We were sitting in a quiet bar in the Saint-Germain-de-Prés neighborhood of Paris. We huddled in a booth in the back. It was just after dinnertime, and I hadn't had a chance to eat. Max was drinking a white Bordeaux. I had a glass of claret.

"That sounds like a compliment," I said, taking a sip.

"I don't know if I have before met a woman so attractive," he said, staring at me. His accent was so thick that I found myself leaning in to hear him.

"Thank you."

"You can act?" he said.

"Better than I look."

"That cannot be so."

"It is."

I saw Max's wheels start turning. "Are you willing to test for a part?"

I was willing to scrub a toilet for a part. "If the part is great," I said.

Max smiled. "This part is spectacular. This part is a movie-star part."

I nodded slowly. You have to restrain every part of your body when you are working hard not to look eager.

"Send me the pages, and we'll talk," I said, and then I drank the last of my wine and stood up. "I'm so sorry, Max, but I should go. Have a wonderful evening. Let's be in touch."

There was absolutely no way I was going to sit at a bar with a man who hadn't heard of me and let him think I had all the time in the world.

I could feel his eyes on me as I walked away, but I walked out the door with all the confidence I had—which, despite my current predicament, was quite a lot. And then I went back to my hotel room, put on my pajamas, ordered room service, and turned on the TV.

Before I went to bed, I wrote Celia a letter.

> *My Dearest CeCe,*
>
> *Please never forget that the sun rises and sets with your smile. At least to me it does. You're the only thing on this planet worth worshipping.*
>
>

All my love,
Edward
>

I folded it in half and tucked it into an envelope addressed to her. Then I turned out my light and closed my eyes.

Three hours later, I was awakened by the jarring sound of a phone ringing on the table next to me.

I picked it up, irritated and half asleep.

"*Bonjour?*" I said.

"We can speak your language, Evelyn." Max's accented English reverberated through the phone. "I am calling to see if you would be free to be in a movie I am shooting. The week after next."

"Two weeks from now?"

"Not even, quite. We are shooting six hours from Paris. You will do it?"

"What is the part? How long is the shoot?"

"The movie is called *Boute-en-Train*. At least, that's what it is called for now. We shoot for two weeks in Lac d'Annecy. The rest of the shoot you do not need to be there."

"What does *Boute-en-Train* mean?" I tried to say it the way he said it, but it came out overprocessed, and I vowed not to try again. Don't do things you're not good at.

"It means the life of the party. That is you."

"A party girl?"

"Like someone who is the heart of life."

"And my character?"

"She is the kind of woman every man falls in love with. It was originally written for a French woman, but I have just decided tonight that if you will do it, I will fire her."

"That's not nice."

"She's not you."

I smiled, surprised at both his charm and his eagerness.

"It is about two men who are petty thieves, and they are on the run to Switzerland when they are distracted by an incredible woman they meet on the way. The three of them go for an adventure in the mountains. I have been sitting here with my pages, trying to decide if this woman can be American. And I think she can. I think it's more interesting that way. It is a stroke of luck. To meet you at this time. So you will do it?"

"Let me sleep on it," I said. I knew I was going to take the part. It was the only part I could get. But you never get anywhere good by seeming amenable.

"Yes," Max said. "Of course. You have done nudity before, yes?"

"No," I said.

"I think you should be topless. In the film."

If I was going to be asked to show my breasts, wouldn't it be for a French film? And if the French were going to ask anyone, shouldn't it be me? I knew what got me famous the first time. I knew what it could do a second time.

"Why don't we discuss it tomorrow?" I said.

"Let's talk tomorrow *morning*," he said. "Because this other actress I have, she will show her breasts, Evelyn."

"It's late, Max. I'll ring you in the morning." And I hung up the phone.

I closed my eyes and breathed in deeply, considering both how beneath me this opportunity was and how lucky I was to be given it. It's a hard business, reconciling what the truth used to be with what the truth is now. Luckily, I didn't have to do it for very long.

TWO WEEKS LATER, I was back on a film set. And this time, I was free of all the buttoned-up, innocent-girl stuff that Sunset had pinned on me. This time, I was able to do whatever I wanted.

It was clear for the entire shoot that Max wanted nothing more than to possess me himself. I could tell by the way he looked at me in stolen glances that part of my allure to Max the director was my allure to him as a man.

When Max came to my dressing room on the second-to-last day of filming, he said, "*Ma belle, aujourd'hui tu seras seins nus.*" I had picked up enough French by then to know he was saying he wanted to shoot my scene coming out of the lake. When you're an American movie star with huge boobs in a French movie, you quickly learn that when French men are saying *seins nus*, they are talking about you being topless.

I was fully willing to take my top off and show my assets if that was what it took to get my name back out there. But by that point, I had fallen madly in love with a woman. I had grown to desire her with every fiber of myself. I knew the pleasure of finding delight in a woman's naked body.

So I told Max I'd shoot it however he wanted but that I had a suggestion that might make the movie even more of a sensation.

I knew my idea was a good one, because I knew how it felt to want to tear a woman's shirt off.

And when Max heard it, *he* knew it was a good one, because he knew how it felt to want to tear *my* shirt off.

In the editing room, Max slowed down my exit from the lake to a snail's crawl and then cut the footage a millisecond before you can see my full breasts. It simply cut to black, as if the film itself had been tampered with, as if maybe you'd just gotten a bad cut.

There was so much anticipation. And it never paid off, no matter how many times you watched it, no matter how perfectly you paused the tape.

And here's why it worked: man, woman, gay, straight, bisexual, you name it, we all just want to be teased.

Six months after we finished shooting *Boute-en-Train*, I was an international sensation.

SINGER MICK RIVA SWEET FOR EVELYN HUGO

Performing last night at the Trocadero, Mick Riva had a few minutes to indulge our questions. Armed with an old-fashioned that appeared not to be his first, Mick was awfully forthcoming . . .

He revealed that he's happy to be divorced from siren Veronica Lowe because, he said, "I didn't deserve a lady like that, and she didn't deserve a guy like me."

And when asked if he's dating, he admitted he's been seeing quite a few ladies but that he'd give them all up for one night with Evelyn Hugo.

The former Mrs. Don Adler has proven to be a very hot commodity these days. Her appearance in French director Max Girard's newest film, *Boute-en-Train*, has spent the summer selling out movie houses all over Europe, and now it's taking the good ol' US of A by storm.

"I've seen *Boute-en-Train* three times now," Mick told us. "And I'll see it a fourth. I just can't get enough of her coming out of that lake."

So would he like to take Evelyn out on a date?

"I'd like to marry her is what I'd like to do."

You hear that, Evelyn?

EVELYN HUGO TO PLAY ANNA KARENINA

Talk of the town Evelyn Hugo has just signed on to play the title role in Fox's epic *Anna Karenina*. She has also signed to produce the picture with Harry Cameron, formerly of Sunset Studios.

Miss Hugo and Mr. Cameron worked together at Sunset on such hits as *Father and Daughter* and *Little Women*. This will be their first project together outside of the Sunset umbrella.

Mr. Cameron, who has made a name for himself in the biz for his great taste and even greater business acumen, is said to have left Sunset over differences with none other than studio head Ari Sullivan. But it appears Fox is eager to be in business with both Miss Hugo and Mr. Cameron, as they have ponied up a substantial fee and a stake in the box office.

Everyone has been watching to see what Miss Hugo's next project will be. *Anna Karenina* is an interesting choice. One thing's for sure, if Evelyn so much as shows a bare shoulder in the flick, audiences will come running.

DON ADLER AND RUBY REILLY, ENGAGED?

Mary and Roger Adler threw a party this past Saturday that was said to have grown a bit out of control! The guests who showed up were surprised to learn that it wasn't just a party for Don Adler . . .

It was to announce the engagement of Don and none other than Sunset Studios' reigning queen, Ruby Reilly!

Don and Ruby have become close after Don's divorce from bombshell Evelyn Hugo almost two years ago. Apparently, Don admitted he had eyes for Ruby way back when she and Evelyn were shooting *Little Women* together.

We are so happy for Don and Ruby, but we can't help but wonder how Don feels about Evelyn's skyrocketing fame. She is the hottest thing under the sun right now, and if we had let her go, we'd be kicking ourselves.

Regardless, best wishes to Don and Ruby! Hopefully, this one sticks!

I was sent an invitation to see Mick Riva perform at the Hollywood Bowl that fall. I decided to go, not because I cared about seeing Mick Riva but because an evening outside sounded fun. And I wasn't above courting the tabloids.

Celia, Harry, and I decided to go together. I would never have gone with just Celia, not with that many eyes on us. But Harry was a perfect buffer.

That night, the air in L.A. was cooler than I had anticipated. I was wearing capri pants and a short-sleeved sweater. I had just gotten bangs and had started sweeping them to the side. Celia had on a blue shift dress and flats. Harry, dapper as ever, was wearing slacks and a short-sleeved oxford shirt. He held a camel-colored knit cardigan with oversized buttons in his hand, ready for any of us who were too cold.

We sat in the second row with a couple of Harry's producer friends from Paramount. Across the aisle, I saw Ed Baker with a young woman who appeared as if she could be his daughter, but I knew better. I decided not to say hi, not only because he was still a part of the Sunset machine but also because I never liked him.

Mick Riva took the stage, and the women in the crowd started cheering so loudly that Celia actually put her hands over her ears. He was wearing a dark suit with a loose tie. His jet-black hair was combed back but just slightly disheveled. If I had to guess, I'd say he'd had a drink or two backstage. But it didn't seem to slow him down in the slightest.

"I don't get it," Celia said to me as she leaned in to my ear. "What do they see in this guy?"

I shrugged. "That he's handsome, I suppose."

Mick walked up to the microphone, the spotlight following him. He grabbed the mic stand with both passion and softness, as if it were one of the many girls yelling his name.

"And he knows what he's doing," I said.

Celia shrugged. "I'd take Brick Thomas over him any day."

I shook my head, cringing. "No, Brick Thomas is a heel. Trust me. If you met him, within five seconds, you'd be gagging."

Celia laughed. "I think he's cute."

"No, you don't," I said.

"Well, I think he's cuter than Mick Riva," she said. "Harry? Thoughts?"

Harry leaned in from the other side. He whispered so softly I almost didn't hear him. "I'm embarrassed to admit I have something in common with these shrieking girls," he said. "I would not kick Mick out of bed for eating crackers."

Celia laughed.

"You are too much," I said as I watched Mick walk from one end of the stage to the other, crooning and smoldering. "Where are we eating after this?" I asked them both. "That's the real question."

"Don't we have to go backstage?" Celia asked. "Isn't that the polite thing to do?"

Mick's first song ended, and everyone started clapping and cheering. Harry leaned over me as he clapped so Celia could hear him.

"You won an Oscar, Celia," he said. "You can do whatever the hell you want."

She threw her head back and laughed as she clapped. "Well, then I want to go get a steak."

"Steak it is," I said.

I don't know whether it was the laughing or the cheering or the clapping. There was so much noise around me, so much chaos from the crowd. But for one fleeting moment, I forgot myself. I forgot where I was. I forgot who I was. I forgot who I was with.

And I grabbed Celia's hand and held it.

She looked down, surprised. I could feel Harry's gaze on our hands, too.

I pulled my hand away, and just as I corrected myself, I saw a woman down the row from us stare at me. She looked to be in her midthirties, with a patrician face, small blue eyes, and perfectly applied crimson lipstick. Her lips turned down as she looked at me.

She had seen me.

She had seen me hold Celia's hand.

And she had seen me pull it back.

She knew both what I had done and that I had not meant for her to have seen it.

Her small eyes got smaller as she stared at me.

And any hope I had that she did not realize who I was went right out the window when she turned to the man next to her, probably her husband, and whispered in his ear. I watched as his gaze moved from Mick Riva to me.

There was a subtle disgust in his eyes, as if he was unsure if what he suspected was true but that the thought in his head made him nauseated and it was my fault for putting it there.

I wanted to slap both of them across their faces and tell them that what I did was none of their business. But I knew I couldn't do that. It wasn't *safe* to do that. I wasn't safe. We weren't safe.

Mick hit an instrumental part in the song and started walking toward the very front of the stage, talking to the audience. Reflexively, I stood up and cheered for him. I jumped up and down. I was louder than anyone there. I wasn't thinking clearly. I just wanted to make the two of them stop talking, to each other or to anyone else. I wanted the gossip game of telephone that had started with that woman to end with that man. I wanted it all to be over. I wanted to be doing *something else.* So I cheered as loudly as I could. I cheered like the teenage girls in the back. I cheered as if my life depended on it, because maybe it did.

"Do my eyes deceive me?" Mick said from the stage. He had his hand over his brow, shading the spotlight from his eyes. He was looking right at me. "Or is that my dream woman right there in the front?"

EVELYN HUGO AND CELIA ST. JAMES SLUMBER PARTIES

How close is too close?

Girl-next-door Celia St. James, with her Oscar win and her trail of hits, has been a longtime friend of honey-blond sexpot Evelyn Hugo. But lately we're starting to wonder if these two aren't up to something.

Insiders are saying the two are quite a pair of . . . thespians.

Sure, plenty of girlfriends go shopping together and share a drink or two. But Celia's car is parked outside Evelyn's home, the one she used to share with none other than Mr. Don Adler, every night. All night.

So what's happening behind those walls?

Whatever it is, it certainly doesn't sound like it's on the straight and narrow.

I'M GOING OUT ON A date with Mick Riva."

"Like hell you are."

When Celia was angry, her chest and her cheeks flushed. This time, they'd grown red faster than I'd ever seen.

We were in the outdoor kitchen of her weekend home in Palm Springs. She was grilling us burgers for dinner.

Ever since the article came out, I'd refused to be seen with her in Los Angeles. The rags didn't yet know about her place in Palm Springs. So we would spend weekends there together and our weeks in L.A. apart.

Celia went along with the plan like a put-upon spouse, agreeing to whatever I wanted because it was easier than fighting with me. But now, with the suggestion of going on a date, I'd gone too far.

I knew I'd gone too far. That was the point, sort of.

"You need to listen to me," I said.

"You need to listen to *me*." She slammed the lid of the grill shut and gestured to me with a pair of silver tongs. "I'll go along with any of your little tricks that you want. But I'm not getting on board with either of us *dating*."

"We don't have a choice."

"We have plenty of choices."

"Not if you want to keep your job. Not if you want to keep this house. Not if you want to keep any of our friends. Not to mention that the police could come after us."

"You are being paranoid."

"I'm not, Celia. And that's what's scary. But I'm telling you, they know."

"One article in one tiny paper *thinks* they know. That's not the same thing."

"You're right. This is still early enough that we can stop it."

"Or it will go away on its own."

"Celia, you have two movies coming out next year, and my movie is all anyone is talking about around town."

"Exactly. Like Harry always says, that means we can do whatever we want."

"No, that means we have a lot to lose."

Celia, angry, picked up my pack of cigarettes and lit one. "So that's what you want to do? You want to spend every second of our lives trying to hide what we really do? Who we really are?"

"It's what everyone in town is doing every day."

"Well, I don't want to."

"Well, then you shouldn't have become famous."

Celia stared at me as she puffed away at her cigarette. The pink of her lipstick stained the filter. "You're a pessimist, Evelyn. To your very core."

"What would you like to do, Celia? Maybe I should call over to *Sub Rosa* myself? Call the FBI directly? I can give them a quote. 'Yep, Celia St. James and I are deviants!'"

"We aren't deviants."

"I know that, Celia. And you know that. But no one else knows that."

"But maybe they would. If they tried."

"They aren't going to try. Do you get that? No one wants to understand people like us."

"But they should."

"There are lots of things we all should do, sweetheart. But it doesn't work that way."

"I hate this conversation. You're making me feel awful."

"I know, and I'm sorry. But the fact that it's awful doesn't mean it's not true. If you want to keep your job, you cannot allow people to believe that you and I are more than friends."

"And if I don't want to keep my job?"

"You do want to."

"No, *you* want to. And you're pinning it on me."

"Of course I want to."

"I'd give it all up, you know. All of it. The money and the jobs and the fame. I'd give it all up just to be with you, just to be normal with you."

"You have no idea what you're saying, Celia. I'm sorry, but you don't."

"What's really going on here is that you're not willing to give it up for *me*."

"No, what's going on here is that you're a dilettante who thinks if this acting thing doesn't work out, you can go back to Savannah and live off your parents."

"Who are you to talk to me about money? You've got bags of it."

"Yeah, I do. Because I worked my ass off and was married to an asshole who knocked me around. And I did that so I could be famous. So I could live the life we're living. And if you think I'm not going to protect that, you've lost your mind."

"At least you're admitting this is about you."

I shook my head and pinched the bridge of my nose. "Celia, listen to me. Do you love that Oscar? The very thing you keep on your nightstand and touch before you go to sleep?"

"Don't—"

"People are saying, given how early you won it, you're the kind of actress who could win multiple times. I want that for you. Don't you want that?"

"Of course I do."

"And you're gonna let them take that away just because you met me?"

"Well, no, but—"

"Listen to me, Celia. I love you. And I can't let you throw away everything you have built—and all your incredible talent—by taking a stand when no one will stand with us."

"But if we don't try . . ."

"No one is going to back us, Celia. I know how it feels to be shut out

of this town. I'm just finally making my way back in. I know you're probably picturing some world where we go up against Goliath and win. But
that's not gonna happen. We'd tell the truth about our lives, and they'd
bury us. We could end up in prison or in a mental hospital. Do you get
that? We could be committed. It's not that far-fetched. It happens. Certainly, you can count on the fact that no one would return our calls. Not
even Harry."

"Of course Harry would. Harry's . . . one of us."

"Which is precisely why he could never be caught talking to us again.
Don't you get it? The danger is even higher for him. There are actually
men out there who would want to kill him if they knew. That's the world
we live in. Anyone who touched us would be examined. Harry wouldn't
be able to withstand it. I could never put him in that position. To lose
everything he's worked for? To quite literally risk his life? No. No, we'd
be alone. Two pariahs."

"But we'd have each other. And that's enough for me."

She was crying now, the tears streaking down her face and carrying
her mascara with them. I put my arms around her and wiped her cheek
with my thumb. "I love you so much, sweetheart. So, so much. And it's
in part because of things like that. You're an idealist and a romantic, and
you have a beautiful soul. And I wish the world was ready to be the way
you see it. I wish that the rest of the people on earth with us were capable
of living up to your expectations. But they aren't. The world is ugly, and
no one wants to give anyone the benefit of the doubt about anything.
When we lose our work and our reputations, when we lose our friends
and, eventually, what money we have, we will be destitute. I've lived that
life before. And I cannot let it happen to you. I will do whatever I can to
prevent you from living that way. Do you hear me? I love you too much
to let you live only for me."

She heaved into my body, her tears growing inside her. For a moment, I thought she might flood the backyard.

"I love you," she said.

"I love you, too," I whispered into her ear. "I love you more than anything else in the entire world."

"It's not wrong," Celia said. "It shouldn't be wrong, to love you. How can it be wrong?"

"It's not wrong, sweetheart. It's not," I said. "*They're* wrong."

She nodded into my shoulder and held me tighter. I rubbed her back. I smelled her hair.

"It's just that there's not much we can do about it," I said.

When she calmed down, she pulled away from me and opened the grill again. She did not look at me as she flipped the burgers. "So what is your plan?" she said.

"I'm going to get Mick Riva to elope with me."

Her eyes, which already looked sore from crying, started to bloom again. She wiped a tear away, keeping her eyes on the grill. "What does that mean for us?" she said.

I stood behind her and put my arms around her. "It doesn't mean what you think it means. I'm going to see if I can get him to elope with me, and then I'm going to have it annulled."

"And you think that means they'll stop watching you?"

"No, I know it means they will only watch me more. But they will be looking for other things. They will call me a tart or a fool. They will say I have terrible taste in men. They will say I'm a bad wife, I am too impulsive. But if they want to do any of that, they'll have to stop saying I'm with you. It won't fit their story anymore."

"I get it," she said, grabbing a plate and taking the burgers off the grill.

"OK, good," I said.

"You'll do whatever you have to do. But this is the last I want to hear about it. And I want it to be over and done with as soon as possible."

"OK."

"And when it's over, I want us to move in together."

"Celia, we can't do that."

"You said this would be so effective that no one would ever mention us."

The thing is, I wanted us to move in together, too. I wanted it very much. "OK," I said. "When it's over, we'll talk about moving in together."

"OK," she said. "Then we have a deal."

I put my hand out to shake hers, but she waved it away. She didn't want to shake on something that sad, that vulgar.

"And if it doesn't work with Mick Riva?" she asked.

"It's gonna work."

Celia finally looked up at me. She was half smiling. "You think you're so gorgeous that no one can possibly resist your charms?"

"Yes, actually."

"All right," she said, rising slightly on her toes to kiss me. "I suppose that's true."

I WORE A CREAM-COLORED COCKTAIL dress with heavy gold beading and a plunging neckline. I pulled my long blond hair into a high ponytail. I wore diamond earrings.

I *glowed.*

THE FIRST THING you need to do to get a man to elope with you is to challenge him to go to Las Vegas.

You do this by being out at an L.A. club and having a few drinks together. You ignore the impulse to roll your eyes at how eager he is to have his picture taken with you. You recognize that everyone is playing everyone else. It's only fair that he's playing you at the same time as you're playing him. You reconcile these facts by realizing that what you both want from each other is complementary.

You want a scandal.

He wants the world to know he screwed you.

The two things are one and the same.

You consider laying it out for him, explaining what you want, explaining what you're willing to give him. But you've been famous long enough to know that you never tell anyone anything more than you have to.

So instead of saying *I'd like us to make tomorrow's papers*, you say, "Mick, have you ever been to Vegas?"

When he scoffs, as if he can't believe you're asking *him* if *he's* ever been to Vegas, you know this will be easier than you thought.

"Sometimes I just get in the mood to roll dice, you know?" you say. Sexual implications are better when they are gradual, when they snowball over time.

"You want to roll dice, baby?" he says, and you nod.

"But it's probably too late," you say. "And we're already here. And here's OK, I suppose. I'm having a fine time."

"My guys can call a plane and have us there like that." He snaps his fingers.

"No," you say. "That's too much."

"Not for you," he says. "Nothing is too much for you."

You know what he really means is *Nothing is too much for* me.

"You could really do that?" you say.

An hour and a half later, you're on a plane.

You have a few drinks, you sit in his lap, you let his hand wander, and you slap it back. He has to ache for you and believe there is only one way to have you. If he doesn't want you enough, if he believes he can get you another way, it's all over. You've lost.

When the plane lands and he asks if the two of you should book a room at the Sands, you must demur. You must be shocked. You must tell him, in a voice that makes it clear you assumed he already knew, that you don't have sex outside of marriage.

You must seem both steadfast and heartbroken about this. He must think, *She wants me. And the only way we can make it happen is to get married.*

For a moment, you consider the idea that what you're doing is unkind. But then you remember that this man is going to bed you and then divorce you once he's gotten what he wants. So no one is a saint here.

You're going to give him what he's asking for. So it's a fair trade.

You go to the craps table and play a couple of rounds. You keep losing at first, as does he, and you worry that this is sobering both of you. You know the key to impulsivity is believing you are invincible. No one goes around throwing caution to the wind unless the wind is blowing their way.

You drink champagne, because it makes everything seem celebratory. It makes tonight seem like an *event*.

When people recognize the two of you, you happily agree to get your picture taken with them. Every time it happens, you hang on to him. You are telling him, in no small way, *This is what it could be like if I belonged to you.*

You hit a winning streak at the roulette table. You cheer so ebulliently that you jump up and down. You do this because you know where his eyes are going to go. You let him catch you catching him.

You let him put his hand on your ass as the wheel spins again.

This time, when you win, you push your ass against him.

You let him lean into you and say, "Do you want to get out of here?"

You say, "I don't think it's a good idea. I don't trust myself with you."

You cannot bring up marriage first. You already said the word earlier. You have to wait for him to say it. He said it in the papers. He will say it again. But you have to wait. You cannot rush it.

He has one more drink.

The two of you win three more times.

You let his hand graze your upper thigh, and then you push it away. It is two A.M., and you are tired. You miss the love of your life. You want to go home. You would rather be with her, in bed, hearing the light buzz of her snoring, watching her sleep, than be here. There is nothing about here that you love.

Except what being here will afford you.

You imagine a world where the two of you can go out to dinner together on a Saturday night and no one thinks twice about it. It makes you want to cry, the simplicity of it, the smallness of it. You have worked so hard for a life so grand. And now all you want are the smallest freedoms. The daily peace of loving plainly.

Tonight feels like both a small and a high price to pay for that life.

"Baby, I can't take it," he says. "I have to be with you. I have to see you. I have to love you."

This is your chance. You have a fish on the line, and you have to gently reel him in.

"Oh, Mick," you say. "We can't. We can't."

"I think I love you, baby," he says. There are tears in his eyes, and you realize he's probably more complex than you have given him credit for.

You're more complex than he's given you credit for, too.

"Do you mean it?" you ask him, as if you desperately hope it's true.

"I think I do, baby. I do. I love everything about you. We only just met, but I feel like I can't live without you." What he means is that he thinks he can't live without screwing you. And that, you believe.

"Oh, Mick," you say, and then you say nothing more. Silence is your best friend.

He nuzzles your neck. It's sloppy, and it feels akin to meeting a Newfoundland. But you pretend you love it. You two are in the bright lights of a Vegas casino. People can see you. You have to pretend that you do not notice them. That way, tomorrow, when they talk to the papers, they will say that the two of you were carrying on like a couple of teenagers.

You hope that Celia doesn't pick up a single rag with your face on it. You think she's smart enough not to. You think she knows how to protect herself. But you can't be sure. The first thing you're going to do when you get home, when this is all over, is to make sure she knows how important she is, how beautiful she is, how much you feel your life would be over if she were not in it.

"Let's get married, baby," he says into your ear.

There it is.

For you to grab.

But you can't look too eager.

"Mick, are you crazy?"

"You make me this crazy."

"We can't get married!" you say, and when he doesn't say anything back for a second, you worry that you've pushed slightly too far. "Or can we?" you ask. "I mean, I suppose we could!"

"Of course we can," he says. "We're on top of the world. We can do anything we want."

You throw your arms around him, and you press against him, to let him know how excited—how surprised—you are by this idea and to remind him what he's doing it for. You know your value to him. It would be silly to waste an opportunity to remind him.

He picks you up and sweeps you away. You whoop and holler so everyone looks. Tomorrow they will tell the papers he carried you off. It's memorable. They will remember it.

Forty minutes later, the two of you are drunk and standing in front of each other at an altar.

He promises to love you forever.

You promise to obey.

He carries you over the threshold of the nicest room at the Tropicana. You giggle with fake surprise when he throws you onto the bed.

And now here comes the second-most-important part.

You cannot be a good lay. You must disappoint.

If he likes it, he'll want to do it again. And you can't do that. You can't do this more than once. It will break your heart.

When he tries to rip your dress off, you have to say, "Stop, Mick, Christ. Get a hold of yourself."

After you take the dress off slowly, you have to let him look at your breasts for as long as he wants to. He has to see every inch of them. He's been waiting for so long to finally see the ending of that shot in *Boute-en-Train*.

You have to remove all mystery, all intrigue.

You make him play with your breasts so long he gets bored.

And then you open your legs.

You lie there, stiff as a board underneath him.

And here is the one part of this you can't quite come to terms with but you can't quite avoid, either. He won't use a condom. And even though women you know have gotten hold of birth control pills, you don't have them, because you had no need for them until a few days ago when you hatched this plan.

You cross your fingers behind your back.

You close your eyes.

You feel his heavy body fall on top of you, and you know that he is done.

You want to cry, because you remember what sex used to mean to you, before. Before you realized how good it could feel, before you discovered what you liked. But you push it out of your mind. You push it all out of your mind.

Mick doesn't say anything afterward.

And you don't, either.

You fall asleep, having put on his undershirt in the dark because you didn't want to sleep naked.

In the morning, when the sun shines through the windows and burns your eyes, you put your arm over your face.

Your head is pounding. Your heart is hurting.

But you're almost at the finish line.

You catch his eye. He smiles. He grabs you.

You push him off and say, "I don't like to have sex in the morning."

"What does that mean?" he says.

You shrug. "I'm sorry."

He says, "C'mon, baby," and lies on top of you. You're not sure he'd listen if you said no one more time. And you're not sure you want to find out the answer. You're not sure you could bear it.

"OK, fine, if you have to," you say. And when he lifts himself off you and looks you in the eye, you realize it has accomplished what you had hoped. You have taken all the fun out of it for him.

He shakes his head. He gets out of bed. He says, "You know, you're nothing like I imagined."

It doesn't matter how gorgeous a woman is, to a man like Mick Riva, she's always less attractive after he's had sex with her. You know this. You allow it to happen. You do not fix your hair. You pick at the mascara flakes on your face.

You watch Mick step into the bathroom. You hear him turn on the shower.

When he comes out, he sits down next to you on the bed.

He is clean. You have not bathed.

He smells like soap. You smell like booze.

He is sitting up. You are lying down.

This, too, is a calculation.

He has to feel like the power is all his.

"Honey, I had a great time," he says.

You nod.

"But we were so drunk." He speaks as if he's talking to a child. "Both of us. We had no idea what we were doing."

"I know," you say. "It was a crazy thing to do."

"I'm not a good guy, baby," he says. "You don't deserve a guy like me. I don't deserve a girl like you."

It's just so unoriginal and laughably transparent, feeding you the same line he fed the papers about his last wife.

"What are you saying?" you ask. You put a little spin into it. You make it sound like you might start crying. You have to do this because it is what most women would do. And you have to appear to him the way he sees most women. You have to appear to have been outsmarted.

"I think we should call our people, baby. I think we should get an annulment."

"But, Mick—"

He cuts you off, and it makes you mad, because you really did have more to say. "It's better this way, honey. I'm afraid I can't take no for an answer."

You wonder what it must be like to be a man, to be so confident that the final say is yours.

When he gets up off the bed and grabs his jacket, you realize there's an element of this that you hadn't accounted for. He *likes* to reject. He *likes* to condescend. When he was calculating his moves last night, he was thinking of this moment, too. This moment where he gets to leave you.

So you do something you hadn't rehearsed in your mind.

When he gets to the door and turns to you and says, "I'm sorry it didn't work out between us, baby. But I wish you all the best," you pick up the phone on the side of the bed and throw it at him.

You do it because you know he'll like it. Because he's given you everything you came for. You should give him everything he came for.

He ducks and frowns at you, as if you're a small deer he has to leave in the forest.

You start crying.

And then he's gone.

And you stop.

And you think, *If only they gave out Oscars for this shit.*

RIVA AND HUGO LOSE THEIR MINDS

Heard of a quickie wedding? How about a quickie marriage? Well, this one takes the cake!

Bombshell Evelyn Hugo was spotted in the lap of none other than her biggest fan Mick Riva last Friday night in the heart of Las Vegas. Card players and dice guys alike were treated to quite a show by the two of them. Canoodling, necking, and drinking up a storm, from the craps table right out the door and down the street to a . . . CHAPEL!!!!

That's right! Evelyn Hugo and Mick Riva got married!

And to make matters even crazier, they promptly filed for an annulment.

The booze seemed to have gotten to their heads—and in the morning, clearer heads prevailed.

With a string of failed marriages between the two of them, what's one more?

EVELYN HUGO'S HEARTBREAK

Don't believe what you hear about Evelyn and Mick's drunken escapades. Mick may get a little too eager with the drink, but those in the know say Evelyn was in full control that night. And desperately wanted to get married.

Poor Evelyn's had such a hard time finding love after Don left her—it's no wonder she would throw herself into the arms of the first handsome man to come along.

And we're hearing she's inconsolable since he left her.

It seems like Evelyn was no more than a night of fun to Mick, but she really thought they had a future together.

We just hope Evelyn can get it right one of these days.

For two months, I was living in near bliss. Celia and I never talked about Mick, because we didn't have to. Instead, we could go wherever we wanted, do whatever we wanted.

Celia bought a second car, a boring brown sedan, and left it parked in my driveway every night without anyone asking questions. We would sleep cradling each other, turning off the light an hour before we wanted to fall asleep so that we could talk in the darkness. I would trace the lines of her palm with my fingertips in the mornings to wake her up. On my birthday, she took me out to the Polo Lounge. We were hiding in plain sight.

Fortunately, painting me as some woman who couldn't keep a husband sold more papers—for a longer period of time—than outing me. I'm not saying the gossip columnists printed what they knew to be a lie. I'm simply saying they were all too happy to believe the lie I was selling them. And of course, that's the easiest lie to tell, one you know the other person desperately wants to be true.

All I had to do was make sure that my romantic scandals felt like a story that would keep making headlines. And as long as I did that, I knew the gossip rags would never look too closely at Celia.

And it was all working so goddamn beautifully.

Until I found out I was pregnant.

"You are not," Celia said to me. She was standing in my pool in a lavender polka-dot bikini and sunglasses.

"Yes," I said. "I am."

I had just brought her out a glass of iced tea from the kitchen. I was standing right in front of her, looming over her, in a blue cover-up and sandals. I'd suspected I was pregnant for two weeks. I'd known for sure since the day before, when I went to Burbank and saw a discreet doctor Harry had recommended.

I told her then, when she was in the pool and I was holding a glass of iced tea with a slice of lemon in it, because I couldn't hold it in anymore.

I am and have always been a great liar. But Celia was sacred to me. And I never wanted to lie to her.

I was under no illusions about how much it had cost Celia and me to be together and that it was going to continue to cost us more. It was like a tax on being happy. The world was going to take fifty percent of my happiness. But I could keep the other fifty percent.

And that was her. And this life we had.

But keeping something like this from her felt wrong. And I couldn't do it.

I put my feet into the pool next to her and tried to touch her, tried to comfort her. I expected that the news would upset her, but I did not expect her to hurl the iced tea to the other side of the pool, breaking the glass on the edge, scattering shards in the water.

I also did not expect her to plunge herself under the surface and scream. Actresses are very dramatic.

When she popped back up, she was wet and disheveled, her hair in her face, her mascara running. And she did not want to talk to me.

I grabbed her arm, and she pulled away. When I caught a glimpse of her face and saw the hurt in her eyes, I realized that Celia and I had never *really* been on the same page about what I was going to do with Mick Riva.

"You slept with him?" she said.

"I thought that was implied," I said.

"Well, it wasn't."

Celia raised herself up out of the pool and didn't even bother to dry off. I watched as her wet footprints changed the color of the cement around the pool, as they created puddles on the hardwood and then started dampening the carpet on the stairs.

When I looked up at the back bedroom window, I saw that she was walking back and forth. It looked like she was packing.

"Celia! Stop it," I said, running up the stairs. "This doesn't change anything."

By the time I got to my own bedroom door, it was locked.

I pounded on it. "Honey, please."

"Leave me alone."

"Please," I said. "Let's talk about this."

"No."

"You can't do this, Celia. Let's talk this out." I leaned against the door, pushing my face into the slim gap of the doorframe, hoping it would make my voice travel farther, make Celia understand faster.

"This is not a life, Evelyn," she said.

She opened the door and walked past me. I almost fell, so much of my weight had been resting on the very door she had just flung open. But I caught myself and followed her down the stairs.

"Yes, it is," I said. "This is our life. And we've sacrificed so much for it, and you can't give up on it now."

"Yes, I can," she said. "I don't want to do this anymore. I don't want to live this way. I don't want to drive an awful brown car to your home so no one knows I'm here. I don't want to pretend I live by myself in Hollywood when I truly live here with you in this house. And I certainly don't want to love a woman who would screw some singer just so the world doesn't suspect she loves me."

"You are twisting the truth."

"You are a coward, and I can't believe I ever thought any differently."

"I did this for you!" I yelled.

We were at the foot of the stairs now. Celia had one hand on the door, the other on her suitcase. She was still in her bathing suit. Her hair was dripping.

"You didn't do a goddamn thing for me," she said, her chest turning red in splotches, her cheeks burning. "You did it for you. You did it because you can't stand the idea of not being the most famous woman on the planet. You did it to protect yourself and your precious fans, who go to the theater over and over just to see if this time they'll catch a half frame of your tits. That's who you did it for."

"It was for you, Celia. Do you think your family is going to stick by you if they find out the truth?"

She bristled when I said it, and I saw her turn the doorknob.

"You will lose everything you have if people find out what you are," I said.

"What *we* are," she said, turning toward me. "Don't go around trying to pretend you're different from me."

"I am," I said. "And you know that I am."

"Bullshit."

"I can love a man, Celia. I can go marry any man I want and have children and be happy. And we both know that wouldn't come easily for you."

Celia looked at me, her eyes narrow, her lips pursed. "You think you're better than me? Is that what's going on? You think I'm sick, and you think you're just playing some kind of game?"

I grabbed her, immediately wanting to take back what I'd said. That wasn't what I meant at all.

But she flung her arm away from me and said, "Don't you ever touch me again."

I let go of her. "If they find out about us, Celia, they'll forgive me. I'll marry another guy like Don, and they'll forget I even knew you. I can survive this. But I'm not sure that you can. Because you'd have to either fall in love with a man or marry one you didn't love. And I don't think you're capable of either option. I'm worried for you, Celia. More than I'm worried for me. I'm not sure your career would ever recover—if your life would recover—if I didn't do *something*. So I did the only thing I knew. *And it worked*."

"It didn't work, Evelyn. You're pregnant."

"I will take care of it."

Celia looked down at the floor and laughed at me. "You certainly know how to handle almost any situation, don't you?"

"Yes," I said, unsure why I was supposed to be insulted by that. "I do."

"And yet when it comes to being a human, you seem to have absolutely no idea where to start."

"You don't mean that."

"You are a whore, Evelyn. You let men screw you for fame. And that is why I'm leaving you."

She opened the door to leave, not even looking back at me. I watched her walk out to my front stoop, down the stairs, and over to her car. I followed her out and stood, frozen, in the driveway.

She threw her bag into the passenger's side of her car. And then she opened the door on the driver's side and stood there.

"I loved you so much that I thought you were the meaning of my life," Celia said, crying. "I thought that people were put on earth to find other people, and I was put here to find you. To find you and touch your skin and smell your breath and hear all your thoughts. But I don't think that's true anymore." She wiped her eyes. "Because I don't want to be meant for someone like you."

The searing pain in my chest felt like water boiling. "You know what? You're right. You aren't meant for someone like me," I said finally. "Because I'm willing to do what it takes to make a world for us, and you're too chickenshit. You won't make the hard decisions; you aren't willing to do the ugly stuff. And I've always known that. But I thought you'd at least have the decency to admit you need someone like me. You need someone who will get her hands dirty to protect you. You want to play like you're all high and mighty all the time. Well, try doing that without someone in the trenches protecting you."

Celia's face was stoic, frozen. I wasn't sure she'd heard a single word I'd said. "I guess we aren't as right for each other as we thought," she said, and then she got into her car.

It wasn't until that moment, with her hand on the steering wheel, that I realized this was really happening, that this wasn't just a fight we were having. That this was *the* fight that would end us. It had all been going so well and had turned so quickly in the other direction, like a hairpin turn off the freeway.

"I guess not" was all I could say. It came out like a croak, the vowels cracking.

Celia started the car and put it in reverse. "Good-bye, Evelyn," she said at the very last minute. Then she backed out of my driveway and disappeared down the road.

I walked into my house and started cleaning up the puddles of water she'd left. I called a service to come and drain the pool and clean the shards of glass from her iced tea.

And then I called Harry.

Three days later, he drove with me to Tijuana, where no one would ask any questions. It was a set of moments that I tried not to be mentally present for so that I would never have to work to forget them. I was relieved, walking back to the car after the procedure, that I had become so good at compartmentalization and disassociation. May it make its way to the record books that I never regretted, not for one minute, ending that pregnancy. It was the right decision. On that I never wavered.

But still I cried the whole way home, while Harry drove us through San Diego and along the California coastline. I cried because of everything I had lost and all the decisions I had made. I cried because I was supposed to start *Anna Karenina* on Monday and I didn't care about acting or accolades. I wished I'd never needed a reason to be in Mexico in the first place. And I desperately wanted Celia to call me, crying, telling me how wrong she'd been. I wanted her to show up on my doorstep and beg to come home. I wanted . . . her. I just wanted her back.

As we were coming off the San Diego Freeway, I asked Harry the question that had been running through my mind for days.

"Do you think I'm a whore?"

Harry pulled over to the side of the road and turned to me. "I think you're brilliant. I think you're tough. And I think the word *whore* is something ignorant people throw around when they have nothing else."

I listened to him and then turned my head to look out my window.

"Isn't it awfully convenient," Harry added, "that when men make the rules, the one thing that's looked down on the most is the one thing that would bear them the greatest threat? Imagine if every single woman on the planet wanted something in exchange when she gave up her body. You'd all be ruling the place. An armed populace. Only men like me would stand a chance against you. And that's the last thing those assholes want, a world run by people like you and me."

I laughed, my eyes still puffy and tired from crying. "So am I a whore or not?"

"Who knows?" he said. "We're all whores, really, in some way or another. At least in Hollywood. Look, there's a reason she's Celia *Saint* James. She's been playing that good-girl routine for years. The rest of us aren't so pure. But I like you this way. I like you impure and scrappy and formidable. I like the Evelyn Hugo who sees the world for what it is and then goes out there and wrestles what she wants out of it. So, you know, put whatever label you want on it, just don't change. That would be the real tragedy."

When we got to my house, Harry tucked me into bed and then went downstairs and made me dinner.

That night, he slept in the bed next to me, and when I woke up, he was opening the blinds.

"Rise and shine, little bird," he said.

I did not speak to Celia for five years after that. She did not call. She did not write. And I could not bring myself to reach out to her.

I knew how she was doing only from what people said in the papers and what sort of gossip was running around town. But that first morning, as the sunlight shone on my face and I still felt exhausted from the trip to Mexico, I was actually OK.

Because I had Harry. For the first time in a very long time, I felt like I had family.

You do not know how fast you have been running, how hard you have been working, how truly exhausted you are, until someone stands behind you and says, "It's OK, you can fall down now. I'll catch you."

So I fell down.

And Harry caught me.

Y OU AND CELIA DIDN'T HAVE any contact at all?" I ask.

Evelyn shakes her head. She stands up and walks over to the window and opens it a crack. The breeze that streams in is welcome. When she sits back down, she looks at me, ready to move on to something else. But I'm too baffled.

"How long were the two of you together by that point?"

"Three years?" Evelyn says. "Just about."

"And she just left? Without another word?"

Evelyn nods.

"Did you try to call her?"

She shakes her head. "I was . . . I didn't yet know that it is OK to grovel for something you really want. I thought that if she didn't want me, if she didn't understand why I did what I did, then I didn't need her."

"And you were OK?"

"No, I was miserable. I was hung up on her for years. I mean, sure, I spent my time having fun. Don't get me wrong. But Celia was nowhere in sight. In fact, I would read copies of *Sub Rosa* because Celia's picture was in them, analyzing the other people with her in the photos, wondering who they were to her, how she knew them. I know now that she was just as heartbroken as I was. That somewhere in her head, she was waiting for me to call her and apologize. But at the time, I just ached all alone."

"Do you regret that you didn't call her?" I ask her. "That you lost that time?"

Evelyn looks at me as if I am stupid. "She's gone now," Evelyn says. "The love of my life is gone, and I can't just call her and say I'm sorry and have her come back. She's gone forever. So yes, Monique, that is something I do regret. I regret every second I didn't spend with her. I regret every stupid thing I did that caused her an ounce of pain. I should have chased her down the street the day she left me. I should have begged her to stay. I should have apologized and sent roses and stood on top of the Hollywood sign and shouted, 'I'm in love with Celia St. James!' and let them crucify me for it. That's what I should have done. And now that I don't have her, and I have more money than I could ever use in this lifetime, and my name is cemented in Hollywood history, and I know how hollow it is, I am kicking myself for every single second I chose it over loving her proudly. But that's a luxury. You can do that when you're rich and famous. You can decide that wealth and renown are worthless when you have them. Back then, I still thought I had all the time I needed to do everything I wanted. That if I just played my cards right, I could have it all."

"You thought she'd come back to you," I say.

"I *knew* she'd come back to me," Evelyn says. "And she knew it, too. We both knew our time wasn't over."

I hear the distinct sound of my phone. But it isn't the familiar tone of a regular text message. It is the beep I set just for David, last year when I got the phone, just after we were married, when it never occurred to me that he'd ever stop texting.

I look down briefly to see his name. And beneath it: *I think we should talk. This is too huge, M. It's happening too fast. We have to talk about it.* I put it out of my mind instantly.

"So you knew she was coming back to you, but you married Rex North anyway?" I ask, refocused.

Evelyn lowers her head for a moment, preparing to explain herself. "*Anna Karenina* was way over budget. We were weeks behind schedule. Rex was Count Vronsky. By the time the director's cut came in, we knew the entire thing had to be reedited, and we needed to bring someone else in to save it."

"And you had a stake in the box office."

"Both Harry and I did. It was his first movie after leaving Sunset Studios. If it flopped, he would have a hard time getting another meeting in town."

"And you? What would have happened to you if it flopped?"

"If my first project after *Boute-en-Train* didn't do well, I was worried I'd be a flash in the pan. I'd risen from ashes more than once by that point. But I didn't want to have to do it again. So I did the one thing I knew would get people desperate to see the movie. I married Count Vronsky."

Clever Rex North

◆

THERE IS A CERTAIN FREEDOM in marrying a man when you aren't hiding anything.

Celia was gone. I wasn't really at a place in my life where I could fall in love with anyone, and Rex wasn't the type of man who seemed capable of falling in love at all. Maybe, if we'd met at different times in our lives, we might have hit it off. But with things as they were, Rex and I had a relationship built entirely on box office.

It was tacky and fake and manipulative.

But it was the beginning of my millions.

It was also how I got Celia to come back to me.

And it was one of the most honest deals I've ever made with anybody.

I think I will always love Rex North a little bit because of all that.

"So you're never going to sleep with me?" Rex said.

He was sitting in my living room with one leg casually crossed over the other, drinking a manhattan. He was wearing a black suit with a thin tie. His blond hair was slicked back. It made his blue eyes look even brighter, with nothing in their way.

Rex was the kind of guy who was so beautiful it was nearly boring. And then he smiled, and you watched every girl in the room faint. Perfect teeth, two shallow dimples, a slight arch of the eyebrow, and everybody was done for.

Like me, he'd been made by the studios. Born Karl Olvirsson in Iceland, he hightailed it to Hollywood, changed his name, perfected his accent, and slept with everybody he needed to sleep with to get what he wanted. He was a matinee idol with a chip on his shoulder about proving he could act. But he actually *could* act. He felt underestimated because he *was* underestimated. *Anna Karenina* was his chance to be taken seriously. He needed it to be a big hit just as much as I did. Which was why he was willing to do exactly what I was willing to do. A marriage stunt.

Rex was pragmatic and never precious. He saw ten steps ahead but never let on what he was thinking. We were kindred spirits in that regard.

I sat down next to him on my living room sofa, my arm resting behind him. "I can't say for sure I'd never sleep with you," I said. It was the truth. "You're handsome. I could see myself falling for your shtick once or twice."

Rex laughed. He always had a detached sense about him, like you could do whatever you wanted and you wouldn't get under his skin. He was untouchable in that way.

"I mean, can you say for certain that you'd never fall in love with me?" I asked. "What if you end up wanting to make this a real marriage? That would be uncomfortable for everyone."

"You know, if any woman could do it, it would make sense that it was Evelyn Hugo. I suppose there's always a chance."

"That's how I feel about sleeping with you," I said. "There's always a chance." I grabbed my gibson off the coffee table and drank a sip.

Rex laughed. "Tell me, then, where will we live?"

"Good question."

"My house is in the Bird Streets, with floor-to-ceiling windows. It's a pain in the ass to get out of the driveway. But you can see the whole canyon from my pool."

"That's fine," I said. "I don't mind moving to your place for a little while. I'm shooting another movie in a month or so over at Columbia, so your place will be closer anyway. The only thing I insist on is that I can bring Luisa."

After Celia left, I could hire help again. After all, there was no longer anyone hiding in my bedroom. Luisa was from El Salvador, just a few years younger than I was. The first day she came to work for me, she was talking to her mother on the phone during her lunch break. She was speaking in Spanish, right in front of me. "*La señora es tan bonita, pero loca.*" ("This lady is beautiful but crazy.")

I turned and looked at her, and I said, "*Disculpe? Yo te puedo entender.*" ("Excuse me? I can understand you.")

Luisa's eyes went wide, and she hung up the phone on her mother and said to me, "*Lo siento. No sabía que usted hablaba Español.*" ("I'm sorry. I didn't know you spoke Spanish.")

I switched to English, not wanting to speak Spanish anymore, not liking how strange it sounded coming out of my own mouth. "I'm Cuban," I said to her. "I've spoken Spanish my entire life." That wasn't true, though. I hadn't spoken it in years.

She looked at me as if I were a painting she was interpreting, and then she said, apologetically, "You do not look Cuban."

"*Pues, lo soy,*" I said haughtily. ("Well, I am.")

Luisa nodded and packed up her lunch, moving on to change the bed linens. I sat at that table for at least a half hour, reeling. I kept thinking, *How dare she try to take my own identity away from me?*

But as I looked around my house, seeing no pictures of my family, not a single Latin-American book, stray blond hairs in my hairbrush, not even a jar of cumin in my spice rack, I realized Luisa hadn't done that to me. I had done it to me. I'd made the choice to be different from my true self.

Fidel Castro had control of Cuba. Eisenhower had already put the economic embargo in place by that point. The Bay of Pigs had been a disaster. Being a Cuban-American was complicated. And instead of trying to make my way in the world as a Cuban woman, I simply forsook where I came from. In some ways, this helped me release any remaining ties connecting me to my father. But it also pulled me further away from my mother. My mother, whom this had all been for at some point.

That was all me. All the results of my own choices. None of that was Luisa's fault. So I realized I had no right to sit at my own kitchen table blaming her.

When she left that night, I could tell she still felt uncomfortable around me. So I made sure to smile sincerely and tell her I was excited to see her the next day.

From that day forward, I never spoke Spanish to her. I was too embarrassed, too insecure of my disloyalty. But she spoke it from time to time, and I smiled when she made jokes to her mother within earshot. I let her know I understood her. And I quickly grew to care for her very much. I envied how secure she was in her own skin. How unafraid she was to be her true self. She was proud to be Luisa Jimenez.

She was the first employee I ever had whom I cherished. I was not going to move house without her.

"I'm sure she's great," Rex said. "Bring her. Now, practically speaking, do we sleep in the same bed?"

"I doubt it's necessary. Luisa will be discreet. I've learned that lesson before. And we'll just throw parties a few times a year and make it look like we live in the same room."

"And I can still . . . do what I do?"

"You can still sleep with every woman on the planet, yes."

"Every woman except my wife," Rex said, smiling and taking another sip of his drink.

"You just can't get caught."

Rex waved me off, as if my worry wasn't a concern.

"I'm serious, Rex. Cheating on me is a big story. I can't have that."

"You don't have to worry," Rex said. He was more sincere about that than anything else I'd asked of him, maybe more than any scene in *Anna Karenina*. "I would never do anything to make you look foolish. We're in this together."

"Thank you," I said. "That means a lot. That goes for me, too. What I do won't be your problem. I promise you."

Rex put out his hand, and I shook it.

"Well, I should be going," he said, checking his watch. "I have a date with a particularly eager young lady, and I'd hate to keep her waiting." He buttoned his coat as I stood up. "When should we tie the knot?" he asked.

"I think we should probably be seen around town a few times this coming week. And keep it going for a little while. Maybe put a ring on my finger around November. Harry suggested the big day could be about two weeks before the film hits theaters."

"Shock everybody."

"And get them talking about the movie."

"The fact that I'm Vronsky and you're Anna . . ."

"Makes the whole thing seem tawdry when our marriage will make it seem legitimate."

"It's both dirty and clean," Rex said.

"Exactly."

"That's your bread and butter," he said.

"Yours too."

"Nonsense," Rex said. "I am dirty. Through and through."

I walked with him to the front door and hugged him good-bye. As he stood in the open doorway, he asked, "Have you seen the latest edit? Is it good?"

"It's fantastic," I said. "But it's almost three hours long. If we're going to get people to buy a ticket . . ."

"We have to put on a show," he said.

"Precisely."

"But we're good in it? Me and you?"

"We're absolutely dynamite."

EVELYN HUGO AND REX NORTH HITCHED!

Evelyn Hugo's at it again. And this time, we think she's outdone herself. Evelyn and Rex North tied the knot last weekend at North's estate in the Hollywood Hills.

The two met during the filming of the upcoming *Anna Karenina* and are said to have fallen in love instantly, smitten with each other even during rehearsals. These two blond lovers are sure to heat up theaters in the coming weeks as Anna and Count Vronsky.

This is the first marriage for Rex, although Evelyn has a couple of failed marriages behind her. This year, her famous ex Don Adler is separating from *Hat Trick* star Ruby Reilly.

With a brand-new movie, a star-studded wedding, and two mansions between them, surely Evelyn and Rex are having the time of their lives.

CELIA ST. JAMES ENGAGED TO QUARTER-BACK JOHN BRAVERMAN

Superstar Celia St. James has been on a hot streak lately in the film department, with her period drama *Royal Wedding* and her stunning turn in the musical *Celebration*.

And now she has even more to celebrate. Because she's found love with New York Giants QB John Braverman.

The two have been spotted in Los Angeles and Manhattan, dining out and enjoying each other's company.

Here's hoping Celia turns out to be a good-luck charm for Braverman. That big diamond on her finger has sure got to feel like a good-luck charm for her!

ANNA KARENINA *WINS BIG AT THE BOX OFFICE*

The eagerly awaited *Anna Karenina* sailed into theaters this Friday and took the weekend.

With rave reviews for both Evelyn Hugo and Rex North, it's no wonder audiences are flocking to the film. Between the world-class performances and the chemistry both on- and off-screen, excitement for the movie has reached a fever pitch.

People are saying a pair of Oscars might be just the perfect wedding gift for the newlyweds.

As a producer on the film, Evelyn stands to make boffo numbers off the box office.

Brava, Hugo!

T HE NIGHT OF THE ACADEMY Awards, Rex and I sat next to each other, holding hands, allowing everyone a glimpse of the romantic marriage we were peddling around town.

We both smiled politely when we lost, clapping for the winners. I was disappointed but not surprised. It seemed a little too good to be true, the idea of Oscars for people like Rex and me, beautiful movie stars trying to prove they had substance. I got the distinct impression that a lot of people wanted us to stay in our lane. So we took it in stride and then partied the night away, the two of us drinking and dancing until the wee hours.

Celia wasn't at the awards that year, and despite the fact that I searched for her at every party Rex and I went to, I didn't lay eyes on her. Instead, Rex and I painted the town red.

At the William Morris party, I found Harry and dragged him into a quiet corner, where the two of us sipped champagne and talked about how wealthy we were going to be.

You should know this about the rich: they always want to get richer. It is never boring, getting your hands on more money.

When I was a child, trying to find something to eat for dinner besides the old rice and dry beans in the kitchen, I would tell myself that if I could just have a good meal every night, I'd be happy.

When I was at Sunset Studios, I told myself all I wanted was a mansion.

When I got the mansion, I told myself all I wanted was two houses and a team of help.

Here I was, just turned twenty-five, already realizing that no amount would ever really be enough.

Rex and I went home at around five in the morning, the two of us downright drunk. As our car drove away, I searched my purse for keys to the house, and Rex stood beside me breathing his sour gin breath down my neck.

"My wife can't find the keys!" Rex said, stumbling ever so slightly. "She's trying very hard, but she can't seem to find them."

"Would you be quiet?" I said. "Do you want to wake the neighbors?"

"What are they going to do?" Rex said, even louder than before. "Kick us out of town? Is that what they will do, my precious Evelyn? Will they tell us we can't live on Blue Jay Way anymore? Will they make us move to Robin Drive? Or Oriole Lane?"

I found the keys, put them in the door, and turned the knob. The two of us fell inside. I said good night to Rex and went to my room.

I took off my dress alone, without anyone there to unzip the back of it. The loneliness of my marriage hit harder in that moment than it ever had.

I caught a glimpse of myself in the mirror and could see, in no uncertain terms, that I was beautiful. But it didn't mean anyone loved me.

I stood in my slip and looked at my brassy blond hair and my dark brown eyes and my straight, thick eyebrows. And I missed the woman who should have been my wife. I missed Celia.

My mind reeled with the thought that she might be with John Braverman that very moment. I knew better than to believe any of it. But I also feared that I didn't know her the way I thought I did. Did she love him? Had she forgotten me? Tears welled in my eyes as I thought about her red hair that used to fan across my pillows.

"There, there," Rex said from behind me. I turned around to see him standing in the doorway.

He had taken off his tux jacket and undone his cuff links. His shirt was half buttoned, his bow tie undone, hanging on either side of his neck. It was the very sight that millions of women across the nation would have killed for.

"I thought you went to bed," I said. "If I'd known you were up, I'd've had you help me get my dress off."

"I would have liked that."

I waved him off. "What are you doing? Can't sleep?"

"Haven't tried."

He walked farther into the room, closer to me.

"Well, try, then. It's late. At this rate, the two of us will be asleep until evening."

"Think about it, Evelyn," he said. The lights streaming in through the windows lit his blond hair. His dimples glowed.

"Think about what?"

"Think about what it would be like."

He moved closer to me and put his hand on my waist. He stood behind me, his breath once again on my neck. It felt good to be touched by him.

Movie stars are movie stars are movie stars. Sure, we all fade after a while. We are human, full of flaws like anyone else. But we are the chosen ones because we are extraordinary.

And there is nothing an extraordinary person likes more than someone else extraordinary.

"Rex."

"Evelyn," he said, whispering into my ear. "Just once. Shouldn't we?"

"No," I said, "we shouldn't." But I was not wholly convinced of my answer, and thus, neither was Rex. "You should go back to your room before we both do something we'll regret tomorrow."

"Are you sure?" he said. "Your wish is my command, but I'd like it very much if you changed your wish."

"I won't change it," I said.

"Think of it, though," he said. He raised his hands higher up my torso, the silk of my slip the only thing between us. "Think of the way I'd feel on top of you."

I laughed. "I will not think about that. If I think about that, we'll both be sunk."

"Think of the way we'd move together. The way we'd be slow at first and then lose control."

"Does this work with other women?"

"I've never had to work this hard with other women," he said, kissing my neck.

I could have walked away from him. I could have slapped him right across the face, and he would have taken it with a stiff upper lip and left me alone. But I wasn't ready for this part to be over. I liked being tempted. I liked knowing I might make the wrong decision.

And it would absolutely have been the wrong decision. Because as soon as I got out of that bed, Rex would forget how badly he'd worked to get me. He'd remember only that he'd had me.

And this wasn't a typical marriage. There was too much money on the line.

I let him flick one side of my slip off. I let him run his hand underneath the neckline of it.

"Oh, what it would be to lose myself in you," he said. "To lie underneath you and watch you writhe on top of me."

I almost did it. I almost ripped my own slip off and threw him onto the bed.

But then he said, "C'mon, baby, you know you want to."

And it became perfectly clear just how many times Rex had tried this before with countless other women.

Never let anyone make you feel ordinary.

"Get out of here," I said, though not unkindly.

"But—"

"No buts. Go on to bed."

"Evelyn—"

"Rex, you're drunk, and you're confusing me for one of your many girls, but I'm your wife," I said, with all obvious irony.

"Not even once?" he said. He seemed to sober up quickly, as if his hooded eyes had been part of the act. I was never really sure with him. You never knew exactly where you stood with Rex North.

"Don't try it again, Rex. It's not going to happen."

He rolled his eyes and then kissed me on the cheek. "G'night, Evelyn," he said, and then he slipped out my door just as smoothly as he'd come in.

THE NEXT DAY, I woke up to a ringing phone, deeply hungover and mildly confused about where I was.

"Hello?"

"Rise and shine, little bird."

"Harry, what on earth?" The sun in my eyes felt like a burn.

"After you left the Fox party last night, I had a very interesting conversation with Sam Pool."

"What was a Paramount exec doing at a Fox party?"

"Trying to find you and me," Harry said. "Well, and Rex."

"To do what?"

"To suggest that Paramount sign you and Rex to a three-picture deal."

"What?"

"They want three movies, produced by us, starring you and Rex. Sam said to name a price."

"Name a price?" Whenever I had too much to drink, I always woke up the next morning feeling as if I were underwater. Everything looked muted, sounded blurry. I needed to make sure I was following. "What do you mean, name a price?"

"Do you want a million bucks for a picture? I heard that's what Don's getting for *The Time Before*. We could get that for you, too."

Did I want to make as much money as Don? Of course I did. I wanted to get the paycheck and mail a copy of it to him with a photo of my middle finger. But mostly I wanted the freedom to do whatever I wanted.

"No," I said. "Nope. I'm not signing some contract where they tell me what movies to be in. You and I decide what movies I do. That's it."

"You aren't listening."

"I'm listening just fine," I said, shifting my weight onto my shoulder and changing the arm that was holding the phone. I thought to myself, *I'm going to go for a swim today. I should tell Luisa to heat the pool.*

"We choose the movies," Harry said. "It's a blind deal. Whatever films you and Rex like Paramount wants to buy. Whatever salary we want."

"All because of *Anna Karenina*?"

"We've proven your name brings people into the theater. And if I'm being entirely clear-eyed about this, I think Sam Pool wants to screw over Ari Sullivan. I think he wants to take what Ari Sullivan threw away and make gold out of it."

"So I'm a pawn."

"Everyone's a pawn. Don't go around taking things personally now when you never have before."

"Any movies we want?"

"Anything we want."

"Have you told Rex?"

"Do you honestly think I would run a single thing by that cad before running it by you?"

"Oh, he is not a cad."

"If you had been there to talk to Joy Nathan after he broke her heart, you'd disagree."

"Harry, he's my husband."

"Evelyn, no, he's not."

"Can't you find *something* to like about him?"

"Oh, there's plenty to like about him. I *love* how much money he's made us, how much he *will* make us."

"Well, he's always done good by me." I told him no, and he walked out my door. Not every man would do that. Not every man had.

"That's because you both want the same thing. You, of all people, should know that you can't tell a single thing about a person's true character if you both want the same thing. That's like a dog and a cat getting along because they both want to kill the mouse."

"Well, I like him. And I want you to like him. Especially because if we sign this deal, Rex and I will have to stay married quite a bit longer than we originally thought. Which makes him my family. And you're my family. So you're both family."

"Plenty of people don't like their families."

"Oh, shut up," I said.

"Let's get Rex on board and sign this thing, OK? Get your agents together to hammer out the deal. Let's ask for the moon."

"OK," I said.

"Evelyn?" Harry said, before getting off the phone.

"Yes?"

"You know what's happening, right?"

"What?"

"You're about to become the highest-paid actress in Hollywood."

For the next two and a half years, Rex and I stayed married, living in a house in the hills, developing and shooting movies at Paramount.

We were staffed up with an entire team of people by that point. A pair of agents, a publicist, lawyers, and a business manager for each of us, as well as two on-set assistants and our staff at the house, including Luisa.

We woke up every day in our separate beds, got ready on opposite sides of the house, and then got into the same car and drove to the set together, holding hands the moment we drove onto the lot. We worked all day and then drove home together. At which point, we'd split up again for our own evening plans.

Mine were often with Harry or a few Paramount stars I had taken a liking to. Or I went out on a date with someone I trusted to keep a secret.

During my marriage to Rex, I never met anyone I felt desperate to see again. Sure, I had a few flings. Some with other stars, one with a rock singer, a few with married men—the group most likely to keep the fact that they'd bedded a movie star a secret. But it was all meaningless.

I assumed Rex was having meaningless dalliances, too. And for the most part, he was. Until suddenly, he wasn't.

One Saturday, he came into the kitchen as Luisa was making me some toast. I was drinking a cup of coffee and having a cigarette, waiting for Harry to come pick me up for a round of tennis.

Rex went to the fridge and poured himself a glass of orange juice. He sat down beside me at the table.

Luisa put the toast in front of me and then set the butter dish in the center of the table.

"Anything for you, Mr. North?" she asked.

Rex shook his head. "Thank you, Luisa."

And then all three of us could sense it; she needed to excuse herself. Something was about to happen.

"I'll be starting the laundry," she said, and slipped away.

"I'm in love," Rex said when we were finally alone.

It was perhaps the very last thing I ever thought he'd say.

"In love?" I asked.

He laughed at my shock. "It doesn't make any sense. Trust me, I know that."

"With whom?"

"Joy."

"Joy Nathan?"

"Yes. We've seen each other on and off through the years. You know how it is."

"I know how it is with you, sure. But last I heard, you broke her heart."

"Yes, well, it will come as no surprise to you that I have, in the past, been a little . . . let's say, heartless."

"Sure, we can say that."

Rex laughed. "But I started feeling like it might be nice to have a woman in my bed when I woke up in the morning."

"How novel."

"And when I thought of what woman I might like that to be, I thought of Joy. So we've been seeing each other. Quietly, mind you. And, well, now I find that I can't stop thinking about her. That I want to be around her all the time."

"Rex, that's wonderful," I said.

"I hoped you'd think so."

"So what should we do?" I asked.

"Well," he said, breathing deeply, "Joy and I would like to marry."

"OK," I said, my brain already kicking into high gear, calculating the perfect time to announce our divorce. We'd already had two movies come out, one a modest hit, one a smash. The third, *Carolina Sunset*, about a young couple who have lost a child and move to a farm in North Carolina to try to heal, ultimately having affairs with people in their small town, was premiering in a few months.

Rex had phoned in his performance. But I knew the movie had the potential to be big for me. "We'll say that the stress of filming *Carolina Sunset*, of being on set and watching each other kiss other people, ruined us. Everyone will feel bad for us but not too bad. People love stories of hubris. We took what we had for granted, and now we're paying the price. You'll wait a little while. We'll plant a story that I introduced you to Joy because I wanted you to be happy."

"That's great, Evelyn, really," Rex said. "Except that Joy's pregnant. We're having a baby."

I closed my eyes, frustrated. "OK," I said. "OK. Let me think."

"What if we just say that we haven't been happy for a while? That we've been living separate lives?"

"Then we're saying that our chemistry has fizzled out. And who's going to go see *Carolina Sunset* then?"

This was the moment, the one Harry had warned me about. Rex didn't care about *Carolina Sunset*, certainly not as much as I did. He knew he wasn't anything special in it, and even if he was, he was all wrapped up in his new love, his new baby.

He looked out the window and then back at me. "OK," he said. "You're right. We went into this together, we'll leave it together. What do you suggest? I told Joy we'd be married by the time the baby comes."

Rex North was always a more stand-up guy than anyone gave him credit for.

"Obviously," I said. "Of course."

The doorbell rang, and a moment later, Harry walked into the kitchen.

I had an idea.

It wasn't a flawless idea.

Almost no idea is.

"We're having affairs," I said.

"What?" Rex asked.

"Good morning," Harry said, realizing he'd missed a large part of the conversation.

"During the course of making a movie about both of us having affairs, we both started having affairs. You with Joy, me with Harry."

"What?" Harry said.

"People know we work together," I said to Harry. "They've seen us together. You've been in the background of hundreds of photos of me. They'll believe it." I turned to Rex. "We'll divorce immediately after the stories are planted. And anyone who blames you for cheating on me with Joy, which we can't deny for obvious reasons, will realize it's a victimless crime. Because I was doing it to you, too."

"This actually isn't a terrible idea," Rex said.

"Well, it makes both of us look bad," I said.

"Sure," Rex said.

"But it will sell tickets," Harry said.

Rex smiled and then looked me right in the eye, put out his hand, and shook mine.

"No one's going to believe it," Harry said as we drove to the tennis club later that morning. "People in town, at least."

"What do you mean?"

"You and me. There are a lot of people who will dismiss it right out of hand."

"Because . . ."

"Because they know what I am. I mean, I've considered doing something like this before, maybe one day even taking a wife. God knows it would make my mother happy. She's still sitting there, in Champaign, Illinois, desperately wondering when I'll find a nice girl and have a family. I would love to have a family. But too many people would see through it." He looked at me briefly as he drove. "Just as I'm afraid too many people will see through this."

I looked out my window at the palm trees swaying at their tops.

"So we make it undeniable," I said.

The thing I liked about Harry was that he was never one step be-hind me.

"Photos," he said. "Of the two of us."

"Yeah. Candids, looking like we've been caught at something."

"Isn't it easier for you just to pick someone else?" he said.

"I don't want to get to know someone else," I said. "I'm sick of trying to pretend I'm happy. At least with you, I'll be pretending to love some-one I really do love."

Harry was quiet for a moment. "I think you should know something," he said finally.

"OK."

"Something I've thought I should tell you for some time."

"OK, tell me."

"I've been seeing John Braverman."

My heart started beating quickly. "Celia's John Braverman?"

Harry nodded.

"For how long?"

"A few weeks."

"When were you going to tell me?"

"I wasn't sure if I should."

"So their marriage is . . ."

"Fake," Harry said.

"She doesn't love him?" I asked.

"They sleep in separate beds."

"Have you seen her?"

Harry didn't answer at first. He looked as if he was trying to choose his words carefully. But I had no patience for perfect words.

"Harry, *have you seen her?*"

"Yes."

"How does she seem?" I asked, and then thought of a better question, one more pressing. "Did she ask about me?"

While I had not found living without Celia to be easy, I did find it *easier* when I could pretend she was a part of another world. But this, her existing in my orbit, made everything I had been repressing come bubbling up.

"She didn't," Harry said. "But I suspect it's because she didn't want to ask, rather than not wanting to know."

"But she doesn't love him?"

Harry shook his head. "No, she doesn't love him."

I turned my head and looked back out the window. I imagined telling Harry to drive me to her house. I imagined running to her door. I imagined dropping to my knees and telling her the truth, that life without her was lonely and empty and quickly losing all meaning.

Instead, I said, "When should we do the picture?"

"What?"

"The picture of you and me. Where we make it look like we've been caught in an affair."

"We can do it tomorrow night," Harry said. "We can park the car. Maybe up in the hills, so photogs can find us but the picture will look secluded. I'll call Rich Rice. He needs some money."

I shook my head. "This can't come from us. These gossips aren't playing ball anymore. They are out for themselves. We need someone else to call it in. Someone the rags will believe *wants* me to get caught."

"Who?"

I shake my head the moment the idea comes to me. I already don't want to do it the moment I realize I have to.

I SAT DOWN at the phone in my study. I made sure the door was closed. And I dialed her number.

"Ruby, it's Evelyn, and I need a favor," I said as soon as she answered.

"I'm open to it," she said, not missing a beat.

"I need you to tip off some photographers. Say you saw me necking in a car up in the Trousdale Estates."

"What?" Ruby said, laughing. "Evelyn, what are you up to?"

"Don't worry about what I'm up to. You have enough on your plate."

"Does this mean Rex is about to be single?" she asked.

"Haven't you had enough of my leftovers?"

"Honey, Don pursued *me*."

"I'm sure he did."

"The least you could have done was warn me," she said.

"You knew what he was doing behind my back," I said. "What made you think he'd be any different with you?"

"Not the cheating, Ev," she said.

And that's when I realized he'd hit her, too.

I was temporarily stunned silent.

"You're OK now?" I asked after a moment. "You got away?"

"Our divorce is final. I'm moving to the beach, just bought a place in Santa Monica."

"You don't think he's going to try to blackball you?"

"He tried," Ruby said. "But he won't succeed. His last three movies barely broke even. He didn't get nominated for *The Night Hunter* like everybody thought. He's on a downward spiral. He's about to be as harmless as a declawed cat."

I felt for him, in some small way, as I twirled the phone cord in my hand. But I felt for her much more. "How bad was it, Ruby?"

"Nothing I couldn't hide with pancake makeup and long sleeves." The way she said it, the pride in her voice, as if admitting that it hurt her was a vulnerability she wasn't willing to give in to, made my heart break. It broke for her, and it broke for the me of all those years ago who did the same thing.

"You'll come over for dinner one of these days," I said to her.

"Oh, let's not do that, Evelyn," she said. "We've been through too much to be so phony."

I laughed. "Fair enough."

"Anybody in particular you want me to call tomorrow? Or just anybody with a tip line?"

"Anybody powerful will do. Anybody eager to make money off my demise."

"Well, that's everybody," Ruby said. "No offense."

"None taken."

"You're too successful," she said. "Too many hits, too many handsome husbands. We all want to shoot you down from the air now."

"I know, dear. I know. And when they're done with me, they'll come for you."

"You're not really famous if anybody still likes you," Ruby said. "I'll call tomorrow. Good luck with whatever it is you're doing."

"Thanks," I said. "You're a lifesaver."

And as we hung up, I thought, *If I'd told people what he was doing to me, he might not have had the chance to do it to her.*

I wasn't much interested in keeping a log of the victims of my decisions, but it did occur to me that if I was, I'd have had to put Ruby Reilly on the list.

I PUT ON A RISQUÉ dress that showed just a little too much cleavage, and I drove up Hillcrest Road with Harry.

He pulled over to the side, and I moved toward him. I'd stuck with nude lipstick, because I knew red would be pushing it. I was careful to control the elements enough but not too much, because I didn't want it to look perfect. I wanted to be sure the photo wouldn't *look* staged. I needn't have been worried. Pictures speak very loudly. In general, we can almost never shake what we see with our eyes.

"So how do you want to do this?" Harry said.

"Are you nervous?" I asked him. "Have you kissed a woman before?"

Harry looked at me as if I was an idiot. "Of course I have."

"Have you ever made love to one?"

"Once."

"Did you like it?"

Harry thought. "That one's harder to answer."

"Pretend I'm a man, then," I said. "Pretend you *have* to have me."

"I can kiss you unprompted, Evelyn. I don't need you to direct me."

"We have to be doing it long enough that when they come by, it looks like we've been here for a while."

Harry messed up his hair and pulled at his collar. I laughed and messed mine up, too. I pushed one shoulder off my dress.

"Ooh," Harry said. "It's getting very racy in here."

I pushed him away, laughing. We heard a car coming up behind us, the headlights shining ahead.

Panicked, Harry grabbed me by both arms and kissed me. He pressed his lips hard against mine, and just as the car passed us, he ran one hand through my hair.

"I think it was just a neighbor," I said, watching the car's rear lights as it made its way farther up the canyon.

Harry grabbed my hand. "We could do it, you know."

"What?"

"We could get married. I mean, as long as we're gonna pretend to do it, we could *really* do it. It's not so crazy. After all, I love you. Maybe not the way a husband is supposed to love a wife but enough, I think."

"Harry."

"And . . . what I told you yesterday about wanting a wife. I've been thinking, and if this works, if people buy it . . . maybe we could raise a family together. Don't you want to have a family?"

"Yes," I said. "Eventually, I think I do."

"We could be great for each other. And we won't just give up when the bloom falls off the rose, because we already know each other better than that."

"Harry, I can't tell if you're serious."

"I'm dead serious. At least, I think I am."

"You want to marry me?"

"I want to be with someone I love. I want to have a companion. I'd like to bring someone home to my family. I don't want to live alone anymore. And I want a son or a daughter. We could have that together. I can't give you everything. I know that. But I want to raise a family, and I'd love to raise one with you."

"Harry, I'm cynical and I'm bossy, and most people would consider me vaguely immoral."

"You're strong and resilient and talented. You're exceptional inside and out."

He had really thought about this.

"And you? And your . . . proclivities? How does that work?"

"The same as it has with you and Rex. I do what I do. Discreetly, of course. You do what you do."

"But I don't want to continue to have affairs my entire life. I want to be with someone I'm in love with. Someone who's in love with me."

"Well, that I can't help you with," Harry said. "For that one, you have to call her."

I looked down at my lap, stared at my fingernails.

Would she take me back?

She and John. Me and Harry.

It could actually work. It could work so beautifully.

And if I couldn't have her, did I want anyone else? I was pretty sure that if I couldn't have her, all I wanted was a life with Harry.

"OK," I said. "Let's do it."

Another car came up behind us, and Harry grabbed me again. This time, he kissed me slowly, passionately. When a guy jumped out of his car with a camera, Harry pretended, just for a split second, that he didn't see him and slipped his hand down the top of my dress.

The image printed in the papers the next week was tawdry, scandalous, and shocking. It showed us with swollen faces and looks of guilt, Harry's hand clearly on my breast.

The next day, everyone was printing headlines that Joy Nathan was pregnant.

The four of us were the talk of the nation.

Unscrupulous, unfaithful, lustful sinners.

Carolina Sunset set a record for the longest stay in theaters. And to celebrate our divorce, Rex and I shared a pair of dirty martinis.

"To our successful union," Rex said. And then we clinked our glasses and drank.

I T IS THREE IN THE morning by the time I get home. Evelyn had downed four cups of coffee and apparently felt wired enough to keep talking.

I could have bowed out at any point, but on some level, I think I welcomed the excuse not to go back to my own life for a little while. Being wrapped up in digesting Evelyn's story means I don't have to exist in my own.

And anyway, it's not my place to go making the rules. I picked my battle. I won. The rest is up to her.

So when I get home, I crawl into bed and will myself to fall asleep quickly. My last thought as I go to sleep is that I am relieved I have a valid excuse for why I haven't responded to David's text yet.

I'm woken up by my cell phone ringing, and I look at the time. It's almost nine. It's Saturday. I was hoping to sleep in.

My phone shows my mother's face smiling at me. It's not quite six her time. "Mom? Is everything OK?"

"Of course it is," she says, as if she's calling at noon. "I just wanted to try to catch you and say hi before you headed out for the day."

"It's not even six A.M. where you are," I say. "And it's the weekend. I'm mostly planning on sleeping in and transcribing some of my hours of Evelyn recordings."

"We had a small earthquake about a half hour ago, and now I can't go back to sleep. How is it going with Evelyn? I feel weird calling her Evelyn. Like I know her or something."

I tell her about getting Frankie to agree to a promotion. I tell her that I got Evelyn to agree to a cover story.

"You're telling me you went up against the editor in chief of *Vivant* and Evelyn Hugo both within twenty-four hours? And you came out getting what you want from everyone?"

I laugh, surprised at how impressive it sounds. "Yeah," I say. "I guess I did."

My mom lets out what can only be described as a cackle. "That's my girl!" she says. "Oof, let me tell you, your father would be beaming right now if he were here. Would just be glowing with pride. He always knew you were going to be a force to be reckoned with."

I wonder if this is true, not because my mom has ever really lied to me but because it's just so hard for me to imagine. I can see my dad thinking I'd grow up to be kind or smart; that makes sense. But I've never thought of myself as a force to be reckoned with. Maybe I should *start* thinking of myself that way; maybe I deserve to.

"I kind of am, aren't I? Don't mess with me, world. I'm out to get mine."

"That's right, honey. That you are."

As I tell my mom I love her and hang up the phone, I feel proud of myself, smug even.

I have no idea that in less than a week, Evelyn Hugo will finish her story, and I'll find out what this has all been about, and I will hate her so much that I'll be truly afraid I might kill her.

Brilliant, Kindhearted,
Tortured Harry Cameron

◆

I WAS NOMINATED FOR BEST Actress for *Carolina Sunset*.

The only problem was that Celia was nominated that year, too.

I showed up on the red carpet with Harry. We were engaged. He'd given me a diamond and emerald ring. It stood out against the black beaded dress I wore that night. Two slits on either side of the skirt went up to my mid-thigh. I loved that dress.

And so did everyone else. I've noticed that when people do retrospectives of my career, photos of me in that dress always make it in somehow. I made sure it would be included in the auction. I think it could raise a lot of money.

It makes me happy that people love that dress as much as I do. I lost an Oscar, but it ended up being one of the greatest nights of my life.

Celia arrived just before the show began. She was wearing a pale blue strapless gown with a sweetheart neckline. The color of her hair against the dress was striking. When my eyes set on her, for the first time in nearly five years, I found myself breathless.

I'd gone to see every single one of Celia's movies, even though I was loath to admit it. So I had *seen* her.

But no medium can capture what it is to be in someone's presence, certainly not someone like her. Someone who makes you feel important simply because she's choosing to look at you.

There was something stately about her, at the age of twenty-eight. She was mature and dignified. She looked like the kind of person who knew exactly who she was.

She stepped forward and took John Braverman's arm. In a tux that seemed to strain at his broad shoulders, John looked as all-American as a husk of corn. They were a gorgeous couple. No matter how false it all was.

"Ev, you're staring," Harry said as he pushed me into the theater.

"Sorry," I said. "Thank you."

As we took our seats, we smiled and waved to everyone seated around us. Joy and Rex were a few rows behind us, and I waved politely, knowing people were watching, knowing that if I ran up and hugged them, people might be confused.

When we sat down, Harry said, "If you win, will you talk to her?"

I laughed. "And gloat?"

"No, but you'd have the upper hand that you seem to so desperately want."

"She left me."

"You slept with someone."

"For her."

Harry frowned at me as if I was missing the point.

"Fine, if I win, I'll talk to her."

"Thank you."

"Why are you thanking me?"

"Because I want you to be happy, and it appears I have to reward you for doing things in your own favor."

"Well, if *she* wins, I'm not saying a single word to her."

"If she wins," Harry said delicately, "which is a big *if*, and she comes and talks to you, I will hold you down and force you to listen and speak back."

I couldn't look directly at him. I was feeling defensive.

"It's a moot point anyway," I said. "Everyone knows they're going to give it to Ruby, because they feel bad she didn't get it last year for *The Dangerous Flight*."

"They might not," Harry said.

"Yeah, yeah," I told him. "And I've got a bridge in Brooklyn to sell you."

But when the lights dimmed and the host came out, I was not thinking that my chances were slim. I was just delusional enough to think the Academy might finally give me a goddamn Oscar.

When they called out the nominees for Best Actress, I scanned the audience for Celia. I spotted her the very same moment she spotted me. We locked eyes. And then the presenter didn't say "Evelyn" or "Celia." He said "Ruby."

When my heart sank into my chest, aching and heavy, I was mad at myself for believing I had a chance. And then I wondered if Celia was OK.

Harry held my hand and squeezed it. I hoped John was squeezing Celia's. I excused myself to the bathroom.

Bonnie Lakeland was washing her hands as I came in. She gave me a smile, and then she left. And I was alone. I sat in a stall and closed the door. I let myself cry.

"Evelyn?"

You don't spend years pining away for one voice not to notice it when it finally appears.

"Celia?" I said. My back was to the stall door. I wiped my eyes.

"I saw you come in here," she said. "I thought it might be a sign that you weren't . . . that you were upset."

"I'm trying to be happy for Ruby," I said, laughing just a little bit as I used a piece of toilet paper to carefully dry my eyes. "But it's not exactly my style."

"Mine either," she said.

I opened the door. And there she was. Blue dress, red hair, small stature with a presence that filled the whole room. And when her eyes set on me, I knew she still loved me. I could see it in the way her pupils widened and softened.

"You are as gorgeous as ever," she said as she leaned against the sink, her arms holding her weight behind her. There was always something intoxicating about the way Celia looked at me. I felt like a rare steak in front of a tiger.

"You're not so bad yourself," I said.

"We probably shouldn't be caught in here together," Celia said.

"Why not?" I asked.

"Because I suspect more than a few people seated in there know what we once got up to," she said. "I know you'd hate for them to think we were up to it again."

This was a test.

I knew it. She knew it.

If I said the right thing, if I told her I didn't care what they thought, if I told her I'd make love to her in the middle of the stage in front of all of them, I just might be able to have her back.

I let myself think about it for a moment. I let myself think about waking up tomorrow to her cigarette-and-coffee breath.

But I wanted her to admit it wasn't all me. That she had played a part in our demise. "Or maybe you just don't want to be seen with a . . . what was the word you used, I believe it was *whore*?"

Celia laughed and looked down at the floor and then back up at me. "What do you want me to say? That I was wrong? I was. I wanted to hurt you like you hurt me."

"But I never meant to hurt you," I said. "Never once would I have done a single thing to hurt you on purpose."

"You were ashamed to love me."

"Absolutely not," I said. "That is absolutely untrue."

"Well, you certainly went to great lengths to hide it."

"I did what had to be done to protect both of us."

"Debatable."

"So debate it with me," I said. "Instead of running away again."

"I didn't run far, Evelyn. You could have caught up with me, if you wanted to."

"I don't like being played, Celia. I told you that the first time we went out for milk shakes."

She shrugged. "You play everyone else."

"I have never claimed that I wasn't a hypocrite."

"How do you do that?" Celia said.

"Do what?"

"Act so cavalier about things that are sacred to other people?"

"Because other people have got nothing to do with me."

Celia scoffed, somewhat gently, and looked down at her hands.

"Except you," I said.

I was rewarded with the sight of her looking up at me.

"I care about you," I said.

"You *cared* about me."

I shook my head. "No, I didn't misspeak."

"You certainly moved on fast enough with Rex North."

I frowned at her. "Celia, you know better than that."

"So it was fake."

"Every moment."

"Have you been with anyone else? Any men?" she asked. She was always jealous of the men, worried she couldn't compete. I was jealous of the women, worried I wouldn't compare.

"I've had a good time," I said. "As I'm sure you've had."

"John isn't—"

"I'm not talking about John. But I'm sure you haven't kept chaste." I was fishing for information that might break my heart, a flaw of the human condition.

"No," she said. "You're right about that."

"Men?" I asked, hoping the answer was yes. If it was men, I knew it didn't mean anything to her.

She shook her head, and my heart broke just a little bit more, like a tear that deepens from strain.

"Anyone I know?"

"None of them were famous," she said. "None of them meant anything to me. I touched them and thought of what it felt like to touch you."

My heart both ached and swelled to hear it.

"You shouldn't have left me, Celia."

"You shouldn't have let me leave."

And with that, I had no more fight in me. My heart cried out the truth through my throat. "I know. I know that. I know."

Sometimes things happen so quickly you aren't sure when you even realized they were about to begin. One minute she was leaning against the sink, the next her hands were on my face, her body pressed against me, her lips between mine. She tasted like the musky creaminess of thick lipstick and the sharp, spiced sting of rum.

I was lost in her. In the feel of her on me once again, the sheer joy of her attention, the glory of knowing she loved me.

And then the door was flung open, and the wives of two producers walked in. We broke apart. Celia pretended she had been washing her hands, and I moved to one of the mirrors and fixed my makeup. The two women talked together, caught up in their conversation, barely noticing us.

They entered two stalls, and I looked at Celia. She looked at me. I watched her turn off the faucet and take a towel. I worried that she might walk right out the bathroom door. But she didn't.

One of the wives left, and then the other. We were finally alone again. Listening closely, we could tell the show had come back from a commercial break.

I grabbed Celia and kissed her. I pushed her up against the door. I couldn't get enough of her. I needed her. She was as much of a fix to me as any drug.

Before I even stopped to consider the danger, I lifted her dress and slipped my hand up her thigh. I held her against the door, I kissed her, and with one hand I touched her the way I knew she liked.

She moaned slightly and put her hand over her mouth. I kissed her neck. And the two of us, our bodies tightly wound, shuddered against the door.

We could have been caught at any moment. If one woman in the whole auditorium chose to visit the ladies' room during those seven minutes, we'd have lost everything we'd worked so hard for.

That is how Celia and I forgave each other.

And how we knew we couldn't live without each other.

Because now we both knew what we were willing to risk. Just to be together.

EVELYN HUGO WEDS PRODUCER HARRY CAMERON

Fifth time's a charm? Evelyn Hugo and producer Harry Cameron married last Saturday, during a ceremony on the beaches of Capri.

Evelyn wore an off-white silk gown and had her long blond hair down and parted in the middle. Harry, known for being one of the better-dressed Hollywood players, wore a cream-colored linen suit.

Celia St. James, America's Sweetheart, attended as the maid of honor, and her fabulous hubby, John Braverman, served as the best man.

Harry and Evelyn have been working together since the '50s, when Evelyn came to fame in such hits as *Father and Daughter* and *Little Women*. They admitted they were having an affair late last year when they were caught in flagrante while Evelyn was still married to Rex North.

Rex is now married to Joy Nathan and the proud papa of their little girl, Violet North.

We're glad that Evelyn and Harry have decided to finally make it official! After such a shocking beginning to their relationship and a long engagement, all we can say is it's about time!

CELIA GOT ABSOLUTELY SMASHED DURING the wedding. She was having a hard time not being jealous, even though she knew the whole thing was fake. Her own husband was standing next to Harry, for crying out loud. And we all knew what we were.

Two men sleeping together. Married to two women sleeping together. We were four beards.

And what I thought as I said "I do" was *It's all beginning now. Real life, our life. We're finally going to be a family.*

Harry and John were in love. Celia and I were sky-high.

When we got back from Italy, I sold my mansion in Beverly Hills. Harry sold his. We bought this place in Manhattan, on the Upper East Side, just down the street from Celia and John.

Before I agreed to move, I had Harry look into whether my father was still alive. I wasn't sure I could live in the same city he lived in, wasn't sure I could handle the idea of running into him.

But when Harry's assistant searched for him, I learned that my father had died in 1959 of a heart attack. What little he owned was absorbed by the state when no one came forward to claim it.

My first thought when I heard he was gone was *So that's why he never tried to come after me for money.* And my second was *How sad that I'm certain that's all he'd ever want.*

I put it out of my head, signed the paperwork on the apartment, and celebrated the purchase with Harry. I was free to go wherever I wanted. And what I wanted was to move to the Upper East Side of Manhattan. I persuaded Luisa to join us.

This apartment might be within a long walk's distance, but I was a million miles away from Hell's Kitchen. And I was world-famous, married, in love, and so rich it sometimes made me sick.

A month after we moved to town, Celia and I took a taxi to Hell's Kitchen and walked around the neighborhood. It looked so different from when I left. I brought her to the sidewalk just below my old building and pointed at the window that used to be mine.

"Right there," I said. "On the fifth floor."

Celia looked at me, with compassion for all I had been through when I lived there, for all I had done for myself since then. And then she calmly, confidently took my hand.

I bristled, unsure if we should be touching in public, scared of what people would do. But the rest of the people on the street just kept on walking, kept on living their lives, almost entirely unaware of or uninterested in the two famous women holding hands on the sidewalk.

Celia and I spent our nights together in this apartment. Harry spent his nights with John at their place. We went out to dinner in public, the four of us looking like two pairs of heterosexuals, without a heterosexual in the bunch.

The tabloids called us "America's Favorite Double-Daters." I even heard rumors that the four of us were swingers, which wasn't that crazy for that period of time. It really makes you think, doesn't it? That people were so eager to believe we were swapping spouses but would have been scandalized to know we were monogamous and queer?

I'll never forget the morning after the Stonewall riots. Harry was at rapt attention, watching the news. John was on the phone all day with friends of his who lived downtown.

Celia was pacing the living room floor, her heart racing. She believed everything was going to change after that night. She believed that because gay people had announced themselves, had been proud enough to admit who they were and strong enough to stand up, attitudes were going to change.

I remember sitting out on our rooftop patio, looking southward, and realizing that Celia, Harry, John, and I weren't alone. It seems silly to say now, but I was so . . . self-involved, so singularly focused, that I rarely took time to think of the people out there like myself.

That isn't to say that I wasn't aware of the way the country was changing. Harry and I campaigned for Bobby Kennedy. Celia posed with Vietnam protesters on the cover of *Effect*. John was a vocal supporter of the civil rights movement, and I had been a very public supporter of the work of Dr. Martin Luther King Jr. But this was different.

This was *our* people.

And here they were, revolting against the police, in the name of their right to be themselves. While I was sitting in a golden prison of my own making.

I was out on my terrace, directly in the sun, on the afternoon after the initial riots, wearing high-waisted jeans and a black sleeveless top, drinking a gibson. And I started crying when I realized those men were willing to fight for a dream I had never even allowed myself to envision. A world where we could be ourselves, without fear and without shame. Those men were braver and more hopeful than I was. There were simply no other words for it.

"There's a plan to riot again tonight," John said as he joined me on the patio. He had such an intimidating physical presence. More than six feet tall, two hundred and twenty-five pounds, with a tight crew cut. He looked like a guy you didn't want to mess with. But anyone who knew him, and especially those of us who loved him, knew he was the first guy you *could* mess with.

He may have been a warrior on the football field, but he was the sweetheart of our foursome. He was the guy who asked how you slept the night before, the guy who always remembered the smallest thing you said three weeks ago. And he took it on as his job to protect Celia and Harry and, by extension, me. John and I loved the same people, and so we loved each other. And we also loved playing gin rummy. I can't tell you how many nights I stayed up late finishing a hand of cards with John, the two of us deadly competitive, trading off who was the gloating winner and who was the sore loser.

"We should go down there," Celia said, joining us. John took a seat in a chair in the corner. Celia sat on the arm of the chair I was in. "We should support them. We should be a part of this."

I could hear Harry calling John's name from the kitchen. "We're out here!" I yelled to him, at the same moment as John said, "I'm on the patio."

Soon Harry appeared in the doorway.

"Harry, don't you think we should go down there?" Celia said. She lit a cigarette, took a drag, and handed it to me.

I was already shaking my head. John outright told her no.

"What do you mean, no?" Celia said.

"You're not going down there," John said. "You can't. None of us can."

"Of course I can," she said, looking to me to back her up.

"Sorry," I said, giving her the cigarette back. "I'm with John on this."

"Harry?" she said, hoping to make one final successful plea.

Harry shook his head. "We go down there, all we do is attract attention away from the cause and toward us. The story becomes about whether we're homosexuals and not about the *rights* of homosexuals."

Celia put the cigarette to her lips and inhaled. She had a sour look on her face as she blew the smoke into the air. "So what do we do, then? We can't sit here and do nothing. We can't let them fight our fight for us."

"We give them what we have and they don't," Harry said.

"Money," I said, following his train of thought.

John nodded. "I'll call Peter. He'll know how we can fund them. He'll know who needs resources."

"We should have been doing that all along," Harry said. "So let's just do it from now on. No matter what happens tonight. No matter what course this fight takes. Let's just decide here and now that our job is to fund."

"I'm in," I said.

"Yeah." John nodded. "Of course."

"OK," Celia said. "If you're sure that's the way we can do the most good."

"It is," Harry said. "I'm sure of it."

We started filtering money privately that day, and I've continued to do so the rest of my life.

In the pursuit of a great cause, I think people can be of service in a number of different ways. I always felt that my way was to make a lot of money and then channel it to the groups that needed it. It's a bit self-serving, that logic. I know that. But because of who I was, because of the sacrifices I made to hide parts of myself, I was able to give more money than most people ever see in their entire lifetime. I am proud of that.

But it does not mean I wasn't conflicted. And of course, a lot of the time, that ambivalence was even more personal than it was political.

I knew it was imperative that I hide, and yet I did not believe I should have to. But accepting that something is true isn't the same as thinking that it is just.

Celia won her second Oscar in 1970, for her role as a woman who cross-dresses to serve as a World War I soldier in the film *Our Men*.

I could not be in Los Angeles with her that night, because I was shooting *Jade Diamond* in Miami. I was playing a prostitute living in the same apartment as a drunk. But Celia and I both knew that even if I had been free as a bird, I could not go to the Academy Awards on her arm.

That evening, Celia called me after she was home from the ceremony and all the parties.

I screamed into the phone. I was so happy for her. "You've done it," I said. "Twice now you've done it!"

"Can you believe it?" she said. "Two of them."

"You deserve them. The whole world should be giving you an Oscar every day, as far as I'm concerned."

"I wish you were here," she said petulantly. I could tell she'd been drinking. I would have been drinking, too, if I'd been in her position. But I was irritated that she had to make things so difficult. I wanted to be there. Didn't she know that? Didn't she know that I *couldn't* be there? And that it killed me? Why did it always have to be about what all of this felt like for *her*?

"I wish I was, too," I told her. "But it's better this way. You know that."

"Ah, yes. So that people won't know you're a *lesbian*."

I hated being called a lesbian. Not because I thought there was anything wrong with loving a woman, mind you. No, I'd come to terms with that a long time ago. But Celia only saw things in black and white. She liked women and only women. And I liked her. And so she often denied the rest of me.

She liked to ignore the fact that I had truly loved Don Adler once. She liked to ignore the fact that I had made love to men and enjoyed it. She liked to ignore it until the very moment she decided to be threatened by it. That seemed to be her pattern. I was a lesbian when she loved me and a straight woman when she hated me.

People were just starting to talk about the idea of bisexuality, but I'm not sure I even understood that the word referred to me then. I wasn't interested in finding a label for what I already knew. I loved men. I loved Celia. I was OK with that.

"Celia, stop it. I'm sick of this conversation. You're being a brat."

She laughed coldly. "Exactly the same Evelyn I've been dealing with for years. Nothing's changed. You're afraid of who you are, and you still don't have an Oscar. You are what you have always been: a nice pair of tits."

I let the silence hang in the air for a moment. The buzz of the phone was the only sound either of us could hear.

And then Celia started crying. "I'm so sorry," she said. "I should never have said that. I don't even mean it. I'm so sorry. I've had too much to drink, and I miss you, and I'm sorry that I said something so terrible."

"It's fine," I said. "I should be going. It's late here, you understand. Congratulations again, sweetheart."

I hung up before she could reply.

That was how it was with Celia. When you denied her what she wanted, when you hurt her, she made sure you hurt, too.

D ID YOU EVER CALL HER on it?" I ask Evelyn.

I hear the muffled sound of my phone ringing in my bag, and I know from the ringtone that it's David. I did not return his text over the weekend because I wasn't sure what I wanted to say. And then, once I got here again this morning, I put it out of my mind.

I reach over and turn the ringer off.

"There was no point in fighting with Celia once she got mean," Evelyn says. "If things got too tense, I tended to back off before they came to a head. I would tell her I loved her and I couldn't live without her, and then I'd take my top off, and that usually ended the conversation. For all her posturing, Celia had one thing in common with almost every straight man in America: she wanted nothing more than to get her hands on my chest."

"Did it stick with you, though?" I ask. "Those words?"

"Of course it did. Look, I'd be the first person to say back when I was young that all I was was a nice pair of tits. The only currency I had was my sexuality, and I used it like money. I wasn't well educated when I got to Hollywood, I wasn't book-smart, I wasn't powerful, I wasn't a trained actress. What did I have to be good at other than being beautiful? And taking pride in your beauty is a damning act. Because you allow yourself to believe that the only thing notable about yourself is something with a very short shelf life."

She goes on. "When Celia said that to me, I had crossed into my thirties. I wasn't sure I had many more good years left, to be honest. I thought, you know, sure, Celia would keep getting work because people were hiring her for her talent. I wasn't so sure they would continue hiring me once the wrinkles set in, once my metabolism slowed down. So yeah, it hurt, a lot."

"But you had to know you were talented," I tell her. "You had been nominated for an Academy Award three times by that point."

"You're using reason," Evelyn says, smiling at me. "It doesn't always work."

IN 1974, ON MY THIRTY-SIXTH birthday, Harry, Celia, John, and I all went out to the Palace. It was supposedly the most expensive restaurant in the world during that time. And I was the sort of person who liked being extravagant and absurd.

I look back on it now, and I wonder where I got off, throwing money around so casually, as if the fact that it came easily to me meant I had no responsibility to value it. I find it mildly mortifying now. The caviar, the private planes, the staff big enough to populate a baseball team.

But the Palace it was.

We posed for pictures, knowing they would end up in some tabloid or another. Celia bought us a bottle of Dom Perignon. Harry put back four manhattans himself. And when the dessert came with a lit candle in the middle, the three of them sang for me as people looked on.

Harry was the only one who had a piece of the cake. Celia and I were watching our figures, and John was on a strict regimen that had him mostly eating protein.

"At least have a bite, Ev," John said good-naturedly as he took the plate away from Harry and pushed it toward me. "It's your birthday, for crying out loud."

I raised an eyebrow and grabbed a fork, using it to scrape a forkful of the chocolate fudge icing. "When you're right, you're right," I said to him.

"He just doesn't think *I* should have it," Harry said.

John laughed. "Two birds with one stone."

Celia lightly tapped her fork against her glass. "OK, OK," she said. "Small speech time."

She was due to shoot a film in Montana the following week. She'd postponed the start date so she could be with me that night.

"To Evelyn," she said, lifting her glass in the air. "Who has lit up every goddamn room she ever walked into. And who, day after day, makes us feel like we're living in a dream."

LATER THAT NIGHT, as Celia and John went out to hail a cab, Harry gently helped me put my jacket on. "Do you realize that I'm the longest marriage you've had?" he asked.

By that point, Harry and I had been married for almost seven years. "And also the best," I said. "Bar none."

"I was thinking . . ."

I already knew what he was thinking. Or at least, I suspected what he was thinking. Because I'd been thinking it, too.

I was thirty-six. If we were going to have a baby, I'd put it off for as long as I could.

Sure, there were women having babies later than that, but it wasn't very common, and I had spent the last few years staring at babies in strollers, unable to focus my eyes on anything else when they were around.

I would pick up friends' babies and hold them tightly until the very moment their mothers demanded them back. I thought of what my own child might be like. I thought of how it would feel to bring a life into the world, to give the four of us another being to focus on.

But if I was going to do it, I had to get moving.

And our decision to have a baby wasn't really just a two-person conversation. It was a four-person conversation.

"Go on," I said as we made our way to the front of the restaurant. "Say it."

"A baby," Harry said. "You and me."

"Have you discussed it with John?" I asked.

"Not specifically," he said. "Have you discussed it with Celia?"

"No."

"But are you ready?" he said.

My career was going to take a hit. There was no avoiding it. I'd go from being a woman to being a mother—and somehow those things appeared mutually exclusive in Hollywood. My body would change. I'd have months where I couldn't work. It made absolutely no sense to say yes. "Yes," I said. "I am."

Harry nodded. "Me too."

"OK," I said, considering the next steps. "So we'll talk to John and Celia."

"Yeah," Harry said. "I suppose we will."

"And if everyone is on board?" I asked, stopping before we got out to the sidewalk.

"We'll get started," Harry said, stopping with me.

"I know the most obvious solution is adoption," I said. "But . . ."

"You think we should have a biological child."

"I do," I said. "I don't want anyone trying to claim we adopted because we had something to hide."

Harry nodded. "I get it," he said. "I want a biological child, too. Someone half you, half me. I'm with you on this."

I raised my eyebrow. "You do realize how babies are made?" I asked him.

He smiled and then leaned in and whispered, "There is a very small part of me that has wanted to bed you since I met you, Evelyn Hugo."

I laughed and hit him on the arm. "No, there is not."

"A small part," Harry said, defending himself. "It goes against all my greater instincts. But it is there nonetheless."

I smiled. "Well," I said, "we will keep that part to ourselves."

Harry laughed and put out his hand. I shook it. "Once again, Evelyn, you've got yourself a deal."

WOULD THE BABY BE RAISED by the both of you?" Celia asked. We were lying in bed, naked. My back was lined with sweat, my hairline damp. I rolled over onto my stomach and put my hand on Celia's chest.

The movie she was doing next was making her a brunette. I found myself transfixed by the golden red of her hair, desperate to know that they would dye it back properly, that she would return to me looking exactly like herself.

"Yes," I said. "Of course. It would be ours. We'd raise it together."

"And where would I fit into all of this? Where would John?"

"Wherever you want to."

"I don't know what that means."

"It means that we would figure it out as we go."

Celia considered my words and stared at the ceiling. "This is something you want?" Celia asked finally.

"Yes," I told her. "Very badly."

"Is it a problem for you that I have never . . . wanted that?" she asked.

"That you don't want children?"

"Yes."

"No, I suppose not."

"Is it a problem for you that I cannot . . . that I cannot give you that?" Her voice was starting to crack, and her lips were starting to quiver. When Celia was on-screen and needed to cry, she would squint her eyes and cover her face. But they were fake tears, generated out of nothing, for nothing. When she really cried, her face remained painfully still except for the corners of her lips and the water brimming in her eyes that stuck to her lashes.

"Honey," I said, pulling her toward me. "Of course not."

"I just . . . I want to give you everything you've ever wanted, and you want that, and I can't give it to you."

"Celia, no," I said. "It's not like that at all."

"It's not?"

"You have given me more than I ever thought I could have in one life."

"You're sure."

"I'm positive."

She smiled. "You love me?" she said.

"Oh, my God, what an understatement," I told her.

"You love me so much you can't see straight?"

"I love you so much that when I sometimes get a look at all the crazy fan mail you get, I think, *Well, sure, that makes sense. I want to collect her eyelashes, too.*"

Celia laughed and ran her hand across my upper arm as she stared at the ceiling. "I want you to be happy," she said when she finally looked at me.

"You should know that Harry and I will have to . . ."

"There's no other way?" she asked. "I thought women were getting pregnant by men just using their sperm now."

I nodded. "I think there are other ways," I said. "But I'm not confident in the security of the situation. Or, rather, I don't know how to ensure that no one finds out that's how we did it."

"You're saying you're going to have to make love to Harry," Celia said.

"You are the person I'm in love with. You are the person I make love to. Harry and I are merely making a baby."

Celia looked at me, reading my face. "You're sure about that?"

"Absolutely positive."

She looked back up at the ceiling. She didn't talk for a while. I watched her eyes as they moved back and forth. I watched her breathing as it slowed. And then she turned to face me. "If it's what you want . . . if you want a baby, then . . . have a baby. I will . . . we will figure it out. I will make it work. I can be an aunt. Aunt Celia. And I'll find a way to be OK with it all."

"And I'll help you," I said.

She laughed. "How do you suppose you'll do that?"

"I can think of one way to make it all a bit more palatable for you," I said, kissing her neck. She liked to be kissed right below and just behind her ear, where her earlobe hit her neck.

"Oh, you are too much," she said. But she didn't say anything else. She did not stop me as I moved my hand across her breasts, down her stomach, between her legs. She moaned and pulled me closer to her, and she ran her own hand down my body. She touched me while I touched her, soft at first and then harder, faster. "I love you," she said, breathless.

"I love you," I said back to her.

She looked into my eyes and made me feel rapture, and that night, in giving of herself, she gave me a baby.

EVELYN HUGO AND HARRY CAMERON HAVE A BABY GIRL!

Evelyn Hugo is finally a mother! At the age of 37, the stunning bombshell is adding "parent" to her résumé. Connor Margot Cameron, 6 pounds, 9 ounces, was born late last Tuesday at Mount Sinai Hospital.

Dad Harry Cameron is said to be "over the moon" about the little bambina.

With a string of hits behind them, Evelyn and Harry are sure to consider the littlest Cameron their most exciting coproduction yet.

I WAS IN LOVE WITH Connor from the moment she looked at me. With her full head of hair and her round blue eyes, I thought, for a moment, she looked just like Celia.

Connor was always hungry and hated being alone. She wanted nothing more than to lie on me, quietly sleeping. She absolutely adored Harry.

During those first few months, Celia shot two movies back-to-back, both out of town. One of them, *The Buyer*, was a movie I knew she was passionate about. But the second, a mob movie, was exactly the sort of work she hated. On top of the violence and darkness, it shot for eight weeks, four in Los Angeles and four in Sicily. When the offer came in, I was expecting her to turn it down. Instead, she took the part, and John decided to go with her.

During the time they were gone, Harry and I lived almost exactly like a traditional married couple. Harry made me bacon and eggs for breakfast and ran my baths. I fed the baby and changed her nearly hourly.

We had help, of course. Luisa was taking care of the house. She was changing the sheets, doing the laundry, cleaning up after all of us. On her days off, it was Harry who stepped in.

It was Harry who told me I looked beautiful, even though we both knew I'd seen better days. It was Harry who read script after script, looking for the perfect project for me to take on once Connor was old enough. It was Harry who slept next to me every night, who held my hand as we fell asleep, who held me when I was convinced I was a terrible mother after I scratched Connor's cheek giving her a bath.

Harry and I had always been close, had long been family, but during that time, I truly felt like a wife. I felt like I had a husband. And I grew to love him even more. Connor, and that time with her, bonded Harry and me in ways I could never imagine. He was there to celebrate the good and support me during the bad.

It was around that time that I started to believe that friendships could be written in the stars. "If there are all different types of soul mates," I told Harry one afternoon, when the two of us were sitting out on the patio with Connor, "then you are one of mine."

Harry was wearing a pair of shorts and no shirt. Connor was lying on his chest. He hadn't shaved that morning, and his stubble was coming in. It had just the slightest gray patch under his chin. Looking at him with her, I realized how much they looked alike. Same long lashes, same pert lips.

Harry held Connor to his chest with one hand and grabbed my free hand with the other. "I am absolutely positive that I need you more than I've ever needed another living soul," he said. "The only exception being—"

"Connor," I said. We both smiled.

For the rest of our lives, we would say that. The only exception to absolutely everything was Connor.

WHEN CELIA AND John came home, things went back to normal. Celia lived with me. Harry lived with John. Connor stayed at my place, with the assumption that Harry would come by days and nights to be with us, to care for us.

But that first morning, just around the time Harry was due for breakfast, Celia put on her robe and headed to the kitchen. She started making oatmeal.

I had just come down, still in my pajamas. I was sitting at the island nursing Connor when Harry walked in.

"Oh," he said, looking at Celia, noticing the pan. Luisa was washing dishes in the sink. "I was coming in to make bacon and eggs."

"I've got it," Celia said. "A nice warm bowl of oatmeal for everybody. There's enough for you, too, if you're hungry."

Harry looked at me, unsure what to do. I looked at him, equally uncertain.

Celia just kept stirring. And then she grabbed three bowls and set them down. She put the pot in the sink for Luisa to wash.

It occurred to me then how odd this system was. Harry and I paid Luisa's salary, but Harry didn't even live here. Celia and John paid the mortgage on the home Harry lived in.

Harry sat down and grabbed the spoon in front of him. He and I dug into our oatmeal at the same time. When Celia's back was to us, we looked at each other and grimaced. Harry mouthed something to me, and even though I could barely read his lips, I knew what he was saying, because it was exactly what I was thinking.

So bland.

Celia turned back to us and offered us some raisins. We both took her up on it. And then the three of us sat in the kitchen, eating our oatmeal quietly, all aware that Celia had staked her claim. I was hers. She would make my breakfast. Harry was a visitor.

Connor started crying, so Harry took her and changed her. Luisa went downstairs to grab the laundry. And when we were alone, Celia said, "Max Girard is doing a movie called *Three A.M.* for Paramount. It's supposed to be a real art-house piece, and I think you should do it."

I had kept in touch with Max, on and off, since he directed me in *Boute-en-Train*. I never forgot that it was with him that I was able to catapult my name to the top again. But I knew Celia couldn't stand him. He was too overt in his interest in me, too salacious about it. Celia used to jokingly call him Pepé Le Pew. "You think I should do a movie with Max?"

Celia nodded. "They offered it to me, but it makes more sense for you. Regardless of the fact that I think he's a Neanderthal, I can recognize that the man makes good movies. And this role is exactly your thing."

"What do you mean?"

Celia got up and took my bowl with hers. She rinsed them both in the sink and then turned back to me, leaning against it. "It's a sexy part. They need a real bombshell."

I shook my head. "I'm someone's mother now. The whole world knows it."

Celia shook her head. "That's exactly why you *have* to do it."

"Why?"

"Because you're a sexual woman, Evelyn. You're sensual, and you're beautiful, and you're desirable. Don't let them take that away from you. Don't let them desexualize you. Don't let your career be on their terms. What do you want to do? You want to play a mom in every role you take from now on? You want to play only nuns and teachers?"

"No," I said. "Of course not. I want to play everything."

"So play everything," she said. "Be bold. Do what no one expects you to do."

"People will say it's unbecoming."

"The Evelyn I love doesn't care about that."

I closed my eyes and listened to her, nodding. She wanted me to do it for me. I really believe that. She knew I wouldn't be happy being limited, being relegated. She knew I wanted to continue to make people talk, to tantalize, to surprise. But the part she wasn't mentioning, the part I'm not even sure she truly understood, was that she also wanted me to do it because she didn't want me to change.

She wanted to be with a bombshell.

It's always been fascinating to me how things can be simultaneously true and false, how people can be good and bad all in one, how someone can love you in a way that is beautifully selfless while serving themselves ruthlessly.

It is why I loved Celia. She was a very complicated woman who always kept me guessing. And here she had surprised me one more time.

She had said, *Go, have a baby.* But she had meant to add, *Just don't act like a mother.*

Fortunately and unfortunately for her, I had absolutely no intention of being told what to do or of being manipulated into a single thing.

So I read the script, and I took a few days and thought about it. I asked Harry what he thought. And then I woke up one morning and thought, *I want the part. I want it because I want to show I'm still my own woman.*

I called Max Girard and told him I was interested if he was interested. And he was.

"But I'm surprised you want to do this," Max said. "You are one hundred percent sure?"

"Is there nudity?" I asked. "I'm OK with the idea. Really. I look fantastic, Max. It's not a problem." I did not look fantastic, nor did I feel fantastic. It *was* a problem. But it was a solvable problem, and solvable problems aren't really problems, are they?

"No," Max said, laughing. "Evelyn, you could be ninety-seven years old, and the whole world would line up to see your chest."

"Then what are you talking about?"

"Don," he said.

"Don who?"

"Your part," he said. "The whole movie. All of it."

"What?"

"You're playing opposite Don Adler."

WHY DID YOU AGREE TO do it?" I ask her. "Why not say you wanted him cut from the film?"

"Well, first of all, you don't go throwing your weight around unless you're sure you'll win," Evelyn says. "And I was only about eighty percent sure that if I pitched a fit, Max would fire him. And second of all, it seemed mildly cruel, to be honest. Don was not doing well. He hadn't had a hit in years, and most younger moviegoers didn't know who he was. He was divorced from Ruby, hadn't remarried, and the rumor was that his drinking had gotten out of control."

"So you felt bad for him? Your abuser?"

"Relationships are complex," Evelyn says. "People are messy, and love can be ugly. I'm inclined to always err on the side of compassion."

"You're saying you had compassion for what he was going through?"

"I'm saying you should have a little compassion for how complicated it must have been for me."

Cut down to size, I find myself staring at the floor, unable to look at her. "I'm sorry," I say. "I haven't been in that situation before, and I was . . . I don't know what I was thinking making any sort of judgment. I apologize."

Evelyn smiles gently, accepting my apology. "I can't speak for all people who have been hit by someone they love, but what I can tell you is that forgiveness is different from absolution. Don was no longer a threat to me. I was not scared of him. I felt powerful and free. So I told Max I'd meet with him. Celia was supportive but also hesitant once she learned

Don had been cast. Harry, while cautious, trusted my ability to handle the situation. So my representatives called Don's people, and we set a time and place for the next time I was in L.A. I had suggested the bar at the Beverly Hills Hotel, but Don's team changed it at the last minute to Canter's Deli. That's how I ended up seeing my ex-husband for the first time in more than fifteen years over a pair of Reubens."

I'M SORRY, EVELYN," DON SAID when he sat down. I had already ordered an iced tea and eaten half of a sour pickle. I thought he was apologizing for being late.

"It's only five past one," I said. "It's fine."

"No," he said, shaking his head. He looked pale but also a bit thinner than some of his recent photos. The years we had been apart had not been good to Don. His face had bloated, and his waistline had widened. But he was still heads and tails more handsome than anyone else in the place. Don was the sort of man who was always going to be handsome, no matter what happened to him. His good looks were just that loyal.

"I'm sorry," he said. The emphasis, the meaningfulness of it, hit me.

It caught me off guard. The waitress came by and asked for his drink order. He didn't order a martini or a beer. He ordered a Coca-Cola. When she left, I found myself unsure what to say to him.

"I'm sober," he said. "Have been for two hundred and fifty-six days."

"That many, huh?" I said as I took a sip of my iced tea.

"I was a drunk, Evelyn. I know that now."

"You were also a cheater and a pig," I said.

Don nodded. "I know that, too. And I'm deeply sorry."

I had flown all the way here to see if I could do a movie with him. I had not come to be apologized to. The thought had never occurred to me. I merely assumed I would use him this time the way I used him back then; his name near mine would get people talking.

But this repentant man in front of me was surprising and over-whelming.

"What am I supposed to do with that?" I asked him. "That you're sorry? What is that supposed to mean to me?"

The waitress came and took our orders.

"A Reuben, please," I said, handing her the menu. If I was going to have a real conversation about this, I needed a hearty meal.

"I'll have the same," Don said.

She knew who we were; I could see it in the way her lips kept trying to hold back a smile.

When she left, Don leaned in. "I know it doesn't make up for what I did to you," he said.

"Good," I said. "Because it really doesn't."

"But I hope it might make you feel a little better," he said, "to know that I know I was wrong, I know you deserved better, and I'm working every day to be a better man."

"Well, it's awfully late now," I said. "You being a better man does nothing for me."

"I won't hurt anyone like I did then," Don said. "To you, to Ruby."

My heart of ice melted briefly, and I admitted that did make me feel better. "Still," I said. "We all can't go around treating people like dog shit and then expecting that a simple *I'm sorry* erases it."

Don shook his head humbly. "Of course not," he said. "No, I know that."

"And if your movies hadn't tanked and Ari Sullivan hadn't dropped you like you got him to drop me, you'd probably still be living high on the hog, drunk as a skunk."

Don nodded. "Probably. I'm sorry to say you are most likely right about that."

I wanted more. Did I want him to grovel? To cry? I wasn't sure. I just knew I wasn't getting it.

"Let me just say this," Don said. "I loved you from the moment I saw you. I loved you madly. And I ruined it because I turned into a man I'm not proud of. And *because* I ruined it the way I did, because I was awful at treating you the way you deserved to be treated, I am sorry. Sometimes

I think about going back to our wedding day and wanting to do it all over again, wanting to fix my mistakes so that you never have to go through what I put you through. I know I can't do that, but what I can do is look you in the eye and tell you from the very bottom of my heart that I know how incredible you are, I know how great we could have been together, I know that everything we both lost was my fault, I am dedicated to never behaving that poorly again, and I am truly, truly sorry."

In all my years after Don, all my movies, all my marriages, I had never once wanted to go back in time in the hopes that Don and I could get it right. My life since Don had been a story of my own making, a mess and a joy of my own decisions, and a string of experiences that landed me with everything I ever wanted.

I was OK. I felt safe. I had a beautiful daughter, a devoted husband, and the love of a good woman. I had money and fame. I had a gorgeous house in a city I had reclaimed. What could Don Adler take from me?

If I had come to see if I could stand him, I found that I could. There was not a bone in my body that was afraid of him.

And then I realized: if that was true, what did I have to lose?

I did not say the words *I forgive you* to Don Adler. I simply took my wallet out of my purse and said, "Do you want to see a picture of Connor?"

He smiled and nodded, and when I showed him her photo, he laughed. "She looks just like you," he said.

"I'll take that as a compliment."

"I don't think there's any other way to take it. I think every woman in this country would like to look like Evelyn Hugo."

I threw my head back and laughed. When our Reubens were half eaten and taken away by the waitress, I told him I'd do the movie.

"That's great," he said. "Really great to hear. I think you and I could really . . . I think we can really give them a show."

"We are not friends, Don," I said. "I want to be clear on that."

Don nodded. "OK," he said. "I understand."

"But I think we can be *friendly*."

Don smiled. "I'd be honored by friendly."

JUST BEFORE SHOOTING WAS SET to commence, Harry turned forty-five. He said he didn't want a big night out or any sort of formal plans. He just wanted a nice day with all of us.

So John, Celia, and I planned a picnic in the park. Luisa packed us lunch. Celia made sangria. John went down to the sporting-goods store and got us an extra-large umbrella to shade us from not only the sun but also passersby. On the way home, he got the bright idea to buy us wigs and sunglasses, too.

That afternoon, the three of us told Harry we had a surprise for him, and we led him into the park, Connor riding on his back. She loved to be strapped to him. She would laugh as he bounced her while he walked.

I took his hand and dragged him with us.

"Where are we going?" he said. "Someone at least give me a hint."

"I'll give you a small one," Celia said as we were crossing Fifth Avenue.

"No," John said, shaking his head. "No hints. He's too good with hints. It takes all the fun out of it."

"Connor, where is everyone taking Daddy?" Harry said. I watched as Connor laughed at the sound of her name.

When Celia walked through the entrance to the park, not even a block from our apartment, Harry spotted the blanket already set out with the umbrella and the picnic baskets, and he smiled.

"A picnic?" he said.

"Simple family picnic. Just the five of us," I said.

Harry smiled. He closed his eyes for a moment. As if he'd reached heaven. "Absolutely perfect," he said.

"I made the sangria," Celia said. "Luisa made the food, obviously."

"Obviously," Harry said, laughing.

"And John got the umbrella."

John bent down and grabbed the wigs. "And these."

He handed me a curly black one and gave Celia a short blond one. Harry took a red one. And John put on the long brown one that made him look like a hippie.

We all laughed as we looked at one another, but I was surprised to see just how realistic they managed to be. And when I put on the coordinating pair of sunglasses, I felt a little freer.

"If you got the wigs and Celia made the sangria, what did Evelyn do?" Harry asked as he took Connor off his back and put her on the blanket. I grabbed her and helped her sit up.

"Good question," John said, smiling. "You'd have to ask her."

"Oh, I helped," I said.

"Actually, yeah, Evelyn, what *did* you do?" Celia said.

I looked up to see the three of them all staring at me teasingly.

"I . . ." I gestured vaguely to the picnic basket. "You know . . ."

"No," Harry said, laughing. "I don't know."

"Listen, I've been very busy," I said.

"Uh-huh," Celia said.

"Oh, all right." I lifted Connor up as she started to frown. I knew it meant tears were coming any moment. "I didn't do a damn thing."

The three of them started laughing at me, and then Connor started laughing, too.

John opened the basket. Celia poured wine. Harry leaned over and kissed Connor's forehead.

It was one of the last times we were all together, laughing, smiling, happy. A family.

Because after that, I ruined it.

D ON AND I WERE IN the middle of shooting *Three A.M.* in New York. Luisa, Celia, and Harry were trading off watching Connor while I was at work. The days were longer than we anticipated, and the shoot ran long.

I played Patricia, a woman in love with a drug addict, Mark, played by Don. And every day, I could see that he was not the old Don I knew, showing up to set and saying some lines with charm. This was striking, superlative, raw acting. He was pulling from his life, and he was putting it on film.

On set, you really hope that it's all coming together into something magical in the camera lens. But there's never any way to know for sure.

Even when Harry and I were producing work ourselves, when we were watching the dailies so often that my eyes felt dry and I was losing track of reality versus film, we were never one hundred percent sure that all the parts were coming together perfectly until we saw the first cut.

But on the set of *Three A.M.*, I just knew. I knew it was a movie that would change how people saw me, how people saw Don. I thought it might just be good enough to change lives, to get people clean. It might just be good enough to change the way movies were made.

So I sacrificed.

When Max wanted more days, I gave up time with Connor to be there. When Max wanted more nights, I gave up dinners and evenings with Celia. I must have called Celia almost every day from the set, apologizing for something. Apologizing that I couldn't meet her at the restaurant in time. Apologizing that I needed her to stay home and watch Connor for me.

I could tell that part of her regretted pushing me to do the movie. I don't think she liked me working with my ex-husband every day. I don't think she liked me working with Max Girard every day. I don't think she liked my long hours. And I got the impression that while she loved my baby girl, babysitting wasn't exactly her idea of a good time.

But she kept it to herself and supported me. When I called to say I'd be late for the millionth time, she would say, "It's OK, honey. Don't worry. Just be great." She was an excellent partner in that regard, putting me first, putting my work first.

And then, toward the end of shooting, after a long day of emotional scene work, I was in my dressing room getting ready to go home when Max knocked on my door.

"Hey," I said. "What's on your mind?"

He looked at me with consideration and then took a seat. I remained standing, committed to leaving. "I think, Evelyn, we have something to think about."

"We do?"

"The love scene is next week."

"I'm aware."

"This movie, it is almost done."

"Yes."

"And I think it is missing something."

"Like what?"

"I think that the viewer needs to understand the raw magnetism of Patricia and Mark's attraction."

"I agree. That's why I agreed to really show my breasts. You're getting what no other filmmaker, including yourself, has ever gotten from me before. I'd think you'd be thrilled."

"Yes, of course, I am, but I think we need to show that Patricia is a woman who takes what she wants, who delights in the sins of the flesh. She is, right now, such a martyr. She is a saint, helping Mark all through the film, standing by him."

"Right, *because* of how much she loves him."

"Yes, but we also need to see *why* she loves him. What does he give to her, what does she get from him?"

"What are you getting at?"

"I want us to shoot something almost no one does."

"Which is?"

"I want to show you screwing because you love it." His eyes were wide and excited. He was creatively enthralled. I always knew Max was a little lascivious, but this was different. This was a rebellious act. "Think about it. Sex scenes are about love. Or power."

"Sure. And the purpose of the love scene next week is to show how much Patricia loves Mark. How much she believes in him. How strong their connection is."

Max shakes his head. "I want it to show the audience that part of the reason Patricia loves Mark is because he makes her orgasm."

I felt myself pulling back, trying to take it all in. It shouldn't have felt so scandalous, and yet it absolutely was. Women have sex for intimacy. Men have sex for pleasure. That's what culture tells us.

The idea that I'd be shown to enjoy my body, to desire the male form just as strongly as I was desired, to show a woman putting her own physical pleasure at the forefront . . . it felt daring.

What Max was talking about was a graphic portrayal of female desire. And my gut instinct was that I loved the idea. I mean, the thought of filming a graphic sex scene with Don was about as arousing to me as a bowl of bran flakes. But I wanted to push the envelope. I wanted to show a woman getting off. I liked the idea of showing a woman having sex because she wanted to be pleased instead of being desperate to please. So in a moment of excitement, I grabbed my coat, put out my hand, and said, "I'm in."

Max laughed and hopped out of his chair, taking my hand and shaking it. *"Fantastique, ma belle!"*

What I should have done was tell him I had to think about it. What I should have done was tell Celia about it the moment I got home. What I should have done was give her a say.

I should have given her the opportunity to express any misgivings. I should have respected that while she had no place to tell me what I could and could not do with my body, I did have a responsibility to inquire about how my actions might affect her. I should have taken her out to dinner and told her what I wanted to do and explained why I wanted to do it. I should have made love to her that night, to show her that the only body I was truly interested in deriving pleasure from was hers.

These are simply things you do. These are kindnesses you extend to the person you love when you know that your job will entail the world seeing images of you having sex with another person.

I did none of that for Celia.

Instead, I avoided her.

I went home and checked on Connor. I went into the kitchen and ate a chicken salad Luisa had left in the fridge.

Celia came in and hugged me. "How was shooting?"

"Good," I said. "Completely fine."

And because she didn't say, *How was your day?* or *Anything interesting happen with Max?* or even *How's next week looking?* I didn't bring it up.

I HAD TWO shots of bourbon before Max yelled "Action!" The set was closed. Just me, Don, Max, the cinematographer, and a couple of guys working lighting and sound.

I closed my eyes and told myself to remember how good it felt to want Don all those years ago. I thought of how sublime it was to awaken my own desire, to realize I liked sex, that it wasn't just about what men wanted, that it was about me, too. I thought of how I wanted to put that seed of a thought into other women's brains. I thought of how there might be other women out there scared of their own pleasure, of their own power. I thought of what it would mean to have just one woman go home to her husband and say, "Give me what he gave her."

I put myself in that place of desperate wanting, the ache of needing something only someone else can give you. I used to have that with Don. I had it then with Celia. So I closed my eyes, I focused in on myself, and I went there.

Later on, people would say that Don and I were really having sex in the movie. There were all sorts of rumors that the sex was unsimulated. But those rumors were complete and utter bullshit.

People just thought they saw real sex because the energy was searing, because I convinced myself in that moment that I was a woman in urgent need of him, because Don was able to remember how it felt to want me before he ever had me.

That day on set, I truly let go. I was present and wild and unrestrained. More than I ever had been on film before, more than I ever have been since. It was a moment of purely imagined reckless euphoria.

When Max yelled "Cut!" I snapped out of it. I stood up and rushed to my robe. I blushed. Me. Evelyn Hugo. Blushing.

Don asked if I was all right, and I turned away from him, not wanting him to touch me.

"I'm fine," I said, and then I went to my dressing room, closed the door, and bawled my eyes out.

I wasn't ashamed of what I'd done. I wasn't nervous for audiences to see it. The tears that fell down my face were because I realized what I had done to Celia.

I had been a person who believed she stuck by a certain code. It may not have been a code that others subscribed to, but it was one that made sense to me. And part of that code was being honest with Celia, being good to her.

And this was not good to Celia.

Doing what I had just done, without her blessing, was not good for the woman I loved.

When we wrapped for the day, I walked the fifty blocks home instead of grabbing a car. I needed the time to myself.

I stopped on the way and bought flowers. I called Harry from a pay phone and asked him to take Connor for the night.

Celia was in the bedroom when I got home, drying her hair.

"I got you these," I said, handing her the bouquet of white lilies. I did not mention that the florist had said that white lilies mean *My love is pure.*

"Oh, my God," she said. "They are gorgeous. Thank you."

She smelled them and then grabbed a water glass, filled it from the tap, and put the flowers in it. "Just for a moment," she said. "Until I have a chance to choose a vase."

"I wanted to ask you something," I said.

"Oh, boy," she said. "Are these flowers just to butter me up?"

I shook my head. "No," I said. "The flowers are because I love you. Because I want you to know how often I think of you, how important you are to me. I don't tell you that enough. I wanted to tell you this way. With those."

Guilt is a feeling I've never made much peace with. I find that when it rears its head, it brings an army. When I feel guilty for one thing, I start to see all the other things I should feel guilty for.

I sat on the foot of our bed. "I just . . . I wanted to let you know that Max and I have discussed it, and I think the love scene in the movie will be more graphic than you and I were thinking."

"How graphic?"

"Something a bit more intense. Something that conveys Patricia's desperate need to be pleasured."

I was lying outright to hide a lie of omission. I was crafting a new narrative, in which Celia would believe that I had asked for her blessing *before* doing what I had already done.

"Her need to be pleasured?"

"We need to see what Patricia gets out of her relationship with Mark. It's not just love. It has to be more than that."

"That makes sense," Celia said. "You're saying it answers the question *Why does she stay with him?*"

"Yeah," I said, excited that maybe she would understand, maybe I could fix this retroactively. "Exactly. So we are going to shoot an explicit scene between Don and me. I'll be mostly nude. For the heart of the movie to really sink in, we need to see the two main characters truly vulnerable together, connecting . . . sexually."

Celia listened as I spoke, letting the words sink in. I could see her grappling with what I was saying, trying to make it fit for her. "I want you to do the movie as you want to do it," she said.

"Thank you."

"I just . . ." She looked down and started shaking her head. "I'm feeling very . . . I don't know. I'm not sure I can do this. Knowing you're with

Don all day, with these long nights, and I never see you, and . . . sex. Sex is sacred between us. I'm not sure I can stand to watch that."

"You won't need to watch it."

"But I'll know it happened. I'll know it's out there. And everyone will see it. I want to be OK with this. I really do."

"So be OK with it."

"I'm going to try."

"Thank you."

"I'm really going to try."

"Great."

"But Evelyn, I don't think I can. Just knowing that you were . . . when you slept with Mick, I was sick for years afterward, thinking about the two of you together."

"I know."

"And you slept with Harry, God knows how many times," she said.

"I know, honey. I know. But I'm not sleeping with Don."

"But you *have* slept with him. You have. When people watch the two of you on-screen, they will be watching something the two of you have already done."

"It's not real," I said.

"I know, but what you're saying to me is that you are prepared to make it look real. You're saying you're going to make it look more real than anything else any of us have done so far."

"Yes," I said. "I guess I am saying that."

She started crying. She put her head in her hands. "I feel like I'm failing you," she said. "But I can't do it. I can't. I know myself, and I know this is too much for me. I'll be too sick over it. I'll make myself ill thinking of you with him." She shook her head, resolved. "I'm sorry. I don't have it in me. I can't handle it. I want to be stronger for you, I do. I know that if the tables were turned, you could handle it. I feel like I'm disappointing you. And I'm so sorry, Evelyn. I will work forever to make it up to you. I'll help you get any part you want. For the rest of our lives. And I'll work on getting there so that the next time this happens, I can be stronger. But . . . please, Evelyn, I can't live through you sleeping with another man. Even if this time it only *looks* real. I can't do it. Please," she said. "Please don't do this."

My heart sank. I nearly vomited.

I looked down at the floor. I studied the way two planks of wood met just under my feet, how the nailheads were just the littlest bit sunken in.

And then I looked up at her and said, "I already did it."

I sobbed.

And I pleaded.

And I groveled, desperately, on my knees, having long ago learned the lesson that you have to throw yourself at the mercy of the things you truly want.

But before I was done, Celia said, "All I've ever wanted was for you to be truly mine. But you've never been mine. Not really. I've always had to settle for one piece of you. While the world gets the other half. I don't blame you. It doesn't make me stop loving you. But I can't do it. I can't do it, Evelyn. I can't live with my heart half-broken all the time."

And she walked out the door and left me.

Within a week, Celia had packed up all her things, at my apartment and hers, and moved back to L.A.

She would not answer the phone when I called. I couldn't get hold of her.

Then, weeks after she left, she filed for divorce from John. When he got the papers, I swear, it was as if she had served them to me directly. It was clear, in no uncertain terms, that by divorcing him, she was divorcing me.

I got John to make some calls to her agent, her manager. He tracked her down at the Beverly Wilshire. I flew to Los Angeles, and I pounded on her door.

I was wearing my favorite Diane von Furstenberg, because Celia had once said I was irresistible in it. There were a man and a woman coming out of their hotel room, and as they walked down the hall, they couldn't stop looking at me. They knew who I was. But I refused to hide. I just kept knocking on the door.

When Celia finally opened it, I looked her in the eye and didn't say a word. She stared back at me, silent. And then, with tears in my eyes, I said, simply, "Please."

She turned away from me.

"I made a mistake," I said. "I'll never do it again."

The last time we had fought like this, I had refused to apologize. And I really thought that this time, if I just admitted how wrong I was, if I gave in, sincerely and with all my heart, she would forgive me.

But she didn't. "I can't do it anymore," she said as she shook her head. She was wearing high-waisted jeans and a Coca-Cola T-shirt. Her hair was long, past her shoulders. She was thirty-seven but still looked like she was in her twenties. She always had a youthfulness to her that I never really had. I was thirty-eight then, and I was starting to look it.

When she said that, I got down on my knees, in the hallway of the hotel, and bawled my eyes out.

She pulled me inside.

"Take me back, Celia," I begged her. "Take me back, and I'll give the rest of it up. I'll give up everything but Connor. I won't ever act again. I'll let the world know about us. I'm ready to give you all of me. Please."

Celia listened. But then she very calmly sat down in the chair by the bed and said, "Evelyn, you are not capable of giving it up. And you never will be. And it will be the tragedy of my life that I cannot love you enough to make you mine. That you cannot be loved enough to be anyone's."

I stood there for a moment longer, waiting for her to say something else. But she didn't. She had nothing else to say. And there was nothing I could say that would change her mind.

Facing reality, I got hold of myself, held in my tears, kissed her on her temple, and walked away.

I got back on the plane to New York, hiding my pain. And it wasn't until I was back in my apartment that I lost it. Sobbing as if she'd died.

That's how final it felt.

I had pushed her too far. And it was over.

T HAT WAS TRULY IT?" I say.

"She was done with me," Evelyn says.

"What about the movie?"

"Are you asking if it was worth it?"

"I guess so."

"The movie was a huge hit. Didn't make it worth it."

"Don Adler won an Oscar for it, didn't he?"

Evelyn rolls her eyes. "That bastard won an Oscar, and I wasn't even nominated."

"Why not? I've seen it," I say. "Parts of it, at least. You're great. Really exceptional."

"You think I don't know that?"

"Well, then, why weren't you nominated?"

"Because!" Evelyn says, frustrated. "Because I wasn't allowed to be applauded for it. It had an X rating. It was responsible for letters to the editor at nearly every paper in the country. It was too scandalous, too explicit. It got people excited, and when they felt that way, they had to blame someone, and they blamed me. What else were they going to do? Blame the French director? The French are like that. And they weren't going to blame the newly redeemed Don Adler. They blamed the sexpot they'd created whom they could now call a tramp. They weren't going to give me an Oscar for that. They were going to watch it alone in a dark theater and then chastise me in public."

"But it didn't hurt your career," I say. "You did two more movies the next year."

"I made people money. No one turns away money. They were all too happy to get me in their movies and then talk about me behind my back."

"Within a few years, you delivered what is considered one of the most noble performances of the decade."

"Yeah, but I shouldn't have had to turn it around. I did nothing wrong."

"Well, we know that now. People were praising you, and the film, as early as the mid-'80s."

"It's all fine in hindsight," Evelyn says. "Except that I spent years with a scarlet A on my chest, while women and men across the country screwed each other's brains out thinking about what the movie meant. People were shocked by the representation of a woman wanting to get fucked. And while I'm aware of the crassness of my language, it's really the only way to describe it. Patricia was not a woman who wanted to make love. She wanted to get fucked. And we showed that. And people hated how much they loved it."

She's still angry. I can see it in the way her jaw tightens.

"You won an Oscar shortly after that."

"I lost Celia for that movie," she says. "My life, which I loved so much, was turned upside down over that movie. Of course, I understand it was my own fault. I'm the one who filmed an explicit sex scene with my ex-husband without talking to her about it first. I'm not trying to blame other people for the mistakes I made in my own relationship. But still." Evelyn is quiet, lost in her thoughts for a moment.

"I want to ask you something, because I think it's important for you to speak directly about it," I say.

"OK . . ."

"Did being bisexual put a strain on your relationship?" I want to make sure to portray her sexuality with all of its nuance, in all its complexity.

"What do you mean?" she asks. There is a slight edge to her voice.

"You lost the woman you loved because of your sexual relationships with men. I think that's relevant to your larger identity."

Evelyn listens to me and considers my words. Then she shakes her head. "No, I lost the woman I loved because I cared about being famous as much as I cared about her. It had nothing to do with my sexuality."

"But you were using your sexuality to get things from men that Celia couldn't give you."

Evelyn shakes her head even more emphatically. "There's a difference between sexuality and sex. I used sex to get what I wanted. Sex is just an act. Sexuality is a sincere expression of desire and pleasure. That I always kept for Celia."

"I hadn't thought about it like that before," I say.

"Being bisexual didn't make me disloyal," Evelyn says. "One has nothing to do with the other. Nor did it mean that Celia could only fulfill half my needs."

I find myself interrupting her. "I didn't—"

"I know you're not saying that," Evelyn says. "But I want you to have it in my words. When Celia said she couldn't have all of me, it was because I was selfish and because I was scared of losing everything I had. Not because I had two sides of me that one person could never fulfill. I broke Celia's heart because I spent half my time loving her and the other half hiding how much I loved her. Never once did I cheat on Celia. If we're defining cheating by desiring another person and then making love to that person. I never once did that. When I was with Celia, I was with Celia. The same way any woman married to a man is with that man. Did I look at other people? Sure. Just like anyone in a relationship does. But I loved Celia, and I shared my true self only with Celia.

"The problem was, I used my body to get other things I wanted. And I didn't stop doing that, even for her. That's *my* tragedy. That I used my body when it was all I had, and then I kept using it even when I had other options. I kept using it even when I knew it would hurt the woman I loved. And what's more, I made her complicit in it. I put her in a position to continually have to approve of my choices at her own expense. Celia may have left me in a huff, but it was a death by a thousand cuts. I hurt her with these tiny scratches, day after day. And then I got surprised when it left a wound too big to heal.

"I slept with Mick because I wanted to protect our careers, mine and hers. And that was more important to me than the sanctity of our relationship. And I slept with Harry because I wanted a baby, and I thought people would get suspicious if we adopted. Because I was afraid to draw attention to the sexlessness of our marriage. And I chose that over the sanctity of our relationship. And when Max Girard had a good idea about a creative choice in a movie, I wanted to do it. And I was willing to do it at the expense of the sanctity of our relationship."

"You're hard on yourself, I think," I say. "Celia wasn't perfect. She could be cruel."

Evelyn shrugs slightly. "She always made sure the bad was outweighed by so much good. I . . . well, I didn't do that for her. I made it fifty-fifty. Which is about the cruelest thing you can do to someone you love, give them just enough good to make them stick through a hell of a lot of bad. Of course, I realized all this when she left me. And I tried to fix it. But it was too late. As she said, she simply couldn't do it anymore. Because it took me too long to figure out what I cared about. *Not* because of my sexuality. I feel confident you're going to get that right."

"I promise," I say. "I will."

"I know you will. And while we're on the subject of how I'd like to be portrayed, there's something else you need to get exactly right. I won't be able to clear things up after I'm gone. I want to know now, I want to be absolutely sure, that you'll represent what I'm telling you accurately."

"OK," I say. "What is it?"

Evelyn's mood turns a bit darker. "I'm not a good person, Monique. Make sure, in the book, that that's clear. That I'm not claiming to be good. That I did a lot of things that hurt a lot of people, and I would do them over again if I had to."

"I don't know," I say. "You don't seem so bad, Evelyn."

"You, of all people, are going to change your mind about that," she says. "Very soon."

And all I can think is, *What the fuck did she do?*

J OHN DIED OF A HEART attack in 1980. He was just shy of fifty. It
didn't make any sense. The most athletic and fit of us, the one who
didn't smoke, the one who exercised every day, he shouldn't have been
the one whose heart stopped. But things don't make sense. And when he
left us, he left a giant-sized hole in our lives.

Connor was five. It was hard to explain to her where Uncle John went.
It was even harder to explain to her why her father was so heartbroken.
For weeks, Harry could barely get out of bed. When he did, it was to
drink bourbon. He was rarely sober, always somber, and often unkind.

Celia was photographed in tears, her eyes bloodshot, walking into
her trailer on location in Arizona. I wanted to hold her. I wanted us all to
see one another through it. But I knew that wasn't in the cards.

But I could help Harry. So Connor and I stayed with him at his apartment every day. She slept in her room there. I slept on the sofa in his
bedroom. I made sure he ate. I made sure he bathed. I made sure he
played make-believe with his daughter.

One morning, I woke up to find Harry and Connor both in the
kitchen. Connor was pouring herself a bowl of cereal while Harry stood
in his pajama bottoms, looking out the window.

He had an empty glass in his hand. When he turned away from the
view and back toward Connor, I said, "Good morning."

And Connor said, "Daddy, why do your eyes look wet?"

I wasn't sure if he'd been crying or if he was already a few drinks into
the day that early in the morning.

At the funeral, I wore a black vintage Halston. Harry wore a black suit with a black shirt, black tie, black belt, and black socks. Grief never left his face.

His profound, guttural pain didn't follow the story we had sold the press, that Harry and John were friends, that Harry and I were in love. Nor did the fact that John left the house to Harry. But despite my instincts, I did not encourage Harry to hide his feelings or decline the house. I had very little energy left to try to hide who we were. I had learned all too well that pain was sometimes stronger than the need to keep up appearances.

Celia was there, in a long-sleeved black minidress. She did not say hello to me. She barely looked at me. I stared at her, aching to walk over and grab her hand. But I didn't take a single step in her direction.

I was not going to use this loss of Harry's to ease my own. I wasn't going to make her talk to me. Not like that.

Harry held back tears as John's casket was lowered into the ground. Celia walked away. Connor watched me watch her and said, "Mom, who is that lady? I think I know her."

"You do, honey," I said. "You did."

And then Connor, my adorable baby girl, said, "She's the one who dies in your movie."

And I realized she didn't remember Celia at all. She recognized her from *Little Women*.

"She's the nice one. The one who wants everyone to be happy," Connor said.

That's when I knew the family I had made had truly disintegrated.

CELIA ST. JAMES AND JOAN MARKER, BEST OF FRIENDS

Celia St. James and Hollywood newcomer Joan Marker have become the talk of the town lately! Marker, best known for her star-making turn in last year's *Promise Me*, is quickly becoming the It Girl of the season. And who better to show her the ropes than America's Sweetheart? Seen shopping together in Santa Monica and grabbing lunches in Beverly Hills, the two can't seem to get enough of each other.

We certainly hope this means the duo are planning a movie together, because that would be a tour de force of performances!

I KNEW THE ONLY WAY to get Harry to start living his life again was to surround him with Connor and work. The Connor part was easy. She loved her father. She wanted his attention every second of the day. She was growing up to look even more like him, with his ice-blue eyes and his broad, tall frame. And when he was with her, he would stop drinking. He cared about being a good father, and he knew he had a responsibility to be sober for her.

But when he went back to his own home every night, a fact still secret from the outside world, I knew he was drinking himself to sleep. On the days he was not with us, I knew he wasn't getting out of bed.

So work was my only option. I had to find something he would love. It had to be a script he would feel passionate about and one with a great role for me. Not just because I wanted a great role but also because Harry wouldn't do anything for himself. But he *would* do anything if he believed I needed him to.

So I read scripts. Hundreds of scripts over the months. And then Max Girard sent me one that he was having trouble getting made. It was called *All for Us*.

It was about a single mother of three who moves to New York City to try to support her children and pursue her dreams. It was about trying to make ends meet in the cold, hard city, but it was also about hope and daring to believe you deserve more. Both of which I knew would appeal to Harry. And the role of Renee, the mother, was honest, righteous, and powerful.

I ran it over to Harry and begged him to read it. When he tried to avoid it, I said, "I think it will finally get me my Oscar." That's what made him pick it up.

I loved shooting *All for Us*. And it wasn't because I finally got that goddamn statue for it or because I became even closer with Max Girard on the set. I loved shooting *All for Us* because while it didn't get Harry to put down the bottle, it did get him out of bed.

Four months after the movie came out, Harry and I went to the Oscars together. Max Girard had attended with a model named Bridget Manners, but he had joked, for weeks before the event, that all he wanted was to attend with me, to have me on his arm. He had even taken to joking that given all the men I'd married, he was crushed that I'd never married him. I had to admit that Max was quickly becoming someone I truly felt close to. So while he did technically have a date, it felt, as we all sat in the first row together, that I was there with the two men who meant the most to me.

Connor was back at the hotel, watching on TV with Luisa. Earlier that day, she had given Harry and me each a picture she had drawn. Mine was a gold star. Harry's was a lightning bolt. She said they were for luck. I tucked mine into my clutch. Harry put his in his tuxedo pocket.

When they called out the nominees for Best Actress, I realized that I hadn't really ever believed I could win. With the Oscar would come certain things I'd always wanted: credibility, gravitas. And if I truly looked inward, I realized I didn't think I *had* credibility or gravitas.

Harry squeezed my hand as Brick Thomas opened the envelope.

And then, despite everything I had told myself, he said my name.

I stared straight ahead, my chest heaving, unable to process what I'd heard. And then Harry looked at me and said, "You did it."

I stood up and hugged him. I walked to the podium, I took the Oscar that Brick was handing me, and I put my hand to my chest to try to slow down my heartbeat.

When the clapping subsided, I leaned in to the microphone and gave a speech that was both premeditated and extemporaneous. I tried to remember what I'd prepared to say all the other times I thought I might win.

"Thank you," I said, looking out into a sea of familiar, gorgeous faces. "Thank you not just for this award, which I will cherish forever, but also for letting me work in this business. It hasn't always been easy, and God knows I've made a bumpy road of it, but I feel so incredibly lucky to live this life. So thank you not just to every producer I've worked with since the mid-fifties—oh, God, I'm really dating myself here—but specifically to my favorite producer, Harry Cameron. I love you. I love our child. Hi, Connor. Go to sleep now, honey. It's getting late. And to all the other actors and actresses I've worked with, to all the directors who have helped me grow as a performer, especially Max Girard, I thank you. By the way, I believe this counts as a hat trick, Max. And there's one other person out there, whom I think of every day."

Ten years before, I would have been far too scared to say anything more. I probably would have been too scared even to say that. But I had to tell her. Even though I hadn't spoken to her in years. I had to show her that I still loved her. That I always would.

"I know she's watching right now. And I just hope she knows how important she is to me. Thank you all. Thank you."

Shaking, I walked backstage and got hold of myself. I talked to reporters. I accepted congratulations. And I got back to my seat just in time for Max to win Best Director and Harry to win Best Picture. Afterward, the three of us posed for photo after photo, grinning from ear to ear.

We had climbed to the very top of the mountain, and that night we stuck our flags into the summit.

S OMETIME AROUND ONE IN THE morning, after Harry had already gone back to the hotel to check on Connor, Max and I were outside in the courtyard of a mansion owned by the head of Paramount. There was a circular fountain, spraying water into the night sky. Max and I sat, marveling at what we had accomplished together. His limo pulled up.

"Can I give you a ride back to your hotel?" he asked.

"Where's your date?"

Max shrugged. "I fear she was only interested in the ticket to the show."

I laughed. "Poor Max."

"Not poor Max," he said, shaking his head. "I spent my evening with the most beautiful woman in the world."

I shook my head. "You are too much."

"You look hungry. Come get in the car. We will get hamburgers."

"Hamburgers?"

"I'm sure even Evelyn Hugo eats a hamburger from time to time."

Max opened the limo door and waited for me to get in. "Your chariot," he said.

I wanted to go home and see Connor. I wanted to watch the way her mouth hung open as she slept. But the idea of getting a hamburger with Max Girard actually didn't sound so bad.

Minutes later, the limo driver was trying to navigate the drive-through of a Jack in the Box, and Max and I decided it was easier to get out of the car and go in.

The two of us stood in line, me in my navy-blue silk gown, him in his tux, behind two teenage boys ordering french fries. And then, when we got to the front of the line, the cashier screamed as if she'd seen a mouse.

"Oh, my God!" she said. "You're Evelyn Hugo."

I laughed. "I have no idea what you're talking about," I said. After twenty-five years, that line still worked every time.

"You're her. Evelyn Hugo."

"Nonsense."

"This is the greatest day of my life," she said, and then she called to the back. "Norm, you have to come see this. Evelyn Hugo is here. In a gown."

Max laughed as more and more people started to stare. I was beginning to feel like a caged animal. It's not something you really ever get used to, being stared at in small spaces. A few of the people in the kitchen came forward to look at me.

"Any chance we could get two burgers?" Max said. "Extra cheese on mine, please."

Everyone ignored him.

"Can I have your autograph?" the woman behind the counter asked.

"Sure," I said kindly.

I was hoping it would be over soon, that we could get the food and go. I started signing paper menus and paper hats. I signed a couple of receipts.

"We really should be going," I said. "It's late." But no one stopped. They all just kept pushing things at me.

"You won an Oscar," an older woman said. "Just a few hours ago. I saw it. I saw it myself."

"I did, yes," I said. I pointed at Max with the pen in my hand. "So did he."

Max waved.

I signed a few more things, shook a few more hands. "OK, I really must be going," I said.

But the mob of people crowded me more.

"OK," Max said. "Let the lady breathe." I looked in the direction of his voice and saw him coming toward me, breaking up the crowd. He handed me the burgers, picked me up, threw me over his shoulder, and walked us right out of the restaurant and into the limo.

"Wow," I said when he put me down.

He got in next to me. He grabbed the bag. "Evelyn," he said.

"What?"

"I love you."

"What do you mean, you love me?"

He leaned over, smooshed the burgers, and kissed me.

It felt as if someone had turned on the electricity in a long-abandoned building. I had not been kissed like that since Celia left me. I had not been kissed with desire, the kind of desire that spurs desire, since the love of my life walked out the door.

And here was Max, two deformed burgers in between us, his warm lips on mine.

"That is what I mean," he said when he pulled away from me. "Do with that what you will."

THE NEXT MORNING, I woke up as an Oscar winner with a precious six-year-old eating room service in my bed.

There was a knock at the door. I grabbed my robe. I opened the door. In front of me were two-dozen red roses with a note that said, "I have loved you since I met you. I have tried to stop. It will not work. Leave him, *ma belle*. Marry me. Please. XO, M."

W E SHOULD STOP THERE," EVELYN says.

She's right. It is getting late, and I suspect I have a number of missed calls and e-mails to return, including what I know will be a voice mail from David.

"OK," I say, closing my notebook and pressing stop on the recording.

Evelyn gathers some of the papers and stale coffee mugs that have accumulated over the day.

I check my phone. Two missed calls from David. One from Frankie. One from my mother.

I say good-bye to Evelyn and make my way onto the street.

The air is warmer than I anticipated, so I take off my coat. I pull my phone out of my pocket. I listen to my mother's voice mail first. Because I'm not sure I'm ready to know what David has to say. I don't know what I *want* him to say, and thus, I don't know what will disappoint me when he doesn't say it.

"Hi, honey," my mom says. "I'm just calling to remind you that I'll be there soon! My flight gets in Friday evening. And I know you're going to insist on meeting me at the airport because of that time I got lost on the subway, but don't worry about it. Really. I can figure out how to get to my daughter's apartment from JFK. Or LaGuardia. Oh, God, you don't think I accidentally booked the flight to Newark, do you? No, I didn't. I wouldn't have. Anyway, I'm so excited to see you, my little dumpling baby. I love you."

I'm already laughing before the message is over. My mother has gotten lost in New York a number of times, not just once. And it's always because she refuses to take a cab. She insists that she can navigate public transportation, even though she was born and raised in Los Angeles and therefore has no real sense of how any two modes of transportation intersect.

Also, I have always hated it when she called me her dumpling baby. Mostly because we both know it's a reference to how fat I was as a child; I looked like an overstuffed dumpling.

By the time her message is over and I'm done texting her back (*So excited to see you! Will meet you at the airport. Just tell me which one*), I'm at the subway station.

I could easily make the argument to myself that I should listen to David's voice mail when I get to Brooklyn. And I almost do. I very nearly do. But instead, I stand outside the stairwell and hit play.

"Hey," he says, his gravelly voice so familiar. "I texted you. But I didn't hear back. I . . . I'm in New York. I'm home. I mean, I'm here at the apartment. Our apartment. Or . . . your apartment. Whatever. I'm here. Waiting for you. I know it's short notice. But don't you think we should talk about things? Don't you think there's more to say? I'm just rambling now, so I'm going to go. But hopefully I'll see you soon."

When the message is over, I run down the stairs, swipe my card, and slip onto the train just as it's leaving. I pack myself into the crowded car and try to calm down as we roar through each stop.

What the hell is he doing home?

I get off the train and make my way to the street. I put my coat on when I hit the fresh air. Brooklyn feels colder than Manhattan tonight.

I try not to run to my apartment. I try to remain calm, to remain composed. *There is no need for you to rush,* I tell myself. Besides, I don't want to show up out of breath, and I really don't want to ruin my hair.

I head through the front entrance and up the stairs to my apartment.

I slip my key into my door.

And there he is.

David.

In my kitchen, cleaning dishes as if he lives here.

"Hi," I say, staring at him.

He looks exactly the same. Blue eyes, thick lashes, cropped hair. He is wearing a maroon heathered T-shirt and dark gray jeans.

When I met him, as we fell in love, I remember thinking that the fact that he was white made things easier because I knew he would never tell me I wasn't black enough. I think of Evelyn the first time she heard her maid speaking Spanish.

I remember thinking that the fact that he wasn't that well read meant he would never think I was a bad writer. I think of Celia telling Evelyn she wasn't a good actress.

I remember thinking that the fact that I was clearly the more attractive one made me feel better, because I thought that meant he'd never leave. I think of how Don treated Evelyn despite her being, arguably, the most beautiful woman in the world.

Evelyn rose to those challenges.

But looking at David right now, I can see that I have hidden from them.

Perhaps my entire life.

"Hi," he says.

I can't help but vomit the words out of my mouth. I do not have the time or energy or restraint to curate them well or deliver them mildly. "What are you doing here?" I say.

David puts the bowl in his hand into the cupboard and then turns back to me. "I came back to iron out a few things," he says.

"And I am something to iron out?" I ask.

I put my bag down in the corner. I kick off my shoes.

"You're something I need to set right," he says. "I made a mistake. I think we both did."

Why, until this moment, did I not realize that the issue is my own confidence? That the root of most of my problems is that I need to be secure enough in who I am to tell anyone who doesn't like it to go fuck themselves? Why have I spent so long settling for less when I know damn well the world expects more?

"I didn't make a mistake," I say. And it surprises me just as much as, if not more than, it surprises him.

"Monique, we were both acting rash. I was upset that you wouldn't move to San Francisco. Because I felt like I had earned the right to ask you to sacrifice for me, for my career."

I start formulating a response, but David keeps talking.

"And you were upset that I would ask that of you in the first place, because I know how important your life is here. But . . . there are other ways to handle this. We can do long-distance for a little while. And eventually I can move back here, or you can move to San Francisco down the line. We have options. That's all I'm saying. We don't have to get a divorce. We don't have to give up on this."

I sit down on the couch, fiddling with my hands as I think. Now that he says it, I realize what has made me so sad these past few weeks, what has plagued me and made me feel so terrible about myself.

It isn't rejection.

And it isn't heartbreak.

It is defeat.

I wasn't heartbroken when Don left me. I simply felt like my marriage had failed. And those are very different things.

Evelyn said that just last week.

And now I understand why it got under my skin.

I have been reeling because I failed. Because I picked the wrong guy for me. Because I entered the wrong marriage. Because the truth is that at the age of thirty-five, I have yet to love someone enough to sacrifice for them. I've yet to open my heart enough to let someone in that much.

Some marriages aren't really that great. Some loves aren't all-encompassing. Sometimes you separate because you weren't that good together to begin with.

Sometimes divorce isn't an earth-shattering loss. Sometimes it's just two people waking up out of a fog.

"I don't think . . . I think you should go home to San Francisco," I say to him finally.

David comes and joins me on the couch.

"And I think I should stay here," I say. "And I don't think a long-distance marriage is the right play. I think . . . I think divorce is the right play."

"Monique . . ."

"I'm sorry," I say as he takes my hand. "I wish I didn't feel that way. But I suspect, deep down, you think it, too. Because you didn't come here and tell me how much you miss me. Or how hard it has been to live without me. You said you didn't want to give up. And look, I don't want to give up, either. I don't want to fail at this. But that's not actually a great reason to stay together. We should have reasons *why* we don't want to give up. It shouldn't just be *that* we don't want to give up. And I don't . . . I don't have any." I'm unsure how to say what I want to say gently. So I just say it. "You have never felt like my other half."

It is only once David gets up off the sofa that I realize I assumed we would be sitting here talking for a long time. And it is only once he puts on his jacket that I realize he probably assumed he would sleep here tonight.

But once he has his hand on the doorknob, I realize that I have put into motion the end of a lackluster life in the interest of eventually finding a great one.

"I hope one day you find someone who feels like the other half of you, I guess," David says.

Like Celia.

"Thank you," I say. "I hope you find it, too."

David smiles in a way that is more of a frown. And then he leaves.

When you end a marriage, you're supposed to lose sleep over it, aren't you?

But I don't. I sleep free.

I GET A call from Frankie the next morning just as I'm sitting down at Evelyn's. I consider putting it through to voice mail, but there's already too much swirling around in my brain. To add *Call back Frankie* might just put me over the edge. Better to handle it now. Have it behind me.

"Hi, Frankie," I say.

"Hey," she says. Her voice is light, almost cheerful. "So we need to schedule the photographers. I assume Evelyn will want them to come to her there at the apartment?"

"Oh, that's a good question," I say. "One second." I mute my phone and turn to Evelyn. "They are asking when and where you'll want to do the photo shoot."

"Here is fine," Evelyn says. "Let's aim for Friday."

"That's three days away."

"Yes, I believe Friday comes after Thursday. Do I have that right?"

I smile and shake my head at her and then unmute Frankie. "Evelyn says here at the apartment on Friday."

"Late morning, maybe," Evelyn says. "Eleven."

"Eleven, OK?" I say to Frankie.

Frankie agrees. "Absolutely fantastic!"

I hang up and look at Evelyn. "You want to do a photo shoot in three days?"

"No, *you* want me to do a photo shoot, remember?"

"You're sure about Friday, though?"

"We'll be done by then," Evelyn says. "You'll have to work even later than normal. I'll make sure Grace has those muffins you like and the coffee from Peet's that I know you prefer."

"OK," I say. "That's fine, but there's still a lot of ground to cover."

"Don't worry. We'll be done by Friday."

When I look at her skeptically, she says, "You should be happy, Monique. You're going to get your answers."

WHEN HARRY READ THE NOTE Max had sent me, he was stunned silent. At first, I thought I had hurt his feelings by showing it to him. But then I realized he was thinking.

We had taken Connor to a playground in Coldwater Canyon in Beverly Hills. Our flight back to New York left in a few hours. Connor was playing on the swings as Harry and I watched her.

"Nothing would change between us," he said. "If we divorced."

"But, Harry . . ."

"John is gone. Celia is gone. There is no need to hide behind double dates. Nothing would change."

"*We* would change," I said, watching Connor pump her legs harder, swing higher.

Harry was watching her through his sunglasses, smiling at her. He waved to her. "Good job, honey," he called out. "Remember to keep your hands tight on the chains if you're gonna go that high."

He had started to control his drinking a bit. He had learned to pick and choose his moments of indulgence. And he never let anything get in the way of his work or his daughter. But I still worried about what he'd do if left too much to his own devices.

He turned to me. "We wouldn't change, Ev. I promise you that. I would live in my house, just like now. You'd live in yours. I'd come by every day. Connor would sleep at my place the nights she wanted. If anything, appearances-wise, it might make more sense. Pretty soon people are going to start asking why we own two different houses."

"Harry—"

"You do what you want. If you don't want to be with Max, don't be. I'm just saying that there are some fairly good reasons for us to get divorced. And not many cons, except that I won't call you my wife anymore, which I've always been so proud to do. But we will still be as we've always been. A family. And . . . I think it would be good for you to fall in love with someone. You deserve to be loved that way."

"So do you."

Harry smiled sorrowfully. "I had my love. And he's gone. But for you, I think it's time. Maybe it will be Max, maybe it won't. But maybe it should be somebody."

"I don't like the idea of divorcing you," I said. "No matter how meaningless it might actually be."

"Dad, watch," Connor said as she flung her legs into the air, swung high, and then leaped, landing on her feet. She nearly gave me a heart attack.

Harry laughed. "Outstanding!" he said to her, and then he turned to me. "Sorry. I might have taught her that."

"I figured."

Connor got back onto the swing, and Harry leaned toward me and put his arm around my shoulders. "I know you don't like the idea of divorcing me," he said. "But I think you do like the idea of marrying Max. Otherwise, I don't think you would have bothered to show me that note."

"Are you really serious about this?" I asked.

Max and I were back in New York, at his apartment. It had been three weeks since he had told me he loved me.

"I am very serious," Max said. "What is the saying? As serious as cancer?"

"A heart attack."

"Fine. I am as serious as a heart attack."

"We barely know each other," I said.

"We have known each other since 1960, *ma belle*. You simply do not realize how much time has passed. That's more than twenty years."

I was in my midforties. Max was a few years older. With a daughter and a fake husband, I thought falling in love again was out of the question for me. I wasn't sure how it would ever happen.

And here was a man, a handsome man, a man I did rather like, a man I shared a history with, who was saying he loved me.

"So you're suggesting I leave Harry? Just like that? Because of what we think might be between us?"

Max frowned at me. "I am not as stupid as you think I am," he said.

"I don't think you're stupid at all."

"Harry is a homosexual," he said.

I felt my body pull back, as far away from him as possible. "I have no idea what you're talking about," I said.

Max laughed. "That line didn't work when we were getting burgers, and it won't work now."

"Max . . ."

"Do you enjoy spending time with me?"

"Of course I do."

"And do you not agree that we understand each other, creatively speaking?"

"Of course."

"Have I not directed you in three of the most important films of your career?"

"You have."

"And do you think that is an accident?"

I thought about it. "No," I said. "It's not."

"No, it isn't," he said. "It's because I *see* you. It is because I ache for you. It is because, from the very moment I set my eyes on you, my body was full of desire for you. It is because I have been falling in love with you for decades. The camera sees you as I see you. And when that happens, you soar."

"You're a talented director."

"Yes, of course, I am," he said. "But only because you inspire me. You, my Evelyn Hugo, are the talent that powers every movie you are in. You are my muse. And I am your conductor. I am the person who brings out your greatest work."

I breathed in deeply, considering what he was saying. "You're right," I said. "You are absolutely right."

"I can't think of anything more erotic than that," he said. "Than being each other's inspiration." He leaned in close to me. I could feel the heat of him on my skin. "And I can think of nothing more meaningful than the way we understand each other. You should leave Harry. He will be fine. No one knows what he is, and even if they do, no one's talking. He doesn't need you to protect him anymore. *I* need you, Evelyn. I need you so badly," he whispered into my ear. The heat of his breath, the way his stubble scratched my cheek, awakened me.

I grabbed him. I kissed him. I pulled my shirt off. I tore his. I unfastened the belt of his pants, flinging the buckle. I ripped apart the button fly of my jeans. I pushed myself against him.

The way he grabbed me back, the way he moved, made it clear he was yearning for me, that he couldn't believe his luck to be touching me. When I pulled off the straps of my bra and exposed my breasts, he looked me in the eye and then placed his hands on my chest as if he'd unlocked a hidden treasure.

It felt so good. To be touched like that. To set free my desire. He lay down on the couch, and I sat on top of him, moving the way I wanted to, taking what I needed from him, feeling pleasure for the first time in years.

It felt like water in the desert.

When it was over, I didn't want to be apart from him. I wanted to never leave his side.

"You'd be a stepfather," I said. "Do you get that?"

"I love Connor," Max said. "I love children. So to me, that is a benefit."

"And Harry will always be around. He will never go away. He's a constant."

"He does not bother me. I've always liked Harry."

"I'd want to stay in my house," I said. "Not here. I won't uproot Connor."

"Fine," he said.

I was quiet. I didn't know exactly what I wanted. Except that I wanted more of him. I wanted the experience of him again. I kissed him. I moaned. I eased him on top of me. I closed my eyes, and for the first time in years, when I closed them, I did not see Celia.

"Yes," I said as he made love to me. "I'll marry you."

Disappointing Max Girard

◆

EVELYN HUGO DIVORCES HARRY CAMERON, TO MARRY DIRECTOR MAX GIRARD

Evelyn Hugo is the marrying kind! After 15 years of marriage, she and producer Harry Cameron are going their separate ways. The two have just come off a winning streak, both taking home Oscar gold earlier this year for their film *All for Us*.

But sources claim Evelyn and Harry have been separated for some time. Their marriage turned into little more than a friendship within the past few years. Some are claiming that Harry has been living in the home of their late friend John Braverman, just down the street from Evelyn.

Meanwhile, Evelyn must have used that time to warm up to Max Girard, her director on *All for Us*. The two have announced plans to marry. Only time will tell if Max is the lucky ticket to happiness for Evelyn. But what we do know is that he will be husband number six.

MAX AND I GOT MARRIED in Joshua Tree, with Connor, Harry, and Max's brother, Luc. Max had originally suggested Saint-Tropez or Barcelona for our wedding and honeymoon. But both of us had just finished movies shooting in Los Angeles, and I thought it sounded nice, just a small group of us in the desert.

I dispensed with white, having long ago stopped feigning innocence. Instead, I wore an ocean-blue maxi dress, my blond hair feathered ever so slightly. I was forty-four.

Connor wore a flower in her hair. Harry stood next to her in dress pants and a button-down.

Max, my groom, wore white linen. We joked that it was his first wedding, so he should be the one to wear white.

That evening, Harry and Connor flew back to New York. Luc flew back to his home in Lyon. Max and I stayed in a cabin, a rare night alone.

We made love on the bed, on the desk, and, in the middle of the night, on the porch underneath the stars.

In the morning, we ate grapefruit and played cards. We flipped channels on the television. We laughed. We talked about movies we loved, movies we'd shot, movies we wanted to make.

Max said he had an idea for an action movie starring me. I told him I wasn't sure I was fit to be an action hero.

"I'm in my forties, Max," I said. We were walking in the desert, the sun beating down on us. I had forgotten the water in the cabin.

"You are ageless," he said to me, kicking up sand as we went. "You can do anything. You are Evelyn Hugo."

"I'm Evelyn," I told him. I stopped in place. I grabbed his hand. "You don't always need to call me Evelyn Hugo."

"But that is who you are," he said. "You are *the* Evelyn Hugo. You are extraordinary."

I smiled and kissed him. I was so relieved to feel loved, to feel love. I was so exhilarated by wanting to be with someone again. I thought Celia would never come back to me. But Max, he was right there. He was mine.

When we got back to the cabin, the two of us were sunburned and parched. I made us peanut butter and jelly for dinner, and we sat in bed and watched the news. It felt so peaceful. Nothing to prove, nothing to hide.

We went to sleep with Max cradling me. I could feel his heartbeat against my back.

But the next morning, when I woke up and my hair was out of place and my breath smelled, I looked over at him, expecting to see a smile on his face. Instead, he looked stoic, as if he had been staring at the ceiling for hours.

"What's on your mind?" I said.

"Nothing."

His chest hair was graying. I thought it made him look regal.

"What is it?" I said. "You can tell me."

He turned and looked at me. I fixed my hair, feeling somewhat embarrassed at how unkempt I looked. He looked back up at the ceiling.

"This is not how I imagined it."

"What did you imagine?"

"You," he said. "I imagined the glory of a life with you."

"And now you don't?"

"No, that's not it," he said, shaking his head. "Can I be honest? I think I hate the desert. There is too much sun and no good food, and why are we here? We are city people, my love. We should go home."

I laughed, relieved that it wasn't anything more. "We still have three days here," I said.

"Yes, yes, I know, *ma belle*, but please, let us go home."

"Early?"

"We can get a room at the Waldorf for a few days. Instead of here."

"OK," I said. "If you're sure."

"I'm sure," he said. And then he got up and took a shower.

Later on, at the airport as we waited to board, Max went to buy something to read on the flight. He came back with *People* magazine and showed me the write-up of our wedding.

They called me a "daring sexpot" and Max my "white knight."

"Pretty cool, no?" he said. "We look like royalty. You look so beautiful in this picture. But of course you do. That's who you are."

I smiled, but all I could think about was Rita Hayworth's famous line. *Men go to bed with Gilda, but wake up with me.*

"I think maybe I will lose a few pounds," he said, patting his belly. "I want to be handsome for you."

"You *are* handsome," I said. "You've always been handsome."

"No," he said, shaking his head. "Look at this photo they have of me. I look like I have three chins."

"It's just a bad picture. You look marvelous in person. I wouldn't change a single thing about you, really."

But Max wasn't listening. "I think I will stop eating fried foods. I have gotten too American, don't you think? I want to be handsome for you."

But he didn't mean handsome for *me*. He meant handsome for the pictures he'd be taking *with* me.

My heart tore just a little as we boarded the plane. It split further and further as I watched him read the magazine during the flight.

Just before we landed, a man flying in coach came up to first class to use the bathroom and did a double take when he saw me. When he was gone, Max turned to me, smiling, and said, "Do you think all these people are going to go home and tell everyone they were on a flight with Evelyn Hugo?"

The moment he was done saying it, my heart had completely torn in half.

*   *   *

IT TOOK ME about four months to realize that Max had no intention of even *trying* to love me, that he was only capable of loving the *idea* of me. And then, after that, it seems so silly to say it, but I didn't want to leave him, because I didn't want to get divorced.

I'd only married a man I loved once before. This was only the second time in my life I had gone into a marriage believing it could last. And after all, I hadn't left Don. Don had left me.

With Max, I thought that something might change, something might click, something might make him see me as I truly was and love me for it. I thought maybe I could love the real him enough that he'd start loving the real me.

I thought I could finally have a meaningful marriage with someone.

But that never happened.

Instead, Max paraded me around town like the trophy I was. Everyone wanted Evelyn Hugo, and Evelyn Hugo wanted him.

That girl in *Boute-en-Train* mesmerized everybody. Even the man who created her. And I didn't know how to tell him that I loved her, too. But I wasn't her.

I N 1988, CELIA TOOK THE role of Lady Macbeth in a film adaptation. She could have submitted herself for Best Actress. There was no other woman with a bigger part in the movie than her. But she must have submitted herself for Best Supporting, because when the ballot came out, that was what she was nominated for. The moment I saw it, I knew it had been her call. She was just that smart.

Naturally, I voted for her.

When she won, I was in New York with Connor and Harry. Max had gone to the awards that year alone. It was a fight between the two of us. He wanted me with him, but I wanted to spend the evening with my family, not in a control slip and six-inch heels.

Also, if I'm being entirely frank, I was fifty years old. There was an entire new generation of actresses to compete with. They were all gorgeous, with smooth skin and shiny hair. When you are known for being gorgeous, you cannot imagine suffering a fate worse than standing next to someone and falling short.

It did not matter how beautiful I used to be. The clock was ticking, and everyone could see it.

My roles were starting to dry up. The parts I was being offered were the mothers of the great roles being offered to women literally half my age. Life in Hollywood is a bell curve, and I had prolonged my time at the top for as long as possible. I'd lasted longer than most. But I had come around the corner now. And they were all but putting me out to pasture.

So no, I did not want to go to the Academy Awards. Instead of flying to L.A. and spending the day in a makeup chair and then sucking in and standing up straight in front of hundreds of cameras and millions of eyes, I spent the day with my daughter.

Luisa was on vacation, and we had not found someone we liked to step in for her, so Connor and I spent the day making a game out of cleaning the house. We made dinner together. Afterward, we popped some popcorn and sat down with Harry to watch as Celia won.

Celia was wearing a yellow silk dress with a ruffled edge. Her red hair, now shorter, was pulled back in a chignon. She was older, certainly, but never more breathtaking. When they called her name, she got up on the stage and accepted her award with the grace and sincerity that audiences had always known her for. And just as she was about to leave the microphone, she said, "And to anyone tempted to kiss the TV tonight, please don't chip your tooth."

"Mom, why are you crying?" Connor asked.

I put my hand to my face and realized that I had teared up.

Harry smiled at me and rubbed my back. "You should call her," he said. "It's never a bad idea to bury hatchets."

Instead, I wrote a letter.

> *My Dearest Celia,*
> *Congratulations! You absolutely deserve it. There is no doubt you are the most talented actress of our generation.*
> *I wish for nothing more than your complete and total happiness. I did not kiss the TV this time, but I did cheer just as loudly as I did the other times.*
>
> > *All my love,*
> > ~~*Edward*~~
> > *Evelyn*

I sent it with the peace of sending off a message in a bottle. Which is to say that I expected no response. But a week later, there it was. A small, square, cream-colored envelope addressed to me.

My Dearest Evelyn,

Reading your letter felt like gasping for air after being trapped under water. I hope you will forgive me for being so blunt, but how did we make such a mess of it all? And what does it mean that we have not spoken in a decade but I still hear your voice in my head every day?

XO,
Celia

My Dearest Celia,

I own all of our missteps. I was selfish and shortsighted. I can only hope that you have found bliss somewhere else. You deserve so much happiness. And I am sorry I could not give that to you.

Love,
Evelyn

My Dearest Evelyn,

You are dealing in revisionist history. I was insecure and petty and naive. I blamed you for the things you did to keep our secrets. But the truth is, each time you stopped the outside world from coming into our life, I felt immense relief. And all my happiest moments were orchestrated by you. I never gave you enough credit for that. We were both to blame. But you were the only one to ever apologize. Please let me rectify that now: I'm sorry, Evelyn.

Love,
Celia

P.S. I watched Three A.M. *some months ago. It is a bold, brave, important film. I would have been wrong to stand in the way of it. You have always been so much more talented than I ever gave you credit for.*

My Dearest Celia,

Do you think lovers can ever be friends? I hate to think of the years we have left in this life wasted by continuing not to speak.

Love,
Evelyn

My Dearest Evelyn,

Is Max like Harry? Like Rex?

Love,
Celia

My Dearest Celia,

I am sorry to say that no, he's not. He is different. But I am desperate to see you. Can we meet?

Love,
Evelyn

My Dearest Evelyn,

To be frank, that news breaks me. I do not know if I could bear seeing you given those circumstances.

Love,
Celia

My Dearest Celia,

I have called you many times in the past week, but you have not returned my calls. I'll try again. Please, Celia. Please.

Love,
Evelyn

"H ELLO?" HER VOICE SOUNDED EXACTLY like it used to. Sweet but somehow firm.

"It's me," I said.

"Hi." The way she warmed up in that moment made me hopeful that I might be able to put my life back together, the way it should have always been.

"I did love him," I said. "Max. But I don't anymore."

The line was quiet.

Then she asked, "What are you saying?"

"I'm saying I'd like to see you."

"I can't see you, Evelyn."

"Yes, you can."

"What do you want us to do?" she said. "Ruin each other all over again?"

"Do you still love me?" I asked.

She was silent.

"I still love you, Celia. I swear I do."

"I . . . I don't think we should talk about this. Not if . . ."

"Not if what?"

"Nothing has changed, Evelyn."

"Everything has changed."

"People still can't know who we really are."

"Elton John is out of the closet," I said. "Has been for years."

"Elton John doesn't have a child and a career based on audiences believing he's a straight man."

"You're saying we'll lose our jobs?"

"I can't believe I have to tell you this," she said.

"Well, let me tell you something that *has* changed," I told her. "I no longer care. I'm ready to give it all up."

"You can't be serious."

"I'm absolutely serious."

"Evelyn, we haven't even seen each other in years."

"I know you were able to forget me," I said. "I know you were with Joan. I'm sure you were with others." I waited, hoping she would correct me, hoping she would tell me there had been no one else. But she didn't. And so I continued. "But can you honestly say that you stopped loving me?"

"Of course not."

"And I can't say that, either. I have loved you every single day."

"You married someone else."

"I married him because he helped me forget you," I said. "Not because I stopped loving you."

I heard Celia breathe deeply.

"I'll come to L.A.," I said. "And you and I will have dinner. OK?"

"Dinner?" she said.

"Just dinner. We have things to talk about. I think we at least owe each other a nice, long talk. How about the week after next? Harry can watch Connor. I can stay for a few days."

Celia was quiet again. I could tell she was thinking. I got the impression that this was a deciding moment for my future, our future.

"OK," she said. "Dinner."

THE MORNING I left for the airport, Max slept in late. He was supposed to be on set later in the afternoon for a night shoot, so I squeezed his hand good-bye and then grabbed my things from the closet.

I couldn't decide if I wanted to take Celia's letters with me or not. I had kept them all, with their envelopes, in a box at the back of my closet. Over the past few days, as I was gathering what I would take, I packed them and then unpacked them, trying to decide.

I had been rereading them every day since Celia and I started talking. I didn't want to be apart from them. I liked to run my fingers over the words, feeling the way the pen had embossed the paper. I liked hearing her voice in my head. But I was flying to see her. So I decided I didn't need them.

I put on my boots and grabbed my jacket, then unzipped my bag and pulled the letters out. I hid them behind my furs.

I left Max a note: "I will be back on Thursday, Maximilian. Love, Evelyn."

Connor was in the kitchen, grabbing Pop-Tarts before heading over to Harry's house to stay while I was gone.

"Doesn't your dad have Pop-Tarts?" I asked.

"Not the brown sugar kind. He gets the strawberry ones, and I hate those."

I grabbed her and kissed her on the cheek. "Good-bye. Be good while I'm gone," I said.

She rolled her eyes at me, and I wasn't sure if it was for the kiss or the directive. She had just turned thirteen, beginning her ascent into adolescence, and it was already breaking my heart.

"Yeah, yeah, yeah," she said. "I'll see ya when I see ya."

I went down to the sidewalk to find my limo waiting. I gave the driver my bag, and at the very last minute, it occurred to me that after my dinner with Celia, she might tell me she didn't want to see me again. She might tell me she didn't think we should talk anymore. I might be on the flight back, aching for her more than I ever had. I decided I wanted the letters. I wanted them with me. I needed them.

"Hold on, one moment," I said to the driver, and I dashed back into the house. I caught Connor coming out of the elevator just as I was going in.

"Back so soon?" she said, her knapsack on her back.

"I forgot something. Have fun this weekend, sweetheart. Tell your dad I'll be home in a few days."

"Yeah, OK. Max just woke up, by the way."

"I love you," I said to her as I pushed the button in the elevator.

"I love you, too," Connor said. She waved good-bye and headed out the front entrance.

I made my way upstairs and walked into the bedroom. And there, in my closet, was Max.

Celia's letters, which I had kept in such pristine condition, were flung about the room, most of them torn from the envelopes as if they were nothing more than junk mail.

"What are you doing?" I said.

He was in a black T-shirt and sweatpants. "What am *I* doing?" he said. "That is too much. You coming in here asking *me* what *I* am doing."

"Those are mine."

"Oh, I see that, *ma belle.*"

I leaned down and tried to take them from him. He pulled them away.

"You are having an affair?" he said, smiling. "How very French of you."

"Max, stop it."

"I do not mind some infidelity, my dear. If it is respectfully done. And one does not leave evidence."

The way he said it, I realized he had slept with people outside our marriage, and I wondered if any woman was ever really safe from men like Max and Don. I thought of how many women out there thought they could prevent their husbands from cheating if only they were as gorgeous as Evelyn Hugo. But it never stopped any man I loved.

"I am not cheating on you, Max. So would you cut it out?"

"Maybe you are not," he said. "I suppose I can believe that. But what I can't believe is that you are a dyke."

I closed my eyes, my anger burning so hot inside me that I needed to check out of the world, to momentarily gather myself in my own body.

"I am not a dyke," I said.

"These letters beg to differ."

"Those letters are none of your business."

"Maybe," Max said. "If these letters are just Celia St. James talking to you about her feelings for you in the past, then I am in the wrong here.

And I will put them away right now, and I will apologize to you immediately."

"Good."

"I said *if*." He stood up and came closer to me. "It is a big *if*. If these letters were sent leading up to you deciding to visit Los Angeles today, then I am angry, because you are playing me for a fool."

I really do think that if I told him I had absolutely no intention of seeing Celia in Los Angeles, if I really sold it well, he would have backed off. He might have even said he was sorry and driven me to the airport himself.

And that was my gut instinct, to lie, to hide, to cover up what I was doing and who I was. But just as I opened my mouth to feed him a line, something else came out.

"I was going to see her. You're right."

"You were going to cheat on me?"

"I was going to leave you," I said. "I think you know that. I think you've known that for some time. I am going to leave you. If not for her, for me."

"For her?" he said.

"I love her. I always have."

Max looked floored, as if he had been pushing me in this game, assuming I'd forfeit. He shook his head in disbelief. "Wow," he said. "Incredible. I married a dyke."

"Stop saying that," I said.

"Evelyn, if you have sex with women, you are a lesbian. Don't be a self-hating lesbian. That's not . . . that's not becoming."

"I don't care what you think is becoming. I don't hate lesbians at all. I'm in love with one. But I loved you, too."

"Oh, please," he said. "Please don't try to make me any more of a fool than you already have. I have spent years loving you, only to find it meant nothing to you."

"You didn't love me for one goddamn day," I said. "You loved having a movie star on your arm. You loved getting to be the one who slept in my bed. That's not love. That's possession."

"I have no idea what you're talking about," he said.

"Of course you don't," I said. "Because you don't know the difference between the two."

"Did you ever love me?"

"Yes, I did. When you made love to me and you made me feel desire and you took good care of my daughter and I believed that you saw something in me that no one else saw. When I believed you had an insight and a talent that no one else had. I loved you very much."

"So you are not a lesbian," he said.

"I don't want to discuss this with you."

"Well, you're going to. You have to."

"No," I said, gathering the letters and envelopes and shoving them into my pockets. "I don't."

"Yes," he said, blocking the door. "You do."

"Max, get out of my way. I'm leaving."

"Not to see her," he said. "You can't."

"Of course I can."

The phone started ringing, but I was too far away to answer it. I knew it was the driver. I knew that if I didn't leave, I might miss my flight. There would be other flights, but I wanted to catch that one. I wanted to get to Celia as soon as possible.

"Evelyn, stop," Max said. "Think about this. It makes no sense. You can't leave me. I could make one phone call and destroy you. I could tell anyone, anyone at all, about this, and your life would never be the same."

He wasn't threatening me. He was simply explaining to me what was so clearly obvious. It was as if he was saying, *Honey, you're not thinking clearly. That won't end well for you.*

"You're a good man, Max," I said. "I can see you being angry enough to try to hurt me. But I've known you to at least *try* to do the right thing most of the time."

"And what if this time I don't?" he said. And there, finally, was the threat.

"I'm leaving you, Max. It either happens now or it happens later, but it's happening sometime. If you decide you want to try to bring me down over it, then I guess that's just what you'll have to do."

When he wouldn't move, I shoved him out of the way and walked right past him out the door.

The love of my life was waiting, and I was going to go get her back.

WHEN I GOT TO SPAGO, Celia was already seated. She was wearing black slacks and a gauzy cream-colored sleeveless blouse. The temperature outside was a warm seventy-eight degrees, but the restaurant's air-conditioning was on high, and she looked just a little bit cold. Her arms were covered in goose bumps.

Her red hair was still stunning but now clearly dyed. The golden undertones that had been there before, the result of nature and sunlight, were now slightly saturated, coppery. Her blue eyes were just as enticing as they always had been, but now the skin around them was softer.

I'd been to a plastic surgeon a few times in the past several years. I suspected she had, too. I was wearing a deep-V-necked black dress, belted at the waist. My blond hair, a bit lighter now from the gray that had been creeping in and cut shorter, was framing my face.

She stood when she saw me. "Evelyn," she said.

I hugged her. "Celia."

"You look great," she said. "You always do."

"You look just like you did the last time I saw you," I said.

"We never did tell each other lies," she said, smiling. "Let's not start now."

"You're gorgeous," I said.

"Ditto."

I ordered a glass of white wine. She ordered a club soda with lime.

"I don't drink anymore," Celia said. "It's not sitting with me the way it once did."

"That's fine. If you want, I can toss my wine right out the window the moment it gets to the table."

"No," she said, laughing. "Why should my low tolerance be your problem?"

"I want everything about you to be my problem," I said.

"Do you realize what you're saying?" she whispered to me as she leaned across the table. The neck of her blouse opened and dipped into the bread basket. I was worried it would graze the butter, but somehow it didn't.

"Of course I realize what I'm saying."

"You destroyed me," she said. "Twice now in our lives. I have spent years getting over you."

"Did you succeed? Either time?"

"Not completely."

"I think that means something."

"Why now?" she asked. "Why didn't you call years ago?"

"I called you a million times after you left me. I practically knocked down your door," I reminded her. "I thought you hated me."

"I did," she said. She pulled back a bit. "I still hate you, I think. At least a little bit."

"You think I don't hate you, too?" I tried to keep my voice down, tried to pretend it was a chat between two old friends. "Just a little bit?"

Celia smiled. "No, I suppose it would make sense that you do."

"But I'm not going to let that stop me," I said.

She sighed and looked at her menu.

I leaned in, conspiratorially. "I didn't think I had a shot before," I told her. "After you left me, I thought the door was closed. And now it's open a crack, and I want to swing it wide open and walk in."

"What makes you think the door is open?" she asked, looking at the left side of the menu.

"We are having dinner, aren't we?"

"As friends," she said.

"You and I have never been friends."

She closed her menu and put it down on the table. "I need reading glasses," she said. "Can you believe that? Reading glasses."

"Join the club."

"I can be mean sometimes when I'm hurt," she reminded me.

"You're not exactly telling me something I don't know."

"I made you feel like you weren't talented," she said. "I tried to make you think you needed me because I made you legitimate."

"I know that."

"But you've always been legitimate."

"I know that now, too," I told her.

"I thought you would call me after you won the Oscar. I thought maybe you would want to show me, you'd want to shove it in my face."

"Did you listen to my speech?"

"Of course I did," she said.

"I reached out to you," I said. I picked up a piece of bread and buttered it. But I put it down immediately, not taking a single bite.

"I wasn't sure," Celia said. "I mean, I wasn't sure if you meant me."

"I all but said your name."

"You said 'she.'"

"Precisely."

"I thought maybe you had another *she*."

I had looked at other women besides Celia. I had pictured myself with other women besides her. But everyone, for what had felt like my whole life, had always been divided into "Celia" and "not Celia." Every other woman I considered striking up a conversation with might as well have had "not Celia" stamped on her forehead. If I was going to risk my career and everything I loved for a woman, it was going to be her.

"There is no she but you," I told her.

Celia listened and closed her eyes. And then she spoke. It was as if she had tried to stop herself and simply couldn't. "But there were *hes*."

"This old song and dance," I said, trying to stop myself from rolling my eyes. "I was with Max. You were clearly with Joan. Did Joan hold a candle to me?"

"No," Celia said.

"And Max didn't hold a candle to you."

"But you're still married to him."

"I'm filing papers. He's moving out. It's over."

"That's abrupt."

"It's not, actually. It's overdue. And anyway, he found your letters," I said.

"And he's leaving you?"

"No, he's threatening to out me if I don't stay with him."

"What?"

"I'm leaving him," I said. "And I'm letting him do whatever the hell he wants. Because I'm fifty years old, and I don't have the energy to be controlling every single thing anyone says about me until I die of old age. The parts I'm being offered are shit. I have the Oscar on my mantel. I have a spectacular daughter. I have Harry. I'm a household name. They will write about my movies for years to come. What more do I want? A gold statue in my honor?"

Celia laughed. "That's what an Oscar is," she said.

I laughed, too. "Exactly! Excellent point. I already have that, then. There's nothing else, Celia. There are no more mountains to climb. I spent my life hiding so no one would knock me off the mountain. Well, you know what? I'm done hiding. Let them come and get me. They can throw me down a well as far as I'm concerned. I'm signed on to do one last movie over at Fox later this year, and then I'm done."

"You don't mean that."

"I do. Any other line of thinking . . . it's how I lost you. I don't want to lose anymore."

"It's not just our careers," she said. "The ramifications are unpredictable. What if they take Connor away?"

"Because I'm in love with a woman?"

"Because they think both her parents are 'queers.'"

I sipped my wine. "I can't win with you," I said finally. "If I want to hide, you call me a coward. If I'm tired of hiding, you tell me they'll take my daughter."

"I'm sorry," Celia said. She did not seem sorry for what she had said so much as sorry that we lived in the world we lived in. "Do you mean it?" she asked. "Would you really give it up?"

"Yes," I said. "Yes, I would."

"Are you absolutely sure?" she asked just as the waiter put her steak down in front of her and my salad in front of me. "I mean absolutely sure?"

"Yes."

Celia was quiet for a moment. She stared down at her plate. She seemed to be considering everything about this moment, and the longer she took to speak, the farther I found myself bending forward, trying to get closer to her.

"I have chronic obstructive pulmonary disease," she said finally. "I probably won't make it much past sixty."

I stared at her. "You're lying," I said.

"I'm not."

"Yes, you are. That can't be true."

"It is true."

"No, it's not," I said.

"It is," she said. She picked up her fork. She sipped the water in front of her.

My mind was reeling, thoughts bouncing around my brain, my heart spinning in my chest.

And then Celia spoke again, and the only reason I was able to focus on her words was that I knew they were important. I knew they mattered. "I think you should do your movie," she said. "Finish strong. And then . . . and then, after that, I think we should move to the coast of Spain."

"What?"

"I have always liked the idea of spending the last years of my life on a beautiful beach. With the love of a good woman," she said.

"You're . . . you're dying?"

"I can look into some locations in Spain while you're shooting. I'll find a place where Connor can get a great education. I'll sell my home here. I'll get a compound somewhere, with enough space for Harry, too. And Robert."

"Your brother Robert?"

Celia nodded. "He moved out here for business a few years ago. We've become close. He . . . he knows who I am. He supports me."

"What is chronic obstructive—?"

"Emphysema, more or less," she said. "From smoking. Do you still smoke? You should stop. Right now."

I shook my head, having long ago given it up.

"They have treatments to slow down the process. I can live a normal life for the most part, for a while."

"And then what?"

"And then, eventually, it will become difficult to be active, hard to breathe. When that happens, I won't have much time. All told, we're looking at ten years, give or take, if I'm lucky."

"Ten years? You're only forty-nine."

"I know."

I started crying. I couldn't help it.

"You're making a scene," she said. "You have to stop."

"I can't," I said.

"OK," she said. "OK."

She picked up her purse and threw down a hundred-dollar bill. She pulled me out of my chair, and we walked to the valet. She gave him her ticket. She put me in the front seat of the car. She drove me to her house. She sat me on the sofa.

"Can you handle this?" she said.

"What do you mean?" I asked her. "Of course I can't handle it."

"If you *can* handle this," she said, "then we can do this. We can be together. I think we can . . . we can spend the rest of our lives together, Evelyn. If you can handle this. But I can't, in good conscience, do this to you if you don't think you'll survive it."

"Survive what, exactly?"

"Losing me again. I don't want to let you love me if you don't think you can lose me again. One last time."

"I can't. Of course I can't. But I want to anyway. I'm going to anyway. Yes," I said finally. "I can survive it. I'd rather survive it than never feel it."

"Are you sure?" she said.

"Yes," I said. "Yes, I'm sure. I've never been more sure about anything. I love you, Celia. I've always loved you. And we should spend the rest of the time we have together."

She grabbed my face. She kissed me. And I wept.

She started crying with me, and soon I couldn't tell whether the tears I was tasting were hers or mine. All I knew was that I was once again in the arms of the woman I was always meant to love.

Eventually, Celia's blouse was on the floor and my dress was hiked up around my thighs. I could feel her lips on my chest, her hands on my stomach. I stepped out of my dress. Her sheets were stark white and perfectly soft. She no longer smelled like cigarettes and alcohol but like citrus.

In the morning, I woke up with her hair in my face, fanned across the pillow. I rolled to my side and curved my body against the back of hers.

"Here is what we're going to do," Celia said. "You're going to leave Max. I'm going to call a friend of mine in Congress. He's a representative from Vermont. He needs some press. You're going to be seen around with him. We're going to spread a rumor that you're stepping out on Max with a younger man."

"How old is he?"

"Twenty-nine."

"Jesus, Celia. He's a child," I said.

"That's exactly what people will say. They'll be shocked that you're dating him."

"And when Max tries to slander me?"

"It won't matter what he's trying to claim about you. It will look like he's just bitter."

"And then?" I asked.

"And then, down the line, you marry my brother."

"Why am I going to marry Robert?"

"So that when I die, everything I own will be yours. My estate will be under your control. And you can keep my legacy."

"You could appoint that to me."

"And have someone try to take it away because you were my lover? No. This is better. This is smarter."

"But marrying your brother? Are you crazy?"

"He'll do it," she said. "For me. And because he's a rake who likes to bed almost every woman he sees. You'd be good for his reputation. It's a win-win."

"All this instead of just telling the truth?"

I could feel Celia's rib cage expand and contract underneath me.

"We can't tell the truth. Did you see what they did to Rock Hudson? If it was cancer he was dying of, there'd be telethons."

"People don't understand AIDS," I said.

"They understand it just fine," Celia said. "They just think that he deserves it because of how he got it."

I rested my head on the pillow while my heart sank in my chest. She was right, of course. The past few years, I'd watched Harry lose friend after friend, former lovers, to AIDS. I'd watched him cry his eyes red out of fear that he'd get sick, for not knowing how to help the people he loved. And I'd watched Ronald Reagan never so much as acknowledge what was happening in front of our eyes.

"I know things have changed since the sixties," she said. "But they haven't changed that much. It wasn't that long ago that Reagan said gay rights weren't civil rights. You can't risk losing Connor. So I'll call Jack, my friend in the House of Representatives. We'll plant the story. You'll shoot your movie. You'll marry my brother. And we'll all move to Spain."

"I'll have to talk to Harry."

"Of course," she said. "Talk to Harry. If he hates Spain, we'll go to Germany. Or Scandinavia. Or Asia. I don't care. We just need to go somewhere where people won't care who we are, where people will leave us alone and Connor can live a normal childhood."

"You'll need medical care."

"I'll fly where I need to. Or we can bring people to me."

I thought about it. "It's a good plan."

"Yeah?" Celia was flattered, I could tell.

"The student has become the master," I said.

She laughed, and I kissed her.

"We're home," I said.

This wasn't my home. We'd never lived here together before. But she knew what I meant.

"Yes," she said. "We're home."

EVELYN HUGO AND MAX GIRARD DIVORCE TURNS UGLY AMID REPORTS OF HUGO CHEATING

Evelyn Hugo is headed to divorce court one more time. She filed papers citing "irreconcilable differences" this week. And while she's an old hand at this, it looks like this one's gonna be a doozy.

Sources say Max Girard is seeking spousal support, and reports have surfaced claiming that Girard is bad-mouthing Hugo all over town.

"He's so angry he's saying just about anything he can to get back at her," an insider close to the former couple says. "You name it, he's said it. She's a cheater, she's a lesbian, she owes him her Oscar. It's clear he's very heartbroken."

Hugo was recently seen out with a *much* younger man last week. Jack Easton, a Democratic congressman from Vermont, is only twenty-nine years old. That's more than *two decades* younger than Evelyn. And if the photos of their evening together out to dinner in Los Angeles are any indication, it looks like a blossoming romance.

Hugo doesn't have a great track record, but in this case, it seems like one thing is clear: Girard's comments certainly sound like sour grapes.

H ARRY WASN'T ON BOARD.
 He was the one piece of the plan that wasn't up to me, the one person I wasn't willing to manipulate into doing what I wanted him to do. And he didn't want to leave everything behind and fly off to Europe.

"You're suggesting I retire," Harry said. "And I'm not even sixty yet. My God, Evelyn. What on earth am I going to do all day? Play cards on the beach?"

"That doesn't sound nice?"

"It sounds nice for about an hour and a half," he said. He was drinking what looked like orange juice but I suspected was a screwdriver. "And then I'd be stuck trying to occupy myself for the rest of my life."

We were sitting in my dressing room on the set of *Theresa's Wisdom*. Harry had found the script and sold it to Fox with me attached to play Theresa, a woman who is leaving her husband while desperately trying to keep her children together.

It was the third day of shooting, and I was in costume, a white Chanel pantsuit and pearls, about to go on set to shoot the scene where Theresa and her husband announce that they are divorcing over Christmas dinner. Harry looked as handsome as ever in khaki slacks and an oxford shirt. He had gone almost entirely gray by then, and I actively resented him for growing more attractive as he aged, while I had to watch my value disappear by the day like a molding lemon.

"Harry, don't you want to stop living this lie?"

"What lie?" he asked. "I understand it's a lie for you. Because you want to make it work with Celia. And you know that I support that, I do. But this life isn't a lie for me."

"There are men," I said, my voice losing patience, as if Harry was trying to pull one over on me. "Don't pretend there aren't *men*."

"Sure, but there is not a single man anyone could draw any sort of meaningful connection to," Harry said. "Because I have only loved John. And he's gone. I'm only famous because you're famous, Ev. They don't care about me or what I'm doing unless it somehow relates to you. Any men in my life, I see them for a few weeks, and then they are gone. I'm not living a lie. I'm just living my life."

I took a deep breath, trying not to get too worked up before having to go on set and pretend to be a repressed WASP. "Don't you care that I have to hide?"

"I do," he said. "You know I do."

"Well, then—"

"But why does your relationship with Celia mean that we should uproot Connor's life? And mine?"

"She's the love of my life," I said. "You know that. I want to be with her. It's time for us all to be together again."

"We *can't* be together again," he said, putting his hand down on the table. "Not all of us." And he walked away.

HARRY AND I were flying home every weekend to be with Connor, and during the weeks we shot, I was with Celia, and he was . . . well, I didn't know where he was. But he seemed happy, so I didn't question it. I suspected in the back of my mind that he might have met someone who was capable of keeping his interest for more than a few days.

So when *Theresa's Wisdom* went three weeks over our shooting schedule because my costar Ben Madley was hospitalized for exhaustion, I was torn.

On the one hand, I wanted to go back to being with my daughter every night.

On the other hand, Connor was growing more and more annoyed by me every day. She found her mother to be the very epitome of embarrassment. The fact that I was a world-renowned film star seemed to have absolutely no effect on just how big of an idiot Connor saw me to be. So I was often happier in L.A., with Celia, than I was in New York, constantly rejected by my own flesh and blood. But I would have dropped it all in a heartbeat if I thought Connor might want even an evening of my time.

The day after filming wrapped, I was packing up some of my things and talking to Connor on the phone, making plans for the next day.

"Your father and I are getting on the red-eye tonight, so I'll be there when you wake up in the morning," I told her.

"OK," she said. "Cool."

"I thought we could go to breakfast at Channing's."

"Mom, no one goes to Channing's anymore."

"I hate to break it to you, but if *I* go to Channing's, Channing's will still be considered cool."

"This is exactly what I'm talking about when I say you're impossible."

"All I'm trying to do is take you to eat French toast, Connie. There are worse things."

There was a knock on the door of the Hollywood Hills bungalow I'd rented. I opened it to see Harry.

"I gotta go, Mom," Connor said. "Karen is coming over. Luisa's making us barbecue meat loaf," she said.

"Wait one second," I said. "Your father is here. He wants to say hi to you. Good-bye, honey. I'll see you tomorrow."

I handed Harry the phone. "Hi, little bug . . . Well, she has a point. If your mother shows up somewhere, that does sort of mean that, by definition, it will be considered a hot spot . . . That's fine . . . That's fine. Tomorrow morning, the three of us will go out for breakfast, and we can go to whatever the cool new place is . . . It's called what? Wiffles? What kind of a name is that? . . . OK, OK. We'll go to Wiffles. All right, honey, good night. I love you. I'll see you tomorrow."

Harry sat down on my bed and looked at me. "Apparently, we are going to Wiffles."

"You're like putty in her hands, Harry," I said.

He shrugged. "I feel no shame in it." He stood up and poured himself a glass of water while I continued packing. "Listen, I have an idea," he said. As he moved closer to me, I realized he smelled vaguely of liquor.

"About what?"

"About Europe."

"OK . . ." I said. I had resigned to letting it go until Harry and I were settled back in New York. I assumed that then he and I would have the time, and the patience, to discuss it in more depth.

I thought the idea was good for Connor. New York, as much as I loved it, had become a somewhat dangerous place to live. Crime rates were skyrocketing, and drugs were everywhere. We were fairly protected from it on the Upper East Side, but I was still uncomfortable with the idea that Connor was growing up so close to so much chaos. And even more to the point, I was no longer sure that a life where her parents were practically bicoastal and she was being cared for by Luisa when we were gone was the best thing for her.

Yes, we'd be uprooting her. And I knew she'd hate me for making her say good-bye to her friends. But I also knew she would benefit from living in a small town. She'd be better off with a mother who could be around more. And to be frank, she was getting old enough to read gossip columns and watch entertainment news. Was turning on the television and seeing her mother's sixth divorce really the best thing for a child?

"I think I know what to do," Harry said. I sat down on the bed, and he sat next to me. "We move here. We move back to Los Angeles."

"Harry . . ." I said.

"And Celia marries a friend of mine."

"A friend of yours?"

Harry shifts toward me. "I've met someone."

"What?"

"We met on the lot. He's working on another production. I thought it was just a casual thing. I think he did, too. But I think I'm . . . This is a man I could see myself with."

I was so happy for him in that moment. "I thought you couldn't see yourself with anyone," I said, surprised but pleased.

"I couldn't," he said.

"And what happened?"

"Now I can."

"I'm thrilled to hear that, Harry. You have no idea. I'm just not sure this is a good idea," I said. "I don't even know this guy."

"You don't need to," Harry said. "I mean, it's not like I chose Celia. You did. And I'm . . . I think I'd like to choose him."

"I don't want to act anymore, Harry," I said.

All through shooting this last movie, I found myself burning out. I wanted to roll my eyes when asked to do a scene more than once. Hitting my marks felt like running a marathon I'd already run a thousand times before. So easy, so unchallenging, so uninspiring, that you resent even being asked to lace up your shoes.

Maybe if I was getting roles that excited me, maybe if I still felt I had something to prove, I don't know, maybe I would have reacted differently.

There are so many women who continue to do incredible work well into their eighties or nineties. Celia was like that. She could have turned in riveting performance after riveting performance forever, because she was always consumed by the work.

But my heart wasn't in it. My heart was never in the craft of acting, only in the *proving*. Proving my power, proving my worth, proving my talent.

I'd proved it all.

"That's fine," Harry said. "You don't have to act anymore."

"But if I'm not acting, why would I live in Los Angeles? I want to live somewhere I can be free, where no one will pay attention to me. Do you remember when you were little, and whether it was on your block or a few blocks down, there was inevitably a pair of older ladies who lived together as roommates, and no one asked any questions because nobody cared? I want to be one of those ladies. I can't do that here."

"You can't do that anywhere," Harry said. "That's the price you pay for who you are."

"I don't accept that. I think it's very possible for me to do that."

"Well, I don't want to do that. So what I'm proposing is that you and I remarry. And Celia marries my friend."

"We can talk about it later," I said, standing up and taking my toiletry bag to the bathroom.

"Evelyn, you don't get to decide what this family does unilaterally."

"Who said anything about unilaterally? All I'm saying is that I want to talk about it later. There are a number of options here. We can go to Europe, we can move here, we can stay in New York."

Harry shook his head. "He can't move to New York."

I sighed, losing my patience. "All the more reason for us to discuss this *later.*"

Harry stood up, as if he was about to give me a piece of his mind. But then he calmed down. "You're right," he said. "We can discuss it later."

He came over to me as I was packing my soap and makeup. He took my arm and kissed my temple.

"You'll pick me up tonight?" he said. "At my place? We'll have the whole trip to the airport and the flight to discuss it more. We can throw back a couple of Bloody Marys on the plane."

"We will figure this out," I told him. "You know that, right? I'm never going to do anything without you. You're my best friend. My family."

"I know," he said. "And you're mine. I never thought I could love someone after John. But this guy . . . Evelyn, I'm falling in love with him. And to know that I *could* love, that I *can* . . ."

"I know," I said, grabbing his hand and squeezing it. "I know. I promise I'll do whatever I can. I promise you we will figure this out."

"OK," Harry said, and then he squeezed my hand back and walked out the door. "We will figure this out."

MY DRIVER, WHO introduced himself as Nick as I got into the back of the car, picked me up at around nine in the evening.

"To the airport?" Nick said.

"Actually, we're going to make a stop on the Westside first," I said, giving him the address of the home where Harry was staying.

As we made our way across town, through the seedy parts of Hollywood, over the Sunset Strip, I found myself depressed about how unseemly Los Angeles had gotten since I'd left. It was similar to Manhattan in that regard. The decades had not been good to it. Harry was talking about raising Connor here, but I couldn't shake the feeling that we needed to leave both big cities for good.

As we were stopped at a red light close to Harry's rented home, Nick turned around briefly and smiled at me. He had a square jaw and a crew cut. I could tell he had probably bedded a number of women based on his smile alone.

"I'm an actor," he said. "Just like you."

I smiled politely. "Nice work if you can get it."

He nodded. "Got an agent this week," he said as we started moving again. "I feel like I'm really on my way. But, you know, if we get to the airport with time to spare, I'd be interested in any tips you have for somebody starting out."

"Uh-huh," I said, looking out the window. I decided, as we drove up the dark, winding streets of Harry's neighborhood, that if Nick asked me again, after we got to the airport, I was going to tell him that it's mostly luck.

And that you have to be willing to deny your heritage, to commodify your body, to lie to good people, to sacrifice who you love in the name of what people will think, and to choose the false version of yourself time and time again, until you forget who you started out as or why you started doing it to begin with.

But just as we pulled around the corner onto Harry's narrow private road, every thought I'd ever had before that moment was erased from my mind.

Instead, I was leaning forward, shocked still.

In front of us was a car. Bent around a fallen tree.

The sedan looked as if it had run head-on into the trunk, knocking the tree down on top of it.

"Uh, Ms. Hugo . . ." Nick said.

"I see it," I told him, not wanting him to confirm that it was really in front of us, that it wasn't merely an optical illusion.

He pulled over to the side of the road. I heard the scrape of branches on the driver's side of the car as we parked. I froze with my hand on the door handle. Nick jumped out and ran over.

I opened my door and put my feet on the ground. Nick stood to the side, trying to see if he could get one of the doors of the crashed car open. But I walked right to the front, by the tree. I looked in through the windshield.

And I saw what I had both feared and yet not truly believed possible.

Harry was slumped over the steering wheel.

I looked over and saw a younger man in the passenger's seat.

Everyone sort of assumes that when faced with life-and-death situations, you will panic. But almost everyone who's actually experienced something like that will tell you that panic is a luxury you cannot afford.

In the moment, you act without thinking, doing all you can with the information you have.

It's when it's over that you scream. And cry. And wonder how you got through it. Because most likely, in the case of real trauma, your brain isn't great at making memories. It's almost as if the camera is on but no one's recording. So afterward, you go to review the tape, and it's all but blank.

Here is what I remember.

I remember Nick breaking open Harry's car door.

I remember helping to pull Harry out.

I remember thinking that we shouldn't move Harry because we could paralyze him.

But I also remember thinking that I couldn't possibly stand by and allow Harry to stay there, slumped on the wheel like that.

I remember holding Harry in my arms as he bled.

I remember the deep gash in his eyebrow, the way the blood coated half his face in thick rust red.

I remember seeing the cut from where the seat belt had sliced the lower side of his neck.

I remember two of his teeth being in his lap.

I remember rocking him back and forth.

I remember saying, "Stay with me, Harry. Stay with me. Stay true blue."

I remember the other man on the road next to me. I remember Nick telling me he was dead. I remember thinking that no one who looked like that could be alive.

I remember Harry's right eye opening. I remember the way it inflated me with hope, the way the white of his eye looked so bright against the deep red of the blood. I remember how his breath and even his skin smelled like bourbon.

I remember how startling the realization was—once I knew Harry might live, I knew what had to be done.

It wasn't his car.

No one knew he was here.

I had to get him to the hospital, and I had to make sure no one found out he'd been driving. I couldn't let him go to jail. What if they tried him for vehicular manslaughter?

I couldn't let my daughter find out her father had been driving drunk and killed someone. Had killed his lover. Had killed the man who he said was showing him he could love again.

I enlisted Nick to help me get Harry into our car. I made him help me put the other man back into the totaled sedan, this time in the driver's seat.

And then I quickly grabbed a scarf from my bag and wiped the steering wheel clean, wiped the blood, wiped the seat belt. I erased all traces of Harry.

And then we took Harry to the hospital.

There, bloodstained and crying, I called the police from a pay phone and reported the accident.

When I hung up the phone, I turned and saw Nick, sitting in the waiting room, blood on his chest, his arms, even some on his neck.

I walked over to him. He stood up.

"You should go home," I said.

He nodded, still in shock.

"Can you get yourself home? Do you want me to call you a ride?"

"I don't know," he said.

"I'll call you a cab, then." I grabbed my purse. I pulled out two twenties from my wallet. "This should be enough to get you there."

"OK," he said.

"You're going to go home, and you're going to forget everything that happened. Everything you saw."

"What did we do?" he said. "How did we . . . How could we . . ."

"You're going to call me," I said. "I'll get a room at the Beverly Hills Hotel. Call me there tomorrow. First thing in the morning. You're not going to talk to anyone else between now and then. Do you hear me?"

"Yes."

"Not your mother or your friends or even the cabdriver. Do you have a girlfriend?"

He shook his head.

"A roommate?"

He nodded.

"You tell them that you found a man on the street and you brought him to the hospital, OK? That's all you tell them, and you only tell them if they ask."

"OK."

He nodded. I called him a cab and waited with him until it arrived. I put him in the backseat.

"What are you going to do first thing tomorrow?" I asked him through the rolled-down window.

"I'm going to call you."

"Good," I said. "If you can't sleep, think. Think about what you need. What you need from me as a thank-you for what you did."

He nodded, and the cab zoomed off.

People were staring at me. Evelyn Hugo in a pantsuit covered in blood. I was afraid paparazzi would be there any minute.

I went inside. I talked my way into borrowing some scrubs and being given a private room to wait in. I threw my clothes away.

When a man from the hospital staff asked me for a statement about what happened to Harry, I said, "How much will it take for you to leave me alone?" I was relieved when the dollar figure he came up with was less than what I had in my purse.

Just after midnight, a doctor came into the room and told me that Harry's femoral artery had been severed. He had lost too much blood.

For a brief moment, I wondered if I should go get my old clothes, if I could give some of his blood back to him, if it worked like that.

But I was distracted by the next words out of the doctor's mouth.

"He will not make it."

I started gasping for air as I realized that Harry, my Harry, was going to die.

"Would you like to say good-bye?"

He was unconscious in the bed when I walked into the room. He looked paler than normal, but they had cleaned him up a bit. There was no longer blood everywhere. I could see his handsome face.

"He doesn't have long," the doctor said. "But we can give you a moment."

I did not have the luxury of panic.

So I got into the bed with him. I held his hand even though it felt limp. Maybe I should have been mad at him for getting behind the wheel of a car when he'd been drinking. But I couldn't ever get very mad at Harry. I knew he was always doing the very best he could with the pain he felt at any given moment. And this, however tragic, had been the best he could do.

I put my forehead to his and said, "I want you to stay, Harry. We need you. Me and Connor." I grabbed his hand tighter. "But if you have to go, then go. Go if it hurts. Go if it's time. Just go knowing you were loved, that I will never forget you, that you will live in everything Connor and I do. Go knowing I love you purely, Harry, that you were an amazing father. Go knowing I told you all my secrets. Because you were my best friend."

Harry died an hour later.

After he was gone, I had the devastating luxury of panic.

IN THE MORNING, a few hours after I'd checked into the hotel, I woke up to a phone call.

My eyes were swollen from crying, and my throat hurt. The pillow was still stained with tears. I was pretty sure I'd only slept for an hour, maybe less.

"Hello?" I said.

"It's Nick."

"Nick?"

"Your driver."

"Oh," I said. "Yes. Hi."

"I know what I want," he said.

His voice was confident. Its strength scared me. I felt so weak right then. But I knew it had been my idea for this call to happen. I had set up the nature of it. *Tell me what you want to keep you quiet* was what I had said without saying it.

"I want you to make me famous," he said, and when he did, the very last shred of affection I had for stardom drained out of me.

"Do you realize the full extent of what you're asking?" I said. "If you're a celebrity, last night will be dangerous for you, too."

"That's not a problem," he said.

I sighed, disappointed. "OK," I said, resigned. "I can get you parts. The rest is up to you."

"That's fine. That's all I need."

I asked him his agent's name, and I got off the phone. I made two phone calls. One was to my own agent, telling him to poach Nick from his guy. The second was to a man with the highest-grossing action movie in the country. It was about a police chief in his late fifties who defeats Russian spies on the day he's supposed to retire.

"Don?" I said when he answered the phone.

"Evelyn! What can I do for you?"

"I need you to hire a friend of mine in your next movie. The biggest part you can get him."

"OK," he said. "You got it." He did not ask me why. He did not ask me if I was OK. We had been through enough together for him to know better. I simply gave him Nick's name, and I got off the phone.

After I set the phone back in the cradle, I bawled and I howled. I gripped the sheets. I missed the only man I'd ever loved with any lasting meaning.

My heart ached in my chest when I thought about telling Connor, when I thought about trying to live a day without him, when I thought of a world without Harry Cameron.

It was Harry who created me, who powered me, who loved me unconditionally, who gave me a family and a daughter.

So I bellowed in my hotel room. I opened the windows, and I screamed out into the open air. I let my tears soak everything in sight.

If I had been in a better frame of mind, I might have marveled at just how opportunistic Nick was, how aggressive.

In my younger years, I might have been impressed. Harry most certainly would have said he had guts. Plenty of people can make something out of being in the right place at the right time. But Nick somehow turned being in the wrong place at the wrong time into a career.

Then again, I might be giving that moment too much credit in Nick's own story. He changed his name, cut his hair, and went on to do very, very big things. And something tells me that even if he had never run into me, he would have made it happen all on his own. I guess what I'm saying is it's not all luck.

It's luck *and* being a son of a bitch.

Harry taught me that.

PRODUCER HARRY CAMERON HAS DIED

Harry Cameron, prolific producer and onetime husband of Evelyn Hugo, died of an aneurysm over the weekend in Los Angeles. He was 58 years old.

The independent producer, formerly a Sunset Studios mogul, was known for shepherding some of Hollywood's greatest films, including the '50s classics *To Be with You* and *Little Women* and some of the most exciting films of the '60s, '70s, and '80s, such as 1981's *All for Us*. He had just wrapped on the upcoming *Theresa's Wisdom*.

Cameron was known for his keen taste and kind but firm demeanor. Hollywood has been left heartbroken with the loss of one of its favorites. "Harry was an actor's producer," said a former colleague. "If he picked up a project, you knew you wanted to be involved."

Cameron is survived by his teenage daughter with Evelyn Hugo, Connor Cameron.

WILD CHILD

BLIND ITEM!

Which precious Hollywood progeny was caught with her pants down? And we mean that literally!

This daughter of a former A++-list actress has been having a rough time. And it appears that instead of lying low, she's going wild.

We hear that at the age of 14, this Wild Child has been MIA from her prestigious high school and is often seen out at one of New York's various high-profile clubs—at which she's rarely, *ahem*, sober. We're not just talking alcohol, either. *There seems to be some powder under your nose there . . .*

Apparently, her mother has been trying to get a handle on the situation, but things hit the fan when Wild Child was caught with two fellow students . . . in bed!

Six months after Harry died, I knew I had no choice but to get Connor out of town. I had tried everything else. I was attentive and nurturing. I tried to get her into therapy. I talked with her about her father. She, unlike the rest of the world, knew he had been in a car accident. And she understood why something like that needed to be delicately handled. But I knew it only compounded her stress. I tried to get her to open up to me. But nothing was helping me get her to make better choices.

She was fourteen years old and had lost her father with the same swiftness and heartbreak with which I had lost my mother so many years before. I had to take care of my child. I had to do something.

My instinct was to move her away from the spotlight, away from people willing to sell her drugs, willing to take advantage of her pain. I needed to bring her someplace where I could watch her, where I could protect her.

She needed to process and heal. And she could not do that with the life I had made for us.

"Aldiz," Celia said.

We were talking on the phone. I had not seen her in months. But we talked every night. Celia helped ground me, helped me to keep moving forward. Most nights, as I lay in bed speaking to Celia on the phone, I could speak of nothing but my daughter's pain. And when I could speak of something different, it was my own pain. I was just starting to come out of it, to see a light at the end of the tunnel, when Celia suggested Aldiz.

"Where is that?" I asked.

"It's on the southern coast of Spain. It's a small city. I've talked to Robert. He has a call in to some friends he knows in Málaga, which isn't too far. He's going to ask about any English-language schools. It's mostly a fishing village. I don't get the impression anyone will care about us."

"It's quiet?" I asked.

"I think so," she said. "I think Connor would have to really go out of her way to find trouble."

"That seems to be her MO," I said.

"You'll be there for her. I'll be around. Robert will be there. We will make sure she's OK. We will make sure she's supported, that she has people to talk to. That she makes the right types of friends."

I knew that moving to Spain would mean losing Luisa. She had already moved with us from L.A. to New York. She wouldn't want to uproot her life again to move to Spain. But I also knew she had been taking care of our family for decades and was tired. I got the impression that our leaving the United States would be just the excuse she needed to move on. I would make sure she was taken care of. And anyway, I was ready to take a more hands-on approach to maintaining my home.

I wanted to be the kind of person who made dinner, who scrubbed a toilet, who was available to my daughter at all times.

"Are any of your movies big in Spain?" I asked.

"Nothing recently," Celia said. "Yours?"

"Just *Boute-en-Train*," I said. "So no."

"Do you really think you'll be able to handle this?"

"No," I said, even before I knew what Celia was specifically talking about. "Which part do you mean?"

"Insignificance."

I laughed. "Oh, God," I said. "Yes. That's about the only part I am ready for."

WHEN THE PLANS were finalized, when I knew what school Connor would go to, what houses we were going to buy, how we were going to live, I walked into Connor's room and sat down on her bed.

She was wearing a Duran Duran T-shirt and faded jeans. Her blond hair was teased at the crown. She was still grounded from when I had caught her having a threesome, so she had no choice but to sit there with a sour face and listen as I spoke.

I told her I was retiring from acting. I told her we were moving to Spain. I told her I thought she and I would be happier living with good people, away from all the fame and the cameras.

And then I very gently, very tentatively, told her that I was in love with Celia. I told her I was going to marry Robert, and I explained why, succinctly and clearly. I did not treat her like a child. I spoke to her as an adult. I finally gave her the truth. My truth.

I did not tell her about Harry, about how long I had been with Celia or anything that she didn't need to know. Those things would come in time.

But I told her what she deserved to understand.

And when I was done, I said, "I'm ready to hear everything you have to say. I'm ready to answer any questions at all. Let's have a discussion about this."

But all she did was shrug her shoulders. "I don't care, Mom," she said, sitting on her bed with her back against the wall. "I really don't. You can love whoever. Marry anybody. You can make me live wherever. Go to whatever school you decide. I don't care, OK? I just don't care. All I want is to be left alone. So just . . . leave my room. Please. If you can do that, then the rest of it, I don't care."

I looked at her, stared right into her eyes and ached for her aching. With her blond hair and her face thinning out, I was starting to fear that she looked more like me than Harry. Sure, conventionally speaking, she would be more attractive if she looked like me. But she *should* look like Harry. The world should give us that.

"All right," I said. "I will leave you alone for now."

I got up. I gave her some space.

I packed up our things. I hired movers. I made plans with Celia and Robert.

Two days before we left New York, I walked into her bedroom and said, "I'll give you your freedom in Aldiz. You can choose your own room. I'll make sure you can come back here to visit some of your friends. I'll do whatever I can to make life easier for you. But I need two things."

"What?" she said. Her voice sounded disinterested, but she was looking at me. She was talking to me.

"Dinner together, every night."

"Mom—"

"I'm giving you a lot of leeway here. A lot of trust. All I'm asking for is two things. One is dinner every night."

"But—"

"It's nonnegotiable. You only have three more years until you're in college anyway. You can handle one meal a day."

She looked away from me. "Fine. What's the second?"

"You're going to see a psychologist. At least for a little while. You've been through too much. We all have. You need to start talking to someone."

When I had tried this before, months earlier, I was too weak with her. I let her tell me no. I wasn't going to do that this time. I was stronger now. I could be a better mother.

Maybe she could detect it in my voice, because she didn't try to fight me. She just said, "OK, whatever."

I hugged her and kissed the top of her head, and just when I was going to let go, she wrapped her arms around me and hugged me back.

E VELYN'S EYES ARE WET. THEY have been for some time. She stands up and grabs a tissue from across the room.

She's such a spectacular woman—by which I mean she, herself, is a spectacle. But she's also deeply, deeply human. And it is simply impossible for me, in this moment, to remain objective. Against all journalistic integrity, I simply care about her too much not to be moved by her pain, not to feel for all she has felt.

"It must be so hard . . . what you're doing, telling your story, with so much frankness. I just want you to know that I admire you for it."

"Don't say that," Evelyn says. "OK? Just do me a favor, and don't say anything like that. I know who I am. By tomorrow you will, too."

"You keep saying that, but we're all flawed. Do you really believe you're past redemption?"

She ignores me. She looks out the window, without even looking at me.

"Evelyn," I say. "Do you honestly—"

She cuts me off as she looks back at me. "You agreed not to press. We'll be done soon enough. And you won't be left wondering about anything."

I look at her skeptically.

"Really," she says. "This is one thing on which you can trust me."

Agreeable Robert Jamison

◆

EVELYN HUGO MARRIES FOR THE SEVENTH TIME

Evelyn Hugo got married this past Saturday to financier Robert Jamison. While this is the seventh trip down the aisle for Evelyn, it is the first for Robert.

If his name sounds familiar, it might be because Evelyn isn't the only member of Hollywood royalty he's linked to. Jamison is an older brother of Celia St. James. Sources say the two met at a party of Celia's just two months ago. They have been falling head over heels in love since.

The ceremony took place at the Beverly Hills court-house. Evelyn wore a cream-colored suit. Robert looked dapper in pinstripes. Evelyn's daughter with the late Harry Cameron, Connor Cameron, was the maid of honor.

Shortly after, the three left on a trip to Spain. We can only assume they are off to visit Celia, who just recently bought property off the southern coast.

CONNOR CAME BACK TO LIFE on the rocky beaches of Aldiz. It was slow but steady, like a seed sprouting.

She liked playing Scrabble with Celia. As she'd promised, she ate dinner with me every night, sometimes even coming down to the kitchen early to help me make tortillas from scratch or my mother's *caldo gallego*.

But it was Robert she gravitated toward.

Tall and broad, with a gentle beer belly and silver hair, Robert had no idea what to do with a teenage girl at first. I think he was intimidated by her. He was unsure what to say. So he gave her space, maybe even more of a wide berth.

It was Connor who reached out, who asked him to teach her how to play poker, asked him to tell her about finance, asked him if he wanted to go fishing.

He never replaced Harry. No one could. But he did ease the pain, a little bit. She asked his opinion about boys. She took the time to find him the perfect sweater on his birthday.

He painted her bedroom for her. He made her favorite barbecue ribs on the weekends.

And slowly, Connor began to trust that the world was a reasonably safe place to open your heart to. I knew the wounds of losing her father would never truly heal, that scar tissue was forming all through her high school years. But I saw her stop partying. I saw her start getting As and Bs. And then, when she got into Stanford, I looked at her and realized I had a daughter with two feet placed firmly on the ground and her head squarely on her shoulders.

Celia, Robert, and I took Connor out for dinner the night before she and I left to take her to school. We were at a tiny restaurant on the water. Robert had bought her a present and wrapped it. It was a poker set. He said, "Take everybody's money, like you've been taking mine with all those flushes."

"And then you can help me invest it," she said with devilish glee.

"Atta girl," he said.

Robert always claimed that he married me because he would do anything for Celia. But I think he did it, in at least some small part, because it gave him a chance to have a family. He was never going to settle down with one woman. And Spanish women proved to be just as enchanted by him as American ones had been. But this system, this family, was one he could be a part of, and I think he knew that when he signed up.

Or maybe Robert merely stumbled into something that worked for him, unsure what he wanted until he had it. Some people are lucky like that. Me, I've always gone after what I wanted with everything in me. Others fall into happiness. Sometimes I wish I was like them. I'm sure sometimes they wish they were like me.

With Connor back in the United States, coming home only during school breaks, Celia and I had more time with each other than we ever had before. We did not have film shoots or gossip columns to worry about. We were almost never recognized—and if people did recognize one of us, they mostly steered clear and kept it to themselves.

There in Spain, I had the life I truly wanted. I felt at peace, again waking up every day seeing Celia's hair fanned on my pillow. I cherished every moment we had to ourselves, every second I spent with my arms around her.

Our bedroom had an oversized balcony that looked out onto the ocean. Often the breeze from the water would rush into our room at night. We would sit out there on lazy mornings, reading the newspaper together, our fingers gray from the ink.

I even started speaking Spanish again. At first, I did it because it was necessary. There were so many people we needed to converse with, and I was the only one truly prepared to do it. But I think the necessity of it was good for me. Because I couldn't worry too much about feeling insecure; I simply had to get through the transaction. And then, over time, I found myself proud of how easily it came to me. The dialect was different—the Cuban Spanish of my youth was not a perfect match for the Castilian of Spain—but years without the words had not erased many of them from my mind.

I would often speak Spanish even at home, making Celia and Robert piece together what I was saying from their own limited knowledge. I loved sharing it with them. I loved being able to show a part of myself that I had long buried. I was happy to find that when I dug it up, that part was still there, waiting for me.

But of course, no matter how perfect the days seemed, there was one ache looming over us night after night.

Celia was not well. Her health was deteriorating. She did not have much time.

"I know I shouldn't," Celia said to me one night as we lay together in the dark, neither of us yet sleeping. "But sometimes I get so mad at us for all the years we lost. For all the time we wasted."

I grabbed her hand. "I know," I said. "Me too."

"If you love someone enough, you should be able to overcome anything," she said. "And we have always loved each other so much, more than I ever thought I could be loved, more than I ever thought I could love. So why . . . why couldn't we overcome it?"

"We did," I said, turning toward her. "We're here."

She shook her head. "But the *years*," she said.

"We're stubborn," I said. "And we weren't exactly given the tools to succeed. We're both used to being the one who calls the shots. We both have a tendency to think the world revolves around us . . ."

"And we've had to hide that we're gay," she said. "Or, rather, I'm gay. You're bisexual."

I smiled in the dark and squeezed her hand.

"The world hasn't made that easy," she said.

"I think both of us wanted more than was realistic. I'm sure we could have made it work, the two of us, in a small town. You could have been a teacher. I could have been a nurse. We could have made it easier on ourselves that way."

I could feel Celia shaking her head next to me. "But that's not who we are, that's not who we have ever been or could ever be."

I nodded. "I think being yourself—your true, entire self—is always going to feel like you're swimming upstream."

"Yeah," she said. "But if the last few years with you have been any indication, I think it also feels like taking your bra off at the end of the day."

I laughed. "I love you," I said. "Don't ever leave me."

But when she said, "I love you, too. I never will," we both knew she was making a promise she couldn't keep.

I couldn't stand the thought of losing her again, losing her in a deeper way than I'd ever lost her before. I couldn't bear the idea that I would be forever without her, with no tie to her.

"Will you marry me?" I said.

She laughed, and I stopped her.

"I'm not kidding! I want to marry you. For once and for all. Don't I deserve that? Seven marriages in, shouldn't I finally get to marry the love of my life?"

"I don't think it works that way, sweetheart," she said. "And need I remind you, I'd be stealing my brother's wife."

"I'm serious, Celia."

"So am I, Evelyn. There's no way for us to marry."

"All a marriage is is a promise."

"If you say so," she said. "You're the expert."

"Let's get married right here and now. Me and you. In this bed. You don't even have to put on a white nightgown."

"What are you talking about?"

"I'm talking about a spiritual promise, between the two of us, for the rest of our lives."

When Celia didn't say anything, I knew that she was thinking about it. She was thinking about whether it could mean anything, the two of us there in that bed.

"Here's what we will do," I said, trying to convince her. "We will look each other in the eye, and we will hold hands, and we will say what's in our hearts, and we will promise to be there for each other. We don't need any government documents or witnesses or religious approval. It doesn't matter that I'm already legally married, because we both know that when I was marrying Robert, I was doing it to be with you. We don't need anybody else's rules. We just need each other."

She was quiet. She sighed. And then she said, "OK. I'm in."

"Really?" I was surprised at just how meaningful this moment was becoming.

"Yeah," she said. "I want to marry you. I've always wanted to marry you. I just . . . it never occurred to me that we could. That we didn't need anyone's approval."

"We don't," I said.

"Then I do."

I laughed and sat up in our bed. I turned on the light on my nightstand. Celia sat up, too. We faced each other and held hands.

"I think you should probably perform the ceremony," she said.

"I suppose I have been in more weddings," I joked.

She laughed, and I laughed with her. We were in our midfifties, giddy at the idea of finally doing what we should have done years ago.

"OK," I said. "No more laughing. We're gonna do it."

"OK," she said, smiling. "I'm ready."

I breathed in. I looked at her. She had crow's-feet around her eyes. She had laugh lines around her mouth. Her hair was mussed from the pillow. She was wearing an old New York Giants T-shirt with a hole in the shoulder. Convention be damned, she never looked more beautiful.

"Dearly beloved," I said. "I suppose that's just us."

"OK," Celia said. "I follow."

"We are gathered here today to celebrate the union of . . . us."

"Great."

"Two people who come together to spend the rest of their lives with each other."

"Agreed."

"Do you, Celia, take me, Evelyn, to be your wedded wife? In sickness and in health, for richer and for poorer, till death do us part, as long as we both shall live?"

She smiled at me. "I do."

"And do I, Evelyn, take you, Celia, to be my wedded wife? In sickness and in health and all the other stuff? I do." I realized there was a slight hiccup. "Wait, we don't have rings."

Celia looked around for something that might suffice. Without taking my hands from her, I checked the nightstand.

"Here," Celia said, taking the hair tie from her head.

I laughed and took mine out of my ponytail.

"OK," I said. "Celia, repeat after me. Evelyn, take this ring as a symbol of my never-ending love."

"Evelyn, take this ring as a symbol of my never-ending love."

Celia took the hair tie and wrapped it around my ring finger three times.

"Say, With this ring, I thee wed."

"With this ring, I thee wed."

"OK. Now I do it. Celia, take this ring as a symbol of my never-ending love. With this ring, I thee wed." I put my hair tie on her finger. "Oh, I forgot vows. Should we do vows?"

"We can," she said. "If you want to."

"OK," I said. "You think of what you want to say. I'll think, too."

"I don't need to think," she said. "I'm ready. I know."

"OK," I said, surprised to find that my heart was beating quickly, eager to hear her words. "Go."

"Evelyn, I have been in love with you since 1959. I may not have always shown it, I may have let other things get in the way, but know that I have loved you that long. That I have never stopped. And that I never will."

I closed my eyes briefly, letting her words sink in.

And then I gave her mine. "I have been married seven times, and never once has it felt half as right as this. I think that loving you has been the truest thing about me."

She smiled so hard I thought she might cry. But she didn't.

I said, "By the power vested in me by . . . us, I now declare us married."

Celia laughed.

"I may now kiss the bride," I said, and I let go of her hands, grabbed her face, and kissed her. My wife.

S IX YEARS LATER, AFTER CELIA and I had spent more than a de-cade together on the beaches of Spain, after Connor had graduated from college and taken a job on Wall Street, after the world had all but forgotten about *Little Women* and *Boute-en-Train* and Celia's three Os-cars, Cecelia Jamison died of respiratory failure.

She was in my arms. In our bed.

It was summer. The windows were open to let in the breeze. The room smelled of sickness, but if you focused hard enough, you could still smell the salt from the ocean. Her eyes went still. I called out for the nurse, who had been downstairs in the kitchen. I think I stopped making memories again, in those moments when Celia was being taken from me.

I only remember clinging to her, holding her as best I could. I only remember saying, "We didn't have enough time."

It felt as if by taking her body, the paramedics were ripping out my soul. And then, when the door shut, when everyone had left, when Celia was nowhere to be seen, I looked over at Robert. I fell to the floor.

The tiles felt cold on my flushed skin. The hardness of the stone ached in my bones. Underneath me, puddles of tears were forming, and yet I could not lift my head off the ground.

Robert did not help me up.

He got down on the floor next to me. And wept.

I had lost her. My love. My Celia. My soul mate. The woman whose love I'd spent my life earning.

Simply gone.

Irrevocably and forever.

And the devastating luxury of panic overtook me again.

SCREEN QUEEN CELIA ST. JAMES HAS DIED

Three-time Oscar-winning actress Celia St. James died last week of complications related to emphysema. She was 61 years old.

From a well-to-do family in a small town in Georgia, the red-haired St. James was often referred to as the Georgia Peach early in her career. But it was her role as Beth in the 1959 adaptation of *Little Women* that brought her her first Academy Award and turned her into a bona fide star.

St. James would go on to be nominated four other times and take home the trophy twice more over the next 30 years, for Best Actress in 1970 for *Our Men* and for Best Supporting Actress for her role as Lady Macbeth in the 1988 adaptation of the Shakespearean tragedy.

In addition to her remarkable talent, St. James was known for her girl-next-door allure and her fifteen-year marriage to football hero John Braverman. The two divorced in the late 1970s but remained friendly until Braverman's passing in 1980. She never remarried.

St. James's estate is to be managed by her brother, Robert Jamison, husband of actress—and St. James's former costar—Evelyn Hugo.

CELIA, LIKE HARRY, WAS BURIED in Forest Lawn in Los Angeles. Robert and I held her funeral on a Thursday morning. It was kept private. But people knew we were there. They knew she was being laid to rest.

When she was lowered to the ground, I stared at the hole in the earth. I stared at the glossy sheen of the wood of her casket. I could not keep it in. I could not keep my true self from coming out.

"I need a minute," I said to Robert and Connor and then I turned away.

I walked. Farther and farther up the winding hillside roads of the cemetery, until I found what I was looking for.

Harry Cameron.

I sat down at his tombstone, and I cried out everything within me. I cried until I felt depleted. I did not say a single thing. I did not feel any need. I had talked to Harry in my head and my heart for so long, for so many years, that it felt as if we transcended words.

He had been the one to help me, to support me, through everything in my life. And now I needed him more than ever. So I went to him the only way I knew how. I let him heal me as only he could. And then I stood up, dusted off my skirt, and turned around.

There, in the trees, were two paparazzi taking my photo. I was neither angry nor flattered. I simply didn't care. It cost so much, caring. I didn't have any currency to spend on it.

Instead, I walked away.

Two weeks later, after Robert and I had gone home to Aldiz, Connor sent me a magazine with the image of me at Harry's grave on the cover. She had attached a note to the front. It said, simply, "I love you."

I pulled off the note and read the headline: "Legend Evelyn Hugo Weeps at Harry Cameron's Grave Years Later."

Even long past my prime, people were still easily distracted from seeing how I felt about Celia St. James. But this time was different. Because I wasn't hiding anything.

The truth had been there for them to grab if they'd paid attention. I had been my truest self, searching for the help of my best friend to ease the pain of the loss of my lover.

But of course, they got it wrong. They never did care about getting it right. The media are going to tell whatever story they want to tell. They always have. They always will.

It was then that I knew that the only time anyone would know anything true about my life was when I told them directly.

In a book.

I saved Connor's note and threw the magazine in the trash.

W ITH CELIA'S PASSING AND HARRY gone and myself finally in a marriage that, while chaste, was stable, my life officially became entirely void of scandal.

Me. Evelyn Hugo. A boring old lady.

Robert and I lived a friendly marriage for the next eleven years. We moved back to Manhattan in the mid-2000s to be closer to Connor. We refinished this apartment. We donated some of Celia's money to LGBTQ+ organizations and lung disease research.

Every Christmas, we threw a benefit for homeless youth organizations in New York City. After years on a quiet beach, it was nice to be members of society again in some ways.

But all I really cared about was Connor.

She had worked her way up the ladder at Merrill Lynch, and then, shortly after Robert and I moved back to New York, she admitted to him that she hated the culture of finance. She told him she had to leave. He was disappointed that she hadn't been happy with what had made him happy; that was obvious. But he was never disappointed in her.

And he was the first person to congratulate her when she took a job teaching at Wharton. She never knew that he had made a few calls on her behalf. He never wanted her to know. He merely wanted to help her, in any and all ways that he could. And he did that, lovingly, until he died at age eighty-one.

Connor gave the eulogy. Her boyfriend, Greg, was one of the pall-bearers. Afterward, she and Greg came to stay with me for a while.

"Mom, after seven husbands, I'm not sure you've had any practice living on your own," she said as she sat at my dining room table, the same table she used to sit at in a high chair with Harry, Celia, John, and me.

"I lived a very full life before you were born," I told her. "I lived alone once, and I can do it again. You and Greg should go live your lives. Really."

But the moment I shut the door behind them, I realized just how huge this apartment was, just how quiet.

That's when I hired Grace.

I had inherited multiple millions from Harry, Celia, and now Robert. And I had only Connor to spoil. So I also spoiled Grace and her family. It gave me happiness to give them happiness, to give them just a little bit of the luxury I'd had for most of my life.

Living alone isn't so bad once you get used to it. And living in a big apartment like this, well, I've kept it because I wanted to give it to Connor, but I have enjoyed some aspects of it. Of course, I always liked it more when Connor would spend the night, especially after she and Greg broke up.

You can make quite a life for yourself hosting charity dinners and collecting art. You can find a way to be happy with whatever the truth is.

Until your daughter dies.

Connor was diagnosed with late-stage breast cancer two and a half years ago, when she was thirty-nine. She was given months to live. I knew what it was like to realize that the one you love would leave this earth well before you. But nothing could prepare me for the pain of watching my child suffer.

I held her when she puked from the chemo. I wrapped her in blankets when she was so cold she was crying. I kissed her forehead like she was my baby again, because she was forever my baby.

I told her every single day that her life had been the world's greatest gift to me, that I believed I was put on earth not to make movies or wear emerald-green gowns and wave at crowds but to be her mother.

I sat next to her hospital bed. "Nothing I have ever done," I said, "has made me as proud as the day I gave birth to you."

"I know," she said. "I've always known that."

I had made a point of not bullshitting her ever since her father died. We had the sort of relationship where we believed each other, believed *in* each other. She knew she was loved. She knew that she had changed my life, that she had changed the world.

She made it eighteen months before she passed away.

And when they put her in the ground next to her father, I broke like I have never broken before.

The devastating luxury of panic overtook me.

And it has never left.

THAT'S HOW MY STORY ENDS. With the loss of everyone I have ever loved. With me, in a big, beautiful Upper East Side apartment, missing everyone who ever meant anything to me.

When you write the ending, Monique, make sure it's clear that I don't love this apartment, that I don't care about all my money, that I couldn't give a rat's ass if people think I'm a legend, that the adoration of millions of people never warmed my bed.

When you write the ending, Monique, tell everyone that it is the people I miss. Tell everyone that I got it wrong. That I chose the wrong things most of the time.

When you write the ending, Monique, make sure the reader understands that all I was ever really looking for was family. Make sure it's clear that I found it. Make sure they know that I am heartbroken without it.

Spell it out if you have to.

Say that Evelyn Hugo doesn't care if everyone forgets her name. Evelyn Hugo doesn't care if everyone forgets she was ever alive.

Better yet, remind them that Evelyn Hugo never existed. She was a person I made up for them. So that they would love me. Tell them that I was confused, for a very long time, about what love was. Tell them that I understand it now, and I don't need their love anymore.

Say to them, "Evelyn Hugo just wants to go home. It's time for her to go to her daughter, and her lover, and her best friend, and her mother."

Tell them Evelyn Hugo says good-bye.

WHAT DO YOU MEAN, 'GOOD-BYE'? Don't say good-bye, Evelyn."
She looks me right in the eye and ignores my words.

"When you put it all together into one narrative," she says, "make sure it's clear that of all the things I did to protect my family, I would do *every one* again. And I would have done more, would have behaved even uglier, if I thought it could have saved them."

"I think most people probably feel the same way," I tell her. "About their lives, their loved ones."

Evelyn looks disappointed in my response. She gets up and walks over to her desk. She pulls out a piece of paper.

It is old. Crinkled and folded, with a burnt-orange hue on one edge.

"The man in the car with Harry," Evelyn says. "The one I left."

This is, of course, the most egregious thing she's ever done. But I'm not sure I wouldn't have done the same for someone I loved. I'm not saying I would have done the same. I'm just saying that I'm not sure.

"Harry had fallen in love with a black man. His name was James Grant. He died on February 26, 1989."

H ERE IS THE THING ABOUT fury.
    It starts in your chest.

It starts as fear.

Fear quickly moves to denial. *No, that must be a mistake. No, that can't be.*

And then the truth hits. *Yes, she is right. Yes, it can be.*

Because you realize, *Yes, it is true.*

And then you have a choice. Are you sad, or are you angry?

And ultimately, the thin line between the two comes down to the answer to one question. Can you assign blame?

The loss of my father, when I was seven, was something for which I only ever had one person to blame. My father. My father was driving drunk. He'd never done anything like it before. It was entirely out of character. But it happened. And I could either hate him for it, or I could try to understand it. *Your father was driving under the influence and lost control of the car.*

But this. The knowledge that my father never willingly got behind the wheel of a car drunk, that he was left dead on the side of the road by this woman, framed for his own death, his legacy tarnished. The fact that I grew up believing he'd been the one to cause the accident. There is so much blame hanging in the air, waiting for me to snatch it and pin it on Evelyn's chest.

And the way she is sitting in front of me, remorseful but not exactly sorry, makes it clear she's ready to be pinned.

This blame is like a flint to my years of aching. And it erupts into fury.

My body goes white-hot. My eyes tear. My hands ball into fists, and I step away because I am afraid of what I might do.

And then, because stepping away from her feels too generous, I edge back to where she is, and I push her against the sofa, and I say, "I'm glad you have no one left. I'm glad there's no one alive to love you."

I let go of her, surprised at myself. She sits back up. She watches me.

"You think that giving me your story makes up for any of it?" I ask her. "All this time, you've been making me sit here, listening to your life, so that you could confess, and you think that your *biography* makes up for it?"

"No," she says. "I think you know me well enough by now to know I'm not nearly naive enough to believe in absolution."

"What, then?"

Evelyn reaches out and shows me the paper in her hand.

"I found this in Harry's pants pocket. The night he died. My guess is that he'd read it and it was the reason he'd been drinking so much to begin with. It was from your father."

"So?"

"So I . . . I found great peace in my daughter knowing the truth about me. There was immense comfort in knowing the real her. I wanted to . . . I think I'm the only person alive who can give that to you. Can give it to your dad. I want you to know who he truly was."

"I know who he was to me," I say, while realizing that that's not exactly true.

"I thought you would want to know all of him. Take it, Monique. Read the letter. If you don't want it, you don't have to keep it. But I always planned on sending it to you. I always thought you deserved to know."

I snatch it from her, not wanting even to extend the kindness of taking it gently. I sit down. I open it. There are what can only be bloodstains on the top of the page. I wonder briefly if it's my father's blood. Or Harry's. I decide not to think about it.

Before I can read even one line, I look up at her.

"Can you leave?" I say.

Evelyn nods and walks out of her own office. She shuts the door behind her. I look down. There is so much to reframe in my mind.

My father did nothing wrong.

My father didn't cause his own death.

I've spent years of my life seeing him from that angle, making peace with him through that lens.

And now, for the first time in nearly thirty years, I have new words, fresh thoughts, from my father.

> *Dear Harry,*
>
> *I love you. I love you in a way that I never thought possible. I have spent so much of my life thinking that this type of love was a myth. And now here it is, so real I can touch it, and I finally understand what the Beatles were singing about all those years.*
>
> *I do not want you to move to Europe. But I also know that what I may not want may very well be the best thing for you. So despite my desires, I think you should go.*
>
> *I cannot and will not be able to give you the life you are dreaming of here in Los Angeles.*
>
> *I cannot marry Celia St. James—although I do agree with you that she is a stunningly beautiful woman, and if I'm being honest, I did nurse a small crush on her in* Royal Wedding.
>
> *But the fact remains that though I have never loved my wife the way I love you, I will never leave her. I love my family too much to fracture us for even a moment of time. My daughter, whom I desperately hope you can one day meet, is my reason for living. And I know that she is happiest with me and her mom. I know that she will live her best life only if I stay where I am.*
>
> *Angela is perhaps not the love of my life. I know that now, now that I've felt real passion. But I think, in many*

ways, she means to me what Evelyn means to you. She is my best friend, my confidante, my companion. I admire the forthrightness with which you and Evelyn discuss your sexuality, your desires. But it is not how Angela and I work, and I'm not sure I'd want to change that. We do not have a vibrant sex life, but I love her the way one loves a partner. I would never forgive myself for causing her pain. And I would find myself desperate to call her, to hear her thoughts, to know how she is, every moment of every day if I was not with her.

My family is my heart. And I cannot break us up. Not even for the type of love that I have found with you, my Harry.

Go to Europe. If you believe it is what is best for your family.

And know that here, in Los Angeles, I am with mine, thinking of you.

Forever yours,
James

I put down the letter. I stare straight ahead into the air. And then, and only then, it hits me.

My father was in love with a man.

I DON'T KNOW HOW LONG I sit on the couch, staring at the ceiling. I think of my memories of my dad, the way he would throw me up in the air in the backyard, the way he would every once in a while let me eat banana splits for breakfast.

Those memories have always been tinged by how he died. They have always had a bittersweetness to them because I believed it was his mistakes that took him from me too soon.

And now I don't know what to make of him. I don't know how to think of him. A defining trait is gone and is replaced by so much more—for better or for worse.

At some point, after I start replaying the same images over and over in my mind—memories of my father alive, imagined images of his final moments and his death—I realize I can't sit still anymore.

So I stand up, I walk into the hallway, and I start looking for Evelyn. I find her in the kitchen with Grace.

"So this is why I'm here?" I say, holding the letter in the air.

"Grace, would you mind giving us a moment?"

Grace gets up from her stool. "Sure." She disappears down the hall.

When she's gone, Evelyn looks at me. "It's not the only reason I wanted to meet you. I tracked you down to give you the letter, obviously. And I had been looking for a way to introduce myself to you that wasn't quite so out of the blue, quite so shocking."

"*Vivant* helped you with that, clearly."

"It gave me a pretense, yes. I felt more comfortable having a major magazine send you than calling you up on the phone and trying to explain how I knew who you were."

"So you figured you'd just lure me here with the promise of a best-seller."

"No," she says, shaking her head. "Once I started researching you, I read most of your work. Specifically, I read your right-to-die piece."

I put the letter on the table. I consider taking a seat. "So?"

"I thought it was beautifully written. It was informed, intelligent, balanced, and compassionate. It had heart. I admired the way you deftly handled an emotional and complicated topic."

I don't want to let her say anything nice to me, because I don't want to have to thank her for it. But my mother instilled in me a politeness that kicks in when I least expect it. "Thank you."

"When I read it, I suspected that you would do a beautiful job with my story."

"Because of one small piece I wrote?"

"Because you're talented, and if anyone could understand the complexities of who I am and what I've done, it was probably you. And the more I've gotten to know you, the more I know I was right. Whatever book you write about me, it will not have easy answers. But it will, I predict, be unflinching. I wanted to give you that letter, and I wanted you to write my story, because I believe you to be the very best person for the job."

"So you put me through all this to assuage your guilt and make sure you got the book about your life that you wanted?"

Evelyn shakes her head, ready to correct me, but I'm not done.

"It's amazing, really. How self-interested you can be. That even now, even when you appear to want to redeem yourself, it's still about *you*."

Evelyn puts up her hand. "Don't act like you haven't benefited from this. You've been a willing participant here. You wanted the story. You took advantage—deftly and smartly, I might add—of the position I put you in."

"Evelyn, seriously," I say. "Cut the crap."

"You don't want the story?" Evelyn asks, challenging me. "If you don't want it, don't take it. Let my story die with me. That is just fine."

I am quiet, unsure how to respond, unsure how I *want* to respond.

Evelyn puts out her hand, expectantly. She's not going to let the suggestion be hypothetical. It's not rhetorical. It demands an answer. "Go ahead," she says. "Get your notes and the recordings. We can burn them all right now."

I don't move, despite the fact that she gives me ample time to do so.

"I didn't think so," she says.

"It's the least I deserve," I tell her, defensive. "It's the fucking least you can give me."

"Nobody deserves anything," Evelyn says. "It's simply a matter of who's willing to go and take it for themselves. And you, Monique, are a person who has proven to be willing to go out there and take what you want. So be honest about that. No one is just a victim or a victor. Everyone is somewhere in between. People who go around casting themselves as one or the other are not only kidding themselves, but they're also painfully unoriginal."

I get up from the table and walk to the sink. I wash my hands, because I hate how clammy they feel. I dry them. I look at her. "I hate you, you know."

Evelyn nods. "Good for you. It's such an uncomplicated feeling, isn't it? Hatred?"

"Yes," I say. "It is."

"Everything else in life is more complex. Especially your father. That's why I thought it was so important that you read that letter. I wanted you to *know*."

"What, exactly? That he was innocent? Or that he loved a man?"

"That he loved *you*. Like that. He was willing to turn down romantic love in order to stand by your side. Do you know what an amazing father you had? Do you know how loved you were? Plenty of men say they'll never leave their families, but your father was put to the test and didn't even blink. I wanted you to know that. If I had a father like that, I would have wanted to know."

No one is all good or all bad. I know this, of course. I had to learn it at a young age. But sometimes it's easy to forget just how true it is. That it applies to *everyone*.

Until you're sitting in front of the woman who put your father's dead body in the driver's seat of a car to save the reputation of her best friend—and you realize she held on to a letter for almost three decades because she wanted you to know how much you were loved.

She could have given me the letter earlier. She also could have thrown it away. There's Evelyn Hugo for you. Somewhere in the middle.

I sit down and put my hands over my eyes, rubbing them, hoping that if I rub hard enough, maybe I can make my way to a different reality.

When I open them, I'm still here. I have no choice but to resign myself to it.

"When can I release the book?"

"I won't be around much longer," Evelyn says, sitting down on a stool by the island.

"Enough with the vagaries, Evelyn. When can I release the book?"

Evelyn absentmindedly starts folding an errant napkin that is sitting haphazardly on the counter. Then she looks up at me. "It's no secret that the gene for breast cancer can be inherited," she says. "Although if there were any justice in the world, the mother would die of it well before the daughter."

I look at the finer points of Evelyn's face. I look at the corners of her lips, the edges of her eyes, the direction of her brows. There is very little emotion in any of them. Her face remains as stoic as if she were reading me the paper.

"You have breast cancer?" I ask.

She nods.

"How far along is it?"

"Far enough for me to need to hurry up and get this done."

I look away when she looks at me. I'm not sure why. It's not out of anger, really. It's out of shame. I feel guilty that so much of me does not feel bad for her. And stupid for the part of me that does.

"I saw my daughter go through this," Evelyn says. "I know what's ahead of me. It's important that I get my affairs in order. In addition to finalizing the last copy of my will and making sure Grace is taken care of, I handed over my most-prized gowns to Christie's. And this . . . this is the last of it. That letter. And this book. You."

"I'm leaving," I say. "I can't take any more today."

Evelyn starts to say something, and I stop her.

"No," I say. "I don't want to hear anything else from you. Don't say another goddamn word, OK?"

I can't say I'm surprised when she speaks anyway. "I was just going to say that I understand and I'll see you tomorrow."

"Tomorrow?" I say, just as I remember that Evelyn and I aren't done.

"For the photo shoot," she says.

"I'm not sure I'm prepared to come back here."

"Well," Evelyn says, "I very much hope that you do."

WHEN I GET HOME, I instinctively throw my bag onto the couch. I am tired, and I am angry, and my eyes feel dry and stiff, as if they have been wrung out like wet laundry.

I sit down, not bothering to take off my coat or my shoes. I respond to the e-mail my mother has sent containing her flight information for tomorrow. And then I lift my legs and rest my feet on the coffee table. As I do, they hit an envelope resting on the surface.

It is only then that I realize I even have a coffee table in the first place.

David brought it back. And on it rests an envelope addressed to me.

> *M—*
>
> *I should never have taken the table. I don't need it. It's silly for it to sit in the storage unit. I was being petty when I left.*
>
> *Enclosed is my key to the apartment and the business card of my lawyer.*
>
> *I suppose there is not much else to say except that I thank you for doing what I could not.*
>
> *—D*

I put the letter down on the table. I put my feet back up. I wrestle myself out of my coat. I kick off my shoes. I lay my head back. I breathe.

I don't think I would have ended my marriage without Evelyn Hugo.

I don't think I would have stood up to Frankie without Evelyn Hugo.

I don't think I would have had the chance to write a surefire bestseller without Evelyn Hugo.

I don't think I would understand the true depths of my father's devotion to me without Evelyn Hugo.

So I think Evelyn is wrong about at least one thing.

My hate is not uncomplicated.

WHEN I GET TO EVELYN'S apartment in the morning, I'm unsure when I even made the actual decision to come.

I simply woke up and found myself on my way. When I rounded the corner, walking here from the subway, I realized I could never have *not* come.

I cannot and will not do anything to compromise my standing at *Vivant*. I did not fight for writer at large to bunt at the last minute.

I'm right on time but somehow the last to arrive. Grace opens the door for me and already looks as if a hurricane hit her. Her hair is falling out of her ponytail, and she's trying harder than usual to keep a smile on her face.

"They showed up almost forty-five minutes early," Grace says to me in a whisper. "Evelyn had a makeup person in at the crack of dawn to get her ready before the magazine's makeup person. She had a lighting consultant come in at eight thirty this morning to guide her on the most flattering light in the house. Turns out it's the terrace, which I have not been as diligent about cleaning because it's still cold out every day. Anyway, I've been scrubbing the terrace from top to bottom for the past two hours." Grace jokingly rests her head on my shoulder. "Thank God I'm going on vacation."

"Monique!" Frankie says when she sees me in the hallway. "What took you so long?"

I look at my watch. "It's eleven-oh-six." I remember the first day I met Evelyn Hugo. I remember how nervous I was. I remember how larger-than-life she seemed. She is painfully human to me now. But this is all new to Frankie. She hasn't seen the real Evelyn. She still thinks we're photographing an icon more than a person.

I step out onto the terrace and see Evelyn in the midst of lights, reflectors, wires, and cameras. There are people circled around her. She is sitting on a stool. Her gray blond hair is being blown in the air by a wind machine. She is wearing her signature emerald green, this time in a long-sleeved silk gown. Billie Holiday is playing on a speaker somewhere. The sun is shining behind Evelyn. She looks like the very center of the universe.

She is right at home.

She smiles for the camera, her brown eyes sparkling in a different way from anything I've ever seen in person. She seems at peace somehow, in full display, and I wonder if the real Evelyn *isn't* the woman I've been talking to for the past two weeks but, instead, the one I see before me right now. Even at almost eighty, she commands a room in a way I've never seen before. A star is always and forever a star.

Evelyn was born to be famous. I think her body helped her. I think her face helped her. But for the first time, watching her in action, moving in front of the camera, I get the sense that she has sold herself short in one way: she could have been born with considerably less physical gifts and probably still made it. She simply has *it*. That undefinable quality that makes everyone stop and pay attention.

She spots me as I stand behind one of the lighting guys, and she stops what she's doing. She waves me over to her.

"Everyone, everyone," she says. "We need a few photos of Monique and me. Please."

"Oh, Evelyn," I say. "I don't want to do that." I don't want to even be close to her.

"Please," she says. "To remember me by."

A couple of people laugh, as if Evelyn is making a joke. Because, of course, no one could forget Evelyn Hugo. But I know she's serious.

And so, in my jeans and blazer, I step up next to her. I take off my glasses. I can feel the heat of the lights, the way they glare in my eyes, the way the wind feels on my face.

"Evelyn, I know this isn't news to you," the photographer says, "but boy, does the camera love you."

"Oh," Evelyn says, shrugging. "It never hurts to hear it one more time."

Her dress is low-cut, revealing her still-ample cleavage, and it occurs to me that it is the very thing that made her that will be the thing to finally take her down.

Evelyn catches my eye and smiles. It is a sincere smile, a kind smile. There is something almost nurturing about it, as if she is looking at me to see how I'm doing, as if she cares.

And then, in an instant, I realize that she does.

Evelyn Hugo wants to know that I'm OK, that with everything that has happened, I will still be all right.

In a moment of vulnerability, I find myself putting my arm around her. A second after I do, I realize that I want to pull it back, that I'm not ready to be this close.

"I love it!" the photographer says. "Just like that."

I cannot pull my arm away now. And so I pretend. I pretend, for one picture, that I am not a bundle of nerves. I pretend that I am not furious and confused and heartbroken and torn up and disappointed and shocked and uncomfortable.

I pretend that I am simply captivated by Evelyn Hugo.

Because, despite everything, I still am.

AFTER THE PHOTOGRAPHER leaves, after everyone has cleaned up, after Frankie has left the apartment, so happy that she could have sprouted wings and flown herself back to the office, I am preparing to leave.

Evelyn is upstairs changing her clothes.

"Grace," I say as I spot her gathering disposable cups and paper plates in the kitchen. "I wanted to take a moment to say good-bye, since Evelyn and I are done."

"Done?" Grace asks.

I nod. "We finished up the story yesterday. Photo shoot today. Now

I get to writing," I say, even though I haven't the foggiest idea how I'm going to approach any of this or what, exactly, my next step is.

"Oh," Grace says, shrugging. "I must have misunderstood. I thought you were going to be here with Evelyn through my vacation. But honestly, all I could focus on was that I had two tickets to Costa Rica in my hands."

"That's exciting. When do you leave?"

"On the red-eye later," Grace says. "Evelyn gave them to me last night. For me and my husband. All expenses paid. A week. We're staying near Monteverde. All I heard was 'zip-lining in the cloud forest,' and I was sold."

"You deserve it," Evelyn says as she appears at the top of the stairs and walks down to meet us. She is in jeans and a T-shirt but has kept her hair and makeup. She looks gorgeous but also plain. Two things that only Evelyn Hugo can be at once.

"Are you sure you don't need me here? I thought Monique would be around to keep you company," Grace says.

Evelyn shakes her head. "No, you go. You've done so much for me lately. You need some time on your own. If something comes up, I can always call downstairs."

"I don't need to—"

Evelyn cuts her off. "Yes, you do. It's important that you know how much I appreciate all that you've done around here. So let me say thank you this way."

Grace smiles demurely. "OK," she says. "If you insist."

"I do. In fact, go home now. You've been cleaning all day, and I'm sure you need more time to pack. So go on, get out of here."

Surprisingly, Grace doesn't fight her. She merely says thank you and gathers her things. Everything seems to be happening seamlessly until Evelyn stops her on her way out and gives her a hug.

Grace seems slightly surprised though pleased.

"You know I could never have spent these past few years without you, don't you?" Evelyn says as she pulls away from her.

Grace blushes. "Thank you."

"Have fun in Costa Rica," Evelyn says. "The time of your life."

And once Grace is out the door, I suspect I understand what is going on.

Evelyn was never going to let the thing that made her be the thing to destroy her. She was never going to let anything, even a part of her body, have that sort of power.

Evelyn is going to die when she wants to.

And she wants to die now.

"Evelyn," I say. "What are you . . ."

I can't bring myself to say it or even suggest it. It sounds so absurd, even the thought of it. Evelyn Hugo taking her own life.

I imagine myself saying it out loud and then watching Evelyn laugh at me, at how creative my imagination is, at how silly I can be.

But I also imagine myself saying it and having Evelyn respond with a plain and resigned confirmation.

And I'm not sure I'm ready to stomach either scenario.

"Hm?" Evelyn says, looking at me. She does not seem concerned or disturbed or nervous. She looks as if this is any normal day.

"Nothing," I say.

"Thank you for coming today," she says. "I know you were unsure if you would be able to make it, and I . . . I'm just glad that you did."

I hate Evelyn, but I think I like her very much.

I wish she had never existed, and yet I can't help but admire her a great deal.

I'm not sure what to do with that. I'm not sure what any of it means.

I turn the front doorknob. All I can manage to squeak out is the very heart of what I mean. "Please take care, Evelyn," I say.

She reaches out and takes my hand. She squeezes it briefly and then lets go. "You too, Monique. You have an exceptional future ahead of you. You'll wrangle the very best out of this world. I really do believe that."

Evelyn looks at me, and for one split second, I can read her expression. It is subtle, and it is fleeting. But it is there. And I know that my suspicions are right.

Evelyn Hugo is saying good-bye.

As I walk into the subway tunnel and through the turnstiles, I keep wondering if I should turn back.

Should I knock on her door?

Should I call 911?

Should I *stop* her?

I can walk right back up the subway steps. I can put one foot in front of the other and make my way back to Evelyn's and say "Don't do this."

I am capable of that.

I just have to decide if I want to do it. If I should do it. If it's the right thing to do.

She didn't pick me just because she felt she owed me. She picked me because of my right-to-die piece.

She picked me because I showed a unique understanding of the need for dignity in death.

She picked me because she believes I can see the need for mercy, even when what constitutes mercy is hard to swallow.

She picked me because she trusts me.

And I get the feeling she trusts me now.

My train comes thundering into the station. I need to get on it and meet my mother at the airport.

The doors open. The crowds flow out. The crowds flow in. A teenage boy with a backpack shoulders me out of the way. I do not set foot in the subway car.

The train dings. The doors close. The station empties.

And I stand there. Frozen.

If you think someone is going to take her own life, don't you try to stop her?

Don't you call the cops? Don't you break down walls to find her?

The station starts to fill again, slowly. A mother with her toddler. A man with groceries. Three hipsters in flannel with beards. The crowd starts gathering faster than I can clock them now.

I need to get on the next train to see my mother and leave Evelyn behind me.

I need to turn around and go save Evelyn from herself.

I see the two soft lights on the track that signal the train approaching. I hear the roar.

My mom can get to my place on her own.

Evelyn has never needed saving from anyone.

The train rolls into the station. The doors open. The crowds flow out. And it is only once the doors close that I realize I have stepped inside the train.

Evelyn trusts me with her story.

Evelyn trusts me with her death.

And in my heart, I believe it would be a betrayal to stop her.

No matter how I may feel about Evelyn, I know she is in her right mind. I know she is OK. I know she has the right to die as she lived, entirely on her own terms, leaving nothing to fate or to chance but instead holding the power of it all in her own hands.

I grab the cold metal pole in front of me. I sway with the speed of the car. I change trains. I get onto the AirTrain. It is only once I am standing at the arrivals gate and see my mother waving at me that I realize I have been nearly catatonic for an hour.

There is simply too much.

My father, David, the book, Evelyn.

And the moment my mother is close enough to touch, I put my arms around her and sink into her shoulders. I cry.

The tears that come out of me feel as if they were decades in the making. It feels as if some old version of me is leaking out, letting go, saying good-bye in the effort of making room for a new me. One that is stronger and somehow both more cynical about people and also more optimistic about my place in the world.

"Oh, honey," my mom says, dropping her bag off her shoulder, letting it fall wherever it falls, paying no attention to the people who need to get around us. She holds me tightly, with both arms rubbing my back.

I feel no pressure to stop crying. I feel no need to explain myself. You don't have to make yourself OK for a good mother; a good mother makes herself OK for you. And my mother has always been a good mother, a great mother.

When I am done, I pull away. I wipe my eyes. There are people passing us on the left and the right, businesswomen with briefcases, families with backpacks. Some of them stare. But I'm used to people staring at my mother and me. Even in the melting pot that is New York City, there are still many people who don't expect a mother and daughter to look as we look.

"What is it, honey?" my mom asks.

"I don't even know where to start," I say.

She grabs my hand. "How about I forgo trying to prove to you that I understand the subway system and we hail a cab?"

I laugh and nod, drying the edges of my eyes.

By the time we are in the backseat of a stale taxi, clips of the morning news cycle repeating over and over on the console, I have gathered myself enough to breathe easily.

"So tell me," she says. "What's on your mind?"

Do I tell her what I know?

Do I tell her that the heartbreaking thing we've always believed—that my father died driving drunk—isn't true? Am I going to exchange that transgression for another? That he was having an affair with a man when his life ended?

"David and I are officially getting divorced," I say.

"I'm so sorry, sweetheart," she says. "I know that had to be hard."

I can't burden her with what I suspect about Evelyn. I just can't.

"And I miss Dad," I say. "Do you miss Dad?"

"Oh, God," she says. "Every day."

"Was he a good husband?"

She seems caught off guard. "He was a great husband, yes," she says. "Why do you ask?"

"I don't know. I guess I just realized I don't know very much about your relationship. What was he like? With you?"

She starts smiling, as if she's trying to stop herself but simply can't. "Oh, he was very romantic. He used to buy me chocolates every single year on the third of May."

"I thought your anniversary was in September."

"It was," she says, laughing. "He just always spoiled me on the third of May for some reason. He said there weren't enough official holidays to celebrate me. He said he needed to make one up just for me."

"That's really cute," I say.

Our driver pulls out onto the highway.

"And he used to write the most beautiful love letters," she says. "Really lovely. With poems in them about how pretty he thought I was, which was silly, because I was never pretty."

"Of course you were," I say.

"No," she says, her voice matter-of-fact. "I wasn't really. But boy, did he make me feel like I was Miss America."

I laugh. "It sounds like a pretty passionate marriage," I say.

My mom is quiet. Then she says, "No," patting my hand. "I don't know if I would say passionate. We just really *liked* each other. It was almost as if when I met him, I met this other side of myself. Someone who understood me and made me feel safe. It wasn't passionate, really. It was never about ripping each other's clothes off. We just knew we could be happy together. We knew we could raise a child. We also knew it wouldn't be easy and that our parents wouldn't like it. But in a lot of ways, that just brought us closer. Us against the world, sort of.

"I know it's not popular to say. I know everybody's looking for some sexy marriage nowadays. But I was really happy with your father. I really loved having someone look out for me, having someone to look out for. Having someone to share my days with. I always found him so fascinating. All of his opinions, his talent. We could have a conversation about almost anything. For hours on end. We used to stay up late, even when you were a toddler, just *talking*. He was my best friend."

"Is that why you never remarried?"

My mom considers the question. "You know, it's funny. Talking about passion. Since we lost your dad, I've found passion with men, from time to time. But I'd give it all back for just a few more days with him. For just one more late-night talk. Passion never mattered very much to me. But that type of intimacy that we had? That was what I cherished."

Maybe one day I will tell her what I know.

Maybe I never will.

Maybe I'll put it in Evelyn's biography, or perhaps I'll tell Evelyn's side of it without ever revealing who was sitting in the passenger's seat of that car.

Maybe I'll leave that part out completely. I think I'd be willing to lie about Evelyn's life to protect my mother. I think I'd be willing to omit the truth from public knowledge in the interest of the happiness and sanity of a person I love dearly.

I don't know what I'm going to do. I just know that I will be guided by what I believe to be best for my mother. And if it comes at the expense of honesty, if it takes a small chunk out of my integrity, I'm OK with that. Perfectly, stunningly OK.

"I think I was just very fortunate to find a companion like your father," my mom says. "To find that kind of soul mate."

When you dig just the tiniest bit beneath the surface, everyone's love life is original and interesting and nuanced and defies any easy definition.

And maybe one day I'll find someone I love the way Evelyn loved Celia. Or maybe I might just find someone I love the way my parents loved each other. Knowing to look for it, knowing there are all different types of great loves out there, is enough for me for now.

There's still much I don't know about my father. Maybe he was gay. Maybe he saw himself as straight but in love with one man. Maybe he was bisexual. Or a host of other words. But it really doesn't matter, that's the thing.

He loved me.

And he loved my mom.

And nothing I could learn about him now changes that. Any of it.

The driver drops us off in front of my stoop, and I grab my mother's bag. The two of us head inside.

My mom offers to make me her famous corn chowder for dinner but, seeing that I have almost nothing in the refrigerator, agrees that ordering pizza might be best.

When the food comes, she asks if I want to watch an Evelyn Hugo movie, and I almost laugh before realizing she's serious.

"I've had the itch to watch *All for Us* ever since you told me you were interviewing her," my mom says.

"I don't know," I say, not wanting to have anything to do with Evelyn but also hoping that my mom will talk me into it, because I know that on some level, I'm not yet ready to truly say good-bye.

"C'mon," she says. "For me."

The movie starts, and I marvel at how dynamic Evelyn is on-screen, how it is impossible to look at anything but her when she's there.

After a few minutes, I feel the pressing urge to get up and put on my shoes and knock down her door and talk her out of it.

But I repress it. I let her be. I respect her wishes.

I close my eyes and fall asleep to the sound of Evelyn's voice.

I don't know when exactly it happens—I suspect I made sense of things when I was dreaming—but when I wake up in the morning, I realize that even though it is too early yet, I will, one day, forgive her.

Evelyn Hugo, Legendary Film Siren, Has Died

BY PRIYA AMRIT   MARCH 26, 2017

Evelyn Hugo died Friday evening at the age of 79. Initial reports are not naming a cause of death, but multiple sources claim that it's being ruled an accidental overdose, as it appears that contradicting prescribed drugs were found in Hugo's system. Reports that the star was battling the early stages of breast cancer at the time of her death have not been confirmed.

The actress is to be buried at Forest Lawn Cemetery in Los Angeles.

A style icon of the '50s, turned sexpot in the '60s and '70s and Oscar winner in the '80s, Hugo made a name for herself with her voluptuous figure, her daring film roles, and her tumultuous love life. She was married seven times and outlived all of her husbands.

After retiring from acting, Hugo donated a great deal of time and money to organizations such as battered women shelters, LGBTQ+ communities, and cancer research. It was just recently announced that Christie's has taken in 12 of her most famous gowns to auction off for the American Breast Cancer Foundation. That auction, already sure to raise millions, will now, no doubt, see soaring bids.

It comes as little surprise that Hugo's will has bequeathed the majority of her estate, save for generous gifts to those who worked for her, to charity. The largest recipient appears to be GLAAD.

"I've been given so much in this life," Hugo said last year in a speech to the Human Rights Campaign. "But I've had to fight tooth and nail for it. If I can one day leave this world a little bit safer and a little bit easier for those who come after me . . . well, that just might make it all worth it."

Evelyn and Me

JUNE 2017   BY MONIQUE GRANT

When Evelyn Hugo, legendary actress, producer, and philanthropist, died earlier this year, she and I were in the process of writing her memoirs.

To say that spending the last couple of weeks of Evelyn's life with her was an honor would be both an understatement and, to be frank, somewhat misleading.

Evelyn was a very complex woman, and my time with her was just as complicated as her image, her life, and her legend. To this day, I wrestle with who Evelyn was and the impact she had on me. Some days I find myself convinced that I admire her more than anyone I've ever met, and others days I think of her as a liar and a cheat.

I think Evelyn would be rather content with that, actually. She was no longer interested in pure adoration or salacious scandal. Her primary focus was on the truth.

Having gone over our transcripts hundreds of times, having replayed every moment of our days together in my head, I think it's fair to say that I might just know Evelyn even better than I know myself. And I know that what Evelyn would want to reveal in these pages, along with the stunning photos taken just hours before her death, is one very surprising but beautifully true thing.

And that is this: Evelyn Hugo was bisexual and spent the majority of her life madly in love with fellow actress Celia St. James.

She wanted you to know this because she loved Celia

in a way that was in turns breathtaking and heart-breaking.

She wanted you to know this because loving Celia St. James was perhaps her greatest political act.

She wanted you to know this because over the course of her life, she became aware of her responsibility to others in the LGBTQ+ community to be visible, to be seen.

But more than anything, she wanted you to know this because it was the very core of herself, the most honest and real thing about her.

And at the end of her life, she was finally ready to be real.

So I'm going to show you the real Evelyn.

What follows is an excerpt from my forthcoming biography, *The Seven Husbands of Evelyn Hugo*, to be published next year.

I have settled on that title because I once asked her if she was embarrassed about having been married so many times.

I said, "Doesn't it bother you? That your husbands have become such a headline story, so often mentioned, that they have nearly eclipsed your work and yourself? That all anyone talks about when they talk about you are the seven husbands of Evelyn Hugo?"

And her answer was quintessential Evelyn.

"No," she told me. "Because they are just husbands. *I* am Evelyn Hugo. And anyway, I think once people know the truth, they will be much more interested in my wife."

ACKNOWLEDGMENTS

It is a testament to the grace, faith, and aplomb of my editor, Sarah Cantin, that when I told her I wanted to do something completely different that hinged on the reader believing a woman had been married seven times, she said, "Go for it." Within the safety of that trust, I felt free to create Evelyn Hugo. Sarah, it is with my most sincere thanks that I acknowledge how lucky I am to have you as my editor.

Big, big thanks must also go to Carly Watters for all that she has done for my career. I feel fortunate to continue working with you on so many books together.

To my incomparable rep team: You all are so good at your jobs and seem to do them with such passion that I feel as if I'm armed at all sides. Theresa Park, thank you for coming aboard and hitting the ground running with a strength and elegance that is truly unmatched. With you at the helm, I feel incredibly confident I can reach new heights. Brad Mendelsohn, thank you for running the show with such a strong belief in me and for dealing with the intricate details of my neurosis with such warmth. Sylvie Rabineau and Jill Gillett, your intelligence and skill are perhaps only outshone by your compassion.

To Ashley Kruythoff, Krista Shipp, Abigail Koons, Andrea Mai, Emily Sweet, Alex Greene, Blair Wilson, Vanessa Martinez, and everyone else at WME, Circle of Confusion, and Park Literary & Media, I am honestly overwhelmed at how seamlessly you all consistently deliver excellence. Special thanks for Vanessa *para el español. Me salvaste la vida.*

To Judith, Peter, Tory, Hillary, Albert, and everyone else at Atria who works to help my books make their way in the world, I thank you deeply.

To Crystal, Janay, Robert, and the rest of the BookSparks team, you are unstoppable, brilliant publicity machines and wonderful humans. One thousand prayer hands emojis to you and all that you do.

To all the friends who have shown up time and time again, to hear me read, to buy my books, to recommend my work to other people, and to surreptitiously put my books at the front of the store, I am forever grateful. To Kate, Courtney, Julia, and Monique, thank you for helping me write about people different from myself. It is a tall order that I take on humbly and it helps so much to have you by my side.

To the book bloggers who write and tweet and snap photos all in the effort of telling people about my work, you are the reason I can continue to do what I do. And I have to give it up to Natasha Minoso and Vilma Gonzalez for just straight killin' it.

To the Reid and Hanes families, thank you for supporting me, for cheering the loudest, and for always being there when I need you.

To my mother, Mindy, thank you for being proud of this book and always so eager to read anything I write.

To my brother, Jake, thank you for seeing me the way I want to be seen, for understanding what I'm trying to do at such a deep level, and for keeping me sane.

To the one and only Alex Jenkins Reid: Thank you for understanding why this book was so important to me and for being so *into it*. But more important, thank you for being the kind of man who encourages me to shout louder, dream bigger, and take less shit. Thank you for never making me feel as if I should make myself smaller to make anyone else feel better. It brings me an absolutely unparalleled amount of pride and joy to know that our daughter is growing up with a father who will stick by her side no matter who she is, who will show her how she should expect to be treated by modeling it for her. Evelyn did not have that. I did not have that. But she will. Because of you.

And lastly, to my baby girl. You were teeny teeny tiny—I believe the size of half the period on the end of this sentence—when I started writing this book. And when I finished it, you were mere days away from making your entrance. You were with me every step of the way. I suspect it was, in no small part, *you* who gave me the strength to write it.

I promise that I will repay the favor by loving you unconditionally and accepting you always, so that you feel strong enough and safe enough to do anything you set your mind to. Evelyn would want that for you. She would say, "Lilah, go out there, be kind, and grab what you want out of this world with both hands." Well, she might not have put as big an emphasis on being kind. But as your mother, I must insist.